Susan Meier is the author of over fifty books for Mills & Boon. *The Tycoon's Secret Daughter* was a Romance Writers of America RITA® Award finalist, and *Nanny for the Millionaire's Twins* won the Book Buyers' Best award and was a finalist in the National Readers' Choice awards. She is married and has three children. One of eleven children herself, she loves to write about the complexity of families and totally believes in the power of love.

Nina Crespo lives in Florida, where she indulges in her favourite passions—the beach, a good glass of wine, date night with her own real-life hero and dancing. Her lifelong addiction to romance began in her teens while on a 'borrowing spree' in her older sister's bedroom, where she discovered her first romance novel. Let Nina's sensual contemporary stories feed your own addiction for love, romance and happily-ever-after. Visit her at ninacrespo.com

Discover more at millsandboon.co.uk

TUSCAN SUMMER WITH THE BILLIONAIRE

SUSAN MEIER

AN OFFICER AND A FORTUNE

NINA CRESPO

MILLS & BOON

First Published in Great Britain 2021
by Mills & Boon, an imprint of HarperCollins*Publishers* Ltd
1 London Bridge Street, London, SE1 9GF

www.harpercollins.co.uk

HarperCollins*Publishers*
1st Floor, Watermarque Building,
Ringsend Road, Dublin 4, Ireland

Tuscan Summer with the Billionaire © 2021 Linda Susan Meier
An Officer and a Fortune © 2021 Harlequin Books S.A.

Special thanks and acknowledgement are given to Nina Crespo for her contribution to *The Fortunes of Texas: The Hotel Fortune* series.

ISBN: 978-0-263-29959-5

TUSCAN SUMMER WITH THE BILLIONAIRE

SUSAN MEIER

For the real Marcia, my bowling bud,
who wanted her own book.

The name is the same,
though the life circumstances are a tad different,
since she doesn't live in a villa in Tuscany.

Kisses, Friend Marcia!

CHAPTER ONE

TRACE JACKSON SLOWED his red Maserati and made the turn at the sign announcing Giordano Vineyards, the property for which he'd assumed ownership that morning. He kept his speed low as he took in the grounds, awestruck by the long rows of grapes, the hills and valleys covered in green grass and trees, and the blue, blue sky.

He was now Trace Jackson, Tuscan vintner. Soon he would be the guy who laughed with tourists at wine-tasting events and the guy who relaxed on the back patio of his villa as evening descended. Holding a glass of red, he would gaze at his beautiful property, not haunted by the past or pushed toward the future, just being himself.

Nothing else.

No more ghosts. No more memories.

The three-story ivory stucco house with dark brown shutters came into view. The vineyard was closed to guests that day while it left the hands of the Giordano family and passed into his. The entire property shimmered with stillness.

He finished the drive down the lane and got out of his car. Taking a long, satisfied breath, he admired the new winemaking facility complete with gift shop and two tasting bars, then the manicured lawn and the multicar garage.

A warm June breeze ruffled his short hair, as he retrieved his bag from the trunk, then half jogged to the villa door. But he stopped and took one more look around the grounds, unable to believe this place was his, that he was about to become a vintner, that he was starting a whole new life. Then he pressed in the numbers for the lock and pushed on the thick wood door.

Glancing around the echoing foyer, he set his bag on a bench in front of the stairway that curled to the second-floor hall. Three tall windows gracefully ascended the wall beside it. The sconce lights between the windows added elegance to the polished space with marble floors and dark-stained steps that complemented the embellished black wrought-iron railing.

A sound in the back had his head jerking to the left. Knowing the house was supposed to be empty, he walked through the bare living room and the almost bare dining room—which still had the long table and chairs that had been negotiated in the sale—toward the great room, where he stopped.

A short, shapely woman stood in front of the wall of windows, staring out at the rows of grapes on a hillside just beyond the manicured lawn. Her hunched shoulders and the way her hands gripped her elbows as if she were hugging herself spoke of sadness or maybe defeat. The room suddenly filled with it. All the joy he'd experienced as he'd gotten out of his car and entered his new home evaporated. Cast away by her sorrow.

Not happy with that or the intruder, he said, "Excuse me?"

His voice echoed around him in the hollow, high-ceilinged room.

The woman slowly turned. Long black corkscrew curls framed a face with delicate features that looked to have been fashioned by the gods. A lightweight pink sweater outlined the kind of curves a man itched to get his fingers on.

His heart jolted and he almost laughed at himself. After his divorce, he'd vowed never to marry again, so he only dated tall, leggy redheads. Women who looked nothing like his blonde ex-wife. He'd never given much thought to brunettes. But this brunette was stunning.

"Signor Jackson?"

When she said his name, he realized she was probably

an employee of the vineyard there to greet him, and he extended his hand to her.

"Yes. But you can call me Trace."

She shook his hand. "I'm Marcia. General manager."

"Oh!" He took a second to process that. He wasn't sure why he'd thought the general manager was a man. But… whatever. They'd had plenty of female executives at the holding company he and his partners had owned until a few months ago. He had no bias. He could work with anybody.

"It's a pleasure to meet you. Thank you for agreeing to stay on and teach me the ropes."

She snorted. "I did not agree."

"But the sales contract—"

Her brown eyes flashed. "My father doesn't ask permission. He also didn't bother to ask forgiveness when I told him I wasn't chattel he could barter in a business deal. He simply told me he'd put it in the clause, and I had to abide by it."

"It's part of the transition. Lots of companies have employees stay behind to help the new owner. Besides, you're not the only one in the agreement. Your brothers are staying too."

"*Si*, they'll stay for a few months. I'll stay a year."

"You're the general manager. Your job's a little more complex than running the wine-tasting room."

She snorted. "You think you're going to pick up how to handle customers in a few weeks?" She shook her head. "It's not as easy as it sounds."

"Doesn't matter. They'll be here tomorrow morning to start showing me their jobs. What I pick up I pick up. What I don't I'll figure out when the time comes."

She shook her head and paced the room. Her body moved fluidly, with a grace and elegance that mesmerized him.

He caught himself, confused by the direction of his thoughts, but more baffled by her. It didn't seem right that someone so angry could make a man's mind go blank from attraction. Especially his. He was all business, no nonsense. He didn't even tiptoe over the line into personal feelings or issues when it came to work.

He blamed his lapse on time zones and hormones. And all that glorious hair. It had been a while since a woman's looks had entranced him. He'd reacted because he hadn't been prepared for it.

No big deal.

She gestured back the way he'd come. "My duties today include showing you around." She gave him a quick once-over and he'd never felt more deficient. "Whether I want to or not."

Okay. So, his general manager's problem went a little deeper than job dissatisfaction. Were he to hazard a guess, he'd say she was more than unhappy to be stuck with *him* for the year her father had promised she would stay at the vineyard.

He headed for the door, thinking through options. He could fire her and hire someone else who knew as much as she did. In this part of Italy, vineyards were everywhere. Surely, he could find a replacement. Or he could feel her out. See just how angry she was and if that anger would spill over into their work. Lots of angry people were competent. Keeping her would be easier than replacing her, but he'd replaced indispensable people before. Because that's what he did. That's why he was successful. He could adapt.

Another situation flitted through his brain. He'd thought he'd adapted to that, but now he wasn't so sure. Still, that was why he was here. In quiet Tuscany. Starting over.

With the right questions, he could probably have Marcia Giordano figured out in ten minutes.

Marcia let Trace Jackson lead the way to the front door and she stifled a groan. The view from the back was even better than the front. Shiny black hair and blue eyes the color of a perfect sky had almost had her forgetting how furious she was with her dad for selling the vineyard. Add tortoiseshell glasses that made him look like a smart, savvy business-man, as well as a gray suit, white shirt and wine-colored tie, and, sure, she might have had the urge to fan herself. Now, she could see his broad shoulders, tapered waist and what appeared to be a very tight butt.

She tamped down the surge of feminine curiosity. This was no time to be soft. This was war. She needed to get this vineyard back into her family's hands to make up for the fact that it was her fiancé, Adam, who had embezzled the money the Giordano family had borrowed to build the new wine facility, forcing her father to borrow more money and getting them so far into debt he had to sell.

That was why *she* had to buy it back.

Not her dad. Not her brothers. *She* had to fix this.

Trace Jackson opened the door and motioned for her to exit first. Politely. Gallantly.

She held back a sigh. She didn't want him to be nice. That would just make this more difficult. "We don't go overboard with courtesies here."

"That's okay. It's kind of ingrained in me."

"Well, out-grain it. Because you and I are competition."

Clearly surprised, he said, "What?"

Holding the gaze of his sexy pale eyes, she decided a strong dose of truth wouldn't just get rid of her attraction. It would also put his guard up so this would be a fair fight. She might need to get the vineyard into Giordano hands again, but she wouldn't cheat, lie or steal. That had been Adam's forte.

"I fully intend to buy this vineyard back from you."

His brow furrowed. "But I just bought it."

"My dad put it up for sale prematurely."

"No. Your dad picked the right time. I saw the books.

Had he waited even another three months, penalties and interest would have bankrupted him."

"Yes, well. I had a source for the money. He should have talked to me, not gone to you."

He crossed his arms on his chest. The blue eyes behind the lenses of his glasses narrowed. "If you had a source for the money, why didn't you bail your dad out *before* he came to me?"

"My friend Janine's mother became ill suddenly, and I couldn't contact her about a loan. That would have been inappropriate."

He lowered his arms. "Oh." But the skepticism hadn't left his voice when he said, "This friend has an extra thirty million dollars hanging around?"

"Actually, she could probably lend me ten times that and not miss it."

His voice hardened. "And how do you intend to pay it back?"

"Profits from the vineyard—and before you ask, she'll give me an interest rate much lower than the bank, making the payments manageable."

He said only, "Hmm," and then he motioned to the door for her to walk outside ahead of him. But he stopped suddenly and said, "Wait a second."

He took off his jacket and tossed it to the bench with a bag that was probably his. Then he loosened his tie. As his hands worked the knot, the fringe of a sleeve tattoo appeared at his wrist.

Her breath caught a little.

She forced air into her lungs, stopping that reaction before it really started. She couldn't be attracted to him. The notion was idiotic. A romance—even a casual affair—was the last thing she wanted or needed right now. Especially with an American like Adam had been. Educated. Gorgeous. Except where Adam had been blond, Trace had black hair. And she'd bet he had dark chest hair and six-pack abs—

This time the wave that hit her was disbelief at her own stupidity. Hadn't falling for one smooth-talking American been enough? Hadn't losing all the money her family had borrowed to pay for the new building taught her a lesson?

A year might have passed, but she still felt the sting of it. She was only now coming back to herself. She wouldn't wreck that over a handsome face.

Sexy or not, Trace Jackson was the opposition. Not quite an enemy but the guy who had her family's business. And she had to wrestle it back—even as she trained him enough that he would see he didn't really want to own a vineyard. Running one wasn't as romantic and easy as everyone thought. The work was hard, hours were long, and tourists weren't always pleasant.

As they made the short walk to the wine building, he rolled his white shirtsleeves to his elbows. Refusing to allow herself a quick look at his tattoos, she opened the door on two long mahogany bars with round tables scattered throughout the sparkling-clean room. The gift shop behind a wall of glass at the far right held everything from single bottles of wine to wineglasses with the silver-and-white vineyard logo, as well as towels, mugs, stoppers and T-shirts, all displayed as if they were fine jewels. Everything about the room screamed sophistication. If it didn't shine like well-polished wood, it glowed from a recent scrubbing.

It was perfect as the initial thing tourists saw. She'd made sure of that, cradling the project with loving hands. Handling every detail. Thinking through every tile and piece of machinery.

Trace strolled the room, smiling, the gorgeous artwork of the tattoos on his forearms revealed for all the world to see. He hadn't gone to the back room of a bar in his city for his art. No. His tattoos had been drawn by a master.

"This room is what sold me on buying the vineyard."

Marcia smiled stiffly. Not merely because it rankled that someone had bought her baby, but because one of those weird whooshes of attraction had roared through her again, causing her blood to tingle and her knees to turn to jelly. A businessman with tattoos? What could be sexier?

She had to take a breath before she could say, "Really?"

He ambled around the silent room, his movements smooth and incredibly male. Especially with his sleeves rolled up.

Annoyed with herself, she forced her eyes away. It didn't matter how sexy he was. He wouldn't be staying.

"This space was filled with tourists the day I walked through with your dad."

Which explained why Marcia hadn't seen him. Her father had probably deliberately mixed him in with the crowd so he wouldn't be noticed. The vineyard's financial troubles had bruised Antonio Giordano's pride, and she knew he blamed her, no longer trusted her and hadn't wanted her opinions. Not even on the sale of the business that was to be her future.

"Everyone was happy, praising the samples they tasted." Trace turned to face her again. "And orders for cases of Giordano's finest flowed as naturally and as freely as the wine."

"We have a very good reputation."

"And I want to make sure that reputation stays intact. That's the wine's biggest selling point. The vineyard's reputation. That's why I won't be renaming it Jackson Vineyards or Trace of Delight Wines."

A spontaneous laugh burst from Marcia and she cut it off. The man was charming and easygoing. But that didn't matter. *Couldn't* matter.

He walked over, met her gaze. "If you intend to buy me

out because you're worried that I'm going to change things, I'm not. I'm a CPA. I know a good deal when I see one. This vineyard is a success. Your dad would have never sold it had it not been for the embezzling."

Her heart stopped. Her breath froze.

He knew about Adam?

Of course he did. A smart businessman would investigate every nook and cranny of the vineyard's history...and its accounting...before buying.

The sale might have been fast, and she might not have been told about it until agreements had already been signed, but she hadn't been made general manager because she was pretty. She'd been educated to build Giordano Wines. She knew business. Some part of her had always realized the new owner would find out about the embezzling. She simply hadn't acknowledged it until this minute.

But now that she had, she would breathe again.

Really.

She forced air in and out of her lungs, accepting the fact that her greatest mistake was a part of the vineyard's history. She'd never escape it. It would follow her like an unwashed dog.

"Anyway, we both know I understand numbers. What I don't know is wine." He pointed to the double aluminum doors in the middle of the far wall. "Let's take a look back there."

Relief that he didn't ask for details about the embezzling poured through her, quelling the wild beating of her heart. Then she realized he'd asked a few questions and moved on as if he either didn't take her seriously about buying the vineyard back from him or didn't see her as a threat.

Something hot and angry flickered through her.

This she wouldn't ignore. This she would handle.

CHAPTER TWO

TRACE FOLLOWED MARCIA to the destemmer, a little clearer about what was going on with her. She was furious that her dad had sold the vineyard out from under her. He would have been too. But he wasn't done figuring her out. It was far-fetched that she had a friend who could lend her the money to buy it back. A thirty-million-dollar loan was a huge favor. More than that, he couldn't understand why she'd want to put herself in that much debt.

She motioned toward the back of the building, to big garage doors. "Grapes come in there. Washed over there. And are brought here for destemming, then poured into the crusher."

Impressed by how new everything was, he inspected the silent machine.

Marcia continued her explanation. "Wine is a five-step process. Picking the grapes, crushing the grapes, fermenting the grapes into wine, aging the wine and bottling the wine. It's not difficult to learn."

He peered over at her. "There might only be five steps, but there are steps within those steps."

She nodded. "Seeds and skin are removed. Yeast is added. But if we take this one process at a time, after we pick the grapes in late summer, early fall, you'll see every step inside each process."

"So, your plan to buy me out is long term? You're not going to hand me a check tomorrow?"

She shrugged. "I'm trying to be fair."

Plus, she didn't have the money. At least not yet. "Fair?"

"I'll give you a whole year to see the process. So, you

can make an informed decision. But I'm betting you'll be out sooner."

He had to hold back a chuckle. Working with a woman who intended to oust him might not be smart, but she wasn't a threat. She couldn't take back the vineyard without him selling it to her. Plus, she knew how to run this place and he didn't. Add in that she was pretty and just miffed enough to be interesting, and this conversation was the best fun he'd had in years. Most things in life were easy to him. Even buying Giordano Vineyards had been nothing but a little research and writing a check. He was thrilled that it came with a puzzle.

He liked puzzles.

"Winemaking isn't as easy as it sounds."

He wandered around the room. "Oh, I get that. Following steps is one thing. But experience, instinct is quite another."

"Exactly."

"And you think I'm going to flub that?"

When she said nothing, he recognized she was smart enough to see he was baiting her and she pulled back. Which was a point in her favor. She might be angry, but she knew how to control it. He decided it was time to be as honest with her as she was being with him. At his old company he'd been known as The Eliminator because he didn't fuss around. He got things out in the open and dealt with them.

"It will take years before I admit defeat. Up to then, I'll just consider myself in the learning curve. I'll never sell this back to you."

"Why don't we cross that bridge when we come to it?"

"Because I'm trying to be as fair as you are, to let you see what you're up against if you seriously think you'll get this vineyard back. I'm a planner. My friends and I owned a huge holding company for supermarket chains. We didn't get to that size by leaving anything to chance."

She frowned. "A holding company for supermarket chains?"

"Enormous corporation. Massive five-year plans and forecasts. Tons of work. This vineyard will be just enough mental stimulation to entertain me and not so much as to make me crazy."

"Your other company made you crazy?"

"No. Not having anything to do after we sold it made me crazy." He wouldn't tell her that having too much time to think about the pain of the past had driven him home. Hoping a visit with his down-to-earth parents would soothe him, he'd brought gifts and planned to stay a few weeks. But his father had made a comment about his son, how everything had worked out for the best after his death, and Trace had melted inside. How could the death of his innocent baby and the end of his teenage marriage have been for the best? He lived with a permanent hole in his heart and a head full of unanswered questions and his parents didn't know what to say, couldn't soothe him. Even now, the memory of his lost child crushed his chest, made it hard to breathe.

He couldn't go back twelve years and change things or even ease the pain, so he'd decided to go forward. Buying this vineyard and moving to Italy was such a huge step, it would shift his thoughts, occupy his brain, calm him again.

He was sure of it.

Marcia's voice tiptoed into the silent room. "If having nothing to do makes you crazy, why did you sell your company?"

He glanced at her, blinking to bring himself back to the present. "Actually, my partners and I received an offer out of the blue. It was higher than any of us believed we'd ever get. We cashed out and became wealthy in the process." He let his gaze cruise the room again. "We'd have been fools not to take it."

He ambled around a bit more, liking the feel of the place and the knowledge that the challenge of running the vineyard would easily get his mind off his past. Then the peace of the area would surely help him get more than an hour or two of sleep every night.

"But that's when I realized too much time on my hands wasn't a good thing. I wanted something to do but not something as extreme as running ten grocery store chains. Almost two hundred stores. Thousands of employees."

"That's a lot of accounting."

He laughed. "It was intense."

She sniffed. "You could have hired people to help."

"Oh, we did," he said, strolling around the big silver machine. "Let's just say you don't get rich by paying other people to do what you can do." He grinned stupidly. "And I like to work."

"Just not too hard."

He laughed again. He should have been annoyed by her impertinence, but he liked her. She had just enough sass to be good as a manager and not so much that she hadn't known to shut up when he baited her.

"Agreed. I like to work, but not too hard."

Her expression soured.

"Sorry to disappoint you."

"Oh, you don't disappoint me. I didn't think it would be easy to get you to sell. But you'll sell." She met his gaze. "I guarantee it."

The competitive streak in him sat up. "So, this is like a bet?"

"No."

"A competition, then? You think you can get me to sell. I think I can get you to like working for me enough that you'll stay on after the year is up." He smiled. "Maybe indefinitely."

"Never happen."

He laughed. "Seriously? Don't tell me that. That just fires my blood. Now for sure I'll beat you."

She held out her hand. "So, what do you say we set terms? If I can't get you to sell, I'll stay on for five years."

Impressed, he considered that. Five years would give him plenty of time to learn how to make wine. Then if she wanted to leave, it wouldn't be a hardship. He reached to shake the hand she held out to him. "Deal."

She drew it back. "Not so fast. If you decide to sell at any time in those five years, you sell only to me...and at three-quarters of the price you paid."

He whistled. "I'll lose twenty-five percent of my investment?"

"That's the deal. Take it or leave it."

He studied her. Five years with her working for him? Teaching him? He'd have no reason to sell. The three-quarters price was irrelevant.

"Deal."

This time when he reached for her hand, she let him take it. When their palms met, electricity shimmied up his arm.

He ignored it. He might be attracted to this brunette, but now they had a bet for the piece of property that was supposed to give him back his sanity.

Not that he thought he'd lose. Her terms were too broad and general. All he had to do was stay owner of the vineyard for five years. Which had been his plan anyway.

One gorgeous, smart Italian woman wouldn't send him packing. Not when he needed the peace and tranquility and the challenge of the bet more than he needed the money.

She took a breath, turned on her heel and walked away.

He stifled a laugh. If she thought treating him poorly would get him to sell, that was adorable. He loved puzzles and competitions. His brain thrived on them. The more she tried to make this difficult, the sharper he'd get and the happier he'd be. And thoughts of his past would all but disappear. She'd just made this deal perfect.

The rest of the afternoon passed quickly, with Marcia showing Trace every piece of equipment, the vats, the storerooms. It was a lot of information, but now that the challenge was on, his brain all but glowed as it sucked up facts and processes.

Tired at the end of the tour, he entered the house through the front foyer, grabbed his jacket and bag, and walked upstairs.

His breathing slowed as he made his way down the hall of the second floor. Doors were closed, but there were four bedrooms on this level and five on the floor above it. And it was all his. The peace and serenity he'd longed for were finally at his fingertips.

Happy, he showered and dressed in jeans and an over-size T-shirt. The plan was to hop in the Maserati and cruise into town for dinner, then a trip to the market for essentials like eggs and bread. He'd bartered with the Giordano family to leave behind some dishes and pots and pans, so all he needed were a few basics. When he returned, he would grab a bottle of wine made at *his* vineyard and settle in on the back patio to bask in his new reality. He would listen to night sounds, savor his wine, then go to bed in the peace and quiet of Tuscany.

And hopefully, he'd sleep.

As he stepped out of the master bedroom, a noise drifted to him. Thinking it might have been the house creaking, he walked down the stairs to the foyer, but he heard another sound. This one was odd like…

Well, he had no idea. It wasn't quite a crash or a bang. But it was loud and coming from the back.

He raced down the hall, following what was now a bunch of clattering noises, and strode into the kitchen to find

Marcia, dressed in jeans and a tank top, looking like she was getting ready to cook.

His brow furrowed as she glanced at him over the long island of the white and stainless-steel kitchen.

"I guessed you would want me to make dinner."

"Can you…? *Should* you?" Holy cow, she looked great. She might be small, but her body packed a punch. Her tank top didn't merely show off ample bosoms; it cinched her tiny waist.

His thoughts paused, then backed up a bit.

She'd changed clothes and was in the kitchen?

Why hadn't she gone home?

Why was she comfortably searching for pots…as if she—?

"Is there food in the fridge?"

She shrugged. "A bit. Mama left a few things."

"Like to make your lunch while you're working?"

She winced. "That and a bit more."

His stomach fell. "Are you still living here?"

She frowned. "I've always lived here."

"Until I bought this house. Then it became mine and your family moved out."

"Oh. I see." She chuckled. "You think because my family has gone, I should have gone." She shook her head. "But no. You kept me on as the employee I've always been, and I've always lived here. Meaning room and board come with the deal I've always had as an employee here." She smiled. "But, if you think about it, if I'm buying you out, there's no point in my moving anyway."

"There's plenty of point! Per our deal, I'm staying at least five years. And I bought this vineyard for peace and quiet. Having somebody live with me sort of ruins that." And was nonnegotiable. If she thought he'd gotten soft because he'd taken her bet, she was wrong. Trace Martin Jackson wasn't soft.

The Eliminator in him came roaring to life. If her living here was part of her plan to edge him out, she had opened a can of worms she should have left closed.

She shook her head. "You think you're staying, but grape harvest might scare you off. It gets rowdy."

"Rowdy?" He walked toward her, but the closer he got the more his nerve endings prickled. He enjoyed a good fight, but these prickles were different. More like prickles of attraction than getting his hackles up to take on the enemy.

He stopped, casually took two steps back, not liking the way the attraction kept weaving between them anytime they were in a room together. "Rowdy won't intimidate me."

"All right. How about this? Guests aren't here only from nine to five. They can stay into the night. It'll be handy to have me around."

His brain stalled. He hadn't thought of that. Mostly because he didn't know anything about running a vineyard. "Okay." Because he didn't want her thinking she'd won, he added, "I'm not getting soft. I simply see your point. Being overconfident about getting me to change my mind will get you into trouble."

She laughed as if she thought him wrong, but when she grabbed a pot handle again, weirdness about her cooking brought The Eliminator back, the guy who saw and solved problems. She might be sleeping in his house that night, but she was still an employee and he would not open himself up to a lawsuit because she thought he "assumed" she would cook. *After hours.* While they were *living together.*

No. This was a problem he would fix immediately.

"You're not cooking."

"What?"

"You're an employee. You're not cooking for the boss." To soften the blow, he added, "I'll take you out for dinner."

She stopped dead in her tracks. "In town?"

"Sure. We can get something to eat, then go to the market, pick up a few things like coffee, cream, eggs, bread and whatever else I think of."

She only stared at him.

Either she really, really liked to cook or she was so accustomed to making her own dinner, she appeared stymied by having a choice. But he wasn't risking a lawsuit. As long as they worked together, she would not cook.

"I can't let you prepare meals for me. I don't know how things are here in Italy, but bosses don't take advantage of employees in the US. Unless they like lawsuits."

"I know. I went to school in the States." She sighed. "It's just that—" Confusion filled her face. Then she rolled her eyes. "Oh, whatever." Setting the pan on the counter, she said, "Let's go."

They walked to his car in silence with him feeling like he'd dodged a bullet about potential lawsuits, until he realized she might have hesitated because she didn't want to go to dinner with *him*. After all, he was her boss. He'd bought her family's vineyard. And they'd already spent a whole darned afternoon together. If nothing else, she was probably sick of him.

He wanted to groan. He'd been so sure when he'd met her that he could figure her out. Then she'd lured him into a bet and now he seemed to have lost his ability to decipher a normal situation.

He almost told her she didn't have to go, but before he got the words out she was in the car. He decided to make the evening fun, to get to know her, and hopefully establish a less confusing work relationship.

They couldn't talk on the drive to town because of the noise of having the car's top down. But as soon as he stopped the engine in the parking lot of a quaint tavern, he said, "This is such a nice little village."

She smiled stiffly. "Yes. It's lovely."

Okay. Getting her to talk might take a bit of work, but he'd faced grumpier employees before.

He opened the thick wooden door of the tavern, but when they entered, the prickly sensation of being watched rolled down his spine. Not only did all eyes turn in their direction, but people stopped talking as they walked to one of the empty tables.

He realized they could be curious about him—the new guy in town—until he saw the waitress get the bartender's attention and point at Marcia.

He winced. He might be new in town, but that went only so far in terms of gossip and curiosity. Marcia's family, on the other hand, had lost their vineyard under truly gossip-worthy circumstances. From the guarded expression on Marcia's face, he knew she felt every eye on her.

He pulled out her chair, then his. "So, this is a nice place."

She looked neither right nor left. She kept her eyes down. And he felt like hell. *This* was why she'd hesitated to come out with him. It had been a year since her employee had vanished with their loan money, but people in this town had long memories. Or maybe nothing more exciting had happened in the twelve months that had passed.

"Every place in Tuscany is beautiful."

Her subdued voice went through him like a knife. Why had he insisted she come with him? He could have let her cook her own meal, gone into town for dinner alone and gone to the market without her. But, no… His big brain always had a plan.

To lighten the mood, he said, "You sound like you should be on their tourism board."

She laughed and he breathed an internal sigh of relief. Then the waitress came over.

"*Ciao*, Marcia!" The smirky little smile she gave Marcia set Trace's teeth on edge. "What can I get you?"

"I'll have a beer," Trace said before Marcia could answer. He'd been the victim of gossip. Whispers. Speculation. Out-and-out lies. He remembered going into the town convenience store the week after Skylar discovered she was pregnant. The hushed shoppers. The clerk who gave him a wide-eyed stare, as if no one else in the world had ever gotten pregnant at eighteen. The gossip that her wealthy parents were furious and looking for ways to get Skylar away from him.

Unfortunately, that part was true.

The waitress laughed. "Beer in wine country?"

"American beer, if you have it." There. If she wanted something to snipe about, he'd just given it to her. "We'll have wine with our meal. Could we have menus?"

The waitress said, "Of course," and sped away.

"That was Gina. She's—"

"A real pain in the butt." Trace finished her sentence with truth to get everything out in the open. That was another thing he'd learned about gossip. Truth usually killed it. "Look, we both know the circumstances surrounding my getting your family's vineyard weren't the best. And you were general manager when one of your employees stole from your family."

Playing with the silverware on the table, Marcia said nothing.

"You shouldn't run. You shouldn't hide. Clearly everybody knows. Let it ebb and flow until it dies out. The more you react, the longer it lives."

She stared at her silverware for a few seconds, then finally looked him in the eyes. "It sounds like you have some experience with gossip."

He winced. Walked right into that one. "That's a story for another time." Or never. Most people could barely remember what they'd done at eighteen. They didn't have to confess getting the daughter of the town rich guy pregnant, talking her into running away and getting married, having a child, losing that child and then divorcing so quickly he wasn't sure either he or Skylar had had a chance to grieve.

He'd taken that loss to community college, drunk a little too much some nights, then finally realized it was better to drown himself in his studies than whiskey. Which was why he'd eventually gotten into Harvard and why he'd become wealthy. He really had learned things.

"Right now, you're having dinner with your boss. He's thanking you for teaching him the winemaking process... And if you were smart, you'd take advantage of the opportunity to get on his good side."

Marcia laughed, and then she winced. Protectiveness raced through him but so did anger. He'd heard the story of the embezzling from her father, but hearing it was totally different from seeing the living, breathing person who took responsibility for it.

She shook her head. "We're in a fierce competition, remember?"

"True. But I love a challenge."

She leaned forward, braced her arms on the table. "Same here."

"That doesn't mean we can't take breaks from it."

Gina returned to the table with two bottles of beer and two menus.

"Not that Marcia needs a menu," the waitress said pleasantly. "She used to come here all the time. Not quite so sociable now."

Marcia's face reddened and Trace thought he'd go through the roof with anger. Gina's snide comments reminded him of his own past again, the insults, the insinuations that the kid in worn sneakers and ripped jeans had wanted a cut of Skylar's family's money, and the fake condolences when his son died.

Gina left to give them time to look at the menu and Trace

said, "Forget all that. You have a much more interesting dinner companion. I might have started out in community college, but I got my MBA from Harvard." He smiled at her. "Go ahead. Pick my brain."

Before she could answer, he glanced down at the menu and his eyes widened. "Oh, my gosh!"

"What?"

"Our wine is here. They serve our wine!"

"It's good business for both us and the tavern. We give them a discount. They direct people to our vineyard."

His eyes glowed. "No. You're missing the point. The company my friends and I owned didn't have products. We were sellers of someone else's goods. This," he said, pointing at the segment of the menu offering Giordano wines, "is mine... Ours," he corrected, acknowledging that he hadn't actually been in on the process yet.

Her frown deepened.

He shook his head and leaned back in his chair. His empathy for her was off the charts, but having lived through something painful himself, he knew she had to let go. Maybe he could help her with that as she taught him how to make wine and run a vineyard.

"Come on. Humor me. This is cool, and I'm sorry, but I'm enjoying it."

"You're allowed to enjoy it."

He grinned. Her acknowledging that was a good first step. He needed to keep her going in that direction. Acceptance sprinkled with forward momentum. "Thanks. I know it probably seems to you like I took advantage of your family's bad luck, but I feel like a kid at Christmas."

"Okay. Now you're pushing it."

"Not really. I'm happy. And you could be too. You seem to have a plan to buy me out." His grin widened. "What more could you want?"

She laughed. "Stop being charming. I don't want to like you."

The little zing of pleasure he got when she said she liked him surprised him. He ignored that in favor of his mission of helping her. "I think you simply don't *want* to be happy. You could put that waitress in her place just by laughing and having a good time."

"I don't want to make a scene."

"A good old-fashioned scene is exactly what you need." When she shook her head, he sighed. "Look, I know that having one of your employees steal from you had to be embarrassing. Maybe even humiliating. But a year's gone by. It almost seems like not letting yourself be happy is your self-imposed penance."

She pulled in a breath. He clearly believed he had her all figured out, but he'd only nipped the tip of the iceberg. Her humiliation wasn't the issue. It was her dad's. Trace kept mentioning that an employee had stolen from them, which probably meant her dad hadn't explained that she'd been *engaged* to that employee.

"There's more to it than that."

"Then tell me."

The exhausted part of her wanted to confide in him. He was a nice guy. Someone who seemed to understand. It might feel good to unburden herself. But he was also the competition. Someone so confident that he'd risked one-quarter of what he'd paid for the vineyard.

All this kindness could all be a trick.

She fiddled with her silverware. "Maybe *that's* a story for another time."

He grimaced. "Got me."

She only smiled, though it was beginning to soak in that what he said was true. She *was* holding back, letting people talk about her, because she felt she deserved it. It might be time to get beyond that, but she couldn't forget her father's shame. Antonio Giordano had lost the vineyard he'd bought when he was a young man and nursed into a thriving business. She'd run it successfully for three years before she'd talked him into expanding and both had realized they needed more help in the office. Another accountant. She'd chosen Adam.

No matter how she sliced it, it was her fault, but her dad's disgrace. Keeping herself as the focus of the incident protected her dad.

Still, Trace's encouragement bolstered her. He eased the dinner conversation back to the vineyard, giving her a chance to display her knowledge, and she wondered if he hadn't done that on purpose too.

She thought of the men she knew…her dad, her brothers, even Adam. Not one of them would have even noticed the humiliation that surrounded her. Yet Trace had.

The drive back to the vineyard with the top down on his Maserati was heavenly and she wondered how she'd been so preoccupied that she hadn't noticed that on the ride into town. The wind lifted her hair, swirled around her. She would never, ever, ever forget how her mistakes had embarrassed her dad—shamed him. But for the twenty minutes it took to get from town to the villa, she let peace wash through her.

She walked to the front door as Trace grabbed his bags from the tiny trunk of his sports car. She hit the code sequence on the keypad of the lock and opened the door. In the kitchen, she helped him stow the coffee, cream, eggs, milk and bread in various places.

With everything done, she wiped her hands down her jeans. "I guess I'll see you in the morning."

He nodded. "See you in the morning."

They both walked out of the kitchen, through the hall, into the foyer and up the stairs.

He winced. "This is awkward."

She tried to laugh but it came out stiff. Knowing he was behind her, his eyes about level with her butt, sent tingles and possibilities careening through her.

"Yeah. We could have saved our good-nights."

"We *should have* saved our good-nights. At least then we wouldn't have been walking in silence."

Glad when they hit the upstairs hall, she marched to her bedroom door. "Good night," she called, thinking he'd walk past her.

He stopped. "Yeah. Good night." He grinned. "Again."

Their situation was funny but not that funny. "You're enjoying this owning-a-vineyard thing a little too much."

"I can't help it. I needed some peace and quiet and now I own it."

It wasn't his first mention that he wanted peace and quiet, but it was the first time she realized there might be a crack in his armor, a reason he longed for peace and tranquility…thousands of miles away from his home. A reason he understood her troubles.

She studied his face, seeing lines she hadn't noticed before.

"I had a great time. Thank you for making my first night a weird kind of celebration."

She remembered how difficult the beginning of their dinner had been. How he'd labored to bring her out of her shell. Such a strange and interesting man. Desperate for privacy, even as he seemed to be clicking with her.

Holding his gaze, looking for answers, she said, "You're weird if you think that dinner was a celebration."

He smiled. "It was just right. Enough wine and conversation to begin my new life."

The *new life* comment raised her curiosity again. He'd helped her that night. Now he was saying she'd helped him. Maybe she wasn't the only one reaching for something.

That was when she realized how close they were standing. As if being drawn together by some unseen force, they'd inched nearer and nearer until they were close enough to kiss.

Their gazes locked and warmth flooded her, along with a quick, quiet wish that he'd touch his lips to hers. She could see in his eyes that he wanted to, and she'd been alone for so long she could barely remember what it felt like to be desired. Their dinner had been the best evening she'd had in forever. An accidental date—

The mere thought of a date with him shot fear through her. Wouldn't she be the biggest loser of all time to fall twice for someone who came to the vineyard?

She would.

She backed away, swiped her gaze across his. Too bad. She sensed he really was nice, but not too nice. More like honest. He seemed to like to deal with people frankly. Plus, he had a story. No one got to be as empathetic as he was without having gone through something himself. She could probably help him as much as he could help her.

But there was always that risk. She wasn't known for being the best judge of character and any guesses she had about him were just that. Guesses.

She turned to her bedroom door. "Good night."

"Good night."

She walked into her room and closed the door softly, not wanting to alert him to the fact that he'd thrown her off her game. But he had. She'd noticed him, sensed things about him, been curious, interested…happy.

All things she was no longer allowed to be.

Not that she intended to be a workaholic for the rest of her life. It was more that she wouldn't permit herself pleasure until she fixed the problems she'd made for her dad.

She kicked off her shoes as she slid her phone out of the

back pocket of her jeans. Hitting Contacts, she searched for Janine's phone number, then let it dial.

Voice mail answered and Marcia's heart stuttered. The way Janine's phone went straight to the recording could be a hint that her mother's condition had worsened. It felt forward to leave a message with such a mundane request. Money might be Marcia's top priority, but that didn't hold a candle to Janine's mother's cancer.

She thought for a second, realizing the voice mail answer could be a matter of time zones or Janine simply being busy. She could even be in the shower. Her call might not be an intrusion at all.

After a deep breath, she said, "Hey, Janine, it's Marcia. I'm hoping things have improved with your mom and I'm so sorry I can't be there with you. I wanted to talk to you, and I know you have other things going on but… We have a little problem at the vineyard. Remember how you've always said you'd be happy to lend me the money to start a business?" She swallowed hard, then trudged on. Trace was a little too charming and she was a little too vulnerable to wait too long with her request. She hated bothering Janine with this, but maybe things had gotten better for her mom. Or maybe Janine needed a diversion.

"I could use that money now." She laughed a bit, trying to dislodge the lump in her throat. "When you have time, give me a call, please."

She hung up feeling like a heel. And why not? She'd trusted Adam, brought him into her family, didn't pay attention to the way her father was beginning to also trust him too much, and he stole from them.

Now she was asking a friend for money at a really bad time for Janine.

How could one mistake, trusting the wrong man, have upended her entire life?

CHAPTER THREE

THE NEXT MORNING, Trace was sitting on the back patio, enjoying his coffee and reading the news on his phone, when he heard the sound of Antonio Giordano's old red truck chugging down the driveway. Right on time. Matteo and Roberto, Antonio's sons, were arriving to run the wine room and teach Trace the ropes.

He set his cup on the table as he slid his phone into his back pocket. By the time he reached the front of the villa, Antonio and his two sons had piled out of the truck.

"*Buongiorno*, Signor Jackson!"

"*Buongiorno*, Antonio!" He was a little confused about why Antonio had arrived but thought maybe he'd simply driven his sons to work.

Antonio pointed to two tall, strapping young men. Both dressed in black trousers and white shirts with sleeves rolled to the elbows, both with curly dark hair. "These are my sons, Matteo and Roberto, who will work for you until the end of the year, per our agreement."

Matteo and Roberto stepped forward to shake his hand. Trace could easily see these two handsome guys flirting with tourists, getting them to open their wallets and buy wine. But also giving the vineyard a reputation for being a fun place, which translated to lots of stars on the review sites.

"After that," Antonio said, "you and the boys will either negotiate to continue their employment or they can move on."

"Yes. That was the deal," Trace said, glad Antonio had come with his sons for the introductions, but his curiosity grew when the older man headed for the wine building. "You're staying?"

Antonio stopped and turned. "I hope you don't mind. I thought you might need some help on your first day. Someone to explain things."

True. He probably would.

"That's great. Thanks."

Antonio started toward the door again. "The first bus of tourists is scheduled to arrive at nine. But stragglers who rent cars can show up at any time all day."

Rushing ahead to beat Antonio to the door, Trace opened it, granting entry to the three Giordano men. "Good to know."

Antonio nodded and Trace walked into the wine room, taking a long drink of air, so happy to be starting his new life that he hated the odd feeling having Antonio around gave him. First, Marcia thought she should get room and board because that was the way it had always been. Now, Antonio was in the wine-tasting room, almost as if he couldn't let go of his old job.

Telling himself to stop being territorial, Trace decided he should look at this in a more positive light. As long as Antonio was at the vineyard, he could pal around with him and learn his role as the happy vintner.

The men walked to the long bar. Behind them, the door opened again, and Trace turned to see Marcia stepping into the wine-tasting room. He hadn't seen her at breakfast, which was basically toast and coffee. She looked amazing in a sleeveless dress that displayed the perfection of her figure.

Attraction rolled through him, but he reminded himself that she had troubles. He might have tried to help her the night before, but after his strange, jumbled feelings at her bedroom door, he wasn't sure getting too close was a good idea. She was an employee. He couldn't be attracted to her.

She smiled at her father. "Papa, I see you and Trace are already getting things set up."

Antonio stepped back, looking away from Marcia. "We're fine. Go to the office and do whatever it is you do back there."

Marcia's spine stiffened but she kept her smile firmly in place. "There is always plenty of work."

She walked to the steel doors behind the tasting bar, pushed through and disappeared.

Trace faced Antonio. "I guess there are offices back there."

Antonio straightened. His eyes narrowed. "She did not show you?"

"She showed me a ton of things yesterday, Antonio." He'd seen the coolness Antonio had for Marcia, but he also saw something more. Maybe a desire to catch her doing something wrong? Trace didn't know. But he didn't like it. Still, he filed it away to think about later. He wasn't letting anything ruin his first real day as a vintner.

"I'm sure she intended to show me the offices today."

He heard the sound of an engine and tires crunching in the parking lot, and he grinned. "But I think it might be more fun to interact with tourists than to go back and look at the books."

Antonio slapped him on the back. "Then let's go greet your first busload of guests."

Marcia sat at her desk, took a long, calming breath and closed her eyes. She couldn't even muster righteous indignation that her father had embarrassed her. She knew she deserved it.

She stayed out of the wine-tasting area, giving her dad space to enjoy the day with Trace. At five o'clock, she left her office through the back entry and headed to the house.

She'd checked her phone a hundred times that day, but there had been no call from Janine.

When she reached her bedroom door, she had an unexpected thought about living here. Her belief about room and board coming with her job might have been valid, but she suddenly wondered if she shouldn't begin searching for an apartment. She hated the idea of moving out of the villa, then moving back, but she had to admit she was attracted to Trace. The night before, standing at her bedroom door, odd feelings kept buzzing between them, tempting her.

She could get past the fact that he was good-looking. She could enjoy his sense of humor and walk away. But those were surface things. There was more to him than met the eye and half of his allure was the fact that she'd have to dig to find the real Trace. The other half was a blissful suspicion that the struggle would be worth it.

She stopped her thoughts, reminding herself she had a job to do—get the vineyard back from him. She chuckled, thinking of the hard work of grape harvest, and envisioned her family in the villa, where they belonged, at Christmastime.

Surely, she could keep her wits about her for six months.

A little after eight o'clock her stomach growled. With the rental cars and buses now gone from the parking lot, she knew her father and brothers would soon be going home, and Trace would be coming in for dinner.

Remembering their meal from the night before, the awkwardness at the tavern, she grabbed a pot from a cabinet beneath the center island, filled it with water and found some of her mother's pasta and a jar of sauce that had been saved from the last big batch her mama made.

By the time Trace came into the kitchen, looking freshly showered, with his dark hair slicked back, the pasta had finished cooking and the sauce was warm.

She smiled, determined to get them back to a normal

working relationship, even if they did live together. "How do you feel about penne for dinner? Mama left a few jars of her homemade sauce behind."

He groaned. "That sounds heavenly." He walked to the stove and sniffed the sauce. "Oh, God." His stomach growled. "I didn't eat lunch. Didn't want to miss a minute of watching your brothers sweet-talk tourists."

She laughed. "Yeah. That can be fun."

He shook his head. "Damn, your brothers are good. I don't think I'll ever be that smooth."

She poured the drained pasta into a big bowl. "I'm sure you would be." She sneaked a peek at him. She could be normal, but she would also keep him on the ropes. Reminding him that they were adversaries would prevent either of them from paying too much attention to their attraction and crossing any lines. "If you were staying."

"Oh, I'm staying. And I'm starving. I'm not going to say no to penne and homemade sauce." He walked to another cupboard, found two wineglasses and stopped. "Should we eat here? At the island?"

"We could eat outside," she suggested. "There are tables out there."

"Yeah, I know. I was out there last night." He quickly added, "And ate my toast there this morning."

He said both casually, but her senses began to prickle, and she forgot all about keeping him on his toes. Had he gone out there after she'd gone to bed? After *he'd* said good-night and gone to his room?

Her intuition begged her to ask why he wanted the quiet. What had happened in his life? He had a story. She knew he did—

But so did she and she didn't want to tell hers. She'd think long and hard before she tried to pry his from him.

He left to get a bottle of wine, and when he returned, he

said, "I just want to go on the record and say I didn't ask you to make dinner."

"Still worried about lawsuits?"

"Is cooking in your job description?"

"No." She winced. "Mostly because I don't really have a job description. That's the problem with a family-owned business. I did things as a daughter that maybe a normal general manager wouldn't have done. But when your home is your work and your work is your home… I guess that's going to happen."

"So, you did cook?"

"Sure. Mama typically made lunch and dinner for my dad and brothers and for everybody during grape harvest. I would help."

He considered that for a second, then frowned. "I think we need to write job descriptions and add in occasional cooking."

She shook her head, but she chuckled. "Americans. You're so lawsuit happy."

He didn't even try to deny it. "That we are."

"Well, in Italy we're not. And I am living here. It's not out of line for me to cook…or for you to cook."

He snorted. "If I cook, you might not be happy."

"Why don't we let me be the judge of that? Particularly since it's the best way to keep things even between us."

He frowned, as he appeared to think that through. "Okay. All that makes perfect sense."

"Good. Then you won't mind if I tell you to get dishes and utensils while I carry the pasta to the table."

"I will not mind at all."

There was a silliness to his voice that almost stopped her in her tracks. But it was after hours and deep down he was a nice guy. She'd seen it the night before at the tavern with the way he'd helped her cope with Gina and even enjoy the evening.

She picked up the bowl of pasta and took it to the back patio. Well-spaced lighting brightened the place just enough that they could see but not so much that it destroyed the ambience of the warm night. She set the bowl on the table and took the dishes from Trace when he brought them.

"I'm going back in for the wine."

"Good."

By the time he returned, the table had been set and Marcia sat facing the house, leaving the view of the pool and the vineyard for him. He poured her a glass of wine, then took his seat. The air had cooled enough to be comfortable. The scent of the earth wafted around them.

"Beautiful night."

She smiled. "Yes."

She scooped out a plate of pasta for him, then one for herself.

He picked up his fork. "Sorry. But I skipped lunch," he said, reminding her that he'd enjoyed watching her brothers work.

She said, "Matteo and Roberto can be very entertaining," as he took a bite of his pasta and groaned.

"That's fabulous."

"Just some stuff Mama left behind for us."

"I wonder how much I'd have to pay her to leave stuff behind every day."

"She would be thrilled to have you ask."

"Maybe I will."

He ate nonstop for a few minutes, pausing only for wine, and she shook her head. "You really were starving."

"I think it's all the fresh air."

Confused by his appreciation of fresh air, she asked, "Where did you live in the States?"

"Manhattan."

"It's nice there?"

"There is no other place in the world like it. There's big money on Wall Street and penthouses for the people who play with it." He paused, thinking before he said, "Central Park. Broadway. And people everywhere."

"You loved it." She paused, then cautiously added, "Even the noise."

"The first day I stepped out of a taxi onto the sidewalk across from our office building, I knew I was home."

She tilted her head as she studied him. The more she heard, the less she understood. "Yet you are here."

He scooped up more pasta. "I told you. We sold the business."

"And you had too much time to think." Questions about him nagged at her again. But she stifled them, picking up her wine and taking a sip. The sky had darkened enough that the moon shone through. And her mother's pasta, as always, was delicious.

She'd appreciated this as a family home, but tonight it suddenly felt like a bachelor's lair. Odd how a change of ownership had shifted the entire feel of the place. Of course, the inside was empty, except for the dining room table, kitchen things, her bed and the bed her parents had left behind for him. They'd also left behind the outdoor tables and furniture. But that was it. Beyond that, the huge villa was a blank slate, waiting to be filled.

"We should go to the city to shop for furniture for you sometime."

He lifted his wineglass. "Really? I was thinking about shopping online."

"You could do that," she readily agreed because she wasn't sure why she'd made the suggestion. The moonlight, the wine, the pasta and her curiosity about him seemed to have moved a few of the walls she'd erected around herself.

As simply and naturally as it had happened, though, she didn't like it. It made her feel easy. Desperate. Susceptible to a little moonlight and a normal conversation, when she needed to be on her guard, and concerned with getting the vineyard back...not wondering about his past or his problems.

Done with his pasta, he tossed his napkin beside his plate and smiled across the table at her. "I'm not much of a shopper."

"I'm not either. It's just that the house feels so different."

He refilled their wineglasses, then leaned in. His smile was warm and encouraging when he said, "Really? How?"

A sense of connection wove through her, reminding her that they shouldn't be making friends. "It feels empty."

He laughed. "It *is* empty." He sat back in his seat. "Truth be told, I thought I'd wait until I got a sense of the place before I furnished it."

"It seems like the right thing to do."

He leaned in. Smiled again. An odd, warm smile that made her feel like he could see directly into her soul. "It *is* the right thing to do."

The same longing she'd felt the night before at her bedroom door tugged at her heart. If she leaned in too, she could brush her lips across his. She imagined his mouth as soft and warm. She could envision his eyes growing smoky with need.

Desire wove through her. She took a breath and deliberately sat back, putting space between them, bringing herself back to reality. He was gorgeous and charming. He might not think he was, but there was something about his very casual way of speaking to her that made her feel like she'd known him forever—or had been destined to meet him.

Which was silly, romantic nonsense. Just as imagining kissing him had been. Still, she refused to be too hard on herself for thinking these things. She'd made the biggest mistake a woman could make. She trusted a man enough that he stole from her family. But she'd vowed she would never be that foolish again. And she wouldn't be. The very fact that she recognized these feelings and could fight them proved she wasn't the same naive girl she had been when Adam had arrived at the vineyard.

She finished her wine, leading Trace into a discussion of the area. When her glass was empty, she wasted no time gathering their dishes and utensils and heading inside.

"Good night," she called as she walked through the door. She could feel bad for leaving so abruptly. Maybe she *should* feel bad. But leaving was the way to fight the longing to kiss him and the connection she felt with him. She wasn't merely attracted to him. She was drawn to him. Something about him—maybe the way he listened with real interest—made her want to trust him. Made her curious about him. Pushed her guard down so far, she'd spoken without reserve. Listened with genuine curiosity.

And one night when she least expected it, he *would* kiss her. He'd almost made a move the night before, so her intuition didn't have to go out on a limb to make that assumption. And then what would she do? Cave? Submit? Give in to the luscious longings?

She straightened her spine, trying to remind herself she was strong, but she also remembered how easy the night had been…with him. Because of him. Under any other circumstances, the connection she felt with him would be welcome. But with all her baggage, this guy could be perfect for her and she wouldn't see it because she couldn't afford to be a fool again.

In her bedroom, she pulled her phone from her pocket, intending to put it on her bedside table, but she paused. She wished she would hear from Janine, but the dimming of the patio lights reminded her she'd left Trace alone in the moonlight. They'd be laughing together right now, if she hadn't scrambled away.

Disappointment tightened her chest. She was tired of

being desperate. Desperate for money. Desperately working to keep her perspective about a man who intrigued her, when he shouldn't.

She just wanted to be normal again.

CHAPTER FOUR

TRACE STAYED ON the patio a few minutes after Marcia went inside. He finished the bottle of wine they'd started, staring out at vineyards lit only by occasional lights that reminded him of streetlights.

After he was sure she'd be upstairs in her room, he headed in. She'd used the excuse of clearing their dishes to get herself away from their conversation, so he only had to dispose of the empty wine bottle. But he also felt weird again. Just as he'd almost kissed her his first night in the villa, he'd been a little too intimate with her at dinner. He hadn't touched her, but he'd leaned forward when she'd spoken, listening intently, lured by the sound of her beautiful, musical voice.

And that was strange. Not something he did. Not how he behaved. He remembered Skylar leaving him at the hospital after they'd been told their infant son was dead, most likely sudden infant death syndrome, but an autopsy would be performed.

She hadn't turned to him for comfort. Hadn't stayed to comfort him. She hadn't come to the apartment for the death scene investigation. She hadn't helped him provide their child's clinical history. She'd walked away from him, their marriage…their *child*…without a backward glance.

The pain of it could still paralyze him. Freeze his breathing. Empty his heart.

Was it any wonder he was calculated, careful about his interactions with women? After such a horrible loss, he let himself be attracted only to women who wanted a good time. Marcia might need a good time, but she was a woman with trouble, and he was a guy who just liked to play. Commitment was hard. Losses always followed. So, he didn't commit. Ironically, the strategy that had kept him happy for over a decade would end up hurting her.

He couldn't hurt her. She'd been hurt enough. Her judgment error had cost her family their vineyard. And now her father barely spoke to her. He wouldn't add to that.

Walking through the empty downstairs, he sniffed a laugh. She was right. The house did feel different. But to him the odd sensation was transition. The house itself was shifting from the home of a big family who had lived there for almost thirty years to the home of a single man, looking for solitude. There'd be a huge change in the way he would furnish it. But there also wasn't anywhere to sit.

He turned and went outside again, realizing how ironic it was that a man determined to stay single had bought a family home. A family business. And was interacting with the family.

He'd had a family.

Lost a family.

Lost every piece of a future he'd wanted so badly his heart still sometimes yearned for it.

The past twelve years, he'd spent every minute of every day too busy to dwell on the horrific loss of his child and the breakdown of the marriage he'd loved, but under the big starlit sky, in the silence of the Italian countryside, it was all he seemed to be able to think about.

Exactly the opposite of why he'd bought this vineyard.

Pulling his phone from his back pocket, he lowered himself to the chair he'd vacated only a few minutes before and set up a video call with his two friends. When Wyatt White and Cade Smith appeared on the phone screen, his world righted. He'd met them at Harvard and, though they hadn't known it, they'd saved him, brought him back to life enough that he could eventually help them set up the corporation that had made them all rich.

Rubbing a beard the same shiny black as his hair, Wyatt looked like he'd been awakened from a nap. Blond-haired, blue-eyed Cade wore a fishing vest and held a beer.

Wyatt peered at Trace. "What time is it there? Shouldn't you be asleep?"

"No. It's not that late." Trace leaned back. He wouldn't tell his friends that the months of no work had him thinking about his past and given him insomnia. They might know about his losses, but his son had died and his marriage had ended over a decade ago. They would think him crazy to be overwhelmed by memories now. He would handle it on his own. Plus, he had a whole new business he could talk about with them. A new home. A new country.

"I just realized I should have called you earlier while it was light so I could give you a virtual tour."

"No worries." Cade grinned. "I plan on coming to visit in a few weeks."

"Don't. I only negotiated to keep the furniture in the master bedroom and enough pots, dishes and glasses to be able to survive. There isn't another bed." Well, there was, but Marcia was sleeping in it—

"You should go shopping."

"Yeah. Marcia said I should start looking for furniture."

Wyatt sat up. "Marcia?"

Trace waved him off. "Marcia's the general manager. I negotiated for her and her brothers to stay on for a few months to help me. The brothers handle the wine room, giving out samples, selling wine. Marcia does the books, supervises all the admin."

Cade frowned. "Meaning she was the boss of the employee who embezzled?"

Trace relaxed. Discussing his new business—even the sensitive parts—was much better than discussing his insomnia or his past. "Yes."

Wyatt tapped a pencil on his desk. "Are you sure she's trustworthy?"

"If I wasn't, I'd have sent her packing yesterday when I met her. She knows everything there is to know about this company and its wine. I haven't gotten the story of the embezzler yet, but it's clear the whole town knows it. Whoever he was, it's obvious he bamboozled Marcia."

Cade whistled. "Didn't take you long to get that gossip."

He shrugged. "As I said, the whole town knows. Waitress at the tavern the other night treated her like a soccer ball, kicking her because she was down."

Wyatt scratched his scraggly beard again. "Sounds like a beautiful place you moved to."

"Actually, it is," Trace insisted. "I feel like the Giordano Vineyards trouble is an isolated incident. Which makes it even juicier gossip because bad things don't happen here."

Cade sniffed. "You don't know that. You said yourself you don't have the whole story."

"Yeah, but I have the gist of it. Marcia was the supervisor for the guy who embezzled. Ultimately, the Giordanos lost their vineyard. Her dad obviously blames her. That's the only reason he could be so angry with her that he barely speaks to her."

Cade came to attention. "Her dad barely talks to her?"

"Emotions are still raw."

Wyatt sat up too. "I thought you said this happened a year ago?"

"It did…but…"

"But?" Cade said.

"But there are still some sensitivities that are obvious when she and her dad are in the same room. They don't talk and the air sort of crackles. That's the part I'm still trying to figure out."

Wyatt pursed his lips. "A place or a person with secrets can bring down even the strongest company."

Suddenly Trace was sorry he'd led them into a discussion of the vineyard. They were taking everything he said the wrong way. "I'm not saying there are secrets."

"But you don't believe you have the whole story?"

Trace's stomach sank. He didn't like the feeling he was getting from his friends, the sense that they were seeing something he'd missed. "You think I should have let her go?"

Cade said, "Once you realized there was something going on that you didn't know, you should have point-blank asked. If you didn't like the answer, you should have fired her."

Wyatt said, "Sorry, Trace. But she sounds like trouble."

Trace stilled. The Eliminator in him *had* come out several times in their initial discussions but she'd tempted him with that bet.

Still, he wasn't often wrong about situations, about people. He did not sense deceit in her. "I don't think *she's* trouble. I think she's *in* trouble. She made a mistake that cost her family too much. And she can't get beyond it because her dad is still angry with her." He smoothed his hand across the back of his neck. "I don't know… I feel like I should help her."

Wyatt's head tilted as if he finally understood. "Ah…"

"Ah?" Trace frowned. "What the hell does 'ah' mean?"

"It means you're up to your normal tricks."

"My normal tricks?"

"Yeah. Mr. Fix-It."

"I'm not Mr. Fix-It. I'm The Eliminator, remember? I don't deal with people's personal problems. I only see and solve business problems. That's why it seems weird that I want to help her."

"Technically, two fighting employees do pertain to your business," Wyatt corrected. "And *you* called yourself The Eliminator. We called you Mr. Fix-It."

Cade said, "You were the one who could walk into a grocery store we'd bought and immediately see how to bring it up to our standards. Sometimes that involved firing a person or two… So we let you call yourself The Eliminator. But, really, you were Mr. Fix-It."

Wyatt snorted. "Which is why your wanting to mend this situation for the poor employee who was bamboozled is right up your alley."

Cade laughed. "You might not be the guy who gets all warm and fuzzy, but you like to fix things."

Trace frowned. If he was a fixer, wanting to help her should feel normal. Yet it didn't. There was something different about it. Something more…personal.

When he finally spoke, it was quietly. "I think what bugs me is that I'm responsible for some of her pain. The vineyard wasn't on the market twenty-four hours before I was in negotiations with her dad. I really did not give her a chance to try to bail them out herself."

"You buying the vineyard saved her family from financial ruin," Cade reminded him.

"Yeah, but it underscored that she made some bad judgment calls—"

"Trace, we've all made bad judgment calls," Wyatt said. "We get beyond them. She will too. But you spending too much time thinking about fixing hers seems like it's taking your focus off where it needs to be."

Trace frowned.

"Did you ever stop to think that if you use all your time trying to reunite two feuding employees, you just might fail or get so exhausted with their drama that you'll run screaming?"

"Are you saying you think they are making me uncomfortable on purpose?"

"Are they?"

His frown deepened. He didn't think so. The Giordanos

were straightforward people. For Pete's sake, Marcia had warned him she was going to try to buy the vineyard back. He didn't think she or her dad would deceive him. But they were so casual and spontaneous, they *did* have Trace behaving differently. And he finally heard what Cade and Wyatt were saying. Whatever his reasons for his need to help Marcia, it was taking his focus off where it needed to be. On running the vineyard.

And that he would fix.

Maybe he was Mr. Fix-It after all?

The next morning when Trace arrived in the kitchen for breakfast, Marcia stood by the toaster. Her bread popped, she set it on a plate, slathered it with butter and brought it to a stool by the island.

"Good morning."

"Good morning."

His deep voice skipped along her nerve endings, reminding her of the intimacy in the moonlight the night before. She struggled not to notice how handsome he looked in his dark trousers and white shirt, and almost smiled at the way he'd dressed like her dad and brothers. Fitting in.

Except he had tattoos. That sexy art that made her wonder if the good guy she kept seeing was actually a bad boy at heart.

The back door opened, and her dad stepped inside. Trace glanced from her to her dad and then back to her again.

Not wanting to cause a scene, she looked away as her father walked to the coffeepot.

"Trace, we should have a fine time this morning. Lots of buses scheduled. Lots of wine will be sold."

Trace's eyes narrowed as he studied her but spoke to her dad. "That's good."

Pouring coffee into a cup he could take into the wine

room, her dad said, "I think I'm beginning to enjoy this role of being here while not really being responsible."

Trace chuckled. "Yeah, that would be nice. All the entertainment of the wine room with none of the worry." He smiled slightly, peeked at her, then spoke to her dad. "But I am kind of curious about how long you intend to be here. I don't have you on the payroll and I'm not sure the budget can handle taking you on."

Antonio laughed and batted a hand. "I don't need to be paid. Being here is fun for me. I like you. I'm happy to help you adjust and learn. Come grape harvest, you'll be glad I'm here."

With that, her dad headed out, without saying one word to her. Not even *good morning*. At the door, he looked back at Trace. "See you in the wine room."

It couldn't have been more obvious that he was still angry with her.

Trace's voice tiptoed into the quiet kitchen. "Last night my friends pointed out that I'm spending a lot of my time trying to fix your problems."

She nearly choked on her coffee. "What? No one asked you to fix my problems!"

"As long as you and your dad work for me, and your dad won't talk to you, your feud is my problem. Technically, I have a general manager who cowers every time a coworker is in the room."

Unable to deny that, she stayed quiet.

"When I told Wyatt and Cade about the tension between you and your father, they called me Mr. Fix-It. They said when I would go into a business, I could look around, pinpoint the trouble, and if it was a person, I'd fire that person." He winced. "That's the reason I thought they called me The Eliminator."

"Eliminator?"

"Yes, because I got rid of trouble." He winced again.

"Sometimes employees. But here's the thing. You have a problem with your dad. He won't talk to you and that hurts you. But I can't fire you. I need you."

She stiffened. "You certainly don't mince words."

"I never do when it comes to a problem. I believe in facing things head-on. That's why I'm telling you all this. There is a problem. We must fix it."

A bad feeling fluttered through her. She remembered how bossy and calculating he'd been the day she'd met him and realized talking to his friends the night before must have reoriented him to the guy he'd been when he worked with them. "Okay."

"I need you here. You're in the agreement of sale. So are your brothers. Your dad is a different matter. I'd be within my rights to ask him not to come here anymore. But I don't want to." He smiled unexpectedly. "He's right. I do like learning from him. I don't want to ban him from the vineyard. Worse, I don't want *that* to be the next rumor that ripples through town. How I kicked him off the vineyard he'd built."

Neither did she. "That gossip would kill my dad."

"Okay, then, what's *your* solution? You're the general manager. How would you handle two fighting employees?"

She took a breath. She hadn't thought her troubles with her dad affected the business. But how could they not? The vineyard was supposed to be a place of relaxation and fun. She was hardly fun when her dad was around.

"I guess my answer has been to stay away from my dad."

He shook his head. "That isn't working. It's a small company. I feel the tension every time the two of you are in a room, and that's taking everyone's focus off our primary goal…which is to make and sell wine. So, either *you* perk up, stop being hurt by things he says or doesn't say, or I'll have to let your dad go."

She blanched. "There have to be other solutions."

"When it comes to people, there are two solutions. Either you two get along or I get rid of one of you. You want your dad to stay? Then you suck it up. I don't want any sad moods, no sad faces. And for God's sake, stand tall when he's around. You're not a coward. In our very first conversation you told me you were going to buy me out and at a twenty-five percent loss. That's the woman I want running the place."

His toast popped. He smeared it with jam, got himself a cup of coffee and walked outside to the patio table.

She blinked. She'd never thought of this situation from a business perspective, only from the vantage point of having hurt her dad. But Trace was right. A good employee worked to get along.

And she absolutely didn't want him asking her dad not to come over. That would be the last straw. At least with Adam having been her fiancé, all the gossip had been directed at her. If the gossip shifted to her dad? The shame of being asked to leave his own vineyard would be impossible to handle.

Her mama arrived later that morning. The gorgeous dark-haired woman from whom Marcia got her beauty and dark eyes sneaked in the back door that led to Marcia's office and enticed her into the kitchen.

Pulling vegetables from a grocery bag, she said, "Your father tells me Trace Jackson is extremely happy and fun to be around."

Which was exactly why she didn't want her dad to leave. He was enjoying himself. Forgetting his troubles. Maybe even beginning to heal from the loss of his business.

"He is when he's in the wine room. He's happy with Dad and the boys. But with me? Not so much."

Mama frowned. "You're the boss. Trace might be owner.

But you're the boss. Are you doing something he doesn't like?"

Only avoiding her dad. She wasn't about to tell her mother that. Or the fact that Trace had been correct. Here she had to stand tall, be the general manager she was trained to be. When she visited her parents in town, at their rental home, then she would be the mouse. Here, she had to be strong Marcia.

"No. He seems to like my work. It's my attitude." She took a quiet breath, then said, "I'm a bit cautious."

Her mother winced. "After Adam, who can blame you?"

Who indeed? Having a lover deceive her, steal from her family, shame her father was such a tangled mess that Trace was right. She was letting business and personal things overlap and now was the time to stand tall.

Like a good parent, Mama changed the subject. "Your dad wants a feast for lunch. He said there's a tourist break between one and two. If stragglers come in, one of the boys can handle them. But he wants to celebrate."

"Celebrate?" She gasped. "Trace buying this vineyard is his loss."

Her mother shrugged. "Maybe it's not so much a celebration as a welcome, then. No one welcomed Trace, and because it was our home, it's our duty."

She considered that and agreed. Maybe it was another step her father needed? A transition of a sort.

"Yes. Papa has been good to him, but no one officially welcomed him."

"See? Mama is always right."

That made her laugh. And feel good. Feel like herself. Even after her sort of scolding from Trace that morning, her sense of self blossomed. The vineyard felt more like the place she loved. Most of the tension went out of her shoulders. The impression that she was moving on filled her. Not in a bad way. In a good way.

The way a strong woman should embrace change.

But her father's celebration didn't go as planned. First, there was awkwardness when her dad took his seat at the head of the dining room table. Realizing that seat no longer belonged to him, he made a production number out of switching places with Trace, giving him the honor of sitting at the head of the table. Then he allowed Trace to pour everyone's wine, settling back with a fake smile.

Shame flitted through Marcia, but remembering Trace's orders from the morning, and the sense of her strength she'd felt about embracing this change, she kept her head high. Her spine straight.

A bus pulled in just as her dad lifted his glass to toast. Matteo pushed his chair back. "I'll get it."

"Good. Great," her dad said, at the same time that Trace said, "Thank you. I appreciate that."

As Matteo scrambled out of the room, her dad said, "Well, it seems nothing is on track today."

"Oh, I don't know," Trace said, lifting his glass. "We had a great morning. We sold lots of wine. But more than that, I saw what a great man you are, Antonio." He lifted his glass a little higher. "To you, Antonio Giordano. A great man. Someone I hope will become a great friend."

Though Trace had intended his toast to be a salute to her dad, he didn't seem to realize he'd stolen her dad's moment. Antonio had wanted the opportunity to be gracious, to welcome Trace, but Trace had toasted him first.

After a stunned second of silence, Marcia said, "Hear. Hear."

Her mother and brother raised their glasses and her father smiled, accepting the salute, but Marcia saw the emptiness in his eyes.

Trace might want to fix things, but he'd just made things worse.

CHAPTER FIVE

ANTONIO'S SILENCE AT lunch was superseded only by his stony silence the rest of the afternoon. It hadn't taken Trace long to figure out that what had started as a way for Antonio's family to welcome him had become difficult for Antonio. He liked Trace, but he'd lost his life's work. That afternoon it was clear the old man was floundering for a place in the world.

After nine, when the sun had long ago set and the night sounds settled in, Antonio's truck chugged its way off Giordano Vineyards and Trace ambled into the house, exhausted. Not from tourists but from trying to make Antonio happy.

With a bottle of red taken from the wine room samples, he walked down the hall, to the kitchen and directly out to the dark patio.

He stopped when he saw Marcia at the table, staring out at the vineyards. He considered turning around but knew the click of the door closing behind him had alerted her to his presence.

He approached the table. "I see we had the same idea."

She smiled up at him. *"Si."* She rose. "I was just leaving."

He groaned. "Ah, come on. Don't do that. I have never felt more like an interloper than I did today with your dad."

"I thought you said you liked having him around."

He sucked in a breath. "My toast at lunch didn't exactly go over well."

"That's because you stepped on my dad's welcome-to-Tuscany toast to you. The lunch was supposed to be our welcome. You rolled right over my dad when he started to speak."

"Yeah. I figured that out. Your dad was low energy all afternoon." He took a seat at the table and poured wine into his glass, then offered it to Marcia. "Share?"

She hesitated but reached for the wine. "Sure." She took a sip and gave it back to him.

"Your brothers looked like they were walking on eggshells. They sold wine, but not like they had this morning." He sighed. "Your dad's behavior just reinforces everything my friends said last night. One difficult employee can make a mess of things for everyone."

He took a drink of wine and returned the glass to her.

"But if you ask him not to come anymore it would break his heart. He can't be the object of any more gossip."

He closed his eyes. He really should not care about that. But he did. And not just because of her dad. Because of her. She'd been different that day. Stronger. Happier. How could he break their unspoken bargain that he'd keep her dad if she changed her behavior around him?

He couldn't.

"So, what we're saying is we have to wait for him to get back to himself."

"Maybe give him a few days?"

He sniffed. "In a few days, he could lose me thousands of dollars."

She caught his gaze, her dark eyes shiny in the moonlight. "You can afford it."

He laughed. "Yeah. I suppose."

She smiled. "Thank you."

His heart softened. Pleasing her felt like Christmas and Easter all rolled into one. And that was wrong too.

He quickly took the conversation back where it belonged. "I suppose I could help things along if I found a way to get him to cheer up."

She rose from her chair. "Good luck with that."

He sucked in a breath. Not only was she being flippant, but she was his general manager, supposed to help him figure things out.

She turned to leave, and he caught her hand, stopping her. When he rose to stand in front of her, he realized she was smiling, and her brown eyes sparkled.

"You're enjoying this."

"Maybe I like that the heat is off me for once. You said you wanted the tension eased between Papa and me. Knowing you're handling Papa is definitely easing mine."

He couldn't help it. He laughed. She had a great sense of humor, but more than that, he liked making her laugh about something that had just that morning had her nervous and on edge.

Still… It wasn't right. He was feeling things he wasn't allowed to feel, definitely mixing business with pleasure, when he knew better.

He shook his head. "I could virtually run our multibillion-dollar conglomerate in my sleep, and your simple family business is breaking all my rules, making me crazy."

She shrugged. Her lips turned up into a smile that stole his breath and made his blood race.

He still held her hand. They stood only a few inches apart. The full moon smiled down on them while the vineyard that was at the center of their problems rustled in the breeze.

But she was smiling. Amused by him.

The humor of it struck him and his own lips rose. "This is crazy."

"There's that word again. You use *crazy* a lot…especially about yourself."

She really was funny. Fun. He felt like he was getting a glimpse of her as she really was, maybe as she had been before their employee embezzled.

With their gazes locked, everything inside him slowed

to a crawl. Warmth suffused him, along with a yearning so pure he couldn't fight it. He inched closer. The connection between them rose, swelling around him, urging him even closer.

"I think I'm going to kiss you."

Her eyes didn't even flicker with surprise. And why would they? They'd been attracted since the second they'd laid eyes on each other.

"You shouldn't."

Her voice was a soft whisper that skipped along his spine, but she didn't move. Didn't step back. Held his gaze. Expectantly.

The hum of whatever it was that buzzed between them drowned out his common sense and reasoning. Simple curiosity filled him, as desire surged in his blood and temptation promised fulfillment, pleasure enough to make it worth the risk.

He lowered his head and kissed her.

He meant it to be a brief kiss, but her lips were soft. And she'd been surprised enough that she'd gasped, opening her mouth the merest bit, enough to take the kiss from innocent to intimate without either of them trying.

He fell into the kiss like Alice down the rabbit hole. Her soft lips tempted him but also slowed him down to savor every movement, every sensation. Not merely her warm lips, but their height difference, the press of her breasts against his body.

His hands moved to her tiny waist, reminding him of her curves, and his nerve endings glittered and shimmied. She was physically perfect, but more than that, she was Marcia. Not a woman in a crowd. Not someone he chose because she didn't look like his ex. But someone he was coming to know. And like. And understand. Which made the kiss striking, important, breathtaking.

He sank even deeper. Thoughts disappeared. Desire lured him on to a place from which there'd be no return.

But she pulled away, bringing him out of his trance and back to the vineyard. The moon. The night sounds. The scent of the cooling earth.

For ten seconds she stood in front of him, her breathing ragged, her eyes confused. Then without a word, she turned and left him on the patio with a million stars winking overhead and one very disapproving moon.

Yeah, he got it.

All of it. Understanding her guilt over losing the vineyard, he should have realized she didn't need kisses or a baffled man acting out of character all over the place, making passes at her. She needed redemption. Peace. A second chance.

His brain stumbled over that realization. His breathing froze.

She *did* need redemption and a second chance.

Trying to solve her feud with her dad, his thoughts had always gone to removing her father from the vineyard. But what if Marcia was the one who should go?

The idea of losing her cut through him. With her kiss still on his lips, his heart stuttered at the notion that he'd never see her again.

But this wasn't his choice. Or at least it shouldn't be. He'd tied her to the vineyard with his need to smooth the transition from the Giordanos' hands to his. But what if that was the very worst thing for her?

After the spectacular kiss, Marcia carefully considered not joining Trace in the kitchen the next morning. No one had ever kissed her with such feeling. First, they'd laughed. Then he'd kissed her and that amazing connection she always felt around him lit like a firecracker, burned through the walls around her soul and awakened something in her.

A longing to be her total self again. Not merely business-woman Marcia. But Marcia the woman. To find a partner. Someone to share her life with. To be in love.

Which was ridiculous. Wasn't going to happen. Everyone in her world knew of her sin, her mistake. She would always be the object of gossip in their little town, and even if they let her alone for a while, the gossip would resurrect every few years. Belittling her. She'd never be her total self again. Never be that overconfident woman again. Never risk falling in love. No matter how much he tempted her.

And he had tempted her.

It was one thing to be drawn into a kiss, lured by needs she hadn't felt in a year. It was quite another to have a sense of completion spin through her. The mastery of his kiss annihilated her senses, then brought them to stunning life again. The way he controlled it all spoke more of his need than words could have. She'd never experienced anything like that with Adam. And maybe that scared her the most. She'd trusted Adam with everything. Trace would demand even more. She knew it in the center of her being.

And a smart woman wouldn't let herself think about *that* too much. The intensity of what he made her feel might tempt her, but he was her boss. He owned her family home. He was strong, bold, remarkable. She was still figuring out how to right her life. They did not belong together.

That was the conclusion that had her turning away from him without a word the night before. There was nothing to be said when two people were so very, very wrong for each other.

She heard the rustling of pots and pans or maybe the coffee maker, and her stomach growled. She was hungry and she needed coffee. Besides, she couldn't avoid him forever.

Particularly since being cool with him that morning could finish the job she'd started when she walked away from him after that spectacular kiss. They did not belong together. She would show him that.

She took a long, life-sustaining breath and walked into the kitchen. "Good morning."

His gaze rose and he gave her a quick once-over as if assessing her mood. "Good morning, yourself. What's on the agenda for the day?"

She hadn't expected him to jump right to business. But why not? She wanted to send a message. This was the perfect way to get things back to normal between them. Rather than apologize for kissing her, question her about why she'd left without a reaction, or kiss her again, he asked about her schedule. Making all those things moot.

Which was good. She should be grateful—

Still, after such a powerful kiss the night before, why *wasn't* he apologizing? The man worried about lawsuits over her cooking. Yet he'd kissed her? Why wasn't he worried that she'd sue him over that? Plus, if he'd decided he liked her enough to kiss her once… Why didn't he want to kiss her again?

She almost groaned. She had to stop thinking like this! She'd made up her mind. They were not right for each other! She should roll with this easy out he was giving them.

She pasted on her professional smile. "Actually, the vineyard is closed on Thursdays. You're free."

"I don't have time to be free!"

His voice was oddly desperate, and she frowned.

"The sales agreement says you can leave in a year. We extended that with a bet, but that doesn't preclude you from giving up when the amount of time in the sales agreement runs out." He paused and caught her gaze. His eyes shifted, changed from aggressive to soft and warm. "And you might want to leave sooner."

Ah, so he hadn't forgotten that kiss after all.

She took a breath, then another, not quite sure what to

say. A romance between them might be foolish, but that didn't mean she hadn't liked the kiss. It had been an entire year since anyone had kissed her. A year since her heart rate had jumped and her bones had melted. A year since anyone had looked at her with interest, let alone acted on it.

He'd made her feel beautiful, desired. The part of her that always went after what she wanted swelled and nudged her to tell him that.

But that would be wrong. They were opposites. People in two different places in their lives. She couldn't fall for him. One of them would surely get hurt.

Finally, she settled on saying, "I'm fine." Something so neutral she let him know she wasn't offended, even as she soothed her aching heart by drawing on her strength of purpose. She would not willingly walk into a complicated situation again.

She reached for a mug and got some coffee, giving him time to process those few simple words, then changed the subject. "Do you want to go over the books today?"

"I went over the books before I bought the place."

She took a sip. "How about a tour through the grapes?"

He frowned suddenly. "I'm sorry. It just hit me that I'm stealing your day off." Taking in her jeans and T-shirt, he waved his hand. "Go do whatever it was you had planned to do today."

He might have tried to make it seem that the look he'd given her was neutral, but something sparked in his eyes. Something strong enough to make her think of that kiss again.

Luckily, her phone pinged with a text. "No. It's okay. If you want to work, we'll work." She pulled her phone from her jeans pocket and tapped the screen. "There *is* a lot for you to learn in a year. I'm happy to teach you."

He snorted. "Are you sure?"

"I'm sure." Seeing the text was from Janine, she took a breath before she tapped the phone to read it.

"I could probably find something else to do." He rose and filled his coffee mug again.

She quickly scanned the text.

Hi. This is Janine's assistant, Carla. She wanted me to text you to let you know she got your message. But we have some sad news. Her mom's lung cancer is not responding to the experimental treatment her doctor had found. They've given her no more than a few months to live.

Marcia about dropped her phone. She knew how close Janine and her mother were. As close as she was to her own mother, she couldn't imagine the heartbreak of losing her.

She will get back to you as soon as she can, but right now she's only going into the office sporadically. She's focusing on her mom.

Marcia typed back.

As she should. Give her my love and tell her that if she needs anything, she should call me.

"Or maybe I *should* take a day off?"

She looked up at Trace. His pretty blue eyes behind the lenses of sexy glasses. His great hair. Those unexpected tattoos. He was a man who kissed with real emotion. He didn't just go through the motions. He *kissed*.

He felt things. And no matter how much she tried to deny it, they had connected.

The need to tell him about Janine raced through her. Not the fact that it could take months before she'd have the money to buy him out, but that her friend was losing her mother. The sadness of it. The awful feeling that life changed too often and when you least needed or wanted it to.

She had the sense that he would understand. But she also recognized he was her competition. Janine had been Marcia's way out—a chance to repair her relationship with her father by giving back the vineyard she'd lost. Now, also, a chance to get away from this man who didn't merely tempt her physically. Something about him made her long to confide. And that was scary. Especially after falling for Adam had nearly ruined her life.

She could hope Janine went into the office looking for a few minutes of normal in a very dark situation and started the ball rolling on giving her the loan, but that was selfish.

She took a breath, shored up her emotions, quickly remembered Trace had said something about taking a day off and forced herself back into their conversation. "Do all-business bosses take a day off?"

Trace sat on one of the stools by the big island again. "I didn't used to." He glanced around. "But I wanted this experience to be different... So maybe I should shake things up? Take the day off?"

"Maybe?"

"Okay. I *probably* should."

She glanced down at her half-empty coffee cup. Becoming friends, getting to know each other, was an unintended consequence of living together, but God help her, she was curious. What kind of guy never took a break?

She turned to refill her cup, hoping to make her comment seem casual, offhand, even though her questions about him were mounting so high she could no longer contain them and had to have at least some answers. "You sound like you've never rested before."

"I took vacations." He sniffed a laugh. "I was actually

here a few years ago. It's part of why I could so easily buy this place. I knew I loved Tuscany."

She sat beside him at the island. "Where else did you go?"

"Key West in Florida with Cade."

"One of your partners?"

"Yes. He loves to fish. Lots of charter boats in Key West. I also spent most Christmases on a tropical island. I'd work Christmas Day." He peeked over at her. "You have to have grocery stores open on Christmas Eve so people can get last-minute ingredients for pies and baked ham. I'd take care of Christmas Eve's accounting on Christmas Day. Then I'd catch a flight or charter a plane and go somewhere warm. Wyatt would take over the day after Christmas. Then after a few days, he'd be off, and Cade would step in."

"Seems like an efficient team."

Something flickered in his eyes. "We were."

"You miss them."

"Yes." He glanced at her again. "As soon as I get furniture, they'll be visiting."

She was surprised at how much that pleased her. She wanted to know about his friends. Who were these people who called him Mr. Fix-It, yet shared responsibilities like brothers? "That'll be nice."

"You think so now. But they will razz the hell out of you."

"Me?" She blanched, her own fears racing back, though they were never far from her brain. "Because someone embezzled on my watch?"

He shook his head and laughed. "No, because you're pretty and funny. You're clearly smart. You said you went to school in the States. They'll like that."

Her heart lifted a bit. "They'll tease me?"

"And love every second of it."

She would too. She would love to be around people who would treat her normally. "They sound like fun."

"They both have a wicked sense of humor."

And now she understood why he was the one who hired and fired employees. The other two were fun. He was the serious one, their counterbalance. "So, you became The Eliminator by default."

He laughed. "Yes and no. I have a more serious side than either one of those yo-yos."

Exactly what she'd thought. Her heart warmed, even though she knew it wasn't wise. Beneath that all-business exterior was a very nice guy. She'd gotten more than one glimpse of him. And she had the sense that no one ever did anything nice for him.

"We could go to Siena."

He peered at her over his coffee cup. "Excuse me?"

"Siena," she said, her confidence growing. "It's an interesting little city. Less crowded than Florence. It would be the perfect break for you."

She watched his face as he considered it and was surprised when his smile grew.

"I do need a day off."

He did. She could tell he did. But so did she. When she was with him, she forgot her past. Forgot to be careful because she'd made a horrible mistake. Some days she needed a break too. Taking him to Siena had the twofold effect of forgetting her troubles and helping him forget his.

"Do you like art?"

He laughed. "I like knowing things, being cultured."

She rose from her seat. "Then we're going to up your culture today."

He laughed again. "Okay."

Her heart fluttered. The joy of doing something for someone else filled her. Along with the freedom of forgetting everything and living in the moment. "Okay."

CHAPTER SIX

"I CAN'T BELIEVE I'm on a bus." Trace glanced around at the passengers in the seats near theirs. Mostly tourists. "It was bad enough you forced me to get on a train, but the bus is like adding insult to injury."

She laughed. "You have to have a special permit to park in Siena. We didn't have one."

Her answer was matter-of-fact, simple. Nothing like the scenery around them. As they pulled into the bus station, he could see the buildings were a complicated collection of various kinds and periods of architecture.

But it was also breathtaking. He'd been to Italy. That's why buying a vineyard had been so appealing. But in this city, Siena, he felt like he was seeing more than tourist attractions. He was seeing the real Italy.

The bus let them off and Marcia pointed. "Let's walk this way."

They began to move, leaving behind tourists poring over maps and brochures, and the ambience of Siena hit him like a punch in the gut. Air rich with the scents of baked goods and pasta swirled around them in a soft breeze. Warm sun beat down on them. The sounds of laughter and delight flowed to them.

The place was old, crowded and filled with the kind of joy that was contagious.

"This is something."

"I'm surprised you didn't stop here on your trip to Italy a few years ago."

He laughed. "I'm guessing I was put off by needing to take a bus after a train."

She laughed too and, in a surprising move, slid her arm

around his at the elbow. Keeping them close, he was sure, so they didn't get separated in the clusters of tourists. But being connected to her made him even happier than he already was.

"This is a place of history." She motioned around with her hand. "It was once bigger than Rome. We have art, architecture, culture."

He followed the movement of her hand, feeling so many things he wasn't sure he could define them. The city was gorgeous. The air vibrated with simple joy. But with Marcia's hand tucked at his elbow, he felt the weirdest kind of peace. He barely knew her. Sure, he'd kissed her. But, really, they'd been in each other's lives only a few days. Yet it felt so right to be with her. To enjoy this city with her.

"Your choice," she said, guiding him into Piazza del Campo. "We can get a quick lunch or sightsee, then eat."

"Let's walk some more." He pointed in front of them. "I'd like to see inside that cathedral."

As they approached it, he googled it on his phone and began to read. "'Siena Cathedral is a medieval church in Siena, Italy, dedicated as a Roman Catholic Marian church, and now named for the Assumption of Mary.'"

They walked inside. Silence and reverence surrounded them, but as they moved farther inside, the sounds of the tourists echoed in the high-ceilinged sections. They didn't talk as they looked at the magnificent arches, the white-and-black marble columns, the mosaics on the floors.

Just seeing the age of everything rendered him speechless.

It wasn't until they got outside that he spoke. "That was amazing." He shook his head. "You are so lucky to live so close to this much history."

"We know. You Americans are babies compared to us."

He peered around. "Yeah, our two hundred years probably seem like a drop in the bucket to most of you."

She laughed and the weird joy filled him again. Her skin was smooth and clear. Her nose pert. Her lips plump and, today, always lifted into a smile. But her eyes held the real temptation. Dark and teeming with emotion, they caught his gaze. Tempted him to linger. To connect.

For ten seconds, he fought the urge to slide his hand around the back of her neck and pull her close for a quick kiss. Only with great determination and the reminder that he wasn't the happy guy she was dealing with today did he keep himself from kissing her long and deep, enjoying the moment. Enjoying *her*. He couldn't draw her into feelings he wasn't sure of himself. Emotions so bold and spontaneous, they took him when he least expected.

But, oh, he wanted to.

They spent more time examining the Palazzo Pubblico and museums. Caught up in the beauty of the area and how easy it was to be with Marcia, he didn't realize the passage of time until she reminded him that they had better get lunch, which would now be an early dinner.

They decided on a restaurant near the tower and ate pasta with Bolognese sauce and roasted chicken.

As they walked out of the restaurant, Trace laughed. "I don't think I'm going to be able to eat again for a year."

She laughed too. "Good, because by the time we get home it will be too late to eat again."

He didn't know why everything she said made him feel light and airy. He would use the word *comfortable*, but it was more than that. She made him forget. His past. The weirdness at the vineyard. Even the fact that he wasn't supposed to like her.

They took the bus to the train talking about what they'd seen, but when they got into the passenger car, silence reigned.

It wasn't strained, but that was the problem. He should be maintaining his distance with her. Instead, he felt like they'd been friends forever. And he shouldn't. He had too much of a past to think he could handle a future. He wasn't giving her back her vineyard. He intended to live at Giordano Vineyards. And just as he'd thought the night before, she should be moving on—

He couldn't fathom it. It might be the right thing for her, but it didn't feel right in general. He knew she needed a second chance. She needed to redeem herself. But in another city where no one would see? The people of her town wouldn't know?

Could her leaving actually be construed as running?

It could. But how could she stay at a vineyard—or in a town—where her sad, angry father reminded everyone of her mistakes?

Staring out the train window, watching the world go by, he saw a for-sale sign on the huge gates of a vineyard. A few miles down the tracks, he saw another.

He frowned. He would have never bought either one of those vineyards. Even from a distance it was clear they needed a lot of work. But he'd bet they'd be much cheaper than Giordano Vineyards had been—

They would be cheap. Probably less than half of what he'd paid for a vineyard that was up and running, making a profit—

His brain began humming.

He glanced at Marcia. Glanced back at the lush Tuscan landscape. Saw the third for-sale sign that whipped by as the train passed it. He thought about Antonio's anguish. His loss. The man was barely in his fifties. He could either let this loss define him or he could start again.

He almost laughed. The answer was so simple it was brilliant.

He faced Marcia. "I've been thinking about your dad."

She shifted to look at him. "Oh, yeah?"

"Yeah, and I think I've come up with an answer to the problem."

"You mean him not being cheerful with tourists?"

"Well, that and your family losing your vineyard."

She quirked an eyebrow.

Not sure if she was interested or perturbed, he plunged on. "If you take all the emotion out of your family's situation, your dad lost a business because he trusted an employee. If you're going to make a mistake, that's the best kind to make. It proves you put yourself out there. And someone else actually did the deed that ruined you."

She snorted. "That's a funny way of looking at it."

"That's an objective way of looking at it. Business is supposed to be objective. Not emotional. Your dad made great wine, had enormous sales, grew healthy grapes. He did everything right but hire that guy… What was his name?"

"Adam."

"Adam. If he hadn't hired Adam, he'd still own Giordano Vineyards. It didn't change his ability to run a vineyard or his smarts about making wine. That one mistake shouldn't run him out of business. In fact, with his know-how and experience, he should get back on the horse."

She furrowed her brow. "We don't have horses."

"Not a real horse. It's an American expression. It means he should take the money he has left over from selling Giordano Vineyards and buy another."

She gasped. "He can't afford another vineyard!"

"Sure he can. Your dad had all kinds of equity in your business. He simply didn't have the cash for big monthly payments on millions of dollars in loans. But what if he didn't borrow any money? What if he bought something for cash?"

Marcia knew what Trace had paid for the business. The overage wasn't enough for what he was suggesting.

"If my calculations are correct, there still isn't enough left over to buy a thriving vineyard."

"No, but there is enough to buy one that needs work. Your dad has seed money. He has two strapping sons. Right now, they work in the wine-tasting room, but they are young enough and strong enough to do a good day's work."

The point of his idea finally breaking through, she sat up on her train seat.

"You agree with me, don't you?"

A little dazed, she gave herself a minute to let the fullness of the suggestion sink in and finally said, "Yes." She winced. "Sort of."

"No *sort of* about it. He comes to Giordano Vineyards every day because he's bored. He's bored because he needs a challenge. He has everything he needs to buy another vineyard—one he can develop again. He's just sulking."

"And mad at me."

"Yeah. No kidding. But he can't use that as an excuse. He should be saying, 'Lesson learned about trusting the wrong person,' and then jumping in to create competition for me."

She laughed and pulled her fingers through her long curls. "It makes perfect sense, but I don't think my dad will go for it."

"Then maybe we help him along?"

She sniffed. "It will be a cold day in hell before my dad listens to anything I suggest."

"So, we don't suggest. We lure."

She frowned.

He shifted on his seat, getting more comfortable. "I'm not saying we trick your father. But once we investigate a few vineyards and pick the best two or three, the ones with the most potential, we could take him to those, telling him I'm thinking of buying a second and need his opinion."

"Then he would point out everything you'd need to do to get it up and running—"

"And hopefully see the opportunity himself. Even if he doesn't buy it, we'll start the wheels turning in that direction. Eventually, he'll see this is what he should do."

She snorted. "Not if I'm involved. As long as we keep me out of it, I think the idea has a chance."

"Look, I get that he's mad at you. Being general manager and giving an employee so much access without controls, the bottom-line fault does rest with you." He frowned. "Why weren't there checks and balances on that money?"

She took a breath. "Adam talked my father out of having them."

Trace blinked. "*Your father* actually gave him full control over the money from that first loan?"

"I don't think my dad realized that was what he was doing."

He waited a few seconds, probably trying to figure out her dad's rationale, and when he couldn't, he said, "What on earth did he think he was doing?"

She took a breath. She hated telling him this, but she couldn't let her father take the blame for her mistake. "Showing his future son-in-law that he trusted him."

The space between them went silent for a second before Trace said, "His future son-in-law?" His eyes narrowed. "You're not telling me what I think you're telling me."

"Adam and I were engaged."

He gaped at her. "You hired someone you were engaged to?"

"No. We hired Adam when we knew we needed to expand. He was a specialist at getting loans at great rates and finding the subcontractors to do the work, all stuff outside the purview of the vineyard."

"He was your project manager?"

"Yes."

"No wonder your dad is so mad…and not at you. He's mad at himself."

She snorted. "Right."

"Oh, sweetie, if he were mad at you, this would be so much easier for him. But mad at himself? He's barely handling it." His voice filled with excitement. "That's the real reason we need to steer him in the direction of a new vineyard."

"For a second chance to prove himself—"

"No. A chance to prove himself *to himself.* Marcia, he's really hurting right now. I'm guessing his pride is stinging so badly he's driving himself nuts. Especially if the guy who took his money really did get off scot-free."

She sighed. "He's being pursued. But by the time we realized what had happened, he'd had eight hours' head start. No one using his name left the country, so we're thinking he has a new identity."

Trace shook his head. "You'll never find him."

"That's what the police say."

"That makes your dad's embarrassment all the worse."

She glanced down at her cell phone—always in her hand as she hoped for good news from Janine—then back at Trace. "If he really needs a second chance, my getting a loan and buying Giordano back for him might actually make things worse."

"Yes. If this is about his pride, your handing back the vineyard might send him into a tailspin. But if he has a chance to start over, that would be totally different."

Trace nudged her shoulder with his. "What do you say?"

With their gazes locked, she thought about that kiss. Warm. Melting. So emotional her heart fluttered just thinking about it. Was it such a good idea to get even more involved with a guy she was so attracted to?

They had a whole year to work together. If they found her dad a new vineyard, a project to help him redeem himself, there'd be no extension of her brothers' time at Giordano Vineyards. Her dad's visits would stop too. It would be her and Trace finding new employees, harvesting the grapes in the fall…doing all the work—

Together.

Her breath shivered at the thought. She knew everything there was to know about the vineyard. She wasn't afraid of that. But there would be no one else to teach him, no one to show him the ropes…except her. They'd spend days together. Just the two of them. Planning. Working. No interruptions from her family.

But she also realized that her dad needed another chance. And she did too. Starting over without her family, hiring new employees, training them, supervising grape harvest—she could do all of that in her sleep. And maybe working with Trace to reboot Giordano Vineyards was *her* second chance.

She got the feeling he already knew that and her respect for him jumped a hundred notches.

Maybe the thing she needed to focus on here was how much working with this very smart Mr. Fix-It would teach *her*.

"I'm in."

CHAPTER SEVEN

TRACE DIDN'T WASTE TIME. As soon as they finished their breakfast Friday morning, he went to the master suite and got his laptop. He pulled up the website of the real estate agency that had found him Giordano Vineyards and brought it to the kitchen. Sliding it to the island in front of her, he stood behind her as she flipped through the properties offered for sale.

"Wow, look at this one." She glanced behind her at Trace. "Why didn't you buy this one?"

It *was* grand. Acres and acres of land. A huge wine building. A villa fit for a king. But the villa sat in the far-left corner, close to the villa of the neighboring vineyard.

"I wanted privacy."

"Really?"

Wow, she smelled great. As if it wasn't difficult enough that visions of her laughing the day before kept rolling through his brain, now her scent teased him.

"Yes."

A strange feeling ruffled through him again when he added how attracted he was to her to how alone they'd be when her dad and brothers stopped coming over.

"You recognize that to make this work, I'll have to let your brothers out of their agreement to work through grape harvest."

"Yes. I figured that out. It's very generous of you."

"It also means you and I will have to work the wine room until I replace them."

She scrolled down the real estate agency's page. "I loved working there. While I was at university, before I transferred to a school in the States, I was head of that room when my dad was unavailable." She peeked over her shoulder at him again. "So much fun. Almost like playing."

He could picture it. Her in the white shirt and dark trousers. All that glorious black hair spilling around her. Smiling at tourists. Chitchatting about the area, the grapes, the process of making wine.

"In other words, you'll be fine with that."

She peeked back at him again. Her dark eyes soft and warm. "Yes. Thank you for letting my dad have my brothers to help him."

Her sincerity touched him more than a thousand sexy sparkles would have. He thought of her dad, the guy she so desperately wanted to help. And now he did too. Not just for Antonio, but for *her*. To help her get her life on track. To give her a second chance to prove herself. With her dad working his own vineyard, she could strut her stuff at Giordano.

"I couldn't enforce that clause in the agreement, knowing your dad needed them."

She laughed. "Where has The Eliminator gone?"

He shook his head. Where had The Eliminator gone?

Worry about the strength of his feelings for Marcia crept into his brain. Half concerned, half determined to help her, he fell to the seat beside hers and grabbed for the easy answer to defuse the conflicting feelings running through him. "I guess I really am more of a Mr. Fix-It."

She studied him for a second. "Something's happening with you."

He sniffed a laugh. "No kidding."

"Want to tell me?"

"Tell you what? That I took one look at you my first day here, knew you had troubles, pretty much decided I should fire you, then you tempted me with a challenge?"

She looked affronted. "You said you like a good challenge."

"I do."

"So that's normal."

"Not really, because I kept seeing your side of the story, got chummy with your dad, saw the rift between the two of you and realized I couldn't fix it short of getting rid of one of you."

Her head tilted. "And you found a way to do it nicely."

"Sure."

He was going way above and beyond his responsibilities, but he couldn't seem to stop himself. He knew it had more to do with liking Marcia than helping her dad, but if he admitted that, then he had to admit his feelings. That wouldn't be good for either him or Marcia—

Especially Marcia.

"It has to be the Mr. Fix-It in me. No other solution made sense until I came up with this."

She smiled and warmth careened through him. "Bet your friends had a field day with deciding to help my dad buy a vineyard."

The warmth grew until it tightened his chest and filled him with the weird sensation he hadn't felt since middle school when he got his first crush on a girl. But he was a player now. That's what his friends said. He didn't do relationships. He just had fun. He could not get involved with this woman.

He also knew that, like gossip, attractions could sometimes be killed with a good dose of reality. Bring the problem out in the open, see it for the preposterousness that it was and end it.

"I haven't had a chance to run this by them yet. Plus, my friends would be more interested in the fact that I like *you*. I've got to admit, it's given me some trouble."

She turned her stool to the left to look at him fully. She

didn't play coy and act as if she hadn't noticed he was attracted to her. He'd kissed her. She knew.

"Try being the woman who was engaged to the man who embezzled from her family."

He hadn't forgotten that. He'd simply been so gobsmacked by it he'd never asked for more explanation. "I can't even imagine."

"I thought we were so in love. I made such a fool of myself." She pulled her fingers through her glorious hair. "We got an apartment in town. Were always at the tavern, playing darts, drinking wine, cuddling up to each other." She shook her head. "I thought I'd found my Romeo."

"Maybe you had? Maybe all that money with no controls simply tempted him too much."

She snorted. "He was the one who talked my dad into no controls, remember?"

He winced. So much for making things look less egregious. "Yeah."

"The fact that he could disappear so easily proves he'd been planning this for a long time." She drew a quick breath. "Now, I feel like an ass when I go into town, knowing people like Gina saw it all, saw how he snookered me." She took a breath. "You'd think I'd be wise enough never to be attracted to a man again."

His breath froze. She might not realize it, but she'd just admitted she was attracted to him too. Still, giving in to these wonderful feelings would only make her situation worse. "So, this is awkward for both of us?"

She laughed. "Yes. Awkward."

She caught his gaze and he saw the debate in her brain by the way her eyes darkened. For a good ten seconds he was sure she would change the subject. Instead, she said, "Awkward but also interesting."

His nerves exploded like little fireworks and he groaned. "Don't say that! I'm having enough trouble dealing with this. We don't need to add telling me you find our attraction interesting. I'll take that as a sign that you're interested in *me*."

"I am interested. You're gorgeous and usually nice."

He shook his head, afraid to answer, afraid he'd say something he'd regret or, worse, draw her in.

"You're also in control most of the time. Very manly. You're absolutely my equal." She smiled at him again. "All things *any* normal woman would be attracted to. Reminding myself of that keeps me from reacting or saying or doing something stupid. I tell myself 'of course you're attracted to him. Every woman in the world would be.'"

He wanted to argue that not every woman in the world would be attracted to him, but pride stopped his breathing until he saw her point. She was gorgeous. Of course he was attracted to her.

"So, those times when I want to kiss you, all I have to say is, 'Of course you want to kiss her. She's stunning and has beautiful hair.'" He paused to let himself run his fingers through the curls, which weren't corkscrew today. They were softer, some of them almost waves rather than curls. "Eyes that spark with fire one minute and fill with warmth the next."

"My eyes do that?"

"Yeah." He leaned closer. "It's why I kissed you. You'd never given even one overt indicator that you were attracted to me, but your eyes have this way of softening that somehow seems like an invitation."

Her lips slowly pulled up into a smile. "Been a long time since someone said anything that romantic to me."

"Well, they should." His hands were on her curls again. Soft, sensual, they tickled his fingers. The urge to kiss her slid through him. His instinct was to fight the sensation, but the curious look in her eyes had him rethinking that. How had he thought getting their attraction out in the open would rob it of its power? Right now, he wanted to kiss her more than he wanted the vineyard—and *that* scared him silly. Get involved with another woman for real? Risk his heart? His sanity? Or wake up one morning and find her gone, his son a mere memory? His heart bleeding from loss?

He rose from his seat. "Tell you what. You go into the office and hunt for vineyards on that computer, and I'll do the same on this laptop. Anything that overlaps, we'll investigate."

She searched his eyes. Trace wasn't sure what she was looking for, but eventually she said, "Sounds good."

She slipped out of the kitchen, leaving him with a terrible feeling in the pit of his stomach. Longing mixing and mingling with fear. He reminded himself that his first marriage hadn't worked out, reminded himself that he'd lost a child. Told himself that Marcia was vulnerable. And a man who never slept more than two hours a night had to be vulnerable too. It wasn't wrong to be attracted to a woman. But letting that attraction drift over into something more emotional was.

He rifled through his soul to find the detached part of himself that could take everything he felt and snuff it out until he was totally empty.

Once he found it, he pulled the laptop closer and began searching for vineyards. But when he walked out to the patio in the middle of the night, unable to sleep, he thought of her. He knew she appreciated his plan to help her dad, but he also knew her attraction was as strong as his.

He told himself to forget that. But he couldn't. Thinking about her, remembering the feel of her hair skimming his fingers, remembering their kiss, her eyes, nudged a lot of bad memories aside.

Staring at the purple sky, he let the sweet thoughts of their kiss surround him, allowed himself the pleasure of remembering it until the sky began to lighten and he went upstairs again.

He didn't try to sleep. He hated the failure of sleep that wouldn't come. Instead, he went to the shower, then dressed for the day.

One of these nights he would sleep. He had to. But if sleep wouldn't take him, having the kiss of a beautiful woman to think about wasn't a bad way to pass the lonely hours.

The only worry was that all that time spent thinking about her might be dangerous. If he let his daydreams go too far, they would eventually edge over into reality.

The following night, when he found himself thinking about her kiss, he forced his thoughts back to finding a vineyard for her dad and his plans became more detailed. If his brain drifted back to Marcia a time or two over the next few days, he didn't worry. He'd think about her dad's new vineyard and be drawn away from thoughts of her. Work always could drown out the part of his brain that wanted too much. As long as he was busy, he was strong. Invincible.

And no longer thinking about his son. Not wondering if there had been something he could have done, something he should have seen the night his little boy had drifted to sleep and simply never woke up.

But soon thoughts of work mingled with thoughts of Marcia because she was part of the vineyard. And thoughts of Marcia tiptoed over into the way she felt in his arms, the glorious softness of her hair, and some nights he let himself go there.

He stayed away when she was in the house. No more dinners. No more sharing wine. But every day it got more and more difficult not to talk to her, and he told himself this was stupid.

They were two consenting adults who liked each other. Surely, they could work this out.

* * *

Thursday afternoon, they took the Maserati down five miles of winding roads to a vineyard where Trace's real estate agent would meet them. Marcia had tried to talk twice, but with wind whipping around them, she gave up and simply enjoyed the ride.

When they arrived at a property with big white iron gates, he rolled the car to an empty security station and hit a button.

"Hello?"

"Hello! Yes! This is Ruth Montgomery. Your real estate agent. I'll open the gate for you."

The old doors pulled apart slowly and Trace inched his car forward on a cobblestone driveway overgrown with grass and weeds. "Love the cobblestone. Needs some TLC though."

"Agreed," Marcia said. "You know, on the subject of work. I was thinking that maybe we should start scouting for people to replace my brothers right now…before they leave."

"Fresh air really does make you think, doesn't it?"

She laughed. Once she'd realized talking was pointless, the air that swirled around the convertible as he drove had made her feel fanciful and pretty, happy in a way she hadn't been in a long time. All because he'd said a few words and touched her hair as if it were spun gold, causing her heart to soften. Though he'd spent a week avoiding her, she'd still had to force her mind to stop thinking about him. Strategizing the impact his plan would have on Giordano Vineyards seemed to be the only way to do that.

"My major takeaway from your idea is that we have to do it right if we're going to do it. Not just set up my dad to be busy and happy again, but make sure your operation stays intact."

He grinned at her. "Because you like me."

Her already soft heart melted. A week apart had done nothing to change their attraction. The first time they were alone together, he flirted with her.

She knew it was wrong. That was why she wouldn't let herself dwell on his admission that he liked her. It was why she wouldn't let herself go over and over the memory of how he'd touched her hair…so reverently, as if he couldn't stop himself.

"I didn't say I liked you. I said you were interesting."

He got out of the car. "Same thing."

"Yes, well, it seems to me that your happiness about that means you like me too."

He closed the door. "Yeah, but you like me enough that you thought you had to stay away from me for a whole week."

She could have told him it hadn't helped. Their curiosity about each other still raged. But she hadn't been the one avoiding him.

"I didn't stay away. *You* stayed away."

He looked at her over the car roof. "And it bothered you, didn't it?"

She stared at him. How was she supposed to answer that?

The villa door opened. Ruth walked out. "Good afternoon!"

A little breathless and extremely confused, Marcia closed her car door and walked around his sleek red vehicle toward the villa, toward Trace.

Her breath fluttered again when he put his hand on the small of her back to guide her to Ruth.

"Good afternoon." He shook Ruth's hand. Glancing at the overgrown trees, he said, "Some of this is nice."

Ruth winced. "Granted, it needs work."

Relieved for the distraction of the vineyard, Marcia looked around in dismay. "A lot of work."

They toured the villa and winemaking facility and would have headed out to the grapes, but Trace shook his head. "We'll keep this on the list in case nothing else pops, but I think there's too much work here."

Ruth smiled. "Okay. On to vineyard number two."

They drove a short distance to the second vineyard, but when Ruth told them the price, Marcia said, "No. That's too far over budget."

"But less work," Ruth reminded her.

Trace said, "Doesn't matter. We're sticking to the budget."

Vineyard three already had an offer. Ruth turned to Marcia. "Your father would have to beat that."

Once again, Trace said, "No."

The fourth was better. "Interesting," Trace said. Then he glanced at her and smiled.

Her breath caught when she realized he was using her own word to covertly flirt with her. She began to wonder if he'd stayed away from her all week because he knew this would happen. The last time they were together he'd flirted. And when they finally spent time together again, he flirted again. Almost as if he recognized he couldn't resist her.

"...but this vineyard would take us over budget too."

Ruth pulled out her phone. "Want to give me some specifics so I can get you closer to what you need?"

He shrugged. "We'll know it when we see it."

Having already locked the villa, Ruth left them with a big smile and a promise to find a few more vineyards to see the following Thursday.

They were silent in the car. With the Maserati's top down, it was a sort of safe zone because they couldn't talk. Couldn't flirt. Unfortunately, that didn't mean her mind didn't drift. She thought of their return to Giordano Vineyards and tried to decide if she should run into the house and to her room as soon as he stopped the car, or if she should continue the flirting game he'd started...see what would happen.

But Trace pulled into the parking lot of the first restaurant they found. They'd had breakfast, but no lunch, and the sun had already begun to set.

"I'm starving."

She sighed. "Me too."

"So, this is good?"

"This is good." She wasn't really 100 percent sure of that, but driving another hour with both of them hungry seemed idiotic.

Without a word, they walked into a cozy space where the hostess led them to a table in the back. She lit the candle. "Enjoy your dinner."

Trace looked around. "Why are Italian restaurants always so romantic?"

Maybe because he was in that mood? And that's why he'd flirted with her?

Not risking the conversation that observation would start, she said, "Has to be the candle."

He laughed. "Everything is kind of cozy."

Too cozy.

"Maybe we should talk about the vineyards we saw today."

"Good idea." He smiled and her heart lurched. He had the prettiest smile. It lit his blue eyes and transformed his entire face.

By the time their food arrived, they had exhausted the topic of the new vineyard. Awkward silence stretched between them. Soon questions about him popped into her mind.

She picked up her wineglass and swirled the red liquid. "You know, it just dawned on me that you know everything about my past, and I know very little about yours."

He gaped at her. "Are you kidding? You know where I went to school. You know about the business my friends and I sold. Hell, you know about my friends."

"You're saying you've told me more than you tell most people."

"Yes!"

She put her elbow on the table and her chin on her closed fist. "Interesting that you've never told me anything about your relationships."

"That's because I don't have relationships."

She found that hard to believe and snickered. "You never have sex?"

He laughed. "I have girlfriends, but not relationships."

Her brow wrinkled.

He sighed. "Look, I don't do relationships because I had some really awful things happen in my past."

"That part I guessed." She waited for him to elaborate. When he didn't, she groaned. "Come on. I didn't have to tell you I was engaged to Adam, but I did."

He took a drink of wine. A few seconds passed. Then he pulled in a breath. "I could buffalo you by saying that when my friends visit, they'll spill the beans. So, I might as well tell you. But the truth is, you're curious because there's something between us, and telling you is fair."

It shouldn't surprise her that he'd admit there was something between them. He'd been pointing that out to her all day. But for it to be a reason for him to tell her his past? The attraction had to be more serious for him than she'd thought.

Her chest tightened, even as her curiosity piqued. Worried he'd back out before he told her anything significant, she swirled her wine in her glass again, pretending it was no big deal. "So, tell me this mysterious past you're so sure your friends will spill."

He sucked in another breath. "I was married."

She smiled and nodded. A really bad marriage explained why he would be gun-shy about relationships. But there was more. She could see it in the sadness in his blue eyes.

Finally, he said, "We had a son and he died."

The words came out in a rush, as if he was afraid that if he didn't say them quickly, he wouldn't say them at all.

Her eyes widened in surprise and horror. "Oh, my God. I'm so sorry."

He looked down at the table. "Please. You don't have to say that. I don't want sympathy."

"It's not sympathy to say that your loss was horrendous."

"You don't know the half of it. My wife's parents hated me. When our son died and she left, I knew they'd tugged her away or she hadn't really loved me in the first place. I was eighteen. I made the funeral arrangements alone. I had to talk to the coroner alone and agree to an autopsy because he died of sudden infant death syndrome." He shook his head. "One day I had everything I wanted. The next it was gone. As if all the good stuff I'd had was a dream and I woke up."

Shock and sadness poured through her. "I'm so sorry."

He leaned back. "No sympathy, remember?"

She did. But how could she feel nothing?

A few seconds went by in silence as he stared at his wine, but the difficulty of his past made it all the more important that he'd told her.

"Thank you."

He looked across the table at her. "For sharing that?" He tossed his napkin beside his plate. "I don't normally tell people. But like I said, what's happening between us is tempting and you shouldn't be tempted by me. Even if I can't resist you, you should resist me. I'm not the kind of guy you're looking for. I'm bitter about some things. Angry about others. And never going to have another serious relationship."

The sadness that coursed through her shattered her heart. For a few minutes, he seemed different. Older. As bitter as he'd told her he was.

While she was still reeling, he led them back into the discussion of what her dad would need in a new business, but unwanted pictures formed in her brain. She could see Trace as a father, loving a little boy he'd bring up to be as smart and confident as he was. She could picture him loving a woman so much that her walking away had devastated him.

Which was why he didn't take much time off. Why he needed to work. Even why the problem of her dad had lured him in. It was a distraction.

By the time they were finished eating, he was back to being himself. He'd encouraged her to talk about winemaking and growing grapes and analyzed everything she'd said. Until he not only seemed to have forgotten their discussion of his past, but they also had a comprehensive list to give to Ruth of what her dad would need in a new vineyard.

"This will help her," Trace said as they walked to his little red car.

"Agreed."

They slid inside. Trace revved the engine and soon they were back on the winding Tuscan road that would take them home.

As always, the wind kept them silent during the ride. Her nerve endings settled. Her heart found substance again, but the oddest emotion filled it. She absolutely did not feel sorry for him, but everything about him finally made sense. Along with that understanding came an enormous respect for him.

And new questions. He didn't have to tell her about his son. He could have told her about his ex-wife and left it at that. He'd told her so she really could know him. All of him. The truth of his pain. But she wasn't entirely sure

he realized that. Or how telling it meant that he'd con-
fided in her.

She didn't wait for Trace to open her car door. When he
got out, she did too, and they walked to the villa door. He
pressed the buttons on the keypad to disable the alarm and
let them into the house. The nearly empty foyer greeted
them. The sounds of silence surrounded them.

He smiled at her. "Shall we say good-night now and be
awkward walking up the stairs together to our rooms?"

She laughed, telling herself that was not flirting. That
was Trace being Trace. Seeing a problem and fixing it. He
knew the things he'd told her could make their next few
days together uncomfortable. He was facing it head-on.

"No." She started up the stairs. "Let's think about something to talk about that doesn't involve the vineyard or my
dad. Then we can say good-night at my room, and you can
move on."

Behind her on the steps, he was quiet. Then he suddenly
said, "It seems wrong."

"What? The vineyard list?"

"No. Us not having anything to talk about." He paused
a second. Then he said, "You can be chatty."

She laughed. "Right. I'm the one who does all the talking."

"I like when you talk. When you tell me things. I loved
seeing Siena and you telling me how to make wine. But
most of all, I liked figuring out your dad's mess with you."

She heard the longing in his voice and felt the pull. The
delicious temptation of a man realizing how much he liked
her and how well they fit. A man who'd suffered a tragedy
a million times worse than her own. A man who'd vowed
never to get involved but couldn't seem to help himself. Because there really was something between them.

"Stop flirting."

"That wasn't flirting." He laughed. "That was me being honest."

"I like when you're honest."

"Maybe it's another thing we have in common. I'm not a fan of insinuation or guessing."

His easy answer seemed to break another barrier. The more they talked, the closer they got. Something neither of them wanted. He was wounded. She'd been deceived. Even if they were willing to risk it, a relationship between them would be difficult.

"We can always go back to talking about vineyards."

"I don't know how many times I can say those white gates needed painting without boring you."

Pleasure came before she could stop it. The deep, empty place inside her filled to overflowing and her laugh echoed down the hall. "Boring me is better than me wondering if you're staring at my butt."

"I hate to tell you this, but I stare at your butt every time I get a chance."

Oh, Lord. He probably believed telling her about his past was enough to stop her attraction. But if he kept saying things like that, she'd be putty in his hands. Those offhand comments made her feel whole, normal. And she wasn't. She'd been preyed upon, used, had a father who'd lost everything because of her.

And Trace wasn't any better. He'd lost a marriage. A child. He'd admitted to being bitter, angry.

They were the worst possible combination.

"Where is the guy who was worried that I'd sue him if he asked me to cook?"

"He got a good look at his bank account and realized he could afford a suit if you decided to go that route." They stopped at her door. "But you won't. Because this is consensual."

Before she could reply, he lowered his head and kissed

her. Warm and sweet, his mouth moved over hers. For ten seconds, he weakened her knees and drew her to a place of complete oblivion.

Then he broke the kiss and smiled down at her. "Right?"

Her head spun. "Right, what?"

"This is consensual."

Once again, he didn't give her time to answer. He kissed her. His lips danced over hers until her breathing shivered in and out of her chest and her arms moved to his shoulders. Her fingers tunneled into the hair at his nape.

His hands slid from her back to her waist and settled there to nudge her closer. She went willingly. Longing opened her heart, then her soul. The strangest thought blossomed. What if two wounded people weren't the worst combination but the best? What if her feelings for him helped him...and his feelings for her helped her?

He deepened the kiss and her thoughts spun away until only feelings remained. His hands skimmed her back, sending tingles shimmying through her as they slid to her butt and back up again.

She put her hands on his cheeks, desperately taking control of the kiss, fearing he would end it. Instead, he stepped closer, pressing against her. Her pulse scrambling, their mouths meeting and withdrawing, tongues twining, she forgot her good common sense and threw herself into the kiss.

It was Trace who eventually backed away.

She stared at him, realizing she'd lost herself, forgotten her mistakes, forgotten those lessons, forgotten *his* pain, *his* misery, forgotten she had to work with him for an entire year.

She shook her head, not sure if it was to pull herself back to reality or if she'd done it to try to rattle some sense into her brain.

His kisses might lure her into believing they weren't the worst possible combination but the best. But she'd have slept

with him if they'd kept going, and that was not something
a smart woman jumped into without thought.

She turned and opened her bedroom door. "Good night,
Trace."

She didn't wait for his answering goodbye. She stepped
into her room and closed the door.

CHAPTER EIGHT

TRACE STARED AT her door for a full minute before he turned and walked down the hall to his room. The day had been long, peppered with work, good conversation and a kind of relaxation he hadn't experienced in years.

Most of their time together he'd told himself he felt better—felt good about himself—because he and Marcia were working toward finding her dad a new vineyard, a new life. Fixing things always gave him a boost. Good deeds added to that. That was why his chest filled with air and his thoughts didn't scatter. He kept his focus.

Then she'd asked him about his life, and he'd told her. Partially to be fair to her, but to remind himself that he didn't get involved with women beyond friendship and good times. He thought his confessions would nip their attraction in the bud.

They hadn't. The temptation to kiss her at her door had been four times as strong. The need to hold her had rattled through him, pushed him when he might have stood firm. The longing to forget everything had sent him over the top and he'd followed instincts he'd been fighting for a long, difficult week.

And it had been glorious.

Luckily, she'd left him standing in the hallway. He might be confused. He might even be confusing her. But eventually she'd come to her senses and had backed off. Exactly what should happen.

He'd told her he would never have another real relationship.

She'd responded like the smart woman that she was.

They could get past a few lush, primal kisses.

He walked into his bedroom. Ordinary, but squeaky clean, the master suite was obviously the former resting place of a husband and wife—

The thought sharpened his nerve endings. Memories of being a husband poured through him and he remembered being married, remembered how Skylar had loved him. How happy they'd been. How being a husband had been an odd combination of responsibility and joy.

Being a dad had been a stronger version of that. Every day after Joshua's birth, he had worked two jobs to earn enough money to support his little family and then come home to their tiny apartment, where happiness had filled his soul.

He glanced around, realized the homeyness of the Giordanos' bedroom was playing a part in bringing back his memories, and knew that once they found Antonio a vineyard, his next project had to be redecorating.

He almost grabbed the homeyness of the villa as his excuse for being overwhelmingly attracted to Marcia, but he knew that wasn't true. He genuinely liked her. She was gorgeous, smart, funny.

Wanting her had nothing to do with the vineyard.

But her longing made the need irresistible. He saw it in her eyes. Every time before he kissed her, they sharpened with desire, but also softened with a yearning to be happy. After a year of her dad's anger, the town's mocking and her own self-recrimination, she needed a little fun, and he was sure that was what tempted him the most.

He liked making her happy, making her laugh.

He dressed in sweatpants and a T-shirt and sneaked out of the bedroom that fueled memories he had to keep at bay. His phone in his pocket, he slid silently through the villa and out to the patio. For hours, he read news on his phone until his eyes drooped enough that sleep might not be far behind.

Returning to the house, he walked past Marcia's door without as much as a glance and dropped face-first on top of the covers on his bed. Sleep took him for a glorious hour and twenty minutes, but when his eyes opened again, the memories popped into his brain, along with the questions that always joined them.

Had he done enough?

Had he missed something the night Joshua died?

How much did Skylar blame him?

Was that why she'd left?

And *that* was why he couldn't get involved with Marcia.

A man who hadn't worked out his past couldn't create a future.

At lunchtime, Marcia waited until she saw her dad and brother Matteo leave the kitchen before she scooted across the parking lot to the villa for a sandwich. She was just about through eating when Trace and Roberto walked in.

Her eyes met Trace's.

The memory of his kisses the night before tightened her chest and sent shivers through her. The honest way he'd told her about his past and then held the odd conversation as they walked up the stairs had connected them. Again. Every time they were bare-bones honest, they seemed to get closer.

And that petrified her. She wanted something to happen between them. Wanted it so badly now that it almost seemed inevitable, but what if she got hurt again? He said he'd never have another real relationship. What if being with him made a fool of her again?

Worse, what if she somehow hurt him? A man already bowled over by sadness and incomprehensible loss didn't need a confused woman pining after him.

She picked up the remains of her sandwich and headed for the door. "Time for me to get back to work. You guys can have the kitchen."

She didn't wait for their goodbyes, just bolted.

But she couldn't avoid Trace that night. When she realized that, she decided to act as if nothing was different between them. He might have kissed her, but she'd been smart enough to back off. He'd told her the truth, warned her off, and she wasn't a silly girl with stars in her eyes, thinking love would conquer their problems. She'd backed off. She'd done the right thing. She could trust herself.

Taking some leftover pasta to the patio table where Trace sat eating a big salad, she said, "We never did talk about replacing my brothers."

He drew in a long breath. "I know. I watched them today, doing their thing, wondering how on earth I can replace that."

Grateful he was acting as normal with her as she was trying to be with him, she laughed. "They are good. But there are lots of other guys around who will be every bit as flirtatious and fun."

"That's great because I'm banking on your brothers helping to turn your dad's new vineyard into a gold mine." He set his fork down. "Speaking of which, Ruth has three properties scheduled for us to see on Thursday."

"She certainly doesn't let any grass grow under her feet."

"No matter which one your dad chooses, her commission will be hefty. I think she wants to be sure she doesn't lose us to another agency."

"Smart."

"Yes. She is."

He grabbed his fork again and continued eating. Marcia dug into her pasta. Normal conversation had calmed the space between them. But as they ate in amicable silence, the night sounds settled in. The sky darkened. The moon rose. The romance of the vineyard began to fill her.

She squeezed her eyes shut to get her bearings, but when she opened them again, she saw Trace and remembered his story. He'd been married too young to really understand all that he'd committed to and he'd lost his son.

Lost his son.

Her heart ached for him. She imagined he could have gotten over the end of his marriage if he hadn't lost a child. She didn't know much about how his son had died. He'd mentioned sudden infant death syndrome, but was there more?

For twenty seconds, she longed to ask for details, but as she tried to skew up her courage, she saw the fatigue in his eyes.

The sorrow.

That unfathomable emptiness. Something she couldn't pretend to understand.

She collected her dish and fork. "Good night. I'll see you in the morning."

He peeked up at her, over his glasses. "Good night."

Her heart fluttered. He was without a doubt one of the most attractive men she had ever met. The thought alone made her race to the door, but in the kitchen she stopped.

She absolutely could not deny her feelings for him. But suddenly instead of being afraid for herself, afraid of being hurt and damaging her reputation even more, she felt his loneliness. She felt his pain. But most of all she felt his need. And knew with absolute certainty that she was approaching this all wrong.

Fate might seem to have brought them together when they weren't a good match. But what if the truth was they were a match, just not a forever match?

Knowing him, working with him, trusting him had already brought her a long way toward healing.

Maybe it was time she helped him?

They might not be a forever couple. But maybe they were the right two people to help each other get to the next step of their lives?

* * *

Dinner had gone so poorly that Trace stayed outside longer than usual. Marcia had been normal one second, nervous the next. It was all he could do to get them through the meal.

When he was sure she was settled in her room, he walked to his, going through the same routine as the night before and returning to the patio once again.

He considered getting a bottle of wine but decided against it. He'd had his years of hard drinking. They'd only given him hangovers, hadn't soothed his mind. He watched the moon for a while, then clicked the app on his phone that brought his book on screen. He loved mysteries. He loved thrillers. With electronic books, he could have hundreds at his disposal in seconds.

He read until the sky became a red swatch. Realizing the sun was about to rise, he retreated to his room and slept at least an hour.

Knowing that was as good as he would get, he changed into his work clothes—black trousers and white shirt to match the crew—and went to the kitchen for coffee. Hungrier this morning, he made himself eggs and toast.

He was giving the eggs a final flip when Marcia walked in.

She stopped abruptly and her eyes widened.

With fear or surprise, Trace couldn't tell. But he had felt the awkwardness when she'd left for her room the night before. One minute he thought being with him scared her silly, the next he'd sensed their connection. The longer they sat together, the more comfortable they got. Even if they didn't want it, something drew them together. They could avoid it, as she had the night before by leaving before things got too comfortable. But they still had to work together. He had to find the sweet spot where they could be good coworkers without tripping over into their attraction—

Without him kissing her.

Technically, this was all his fault.

He nudged his head toward his fried eggs. "Want these?"

She licked her lips. Part of him stared at that. She had thick, wonderful lips on a skilled mouth made for kissing.

The other part focused on her hesitation, the way she was nervous around him.

He shrugged. "I don't usually eat breakfast, but I'm hungry today. I only had salad last night."

"I'm hungry too." She'd finally spoken. Her voice hadn't shivered. She hadn't avoided his eyes.

"You take these, and I'll make myself two more."

"I couldn't!"

"Why not? We're partners in crime."

Her face scrunched. "Partners in crime?"

"Getting a vineyard for your dad? Already deciding your brothers' fate? We're like two evil geniuses."

She laughed.

"If you can't share eggs with a partner in crime, who can you share eggs with?"

She laughed again.

He held up the plate. "Come on. Take them before they get cold."

She reached for the eggs. "They smell wonderful."

"As I recall, you only had a little bowl of pasta last night."

"True."

"Which means, we either have to eat bigger dinners or plan to eat breakfast every day."

"Good point."

He nudged his head toward the toaster on the back counter. "There's toast too."

She found utensils and took her eggs and toast to the island. He made himself two eggs and more toast and sat beside her.

Tension wedged between them, but she smiled at him. "What's on your agenda today?"

"Working in the wine room. I'm finally making the connection that understanding what people want is the key to a good product."

She laughed. "No kidding."

He waved his hand in dismissal. "It's neither as simple nor as trite as you're trying to make it."

She smiled at him. "Sure it is."

Something woke inside him. That urge again to run his fingers through her hair. Brush a light kiss across her mouth.

He quickly looked away, but she slid her hand on top of his where it lay by his plate.

"Don't sell yourself short."

The need became a tightening. Not just in his chest, but all his muscles. Almost as if his body was resisting her compliment.

"I don't. Not often. But when I start something new, I realize I have a lot to learn."

She smiled again, holding his gaze. The connection surged between them. Everything he felt for her whooshed through his blood. He'd never experienced this kind of attraction for a woman before.

He bounced off his seat. "I've gotta go to work."

"Okay." When he reached for his plate, she caught his hand and squeezed. "Go ahead. I'll take care of this."

His breath shimmied. Every time she touched him, his entire body burst into flames. He raced out to the wine-tasting bars and tried not to watch her office door that morning, but it was no use. She'd been so different at breakfast—so open—that confusion took all his brainpower.

That afternoon, he noticed her retreating to the villa long before tourists had stopped arriving. About twenty minutes later, she walked out the front door, got into her car and left.

His heart dropped. Did he make her so nervous that she was leaving—?

To eat in town?

No. She would not eat in town. She might take a drive to avoid him—

But he had not made her nervous that morning. If anything, she'd been oddly calm. She'd spoken naturally. Touched his hand. *Squeezed* his hand once.

If she'd left, it wasn't because she was angry with him. So, what was it?

An hour later, she returned with four bags of groceries. He froze. She'd gone shopping?

She'd only gone shopping.

The relief was so intense, he laughed. Shame on him for making a big deal out of nothing.

Antonio said, "That's right! Laugh! We have a great crowd tonight."

"Actually, Antonio, I'm kind of tired. I think I'll go in for the night and let you handle this."

He straightened with pride. "Absolutely."

After saying good-night to Matteo and Roberto, he headed for the house. He didn't shower. Didn't change. Just marched to the kitchen, where Marcia was putting away her purchases.

He had absolutely no idea what he was doing. Mostly because she'd changed the game that morning and he couldn't figure out why. "I can pay for those."

She shook her head. "No. You bought last time."

He frowned. "I'm the boss. I own the house. Food is my responsibility."

She glanced over, smiled. "No. You said we were partners in crime. As a partner, I can buy food once in a while."

He could drown in her eyes. He could drown in her, lose his troubles, live in the moment—

He sucked in a breath. Thoughts like that weren't helping anything. "Okay."

He walked to the grocery bags. Peering inside, he paused, then laughed. "Your mother's pasta."

"I called her this afternoon. I told her I'd be making a grocery run. Since we're also feeding my father and two hungry brothers, she suggested I stop by for a few bags."

He looked up and saw Marcia smiling at him. Temptation rumbled through him.

"Which would you like tonight? Spaghetti or tortellini?"

He suddenly realized she'd done this to surprise him. Not because she owed him but because she liked him. The possibility made his soul do a cartwheel. He'd warned her off, told her his awful past, but she hadn't reacted with sorrow or pity. She'd gotten him some of her mother's pasta.

Such a normal, easy, wonderful thing. "Can I help with anything?"

"Not tonight." She pointed at the door. "Go get your shower. Take a break."

Her brown eyes sparked with mischief, enhancing the beauty of her delicate features. Softness and femininity surrounded her, as if the shift from the office to their home had somehow made her more womanly.

His chest froze even as his blood turned to molten lava. He had to stop thinking like that or he'd find himself kissing her again. So, she'd done a nice thing for him? She was a nice person. It was not a big deal.

He left the kitchen, went to his room, got a shower and put on comfortable shorts and a T-shirt before he walked out to the patio, where a bowl of pasta sat on the table, along with a bottle of wine. She lit a fat candle.

Confusion rippled through him as he walked up to the table. She'd also changed into a pretty pink dress. "This is nice."

She smiled again. "Thanks."

The sound of her dad's old truck leaving made him realize how alone they were. They'd been alone every other night. But she was different today. Confusing him.

He pulled out her chair, then his. The pool sparkled in the moonlight. Only the candle lit their dinner space.

When he tasted the pasta with homemade sauce, hunger obliterated all thought. He ate four bites before he glanced over at her.

"This is fabulous. Thank you."

Her warm smile appeared slowly. "You're welcome." She picked up her fork and joined him in eating the pasta while drinking Giordano Vineyards' wine.

She asked about his day and he asked about hers, working to keep the conversation neutral. Soon they were sipping more wine than taking bites of pasta and eventually both pushed away their plate.

The flame of the candle danced in a light breeze, but it wouldn't have mattered if it extinguished. Moonlight lit the patio, the pool, the vineyards beyond.

Peace settled over him.

He drew a breath, then another. This was why he'd bought this vineyard, but he also liked Marcia. Meeting her, getting to know her, had been a delightful bonus. She set her hand on top of his again and he stared at it for a second as desire shimmered through him. He glanced around the dark patio, looked at the candle, frowned at his empty pasta plate.

She'd really gone out of her way to make this night special—

Was she seducing him?

Nah. Couldn't be. The things she'd done were too ordinary. Plus, Marcia was kind. Generous. Preparing this dinner could be construed as nothing more than Marcia being kind to him—

But she was also attracted to him. And after the way he'd kissed her, she had to know he wanted her. Though putting her hand on his seemed innocent, for someone like Marcia it might actually be a big deal.

A sign. A *move*.

Meaning the next move was his.

He took a breath. There was only one way to find out.

"You look beautiful tonight."

With her untamed hair flowing around her like a black cloud and the straps of her little sundress skimming her shoulders, she looked like a goddess.

"Thank you."

"Had I known we were dressing for dinner, I'd have worn something better than shorts."

She braced her elbow on the table and leaned in toward him. "I like you in shorts. You look comfortable." She smiled. "Happy."

"You make me happy." He said the words before he had time to really think them through, but he realized he wouldn't take them back. This was Marcia. Special. Fun. Wonderful. And if she wanted to take what they had and run with it, he wanted that too. Telling her about his marriage, he'd laid to rest any unrealistic expectations. If she was leading them where he suspected she was leading them, it was with everyone's eyes wide open.

He reached over and took her hand. "You make me *very* happy."

She smiled at him. Moonlight winked at him off the water in the pool. The scent of the rich earth wafted around them.

But the area was silent. There wasn't anyone around for miles.

They could take forever being polite and kind, dancing around what they wanted. Or he could simply take them where they wanted to be without all the hassle and confusion.

He pushed back his chair, rose, kicked off his shoes, scooped her up off her seat, turned and jumped into the pool.

She squealed through a bubbly laugh. "What are you doing?"

He eased her out of his arms but kept his hold on her hands as she moved through the water. "I'm not sure. Stop me."

"Stop you?"

"Or don't."

He leaned over and kissed her. When he pulled back, he removed his glasses and set them on the edge of the pool before he yanked his wet shirt over his head and tossed it to the stone patio. "There's still time to back out. My shorts are next, then your dress."

Her eyes bulged. "What?"

"Say the word and I stop."

He waited, standing in chest-deep water with her before him. The choice in her hands.

"Things felt different between us today." He reached over and lifted her chin. "You made them feel different."

"*Si.*"

"Because?"

"Because I like you and maybe I think I finally realized that some things aren't meant to last forever."

He inclined his head. "Maybe."

"Doesn't make them any less real or any less important." Her eyes softened. "They are what they are."

She leaned forward and kissed him, resting her hands on his chest.

He let her lead, and when she finally broke the kiss, their eyes met again. He skimmed the lightweight dress over her head, tossing it over to his shirt.

She stood before him in only panties the same pale pink of her dress. He hadn't realized she was braless.

"Wow." He paused only a second before he said, "There's still time to change your mind."

She laughed. "No. We both want this. We're two adults

who were lucky to find each other. We may not have a future, but we do have now."

He totally understood. It was how he lived his entire life. Forget the past. Don't think about the future. Just take now.

His hands on her elbows, he pulled her to him for a kiss, letting her breasts bump his chest as they floated in the warm pool water.

Everything inside him began to hum. With one smooth move, he got rid of his shorts and eased her against him again. Long and deep, their kisses fueled the fire as he let his hands roam her curves. He broke the kiss and lowered his head to her breast. At the first touch of his lips to her soft skin, his breathing bottomed out. She was perfection.

Her hands found his back, sliding along the slick skin and sleek muscles, and lower. His hands glided along her back to her bottom. Realizing she still wore the pale panties, he peeled them away. His hands went lower. Their kiss deepened as arousal spiked through him and the water perfectly aligned them.

As if they'd done it a million times before, their bodies gracefully merged. The lapping water created a soothing rhythm that grew more and more frantic as need rose until it crested, sending both of them over the edge.

CHAPTER NINE

THEY FLOATED ON the water for a good twenty seconds before either of them could move. Then he caught her elbows again and pulled her to him for another long, lingering kiss.

Marcia let herself fall into it. Passion slowly built between them, but she pushed back, angling herself away from him.

"It's getting chilly."

He laughed. "I didn't notice."

She swam to the edge of the pool and lifted herself out. "I'll race you to my room." She turned and headed for the door.

His confused expression gave way to a hearty laugh. She loved hearing him laugh. Loved seeing him so relaxed and happy. And knew she'd been right the night before. This was why fate brought them together. Not for forever, but for now.

"You have a head start!"

She stopped. Putting her hands on her hips, she frowned. "Okay. To balance things out, I'll grab our clothes. But you have to get the ones still in the pool."

With one quick swoop, she lifted his wet shirt and her dripping dress and raced into the house. She tossed both into the sink as she passed it and ran through the kitchen and hall to the steps. Hearing the door close in the kitchen again, signaling that he was right behind her, she ran up the stairs.

She let the door to her bedroom open and rifled through a box in her bureau for a condom, which she tossed on the bedside table before she pulled down the covers on her bed.

Gloriously naked, he finally made it to her room. Once

again wearing his glasses, he spotted the condom and winced. "I guess we got a little carried away out there."

"It's not a big deal." She cleared her throat. "I'm on the pill. And I obviously haven't had sex recently."

He fell to the bed beside her. "Me neither."

"Oh, don't tell me Mr. Affair-No-Relationships hasn't been having some fun."

"It's been a weird few months since we sold the business. The year before that I hadn't had time for a vacation. Not even a weekend trip. My life pretty much revolved around work."

She pulled him down for a kiss. "So I gathered."

She didn't really want to talk and neither did he. It had been so long since she'd been held, caressed...worshipped the way he touched her. A whirlwind of feelings tried to overtake her, but she flicked them away. For once in her life she didn't want the burden of perfection or the future. Looking for the perfect guy had led her straight into the arms of someone playing a role, pretending to be the real thing so he could gain her trust and then steal from her family.

There would be no more of that in her life.

She didn't know how she'd get herself back into normal relationships, how she'd learn to discern a good guy from a bad guy, but right now, it didn't matter. They liked each other and were good for each other. This was a good thing.

He kissed her neck and she laughed. *A very good thing.*

They played for what seemed like hours, didn't talk, except to say words of happiness, then fell asleep in each other's arms.

Hours later, Trace woke suddenly and sprang up in her bed. *Her bed.*

Morning light came through the window. The sound of her dad's old truck rolled up the vineyard lane.

He jumped out of bed. "Get up! We're late. Your dad's here."

Her eyes opened slowly, sleepily. In the pale morning light, her skin shimmered, her eyes sparkled.

His frenetic search for clothes halted. He bent down, kissed her thoroughly, then ran to the door. "I'm sorry, but your dress and my shorts are in the kitchen sink. Your dad doesn't always come in but I'm not a lucky person. Today will be the day he pops in for a cup of coffee." Especially if their lateness gave him reason to come searching for them. "I don't want to have to explain a dress and shirt in the sink."

She laughed and he raced to his bedroom for shorts and a T-shirt, which he hopped into on his way downstairs. In the kitchen, he tossed the still-wet clothes into a plastic garbage bag and threw them into the laundry room.

Attempting to make everything appear normal, he hurriedly made a pot of coffee and put two slices of bread in the toaster.

Her dad walked in through the back door. "What's this? We're wearing shorts now?"

"No. I slept in." He nodded toward the coffee maker. "Needed coffee more than I needed a shower. Grab a cup."

"I think I will do that."

His toast popped as her dad retrieved a mug and filled it with coffee, which he left black. Trace eased to the toaster, pulled out his bread and slathered it with butter, then poured himself a cup of coffee.

Antonio smiled at him.

He smiled back. Nerves shimmied through him. Not because he was worried Antonio had seen or guessed something had happened between him and Marcia, but because this was the kind of close call he hadn't thought about the night before. It was archaic and weird to even consider that Antonio would go all medieval on him. But who knew how a dad would react to finding his daughter in bed with—

Holy hell. *He'd awoken in a bed.*

He'd slept through the night!

That was the reason he'd never thought about this scenario. He'd never considered that he'd sleep through the night. He'd assumed he'd wake after twenty minutes.

He scrubbed his hand along the back of his neck.

He'd slept through the night.

"Why you sleep in?"

His gaze jumped to Antonio's. A lie easily slid off his tongue. "One too many glasses of wine, I guess."

Antonio laughed. "One of the hazards of owning thousands of bottles." He peered at Trace. "Though you do look well rested. Not so tired around the eyes." He nudged Trace. "Maybe you need more wine."

Trace only stared at him. It was so unusual for him to sleep through the night he almost couldn't reconcile it in his brain. But he couldn't make too much of it. Especially when he didn't want Marcia's dad thinking too much about the living arrangements here at Giordano Vineyards. And he needed to get dressed because they had work to do.

He finished his toast as Antonio sipped coffee. Then he rose from his seat. "You go ahead out to the wine room and I'll get dressed."

"Don't forget to shower."

Trace peeked at Antonio. "Do I smell that bad?"

He laughed. "No, but you said you didn't shower."

The man had a brain like a steel trap. Another reason to remember to be cautious around him. "Okay." He headed for the door. "Give me twenty minutes."

"You should be done right about when our first tourists arrive."

He pushed on the door. "Great. I'll see you then."

* * *

That night, he stayed in the wine room until the tourists were gone. Expecting Marcia to already be in bed, or at least to have eaten, he was surprised to find her in the kitchen.

"No pasta tonight. It's late," she explained. "I was thinking grilled cheese sandwiches."

His stomach growled. He hadn't yet come up with a plan to keep their affair a secret from her dad. But her dad was gone. That worry was something to ponder tomorrow.

"I haven't had a toasted cheese sandwich since I was a kid. I would love one."

"Good. You go get some wine and take it outside. I will bring out sandwiches."

By the time he had a bottle of wine, she was walking out the back door with a plate of sandwiches.

Sitting at the seat he now considered "his" at the outdoor table, he took a sandwich. "Nice night."

She smiled at him. "Yes. Very nice."

He'd be an idiot to misinterpret the gleam in her dark eyes, but his awkward feelings during his encounter with her dad that morning poured through him. Technically, if Antonio discovered their affair, he could think Trace was using Marcia, a woman who'd been hurt so much she was easy prey.

He wasn't sure that he wasn't using her. Though, he had no idea. Everything with her felt different. Special. Original. He'd married so young, then had a spotted relationship with women after that. No real feelings. Just fun. That's what she'd said she wanted and he did too.

All he could do was let this play out.

And hope her dad didn't find out.

They ate their sandwiches talking about their days. When Marcia was done, she rose. She took her wineglass and walked over to a chaise. She sat, stretched out her legs and patted the spot beside her.

"Let's enjoy the night."

As if hypnotized, he rose and slid down on the chaise with her.

"How does our moon compare with yours in Manhattan?"

He snorted. "We rarely see it. Too many tall buildings and light pollution. It has to be big and full before anyone even notices it."

"That's too bad. It's beautiful, don't you think?"

He settled back, got comfortable as he gazed at the moon and the stars twinkling in the dark sky. "Yes. It is beautiful."

She took a breath, nestled beside him. "This is why you bought the place... *Si?*"

"Si." Something about her soft words made him relax again, ease a little farther into the soft cushion.

"We have to be careful not to fall asleep here."

He laughed. "Oh, absolutely. It hit me today that your dad might not be happy with the shift in our relationship."

"Maybe."

"Oh, no *maybe* about it. The last man you guys let into your inner circle robbed you blind and broke your heart."

"You won't break my heart."

He smiled and shook his head. "You're very trusting."

"I trust myself. I'm pretty sure neither one of us believes this is permanent. For now—tonight—" She sat up and looked down at him. "What do you say we just enjoy the stars?"

He studied her beautiful dark eyes. Something warm and soft shifted through him. The urgency that usually caused him to look for answers, new ways of doing things, new things to do, fluttered away. His limbs relaxed. His head emptied.

He couldn't remember the last time that had happened.

After ten minutes, they began to kiss. Then she rose from the chaise and took his hand, leading him to her room.

Thursday morning, they woke early, ate breakfast and hopped into Trace's car to visit the next two vineyards on Ruth Montgomery's list.

Marcia punched the first address into her phone as he started the car. "This vineyard is two hours away!"

"Is that a problem?"

She thought for a second. "If my parents buy it, they will have to leave their friends."

He laughed. "Is *that* a problem?"

"I don't know. I haven't had time to give it any thought."

His eyes twinkled with mischief. She'd never seen him so happy or so comfortable. Pride filled her. She might not know the depth of his pain, but from the way he'd behaved when he arrived, it had to be deep and strong.

And she helped him forget. If only for a few weeks or a few months. Plus, getting her mind off herself and focusing on someone else was the best thing that had ever happened to *her*. She felt better too. Strong and smart. As capable as she'd felt before Adam.

He caught her hand and brought it to his lips for a light kiss. Her heart all but chugged to a stop at the romance of it. An odd hope filled her chest. She reminded herself that he'd been clear about not wanting a real relationship, and she would honor that.

But she was also aware that things had happened between them naturally. Spontaneously. And he was so different. Enjoying himself as much as she was. Falling into the romance like a man truly smitten.

Questions filled her brain.

What if this was more than two attracted people trying to ease their loneliness, forget their pasts?

What if it was real?

She stopped her thoughts. Not because she didn't want it to be real but because part of her wanted it too much and she knew exactly how hurt she would be if she expected things that couldn't happen. Right now, she was happy. He was happy. And that was what counted.

"Okay, so we'll go look at the vineyard, and if it's great, then we'll think through the problem of your parents having to move so far away. If it's not, then there's no need to think through a problem that doesn't exist."

That was exactly the same way she would handle this relationship. As long as this was working, there was no reason to question it or dissect it.

Relief fluttered through her, an unexpected benefit of no expectations. Details didn't matter. None of it mattered. Only the present moment.

The new vineyards Ruth showed them were a bust. Desperately trying to make a sale, Ruth had them trudge all over the rows of grapes on the last vineyard, clearly hoping something about it would make it a contender. But nothing popped. If anything, the tour made it even more obvious why they wouldn't want it.

By the time they got back to Trace's Maserati, they were tired and hot and had a long trip ahead of them.

He paused three steps away from the car door. "Hey, wanna drive?"

Her eyes widened. "This Maserati? Absolutely."

He tossed her the keys. "Okay."

They switched sides and she slid onto the driver's seat of the sleek sports car. She lovingly caressed the leather steering wheel. "I can't believe you're letting me drive."

"We just had one of the worst days of our lives. Walking in heat. Looking at vineyards that absolutely wouldn't work. I thought this would cheer you up."

Grateful, she smiled at him. He returned her smile. Simply. Easily.

And maybe that was the best thing about no expectations. With no worries of setting precedents, they did what they felt. Not afraid she would expect to always be able to drive, he asked her if she wanted to. Being in the moment, spontaneous, was wonderful.

She cautiously drove down the vineyard lane and onto the country road. Trace pulled out his phone. He loved having given her that gift, but he really wanted her to drive so he could find a place to stay the night. He would ask her opinion on it, but he wasn't armed with enough information to persuade her if she argued. He'd tell her once he found a place. Then he'd have something to tempt her with.

Using his phone, he located a bed-and-breakfast only a few miles up the road.

"Hey, look at this. There's a B&B a mile or so ahead of us."

She paused in enjoying her driving to frown at him. "What?"

"I found a bed-and-breakfast." He sighed. "I'm exhausted. You have to admit that after trudging through that last vineyard you are too. We have a two-hour drive ahead of us. Too long, I think, when there's a place we can rest nearby."

She didn't reply, but her face scrunched.

"Since finding your dad a new vineyard is my mission, I will pay for both rooms."

Her already big eyes widened. "You don't have to pay! I have money!"

Her tone clearly said he'd insulted her, and his brow wrinkled. If she wasn't worried about money, then what was she worried about?

He thought for a second and realized the only thing he'd

seen her fear in the weeks he'd known her was the gossip she encountered in town.

But how could she be worried about someone seeing them together when the bed-and-breakfast was a two-hour drive away?

Maybe a friend might tell a friend?

She drove the car into the parking area for the small, quaint bed-and-breakfast, and he opened his mouth to reassure her, then shut it again. How could he assure her no one would find out?

He couldn't.

He almost groaned. He didn't want to drive the hours they needed to get home... But he also didn't want to embarrass her.

Still, wasn't it far-fetched to think a friend of a friend would have a friend who would find out they'd spent the night in a bed-and-breakfast two hours away?

She hopped out of the car and headed for the entrance with him on her heels.

"We'll get separate rooms. Then if anyone finds out, we can tell them about our vineyard search."

"And ruin your plan about having my dad think he decided to buy a vineyard all on his own?"

"Hey, we have a backup story, remember? *I'm* looking for a second vineyard."

She stopped at the door and shook her head. He thought she was going to argue, but she stepped through. As they entered the cool foyer, a man walked through an opening behind a small check-in desk.

"We don't have a reservation. We're hoping you have a vacancy," Trace said.

"*Si. Si.* I will check." He riffled through a book, turning the big pages with a flourish. "Tourists?"

He almost said yes, but despite his easy half-truths with her dad, he wasn't the kind of person to lie. Fortunately, he didn't mind massaging the truth. He could be vague enough that the clerk wouldn't figure out who they were. Especially if they used only one credit card. His. No matter how snippy she got about him paying for their rooms, he would pay.

"We're from a few hours south of here. We went looking at two vineyards, hoping to buy."

The man peeked up. "But no luck?"

"No luck."

"You have luck now though." He turned the book toward Trace. "I have a room for a lovely married couple. Soaking tub. Soft comforter." He smiled.

Trace blinked, then glanced at Marcia, whose only reaction was a widening of her eyes.

The clerk gave her a soft look. "Newlyweds?"

Taking the plunge, not at all unhappy at the clerk's misreading everything, Trace signed the book. "Something like that." He handed his credit card to the older gentleman, who saw his name but not Marcia's.

All problems solved.

They headed upstairs behind the clerk, who finally realized they had no luggage.

Trace said, "We were expecting to go back tonight. Didn't realize how far we'd driven."

"Ah. If you want, I can toss your clothes in the washer."

"No, we'll be fine."

The clerk left, closing the door behind him, and Marcia burst into giggles. "How does it feel to be a newlywed?"

He knew, of course. Her silly question brought back a million feelings. Old emotions about a situation that suddenly seemed so, so far in the past.

"It's not bad," he said, walking over to her, refusing to let his memories mar the moment. He scooped her into his arms and kissed her. "Especially since it comes with you."

"Though we're going to have to put these dirty clothes

back on tomorrow morning, I still think it would be a good idea for us to shower first."

"Oh, I do too."

She laughed and led him into a quaint bathroom where he kissed her senseless so neither one of them would think of anything but the current minute.

CHAPTER TEN

THEY WOKE THE next morning to birds chirping outside their window. And wonderfully rested. He'd slept through the night—

Again.

She nestled against his side. Warmth careened through him, but so did contentment. The peace he'd been searching for for years wove through him, calming his nerves, making him feel normal again.

"I'm not ready to go home yet."

He wrapped his arms around her. "Neither am I."

"But we can't stay. We barely have time to get home before Papa and the boys get there."

"I know." But, oh, he wanted to stay. He almost felt he was living a fantasy, something so good, so perfect, it couldn't be real. He glanced at his phone. When he saw the time, his eyes bulged. "Oh, damn. Your dad will be at the vineyard in a little over an hour."

She groaned. "And we have a two-hour drive!"

"Exactly."

He expected her to hop out of bed. Instead, her mood changed, shifted, and she laughed. "Maybe we're thinking about this all wrong." She nuzzled his neck. "He does know how to open and run the wine bar."

His hand slid down her side. "True." He drew in a breath, ridiculously tempted by her softness. "There's only one problem. We would have to explain why we weren't there this morning."

"You do need furniture."

Confused, he looked down into her brown eyes. "What does that have to do with anything?"

"We could say we got up early and went to look at things for the house."

He rolled out of bed before he could be lured into doing something that would only add time to an already iffy schedule. The realization that they would be out-and-out lying to her dad again sent an odd sensation through him.

A knock on the door had him scurrying for his pants. He jumped into them while Marcia raced into the bathroom. When he opened the door, the bed-and-breakfast owner beamed at him over a room service cart.

"I have fruit and coffee."

A bit surprised, Trace said, "Thank you."

The owner winked at him. "On the house, since we suspect you won't be coming down for breakfast."

Trace laughed. "Actually, we won't. We have to get on the road ASAP. Is there anything I need to sign to check out?"

"No. I have your card number. You can leave whenever." He smiled broadly. "But if I had such a beautiful wife, I wouldn't let this opportunity pass."

Trace chuckled as the older man walked out of the room. He wondered why he was letting such a great opportunity pass. Then he remembered her dad and the lie that just didn't sit right and decided they needed to get moving.

But the owner's comment about Marcia being his wife also hit Trace funny. When he thought *wife*, he thought of Skylar. He couldn't picture Marcia as his wife... But he could picture her as *a* wife.

Somebody's beautiful wife.

A woman a man committed to not because she was gorgeous—though she was. But because she was kind, generous, wonderful.

She came out of the bathroom fully dressed and the sight of her stole his breath. The room immediately filled with light and happiness.

"Aren't you ready?"

He stood like a yutz, barefoot, bare-chested, because his brain had been lollygagging. Stalled because the B&B owner had assumed Marcia was his wife.

He couldn't believe his brain stumbled over that.

But he suddenly realized why it had. If Trace were in the market for a wife, *she* would be a strong candidate.

He chuckled inwardly at his choice of words and realized why he'd never marry again. No woman would want to be thought of as a strong candidate.

He pulled his shirt over his head and looked under the bed for his socks. "Be ready in two minutes." He peeked up at her again. Her glorious black hair and warm brown eyes. "Pour us a cup of coffee and maybe grab some fruit for the road."

"Okay."

The owner had kindly left both china and paper plates, lovely cups and take-out cups. Marcia poured coffee for them in the take-out cups and gathered some fruit, surreptitiously watching Trace rummage beneath the bed for his socks.

The sadness had been gone from his eyes when she came out of the bathroom. She'd seen peeks of his sorrow the day before, even a glimpse of it that morning, when she was trying to convince him they could stay. But to her great relief, it was gone.

It didn't puzzle her that he had sad days. If she was reading the situation correctly, he'd covered his grief with work, and now that he didn't have the mind-numbing, long hours that running a conglomerate entailed, he had moments when the past sneaked up on him.

She got it. He hadn't fully processed his past. The loss of a child. The breakdown of a marriage. She didn't know how to help him with that, but she did know how to make him smile. Which, in the end, might be how he would eventually adjust to his losses. Whether he saw it or not, she was good for him. And that was good for her. They were both moving on—

Except just as he had moments of sorrow, she had moments of *what if*. What if this was real? What if they were crazy not to see that?

She shook her head to clear away those thoughts. If it was real, it would last. That was not a question for two people who'd known each other only a few weeks.

The drive back was fun. With the car roof up for safety purposes, they sipped coffee and ate fruit, working not to spill anything on the beautiful leather of his car seats. Though he would groan every time she bobbled a grape and slowed the car's speed when she took a sip of coffee, he also laughed.

She kept the drive light, knowing this was what he needed. Silliness strong enough that he could see life goes on.

He drove the car into the Giordano Vineyards parking lot, easing past buses and rental cars galore.

Trace whistled. "Wow. Looks like our best day ever."

"It's Friday," she reminded him as he pulled into a parking spot. She opened her door to get out and spoke to him over the roof of his car. "Always a big day."

"I'm going to skip a shower and just jump into my vintner clothes."

He walked around to her side of the car and she smiled at him. The door of the wine room exploded open and Antonio burst out.

"Where the hell were you?"

Trace faced him with a laugh. "Relax, Antonio. We were—"

"You were nowhere in town! The villa was dark and empty all night." He turned his heated gaze on Marcia.

"Where were you?" He stalked toward her, his eyes shooting fire. "Wasn't it enough to bring scandal and shame on our family once? Do you plan to live this way?"

Trace stepped in between them. "Okay, let me stop you before you embarrass yourself. We were out looking for—"

She waited expectantly for him to say *furniture*. Instead, after a pause, he said, "Vineyards for you."

Marcia gaped at him. That wasn't the cover story they'd created.

"We'd traveled pretty far the day before and had to stay over."

Looking like a bull ready to charge, her dad faced Trace. "Stay over?"

"A B&B. It was the first thing we came to."

She'd never seen anybody keep his cool in the face of her dad's anger, and her mouth almost fell open in awe.

Trace waited a few seconds for her dad to answer, but Marcia didn't believe he was going to. His eyes were dark spears aimed at her, the poison of accusation smearing the tips. This was it. The big fight she'd always expected to have with her dad. Except it wouldn't be a fight. Anything he had to say would be the truth. She'd fallen victim to a con man. He'd stolen from them. Nearly bankrupted them. And now she was sleeping with Trace.

Anything he said, she deserved.

Trace shook his head. "Earth to Antonio. How did you miss that I just told you we were looking for a vineyard for you?"

Antonio glanced at him, confused. "What?"

Marcia blinked. She didn't know what Trace was doing. But he'd taken her father's attention off her, off the butt kicking she knew she deserved.

Trace pulled his phone out of his pocket and tapped his contacts. "Hey, Ruth. It's Trace Jackson. I think Antonio is finally ready to start looking at vineyards. How about the one with the white gates?"

Marcia held back a gasp. Not only was he taking the heat off her, but he was removing her dad. Not letting him have the screaming fit he so clearly wanted to have.

"That's great." He disconnected the call, caught Antonio's arm and led him to his car.

Marcia stepped out of the way.

"This vineyard needs oodles of work. But—" he pointed to the wine-tasting room entrance "—you've got two healthy young sons in there who could help you fix it up."

Antonio peered back at the wine building. "I do not understand."

"Get in," Trace said amicably. "We won't put the top down so I can explain things to you. But on the way home, top down. You're gonna love this car."

Marcia stared after them as they drove away. She finally noticed that she hadn't been invited along, even though she had been a big part of building Giordano Vineyards—

But maybe she didn't need to be a part of building the new vineyard? Maybe what *she* needed was to separate herself. Her entire life she'd been in training to take over the family vineyard, but it came at a price. She'd been so focused, so sheltered, that she'd fallen victim to a charlatan. And now that she was finally finding herself, finding her footing, she didn't want to go backward.

She didn't want to lose her family, but she did want to be herself. Her real self.

Whether he knew it or not, Trace had just saved her. And not with a lie or made-up story. Simply by forcing her dad to move forward.

Forcing her to move forward too.

By separating her from the new vineyard.

Trace Jackson, Mr. Fix-It, had to be the most amazing man she'd ever met.

She squeezed her eyes shut as the questions from the bed-and-breakfast poured through her again. *Was this real?*

She groaned. It almost didn't matter if it was real. She was falling in love. How could she not? The man was wonderful.

But that was wrong. So wrong.

If she didn't collect herself, she was going to end up hurt when their time together ended—

Unless it didn't end?

Unless he did all these nice things for her because he was falling in love too?

CHAPTER ELEVEN

TRACE WAITED ONLY until they were out of the lane to Giordano Vineyards before he pulled the car to the side of the road and faced Antonio.

"You will never yell at Marcia like that again."

Antonio's eyes narrowed and his chin lifted. "She is my daughter."

"And your employee. Technically when she got involved with the guy who stole from you, she was more employee than daughter."

Antonio snorted.

Trace paused a second. Nothing Marcia had told him had ever been in confidence. Still, he thought of her feelings, what needed to be said, what didn't, before he spoke.

"Do you know she was trying to buy the Giordano Vineyards back from me?"

Antonio peered over at him. "She doesn't have that kind of money."

"She says she has a friend who could lend it to her."

Antonio inhaled sharply. "Janine." He shook his head. "But her mother is sick... If I remember correctly, she has cancer." He scrubbed his hand across his mouth. "Marcia wouldn't bother them in their time of trouble."

"That's probably the only reason she hasn't actually made an offer."

Antonio gave him a confused look. "And you would have sold it back to her?"

"Nope. Sorry. A deal is a deal. But it only took me a few days to realize you weren't mad at Marcia for the embezzling mess as much as you are angry with yourself."

When Antonio said nothing, Trace said, "You trusted him too."

"Si."

"So, stop being angry with her. Or projecting your anger with yourself onto her and do something."

Antonio laughed and speared him with a sly look. "You mean like buy another vineyard."

"You're still young. You've got two healthy sons. And you are not happy as a retired man."

He snorted.

"Are you?" Trace prodded. "You come to work for me every day as if you can't decide what to do with yourself."

Antonio straightened. "I'm helping you get established."

"Pfft." Trace shook his head. "I could hire thirty people to run Giordano Vineyards."

"You would lose money."

"And I wouldn't care. Because I have more than enough for three lifetimes." He peered at Antonio. "Look. I love having you and your sons around, but I don't need you and you *do* need something else in your life."

He turned and restarted the car's engine, heading for the vineyard with the white gates, which was only a few miles away. "I'd originally nixed the vineyard we're going to see, but I think I spoke too soon."

"Why did you not think it right?"

"It's run-down. Really run-down. But the more vineyards I saw, the more I realized nothing else had quite the right set of specifications."

"*You* know what *I* need."

Trace laughed. "I'm a fixer," he said, and for once he didn't hate the sound of it on his tongue. "I see things objectively."

Antonio sniffed. "You see my daughter objectively?"

"Of course. I could tell on day one that she was determined to make it up to you that she'd lost your vineyard."

He peeked at Antonio as he sped down the road. "She's got a lotta spunk, that one. Told me she'd run me off in less than a year."

Antonio laughed.

"That's why I involved her in the search for a new vineyard for you. She needed to feel that she was doing something to make up for hurting you."

Antonio said nothing.

"She's a good person."

"Which is why I don't want you to hurt her."

The comment surprised Trace, but when he considered it, he didn't know why he thought it had come out of the blue. He wasn't the only perceptive human being in the world. Though he and Marcia had been careful, discreet, fathers had an instinct.

"I'm not going to hurt her."

But he was. He *knew* he was. That was what all the memories of Skylar were about. Except in this case, he wasn't the one who got hurt. He was the passive, not committed one, in it only for the fun side of the affair.

Things he hadn't wanted to admit to himself shuffled through his brain. How Skylar loved rebelling. How she'd loved his devotion to her. How she'd been able to leave their marriage without pain, without a sense of a loss of anything except their son. When Joshua had died, the fun had gone out of her rebellion and been replaced by the stark and terrible reality that real life wasn't always a joyride.

Hating how those thoughts pinched his chest and made him want to punch something, he shut them down. Shoved them aside. Refused to give them space in his brain.

"Yes. You are going to hurt her," Antonio assured him. "Maybe not this week or this month or even this year. But you will move on."

"I don't want to move on. I like it here. I like the peace and quiet."

"And the slow pace?" Antonio laughed. "You tell me I need something more, but what about you? How long until you want to get your hands on another billion-dollar opportunity? How long until a man with your education and instincts starts looking at every business he sees as a chance to make another big score?"

Trace squirmed in his seat. "So far I haven't wanted one."

Antonio snorted. "So far… That's precious. You might as well admit that something is going to tempt you away eventually. And knowing that, any relationship you have with my daughter is temporary."

Trace bit his lower lip to keep from lying. He'd put this man on the ropes professionally, was taking him by the hand, telling him he needed to buy another vineyard, grab the reins of his life. He could not tell him he wasn't going to hurt his daughter any more than he could profess that he wouldn't leave Tuscany one day, wouldn't find an opportunity that would lure him back to luscious Manhattan, where he could get a pizza at any time of the day or night, go to the theater or the Metropolitan Museum of Art.

Except…

He slept when he was with Marcia.

But he also slept when he was working his brain to exhaustion. And there might come a time when a company, a challenge, a chance to be himself again might tempt him more than Marcia.

Oh, God. He *was* using her.

Trace and Antonio returned to Giordano Vineyards a little after five. Antonio had loved White Gates Vineyards—he'd decided to name it that because it fit—and he'd instructed Ruth to make an offer. The real estate agent for the vineyard owner was excited that someone was finally interested, and claimed the owner was eager to sell. So, they'd waited in Ruth's office until the acceptance came through.

The happy pair walked into the wine-tasting room together, all smiles. No hint that Trace all but vibrated with confusion and self-loathing about his relationship with Marcia.

"Hey, everybody," Antonio shouted, commanding the attention of the thirty or so people in the room, including his sons. "I just bought another vineyard."

His sons' eyes popped, but the tourists in the crowd began slapping his back, congratulating him and toasting the new venture.

Trace laughed. Despite their conversation about Marcia as they drove to White Gates, their afternoon had been fun. He liked Antonio. He enjoyed his happiness.

Another bus pulled in and the excitement of the moment took a back seat to work. Trace welcomed the new group while Matteo and Roberto wrote orders from the group getting ready to leave. He and Antonio worked side by side, laughing, involving tourists in their fun, as they poured samples of each kind of wine.

It was eight o'clock before he was able to get away. Antonio promised he and his sons would close the room after the last group left. He hated leaving Antonio with work that was essentially his and his alone now. But all day, he'd gotten shots of memory that about killed him.

Every time he thought about Antonio's accusation that he'd leave, which made him realize he was using Marcia, his brain would jump to Skylar, the new way he was beginning to see her. He couldn't hate her. He'd never hated her, not even for leaving him. She'd been eighteen at the time. *Eighteen.* Too young to bear the burdens of a lost child when their relationship had been nothing but a rebellion against her parents.

He'd loved *her.* Purely. Innocently. He was the one who'd made the big plan to get married when she'd discovered she was pregnant. With time providing perspective, he could remember how her agreement had been a wobbly one. He couldn't hate her for something the Mr. Fix-It in him had orchestrated.

Particularly since his manipulations hadn't gotten the good outcome his older, wiser self got when he intervened to fix business problems. The end of his marriage had been an unmitigated disaster.

Skylar's allegiance clearly hadn't lain with him. A few days after Joshua's death, when he'd realized she wasn't coming back to their apartment, he'd called her and forced her to talk with him. She'd calmly, rationally explained that without their child there was no reason for them to be together. He'd argued that that was her parents talking, but something had changed in her voice. He'd heard a tiredness…

In a way, he supposed he'd always known she didn't love him.

So why did it still torment him?

Twelve years had gone by. He'd spent the bulk of them fine. Busily building his real life.

Why was all this tormenting him now? He could say that without the work of the corporation his brain had too much time to think. But there was more. He knew there was more. And if he used Marcia to stop the pain, would he actually delay figuring all this out?

Not hearing a sound in the house when he entered, he took the steps two at a time and ambled down the hall to the master suite, where he showered and changed into comfortable clothes.

When he returned downstairs, the place was silent, confusing him. He made himself a sandwich in the kitchen, which he took to the patio. He saw Marcia lying on a chaise by the pool and knew why the house had been silent.

She'd been out here.

Her tiny bikini hid nothing. Moonlight sparkling off the water in the pool brought back memories of the first time they'd made love. How he'd picked her up and jumped into the warm water with her.

His breaths bubbling in his chest, he sat on the chaise beside hers. Memories of Skylar colliding with memories of Marcia vibrated through him. He'd never before compared another woman to Skylar.

And he wondered if that wasn't also a piece of this puzzle.

"Hey."

Her eyes opened and she smiled at him. Her face was perfection. Dark, sensual eyes. A pert nose. Full, lush lips.

"Hey."

He swallowed a swell of emotion that threatened to overwhelm him. Touching her velvet skin took him to another place. Sleeping next to her brought him peace.

But wasn't that actually the problem?

She gave him the one thing he'd longed for—rest—when maybe what his brain really needed was to be pushed to the limit, forced to face a dark demon that robbed him of sleep but wouldn't show itself.

Not able to think that through now, he pushed the horrifying thought away. What more could he possibly have to face than the loss of a child?

"Your dad bought White Gates Vineyards."

She sat up. "The first one we looked at?"

"Yep. He named it White Gates Vineyards."

"Oh, my gosh! He really did it?"

Trace caught her gaze. "And he's happy."

Her eyes softened. "He is?"

"He is. I explained my reasoning for looking for a new vineyard for him and he agreed. I told him that the way he spent so much time at Giordano Vineyards proved he needed something to do. I also told him that creating a second successful vineyard would get him beyond the mistake of trusting Adam."

"How'd he take it?"

"He listened." And threw accusations back at Trace about his daughter. But Trace wouldn't tell her that. A conversation a man has with the father of the woman he's sleeping with was a delicate thing. A father always knew his daughter would make her own choices, but the man sleeping with that daughter always knew the dad would kick his ass—or somehow make his life miserable—if he hurt her. Dads didn't like daughters setting themselves up to be hurt by a con man…or a rogue. He might not be a con man, but he supposed he fell into the rogue category.

Skylar's dad had chosen to freeze him out. And in the end, it had worked. When push came to shove, Skylar went home.

Marcia's dad had simply called him out. And that was working too. He couldn't go on sleeping with her now that he knew he'd eventually hurt her. As Antonio said, he'd leave someday. He'd be the Skylar in their relationship.

Not because he was cold and heartless, or too young to make a choice, but because until he really understood what his brain was trying to tell him, he knew he didn't deserve someone like Marcia. Sweet, fierce and longing to make a future, she would want children. She didn't have to say it. Her love and loyalty to family said it for her.

While he couldn't even think about children without cold dread washing over him, freezing his brain on one thought: he'd failed as a father.

He could not tie her to him.

He finished his sandwich and rose from the chaise. "Anyway, just thought you'd want to know."

Marcia's head tilted. "Where are you going?"

His heart stuttered. Every fiber of his being wanted to

stay. He loved being with her. Loved how he felt with her. But if a man who could not commit continued sleeping with a woman who needed a commitment, he would be leading her on. And he was not the kind of guy who led someone on or lived a lie.

"Inside. Maybe I'll get a beer. I don't know."

His words seemed to hang in the air, creating an odd sensation that fluttered through him. He was saying one thing, when he wanted another. He was so accustomed to taking her in his arms, laughing with her, making love like goofy puppies, that it seemed wrong to leave.

But he couldn't stay. Not because Antonio had been correct. That he would someday find another project, hire sufficient staff for Giordano Vineyards and leave without a backward glance. Because of Marcia. He did not want to be the source of new pain for her—

"Stay with me."

Temptation rose again. But that was the problem. She was perfect. Easy for a man to desire.

And he was nothing. The guy who sweet-talked his girlfriend into marrying him. How could he ever believe he deserved to be trusted? How could *he* ever trust *himself* to be even a halfway decent partner to a woman who merited so much more?

He silenced his longings, the voice that begged him to take a chance. On what? On forever? He would never have forever. He'd had that shot and he'd blown it.

Was that what his brain wanted him to remember? That he'd lost his chance? That his life was best spent working?

Which would make Antonio right. His psyche was telling him he needed to find new work, a bigger company to run. Not to mess around with a woman who merited better.

"We have a busy day tomorrow. At some point, I think you and your dad need to talk. Then your dad and I need to make preliminary plans for what to do with White Gates. I'll need some sleep."

He shrugged and almost turned to go into the house. But he saw the hurt in her dark eyes and bent down to kiss her. "I'll see you in the morning."

"Okay."

He walked inside the villa reminding himself that he'd finally gotten this family back on its feet. He would not do anything to jeopardize that. He wouldn't use Marcia. He would end their relationship before she was so involved that she got hurt when he found another business deal, grew tired of Tuscany or simply decided to return to Manhattan.

Because it no longer seemed far-fetched that he should leave. In fact, going back to Manhattan might be the answer he'd been searching for all along.

CHAPTER TWELVE

MARCIA WOKE THE next morning disoriented. Without opening her eyes, she reached for Trace, but he wasn't there. The day before had been exhausting. Her dad had all but accused them of having an affair—which they were, but it wasn't something anyone liked shouted across a crowded vineyard parking lot packed with tourists.

Trace had needed to get his bearings. She totally understood.

She left her bed, showered and dressed in a soft floral shirtwaist dress. She also had some things to adjust to. Her dad was back to being a businessman, and her brothers would be leaving. She and Trace had tons of work to do. It was time to get her head in the game.

He wasn't in the kitchen when she arrived, but a pot of coffee told her he'd been there. She grabbed a mug and filled it, then walked to her workspace. As she suspected, Trace and her dad were in her dad's old office. Trace sat at the desk, his fingers on the keyboard of a laptop. Her dad stood over his shoulder, pointing at something on the screen.

When she closed the door, Trace looked up. "We're creating a budget. Wanna join us?"

She took a soft breath, her gaze jumping to her father. "I don't know—"

"Please," her dad said. "We could use your help."

Her heart skipped a beat. She knew this was as close to an apology as she'd ever get. But acceptance, a welcome back to the fold, was better than a platitude.

She walked to the desk, glanced at the screen and began giving recommendations. Adam might have gotten their first loan and created the renovation plans, but she'd worked with him on hiring a general contractor and organizing a huge revitalization of Giordano Vineyards. She'd also had to assume his end of the responsibilities, including getting a second loan, when he skipped town. Her former fiancé might have hurt them, but she'd gained experience, and now she, her dad and Trace would put it to good use.

Her shame and apprehension fell away and were replaced by a burst of self-esteem. She didn't need Trace pointing the way anymore. She could do this. Herself.

She also didn't *need* Trace personally. So much stronger than when she'd met Adam, she knew the difference between hero worship and real feelings, and what she felt for Trace was deeper, richer, more profound than anything she'd ever felt for Adam.

Her heart caught. She tried to tell herself she'd come to yesterday's conclusion that she loved him too quickly…

But that was a lie. These feelings were strong and real. She loved him.

Was it another mistake? He never said he loved her. He'd all but closed the door on a future. She'd started their affair knowing it would be temporary. She'd even told him that. How had she fallen in love?

She fought the urge to squeeze her eyes shut. She couldn't think about this now. There was work to be done. She needed her focus, first, to help her dad create a plan of action for the new vineyard. Second, to work with Trace to hire the people they would need to keep Giordano Vineyards bustling and prosperous once her father and brothers moved on.

Her dad pondered every choice with the enthusiasm of a man who'd gotten a second chance at life, but Trace was all business. No smiles. No chitchat. No joking around.

At first, she chalked that up to the presence of her father and Trace's sincere desire to help him become successful. But when she left for lunch, he didn't follow. He went into the wine-tasting room. He helped her brothers work with tourists until late, a common occurrence on weekends.

Her thoughts tripped over into the situation that had tried to overwhelm her that morning. They had begun their affair with no promises. She wasn't allowed to change her mind. Particularly since he was behaving differently. Now that they had handled her father's troubles, he'd pulled away. As if her family's problems had been the draw, not her.

The conclusion emptied her heart, hollowed out her chest.

She couldn't be angry with him. She'd been the one to set the terms. He'd given her a couple of weeks of fun, of happiness.

But she could be angry with herself for letting it become more than he'd intended.

More than *they'd* intended.

Deciding not to dwell on it, but to wait to see how things went after her dad and brothers left, she showered, changed into a simple nightshirt and grabbed the novel she'd been reading from the bedside table.

Minutes of waiting became an hour.

One hour turned into two.

She fell asleep reading and woke alone again.

This time, there was no waffling, no confusion about what was going on. He was absolutely avoiding the personal side of the relationship.

She thought of Adam, how she'd been so blind, and for a split second was proud she wasn't such a chump this time. But the loss hit her before she could stop it. The thought that she would work with him every day and never touch him, never kiss him, never have another intimate talk.

She reminded herself they had made no promises. They'd mutually decided to live in the moment, and now he was walking away.

She either had to accept that or be a chump again.

And that was one lesson she'd vowed never to repeat.

She would not be a chump. She would not be the weeping woman, cast aside by a man. She'd entered their affair with her head high. She would keep it high.

Monday morning, Trace worked with Antonio. The all-cash offer for White Gates might get Antonio the vineyard, but he'd need a loan to make repairs to buildings and grapevines that had been abandoned.

After creating the long list of repairs and a spreadsheet with the estimated cost to make them, Trace sat back in his desk chair. "I'm lending you the cash."

Antonio waved his hand in dismissal. "You've done enough."

"No bank is going to give you a no-interest loan."

"So why would *you*?"

"Because we're friends."

Antonio pondered that for a few seconds. "Say more."

"Hey, we're two guys who own vineyards a few miles apart. An alliance works for us."

Antonio chuckled. "True."

"So, let me call my lawyers and get papers ready."

Antonio grinned. "I would argue, but you would argue more. So, I concede. I will take your loan. But it *is* a loan. Not a gift."

Trace held out his hand and they shook on it. "Okay. I'll also have the lawyer create a payment schedule."

Antonio left for lunch, but Trace didn't follow. When he didn't sleep, he didn't seem to get hungry. He headed into the wine-tasting room to do his fair share.

In the early evening, Roberto and Matteo took pity on him and Antonio and shooed their dad home even as they told Trace he looked too tired to be nice to tourists. He laughed, but he also didn't leave.

After ten, he ambled into the house, made a sandwich

and took it to the master suite, eating it as he shucked his clothes.

The food made him feel marginally better. But he didn't wait to see if he could sleep. He headed for the pool patio. The dimmed lights provided enough illumination that he made his way to the first table. He sat, but a movement to the right caught his attention.

He glanced up and saw Marcia sleeping on the chaise.

Tonight, she wasn't wearing a bikini. A big T-shirt fell to her knees. He laughed. Only on Shortie-McShort Marcia would a T-shirt cover her from neck to knees.

He walked over. "Hey, sleepyhead. Unless you're planning on staying here all night, you should go upstairs."

She took a long breath and stretched. Trace's heart stumbled. She looked so sweet, so innocent…and yet somehow so sexy. Lifting her arms above her head, she stretched the T-shirt enough that it molded itself to her breasts, her tiny waist, her round hips.

He blew his breath out in a long sigh, forcing his thoughts back where they belonged. He was bowing out before he hurt her. He'd made too many mistakes when it came to romance and didn't deserve the kind of love she would give him. Total. Complete. And oh, so sweet.

He shook her shoulder. "I mean it. It gets cold out here at night."

"Just a few more minutes, Mama."

He laughed. "I'm not your mom."

"You sure sound like it."

He laughed and, realizing she was more awake than he'd thought, he put out his hand. "Come on. Let me help you up."

She took a breath, opened her eyes. For twenty seconds she held his gaze.

Everything inside Trace stilled. He wanted to sit beside her on the chaise, toss the T-shirt and make love in the moonlight.

She did too. He could see it in her eyes, sense it in her hesitancy.

He took a breath.

She took a breath.

He wasn't entirely sure what he'd do if she made the first move. Part of him wished she would. Wished she'd say or do something—anything—that he could blame for his inability to resist her.

But she said nothing. She didn't even take the hand he'd extended. She shifted on the chaise so she could rise without his help.

Then she headed for the back door. "Good night, Trace."

He swallowed. "Good night."

The door opened and she walked inside the house.

Longing ruffled through him. But, tonight, she'd been the one to walk away. He loved her strength. Loved that she probably realized he'd ended their affair, but she wasn't pouting or arguing. She'd simply moved on.

He frowned. He didn't know any of that. He hadn't told her about the chat with her dad. For all he knew, *she'd* ended the affair.

The thought burned through him like a hot knife through butter.

He told himself that was crazy. The end had been sensible. It didn't matter who stopped things. Everything that was happening was good. Right.

He took a long breath, then another to quell the pain. He told himself they hadn't been together long enough for him to feel this kind of loss.

Ignoring all of it, he walked back to the patio table, but his thoughts wouldn't leave him. He could picture Marcia and a couple of cute kids playing in the pool.

He frowned, staring at the moonlight twinkling off the

pool. If he went back to Manhattan, she'd remain general manager of Giordano Vineyards and, of course, he'd insist she live in the villa. She and her kids would swim in the pool. Laughing. Happy.

His heart froze. His breathing stopped. But he dispatched the pictures to the far corner of his brain. He didn't need to envision what he'd be missing. Part of him already knew.

The next morning, she was in the kitchen when he stumbled in after forty-five minutes of sleep.

She looked sleek and professional with her hair gathered on top of her head and a slim yellow dress riding her curves. She smiled, said, "Good morning," then carried a mug of coffee out the back door, probably on her way to her office.

When the door closed behind her, he whistled. "Holy hell. That woman is on fire."

And he was resisting her. Not because he was strong, but for her. He hadn't needed to go so far as to picture her with another man's children, but he got the gist of it. He wasn't the only one moving on.

The thought stung, but it was yet another thing he had to get accustomed to. And he could not do something foolish before his time at Giordano Vineyards was up. They'd spent the past weeks ensuring Antonio's future and neglected his own business. He had a few more days' work for White Gates before he could shift back to Giordano Vineyards. So he had to suck it up.

Still, the sense of loss vibrated through him, along with fear that he'd have to watch her fall in love with someone else. Ignoring both, he headed to his office, thanking God there were one-year and five-year plans to create for White Gates Vineyards that morning. Antonio was taking his wife to tour the vineyard, so Trace would have something to occupy his mind other than Marcia moving on without him.

His plan to get his focus off what he was missing seemed like it would work, until he remembered Marcia sat in the office in front of his. That was good for when he had questions, but bad when their hands brushed, or when he couldn't keep his eyes off her. She met with suppliers and he surreptitiously watched her sweet-talk them into giving her a better deal. He watched as she had a video call with a graphic artist, wanting to surprise her parents with the perfect logo for White Gates Vineyards.

When the artist disappeared from her computer screen, he rose from his seat and leaned against the door frame between the two rooms. "You're very kind."

She sniffed a laugh. "You wouldn't help your parents if they bought a new business?"

He frowned. "My dad doesn't have that kind of ambition."

"Maybe this is why you hijacked my dad."

He laughed. "I didn't hijack him." He shrugged. "He's my friend."

"I'm not concerned about your love for spending time with my dad as much as I'm curious about your distance from your parents."

He walked from the doorway to sit on the corner of her desk. There was no reason for secrets between them. He intended to go back home, and she'd be moving on without him. In some ways, he actually believed he owed her more explanation about his life, so she'd see his leaving was for the best.

"The last time I was home, my dad said something that about flattened me."

"Must have been something awful."

He picked up her pen, then caught her gaze. "He said my son's death was a blessing in disguise."

Her breathing jerked, so when she spoke, the word came out in a horrified gasp. "What?"

He pretended indifference. "I know. It was hard to hear." He looked down, then caught her gaze again. "My mother tried to explain that what my dad meant was that my ex and I had both moved on and become very successful."

"I'm sure that's true."

"It might have been what he meant, but it's not what he said, and what he said took me so much by surprise I reacted viscerally, from the gut."

"Of course you did! You loved your son. You *miss* your son."

"I do miss my son, but not in the way you might think." He sighed and looked her in the eye again. "I'm not nuts. I don't think about him all the time, but sometimes I miss who he could have been. I miss the chance to teach him how to throw a ball. I miss that wonderful moment when you realize your kid is gifted in math or good with pets or kind to other kids. I long to see who he might have been."

"That makes sense."

"Really?" He snorted. "*Twelve years* have gone by. This sudden burst of yearning makes *no* sense."

"You said yourself that it started when you had time on your hands to think about it. Maybe avoiding it for twelve years only delayed it."

He shifted on her desk. That's what he'd thought. But now instinct was telling him it was something more, even as it told him he could talk about it with Marcia. She'd always been candid with him. Honest. Open. Never judging.

And maybe that's why she tempted him so much.

"I did say that."

"So why don't you believe it?"

He tapped her pen on the desk. "I have a sense that it's something more."

"More?"

He shrugged, not wanting to talk about this anymore because he suddenly felt foolish. "You know… I'm probably looking for something that isn't there. Just as you said, I was fine until I stopped working."

She laughed. "You are a very smart guy. A perceptive guy. You should take your own advice. Listen to your own reason."

He pulled in a slow breath. Regardless of what he'd said to Marcia, his reason insisted there was more behind his inability to sleep than lack of things to do. He had tons of work to do with White Gates and Giordano Vineyards… yet he hadn't slept the night before—

"We should do something fun tonight. Maybe go to Florence for dinner."

Her shift of topic surprised him so much he blinked. "I don't want to entertain myself to make things go away."

"Oh, really, Antonio?"

He frowned at her.

"My father did not want to buy another vineyard to make himself feel better over losing this one. You forced him." She rose from her seat. "So tonight I'm forcing you to do the thing you really need. Relax. Be ready to drive me to Florence tonight at six. Dress up. We're going somewhere nice."

With that, she picked up her coffee mug and walked out of her office.

He watched her go. Half amused, half confused. It was interesting that she didn't try to talk him out of his grief or even tell him it was time to move on. She'd seen him floundering and made plans for dinner. Technically, she'd thrown what he'd done with her dad back at him. She'd made the plan and guided him to it.

He laughed and returned to Antonio's office—now his office, he supposed—to finish his work.

Her dad arrived at three and Trace showed him the plans for White Gates. He approved, liking how Trace had gone back into Giordano Vineyards' history and mimicked a lot of what Antonio had done the first time around.

"Except, I didn't have so much cash." He shook his head, remembering. "I was always going to the bank for money."

Trace glanced at the old records that he had spread out on the desk. "Every five years isn't always."

"No. But I was never debt free. I'd pay off a loan and get another."

"To build things up." He glanced at his watch, saw it was almost five and rose. Clasping Antonio's shoulder for a quick squeeze, he said, "We'll refine those plans tomorrow after you have a chance to think them through."

Antonio said, "Thank you."

"For helping a friend?" He batted his hand. "No thanks necessary."

"Thanks are always necessary. Appreciation and respect make the world go round."

He hadn't thought of it like that, but he supposed Antonio was right.

So why was he going out with this man's daughter again? Thoughts of their evening together had about ruined his concentration that afternoon. Especially when he saw Marcia leaving early, obviously to get ready. His nerves had spiked. His thoughts had spiraled. He'd had trouble keeping his mind on his discussions with Antonio.

But he couldn't talk himself into refusing her invitation. Not because they'd been lovers, but because he liked her. They were *friends* too. He wasn't merely friends with Antonio. He and Marcia were friends.

Walking into the villa, he reminded himself of his plan to keep his distance but decided that a nice night out, not as lovers, but as friends, might be exactly what they needed to complete the transition.

Marcia tried not to be nervous as she descended the steps to the foyer, where Trace awaited her. He wore a dark suit, white shirt and aqua tie. With his dark hair slicked back and his hands tucked into his pants pockets, he looked casually sexy.

Her heart stuttered but she told herself to stop being silly. Mr. Fix-It had done everything he'd intended. He'd found her dad a new vineyard. He'd helped her get back to being confident and strong. Now someone needed to help him.

She'd seen the confusion that overtook him that afternoon when he spoke of his son. She'd seen his difficulty keeping his focus. Tonight, she would provide him with a pleasant-distraction evening. No romance. No pressure. Just a nice time.

At the bottom of the steps, he caught her hand and brought it to his lips, kissing the knuckles. "Am I going to have to fight off men who will try to steal you?"

Her heart knocked against her ribs. The thought that he might be jealous filled her with hope that she'd misread the past few days. But deep down she knew she hadn't.

So, she went along with his teasing. "What a delicious idea."

He opened the villa door for her. "Delicious?"

"Oh, come on. It would be a hoot to have men fighting over me. Let me have some fun."

He laughed. "Now, isn't that a welcome change in attitude?"

Her heart drooped. She loved his teasing, but the way he had no problem with her being with other men was oh, so hard to take. Still, she wasn't a child. He was done with their affair. She might not know why, but she knew he'd withdrawn. And she also knew he was going through something difficult.

If it killed her, she would give him a lovely, happy evening to ease a bit of his sorrow and his confusion over that sorrow.

They drove to the city, top down, air blowing around them. She led him along the crowded Florence sidewalk to the restaurant. The street smelled of the earth and delicious food, especially freshly baked bread. The sun had gone down, but the heat of the day remained, giving the air a feel that was unique to Tuscany. Her cares melted away. Happiness bubbled inside her.

She'd forgotten how much she loved Florence.

After confirming their reservations with the hostess, they were escorted to a table outside. The lights of the city blinked at them.

"I'm sorry," she said, as they were seated. "Beyond all those twinkling lights are mountains. It's too late for the breathtaking view."

"No worries." He toyed with his wineglass. "The view from where I'm sitting is gorgeous."

Her heart squeezed with longing that she had to squelch. Flirting Trace was back. But this dinner, this trip away from the vineyard, wasn't about her. It was about him. He liked to flirt. If it was part of how he forgot his troubles, she would let him.

The waiter arrived with a bottle of wine. She knew it was expensive from the label, but Trace didn't even blink. The waiter poured two glasses and left menus.

Trying to be subtle, she said, "I'm paying for this dinner."

He laughed. "Seriously?"

"Yes!" She thought for a second, then said, "In your normal life, you pay for everything, don't you?"

He shrugged. "I have the money. Lots of people I know don't."

She sat up in her seat. "Well, you're not paying tonight. I asked you out. I pay." Realizing what she'd said, she squeaked. "Not that I'm saying this is a date." She felt her face redden. "It's not."

He reached across the table and took her hand. "Relax."

She sucked in a breath. He was right. Antsy, nervous, guilt-ridden Marcia was gone. This was not the time to revive her. "Yes. Let's both relax."

They talked like friends as the waiter brought several courses of dinner. The moon rose. The night sounds changed. Even the dining area of the restaurant had a hushed reverence to it, as the city slowed down, getting ready to sleep.

As they drove home, they talked some more about her parents, her life. Her teen years seemed to particularly amuse him, and she almost asked about his...about stupid teenage things he'd done... Then she remembered he'd gotten his girlfriend pregnant at eighteen, married her and ultimately lost his child. Careful not to go there, she asked about how he'd met the friends he'd gone into business with.

"Harvard. I seriously studied. They goofed off. But when the time came, and the opportunity was right, Wyatt borrowed a hundred million dollars from his parents to buy the two grocery store chains that started us off."

She gaped at him. "He borrowed a hundred million dollars?"

"For two grocery store *chains*. Each chain had over thirty stores. That kind of business doesn't come cheap." He gave her the side-eye. "Plus, he borrowed it from his parents. Which turned out to be great incentive. He absolutely could not fail."

"I suppose not. A hundred million dollars is a lot of money."

"It wasn't about the money. This was about his dad's wealthy family calling him a slacker."

"Interesting."

"He had something to prove."

"So, he put together a good team to make sure he succeeded."

"Exactly."

She smiled at him. She loved how he loved his friends. Respected them. "Have they set a time to visit?"

"No." He paused. "I haven't gotten furniture yet."

She laughed with glee. "Have they ever heard of a hotel? They don't have to stay with you to visit you."

He frowned. "I guess not."

"Let's arrange it."

"Okay."

Content, Trace glanced over at her and his empty heart filled. He loved when someone saw something he didn't. But he also liked that she really had paid. That she didn't make him feel bad that their affair had ended. It felt like balance. Like the whole world didn't rest on his shoulders.

The urge to reach over and take her hand whispered through him. He ignored it. But the light from the dash illuminated her face, her red dress, her shapely legs, and his breath shivered into his lungs. He'd touched every inch of her, but now, suddenly, he wasn't allowed.

That part seemed off. Like a piece of a puzzle that fits in the available space but doesn't match the colors around it.

She talked nonstop for the rest of the ride home. Mostly drawing out information about Cade and Wyatt, then deciding on the best places to take them when they visited.

She made them sound like a team and Trace licked his suddenly dry lips. Aside from a business partnership, he'd never been a part of a team. He and Skylar certainly weren't a team. He'd always felt a bit of distance with his parents and his sisters. But Marcia's lovely, lilting voice flowed through him like cool water to quench the thirst of a man who lived in a desert. He didn't feel alone. Or lonely. A quiet contentment filled his soul.

He almost hated it when the Giordano Vineyards sign came into view. He slowed his speed as they drove down the long lane, delaying the inevitable end of their trip. But they were in the parking lot soon enough. The car stopped. Their evening was over.

They got out, her face beaming with happiness, and he wondered if his face looked that joyful, that content.

To keep his hand from reaching for hers, he busied himself loosening his tie as they walked to the front door. He took off his jacket and rolled his shirtsleeves as they ambled down the hall to her bedroom.

When they reached it, he stopped with her. "Thank you. I know you wanted to help me keep my mind off the past, and it worked."

"You are not the only Mr. Fix-It."

"Actually, I think you'd be Ms. Fix-It."

She laughed. His quiet soul warmed again. Because they'd been intimate, his body was having difficulty understanding why he couldn't kiss her. Why he couldn't touch her, lie down with her, sleep with her—

Because he had troubles. Something about his past had a hold on him and wouldn't let go. If he couldn't escape it in such a beautiful place as Tuscany, he was beginning to worry it would always haunt him. He was lost, confused and wounded enough that he'd never be able to give her what she needed. A solid marriage. Kids.

Joshua popped into his mind…then his failures.

She placed her palm on his cheek. "Stop thinking. Don't drag yourself back to the past."

He swallowed hard. "Easy for you to say."

"No. Easy for you to say too."

His eyes searched hers. "I could say anything I wanted, but that wouldn't make it real. What's real is what sits inside my chest every time I think of my son…my failures."

"Maybe tonight, don't think of them."

He swallowed hard. He'd give anything for his thoughts to stop cascading back to his past.

"I think you walked away from us because your past makes you believe you will hurt me." Her head tilted. "But what if I hurt you?"

He laughed.

She shook her head. "So much pride."

"It's not pride."

"Silly man. You are not perfect. I am not perfect. Life is not perfect. One of these days I could walk away from you. You don't know that I won't. Neither one of us can tell the future, yet you live it in your head, thinking through every possible bad thing and running from them. Never once considering that the events you expect might never happen."

He sucked in a breath.

She smiled. "Just kiss me. Let go. Let the future take care of itself."

He wanted nothing more than to kiss her and he knew what she was saying. He did always expect the worst. Except in his businesses—

What if that was the problem? He didn't fear his business life. That always worked out. His personal life scared him witless. Without all his mind-numbing work, he'd had a chance to have a personal life, but his brain couldn't handle it. It kept going back to his past, reminding him of his failures...

The answer seemed so obvious that he almost laughed.

Confusion disappeared and was replaced by hope, which seemed so simple...too simple. Yet people walked out on limbs every day.

Why couldn't he?

Why *shouldn't* he?

"Okay." She rose to her tiptoes. "Then I will kiss you."

The kiss was soft, soothing. He let her lead him until his breathing slowed and he couldn't think of anything but how much he liked her. He broke the kiss, pulled back, gazed into those soft eyes again.

She smiled at him. "Maybe the answer is to take things one step at a time. What if we pretended we just had tonight? What if everything didn't have to be serious?"

"Then I'd do this." He ran his fingers under the rim of her dress, where it stopped at the top of her arm. "And probably this," he said, gliding his hands to her hair. He luxuriated in the soft curls. Their gazes locked. The air crackled with possibility. But honesty sneaked up again and wouldn't let him play her game.

"I don't want to hurt you."

"I know." She shrugged daintily. "I've been hurt, remember? And I survived." She waited a beat. "Because you helped me to see that I needed to stand tall. Be strong. Now I am strong."

"You are."

"So, trust me. Trust us."

He lowered his head and kissed her like a starving man. Need poured through him, along with a sense he couldn't ever remember feeling. No pressure. No expectations. Just this minute.

He heard the sound of her bedroom door opening and pulled back. "Did you kick your door open?"

She laughed. "Yes, and backward."

"You are full of surprises." And hope and impossible joy mixed with common sense. When he didn't look forward, he couldn't look back. His mistakes didn't remind him of how easy it was to lose everything. He didn't see hurt or pain or the guilt that reflection always brought. He simply saw her.

She took his hand and led him into her room, then slapped his hands away when he reached to unbutton his shirt. Her nimble fingers worked the buttons, grazing his skin just enough to raise goose bumps and make him eager to be flesh against flesh with her. As she pulled his shirt from his trousers, he reached around and undid the zipper of her dress. One pass of his hands across her shoulders and the simple garment fell away, pooling at her feet.

He eased his hands under her hair and lifted it as he bent to kiss her. Silence and peace surrounded them.

And something more.

It wasn't the quiet contentment he'd felt before. He wouldn't call it serenity. It was more like normalcy…a sense of ordinary perfection that surrounded them like the glow of moonlight. As if he was exactly where he was supposed to be.

That fueled the fire of his need, but he refused to rush. With all the confusion in his life, his need to see and feel secure in his future, he never knew what it was like to feel normal. So, he went slowly, touched every inch of her soft skin, tortured her with teasing kisses and touches meant to send prickles of arousal through her.

He made love to her. Not in the childish, frenetic way he had with Skylar. Not in the sophisticated, practiced way he did with the women he dated. But as himself.

It almost did him in. As they soared to the heights and came back down again, he didn't know whether to laugh or weep. They nestled comfortably on the fat down pillows of her antique bed, and though sleep wanted to take him, for the first time in decades he fought it. He didn't want to miss a minute of "normal" with her. He lay quiet and content, waiting for his body to recharge in order to do it all again.

"So…" She hesitated. "Why don't you tell me about your wife?"

He laughed. With her nestled against him and his eyes closed, he suddenly understood the meaning of pillow talk. "Seriously? You want to discuss my ex after *that*?"

"If by 'that' you mean sex, then talking about your ex is tacky. If by 'that' you mean making love, then discussing your past is perfectly reasonable." She angled herself on her elbow. "Trace, you've done wonderful things for me. You gave me back my strength, my courage, my sense of self. And I've helped you too. But there's still something. Something deep that holds you back. Something that made me have to talk you into my room tonight... I want to hear."

He took a breath. With her on her elbow beside him, he didn't feel the weird sense that there was something he was supposed to be feeling or figuring out. His past was the past.

He turned until he could lay flat on his pillow, with one arm across his forehead. "The story doesn't paint me in a very good light."

Marcia lay down and snuggled against him again, realizing he might need some space to tell this part of his story. Not eye contact. "I don't care. I want to know."

He didn't say anything for a few seconds. Then he sighed. "Okay. You know how my friends call me Mr. Fix-It?"

She laughed. "After the way you handled my dad, I'd say the title's accurate."

"I think I've always had a little bit of that skill, and before I found the right way to channel it, I used it for different things."

That puzzled her enough she levered herself to her elbow again so she could look down on him. "Different things?"

"To sweet-talk teachers into giving me extra time for projects or letting me do projects for extra credits, so I could obliterate the competition for valedictorian."

She laughed. "I can see you being a charmer."

"I was more than a charmer." He grimaced. "I don't want to say I manipulated people. But my talent seemed to go through phases before it found its true use."

She was glad he called his skill a talent and didn't think himself a bad kid because he'd gone after what he wanted. Still, putting everything together in her head, a not-quite-so-kind picture formed of how he saw himself. "You think you manipulated your ex-wife?"

"I wanted her. She was beautiful and smart and so damned fun to be around that I couldn't get enough of her." He drew in a long breath. "My family was good. But my dad had worries. I won't say he was a grouch, but he was a serious guy. My mom bustled about, trying to make everything perfect for him. My two sisters always had their noses in a book." He shrugged. "Skylar was free. She didn't worry. She had a place already secured in an Ivy League college. She didn't have to be concerned about grades or even SAT scores."

Marcia could picture it. A home where everyone was strung tight like a violin string and the introduction of a pretty girl who was the antithesis.

His voice softened. "She made me laugh. It was impossible not to love her. And I knew she was what I needed in my world."

"I think that's normal, Trace."

"Yes and no. I made elaborate plans to be around her. Being in the hall outside the door of her classes when she came out so I could walk her to her next class." He snorted. "I actually joined glee club."

She could picture that too and it made her laugh.

"But as direct as all that sounds, I like to think I wasn't obvious or obnoxious. We were friends before we became a couple and a couple for months before we became lovers."

She braced herself up again so she could study his face as he stared at the ceiling. "All still sounds normal."

"I guess the bad part starts when she got pregnant. Her parents were furious. Mine thought I'd ruined my bright future." He looked up at her. "I had scholarship offers. They thought I'd blown that."

"Had you?"

He winced. "After I talked Skylar into marrying me,

yeah. I had. Because her parents disowned her. I hadn't wanted them to support us, so I was sort of glad. It gave me a way to prove myself. And I did. With two part-time jobs, I made enough for us. But having two jobs and the responsibilities of a marriage and a baby, I didn't have time for school. We figured I'd go later, when things calmed down. But I lost the scholarships."

"Trace, all that is to be expected. I don't really see any manipulation."

"The manipulating happened when I talked her into marrying me. Her parents disowning her and me losing scholarships showed how badly I failed at trying to come up with a plan."

"You were eighteen."

"I talked her into doing things she didn't want to do."

"What things?"

He met her gaze. "She didn't want to get married. I talked her into it. Made promises." He waited a beat. His face shifted as he thought through what he would say next. "When Joshua died, all my promises meant nothing. She didn't have the same feelings for me that I had for her, so she bailed."

"That's on her."

"No! Don't you see? She never loved me. She loved the idea of doing the opposite of what her parents wanted her to do. I took advantage of that. I gave her the path to rebel. And in the end, I got hurt."

"She's starting to sound like the bad guy here."

"Really? What if I hadn't provided the path for her to rebel? What if she'd had Joshua while living with her parents? What if they'd hired a nanny so she could stay in school? What if someone had been there for Joshua the night—" He paused and swallowed, seemingly unable to get out the words *the night Joshua died*. Instead, he said, "*That* night?"

"Oh, Trace…" Her voice caught as the truth of what he was saying made her brain stumble. "You're blaming yourself for your son's death?"

He combed his fingers through his hair. "Sort of. I don't know. Possibilities always race through my head."

"Which is why you don't sleep."

He didn't say anything, just stared at the ceiling.

"You thought I was hard on myself?" She shook her head. "You are a hundred times worse to yourself."

She bent down and kissed him. Not for sex. Her heart burst with pain for him and the most basic kind of love: the connection of understanding combined with the longing to make him feel better.

The weirdest sensation trembled through Trace. He'd felt empty, cold, telling her his story, but as she kissed him, the cold dissolved in the face of her warmth. The emptiness edged away. Honesty opened a door. For the first time in his life he wasn't alone. She didn't have to say it. He didn't have to ask. They were partners.

He'd joked about it before, about them being partners in crime, but now he felt it.

He rolled her to her back and deepened the kiss. His past didn't melt away, didn't become irrelevant. He would carry the loss of his son forever, but he'd also carry the lessons learned from his mistakes, which made him a better man.

A man who might be able to commit again.

The thought tiptoed through his brain, and he savored it. Reveled in it. The emotion of making love became wild abandon and they rode the wave until they collapsed, exhausted, onto the softness of her bed.

What he felt for her went beyond what he'd ever felt with another person, and he had to wonder if this wasn't real love. Not just attraction. Not friendship. But a bonding of hearts and souls and purpose.

Purpose.

To run a vineyard together?

To marry and…

Have a family?

He might be coming to terms with his past, but the idea of having another child froze his limbs, stopped his heart.

He might forgive himself for losing Joshua. He might even see the potential for a future with Marcia. But he couldn't have another child, let alone enough children to fill the bedrooms of Giordano Vineyards' villa.

And Marcia would want children, a family. She loved family.

This was the thing that always stopped him in his tracks and caused his hesitation. *This* was what had made him really listen to her father's warnings about getting involved with her.

He couldn't give her what she wanted…what she needed. A family. He'd had his. And he'd blown it in the worst possible way. He absolutely would not have another child. He could go only so far with her before he began stealing away her dreams.

Stealing her dreams, the way he had stolen Skylar's.

That's why he shouldn't have let Marcia seduce him that night. Why he would stay away from her from now on. Loving Marcia when he couldn't give her what she wanted was as selfish, as wrong as talking Skylar into marrying him had been.

CHAPTER THIRTEEN

MARCIA SLID OUT of bed the next morning, letting Trace sleep. She showered, dressed and went to the kitchen, where she made a pot of coffee. Using her phone, she read her to-do list for the day.

When the kitchen doorknob rattled, her head jerked up and she saw her dad, trying to get in.

She walked over and opened the locked door. "Good morning, Papa."

He kissed her cheek. "Good morning. So where is Trace?"

She shrugged but grinned mischievously. "It's not my day to watch him."

He poured himself a cup of coffee. "Wherever he is, the three of us need to get together sometime today to talk about what you and Trace will need to have in place before the boys and I leave next week."

Her eyebrows rose. "Next week?"

"Yes." Mug of coffee in hand, he leaned against the kitchen counter. "I talked to Roberto and Matteo and they have a few friends who can fill in for them while you hire others."

A bit taken aback but liking the idea of finally moving on to what she and Trace needed to do for Giordano Vineyards, she said, "That's good."

Fully dressed, Trace walked into the kitchen, "What's good?"

"Matteo and Roberto have friends who can fill in in the wine room."

Trace paused on his way to the coffeepot. "Oh, yeah?"

"Si." Antonio took a sip of coffee. "We need to be at White Gates next week."

He held Antonio's gaze. "Do you trust these friends?"

"Roberto and Matteo do. Plus, they are temps. People who can work for you while you find permanent replacements for Roberto and Matteo."

"And it's tourist season," Marcia put in, loving the way she and her dad had gone back to normal, all because of Trace's keen powers of observation. "But grape harvest is coming up. We have to be fully staffed by then."

Trace finished the walk to the coffee maker. "Sounds good."

Antonio nodded. "Sounds good."

Marcia smiled. The plan might be solid, but they also sounded like a team. Like coworkers who wanted what was best for everyone. Her heart expanded again. Everything was right in her world.

Her dad put his coffee cup in the sink and headed for the door. "It's almost time for the first bus."

Trace laughed. "I'll be out in a minute."

When her dad was gone, he poured himself a cup of coffee but stayed staring at the wall.

She walked up behind him and slid her arms around his waist, pressing her cheek to his back.

"I liked how much we sounded like a team."

He didn't turn around. "We always do."

He said it casually, but without emotion. After everything they'd shared the night before, she thought he'd be more open this morning. Still, what he'd told her after they'd made love hadn't been easy. It might take years for him to really be able to give himself to her, but she was patient. He deserved for her to be patient with him.

Later that afternoon, Trace sat behind his desk, putting the finishing touches on the plans for Giordano Vineyards. He'd made the necessary adjustments and now everything was set.

He could leave. Marcia could now run the vineyard

alone. Yes, she'd have to hire staff, but Trace didn't need to be here to help her. She'd run this business with her dad for years. And with his one-year and five-year plans written for her to follow, he could be on the next plane back to Manhattan.

The thought froze him because he had nothing to go back to. But after the connection he and Marcia had made the night before, he knew they had fallen in love. He also knew that he could not have another child. Could not be a dad again. Which meant he could not give her a normal marriage. He couldn't give her children to fill Giordano Villa, the chaotic noise of her own family. Being around a child, even his own child, would be too painful. There'd be too many reminders of his lost son. He'd wear the guilt like a cloak, and that would cheat any kids he had with Marcia.

It was a vicious cycle.

Which was why leaving was the right thing to do.

He was just about to ask Marcia to come into his office, but he decided to make a call first. He casually rose and closed his office door, then called Wyatt and Cade from his laptop.

Wyatt said, "What's up?"

Trace laughed. "What do you mean what's up? Can't I just call to chat?"

Cade laughed. "No. You don't do things like that. Did you call to invite us to visit?"

Trace winced. "No, I still don't have furniture. Plus, I'm about to make arrangements to fly back to Manhattan this afternoon."

Wyatt sat up. "What?"

"There's not as much work here at the vineyard as I'd anticipated. Plus, Marcia's an experienced general manager." He shrugged. "It's been like a long vacation, but I'm ready to come home." He took a breath. "Actually, I'm ready to come back to work."

Cade quietly said, "You are?"

"Yeah." Trace said it eagerly, brightly, like buying a new business would be an adventure.

Wyatt cleared his throat. "Actually, we've already started something."

Trace frowned. "Without me?"

"Don't get your panties in a twist," Wyatt said. "We intended to call you once we had all the ducks in a row."

Cade sat taller. "I found a little manufacturing company that's undervalued."

"And once he found that," Wyatt said, "we focused our search and we found two other, similar businesses that we could buy and group together with the first one."

"They're all small," Cade continued, picking up where Wyatt left off. "We'll get only the one cheap."

"Yeah, we'll be paying full price for the other two," Wyatt agreed. "But it doesn't matter. The minute we group them, the value rises. We go in, clean up production, figure out a strategy that uses all three companies, and edge our way up the ladder in the market."

Trace's senses perked up. "These are manufacturing plants?"

Cade said, "Yes."

"What do they make?"

"A few things. We'll be bidding on government contracts."

He thought of Marcia, thought of leaving her, then reminded himself that she was better off without him. She'd find a man who wanted kids, fill the villa and have the kind of life she wanted.

"We haven't put in any bids or made any moves to buy them. If you think we're idiots, we can back off," Wyatt said with a laugh.

"But it does feel right," Cade said, his voice filled with temptation.

Trace's thoughts about Marcia faded away as his brain fully focused on the new businesses. Exactly what he wanted…what he *needed*. Not even twenty minutes to regret his decision to leave Giordano Vineyards, no time to change his mind and lots and lots of work to fill his brain. "How much money are we talking?"

"That's just it. If the three of us go together to buy these three companies, we don't even dent what we got for the sale of Three Guys Holding Company."

"It's like your vineyard," Wyatt said. "You paid only a drop of what we made from Three Guys and now that turkey will become a cash machine for you."

He didn't like the idea of thinking of Giordano Vineyards as being a cash cow. It was a home first and foremost… exactly why he had to leave. It couldn't be a home again until he gave Marcia the freedom to make it a home.

"I say we do it."

Cade laughed. "Really? We thought you'd tell us to take a hike."

"No. We're businessmen, not people of leisure. It's time to get back to work."

And now he was committed. No way to change his mind about leaving. After disconnecting the call, he searched for a flight out but couldn't get a seat until the next day. But that was okay—he could pack and be gone by noon.

Trace stayed in the wine room the rest of the afternoon and evening. When he entered the house, he turned and went to the master suite.

Marcia knew he wanted to shower, but he didn't come downstairs again. When waiting seemed foolish, she walked to her room. For a second, she debated going to *his* room, but something stopped her. He was absolutely a man of moods. Giving him space had worked so far. Like always she'd let him think this through.

The next morning, she found him at the desk in the office behind hers.

"Good morning."

He glanced up with a smile. "Good morning. Could you come in here, please?"

"Sure." Taking her coffee cup with her, she ambled into his office and sat on one of the chairs in front of his desk. "What's up?"

"I called my friends yesterday."

She gasped happily. "To invite them to visit?"

He folded his hands on his desk in front of him. "No. Basically, I was going to talk to them about looking for another investment. Turns out they'd already been looking. They've found a few businesses they want to buy to create a new company."

His answer was so unexpected, she blinked. "What?"

He chuckled. "I know! A ton of work. Reorganization. New corporation papers." He shook his head. "I see months of seven-day weeks ahead of us."

It took a second before she fully understood what he was saying. "You are leaving?"

"Yes. I have a flight out this afternoon."

Her heart stopped. "This afternoon?"

"Marcia, you are perfectly capable of running Giordano Vineyards. Your brothers can help you find the new employees we need. Your dad is good on his own—"

"Oh, so your work here is done?"

Clearly not happy with her interruption, he said, "Yes and no. I'll be back."

"When?"

"I'd say six months."

She gaped at him. "Six months!"

"Just for a review. Not to take over. You're going to be fine. You ran this vineyard for your dad. You know—"

"Stop! Just stop acting like this is a work issue for me.

I can run this place in my sleep…and without you. You're avoiding or ignoring the fact that there was something between us."

He pulled in a breath. "Maybe avoiding. But not ignoring. Yesterday, I came face-to-face with the fact that we needed to decide if you and I were headed somewhere or not."

"I thought we'd realized that thinking too much didn't work."

"The choice of spending a night together is very different than the making a choice that affects your whole life."

"And, obviously, you made the decision."

"I can't give you what you want."

"Oh, and what do I want?"

"Kids. A happy marriage." He shook his head. "I can't give you that."

"I didn't ask you to."

"No. But without even thinking too hard, I realized that if we kept going the way we were, no promises, no worries, years could go by. Years you would waste with a man who will never change his mind."

"You don't know that."

"Actually, I do."

Pain sliced through her chest like a knife. The impossibility of his actions rattled through her until she wondered why she was surprised. He'd never been able to take those final steps, to say he loved her…

Hell, for all she knew, he'd talked himself out of loving her.

There had always been something between them. Not quite a wall. Not as common as a barrier. A missing link.

"Do you really want to be with someone who is this much work? Always having to worry about my feelings, my past?"

Her eyes filled with tears, but she stopped them. "I never thought of you as work."

He rose from his seat. "Loving me has to be work, Marcia. I'm moody and demanding."

"You're also sweet and kind."

He shook his head. "More moody and demanding." He caught her gaze. "You deserve better."

She pushed herself out of her chair, forced herself to think like the smart woman she was. "I do deserve better." Though right at this moment that wasn't the issue. She'd pushed him the night before, tried to show him the way back to a good life. And he'd followed her, but this morning he'd had second thoughts.

She suddenly saw what he was saying. She wanted to be loved for real. Forever. He was telling her he couldn't do that. If she accepted that, she accepted less than what she wanted.

He walked around the desk. "I can see in your eyes that you agree." Stopping in front of her, he lifted her face with one finger under her chin and said, "You make me forget. You make me happy. But part of me knows I don't deserve to be happy and that's the part that will always hold back. You deserve so much better."

She pulled away. The thudding of her heart in her chest slowed to a crawl. Her limbs felt like lead. She'd known all this, figured it out bit by bit, but had thought her love would be enough to keep him, to bring him back to life.

She might not be a chump this time, but once again she'd totally misread a situation.

He bent to retrieve a briefcase from beneath his desk, then stopped beside her again. "Fill the house with kids. Make the vineyard a home again. Enjoy this life."

Her lips trembled. "It's your life."

"I had thought it might be. Until I met you and realized it belonged to you."

"With you?"

He shook his head. "No. If I stay, I'll only hurt you."

He bent and placed a gentle kiss on her mouth. Then he turned and left.

Her tears spilled over. Part of her begged her to run after him, to convince him to stay. The bruised and battered part simply couldn't do it. Adam had stolen from her family and made her a laughingstock. Trace had given her back her dignity. If she raced out, she'd lose it again.

As the reality of him leaving sank in, pain assaulted her and she realized her pride didn't matter. Then she heard the sound of her dad's old truck chugging into the parking lot and from the window watched Trace toss his things inside. And just that quickly he was gone.

Pain ripped through her. The tears that had been silently falling became gut-wrenching sobs. She raced out of the wine building through the back door and into the kitchen and found a note on the center island.

"I know how you felt about the Maserati. It's yours. Love, Trace."

She crumpled the note into a ball and would have tossed it into the trash, but she remembered the word *love* and swallowed hard. He had loved her after all.

But she hadn't been able to love him enough to heal the wounds that might forever haunt him.

She could not heal him. He could only heal himself.

CHAPTER FOURTEEN

TRACE DEPLANED AND had a car waiting to take him straight to Manhattan to the new offices Cade and Wyatt had rented. There'd be no furniture, but he was growing accustomed to empty or nearly empty rooms. Plus, he had a laptop. He could work anywhere.

And he needed to work. The flight from Italy to the United States had been long and lonely. With so much time on his hands to think, he'd about driven himself crazy.

Marcia's sadness had burned through him. Especially the pain that vibrated through her voice. Pain he had inflicted. The only comfort he had was knowing he would have ruined her life if he'd stayed. What wife wanted a husband who could never be happy? What woman wanted a man whose needs would always come before hers?

There wasn't a question in his mind that he'd done the right thing.

Using a private code, he rode the elevator of the new building to the fiftieth floor and got off to the sounds of silence.

He leaned out and tried to see down the long hall. "Hello!"

No one answered.

Knowing Wyatt and Cade were supposed to be there, he called again. "Hello?"

"Back here."

That answer had come from Wyatt, but Cade appeared from behind the half wall in the empty reception area.

His voice a rushed whisper, he said, "Dude, I'm glad I caught you."

Trace laughed. "Really? Whispers? Are we keeping secrets from each other now?"

Cade made a frantic motion for Trace to lower his voice. "In the last forty-eight hours, we've talked to you, rented this space, put offers in on three companies and discovered Wyatt has a daughter."

Trace's eyes bulged. "What?"

Cade made the lower-your-voice motion again. "You need to be happy for him."

Confused, Trace whispered, "I do?"

"He was gobsmacked. Long story short, last year's girlfriend never told him she was pregnant."

"Okay—"

"What are you two doing out here?" Wyatt walked up the hall carrying a baby girl. He looked from Cade to Trace. "Gossiping?"

Cade shook his head. "No. No. We were just saying hello."

"So, you weren't telling him how my ex sprang a baby on me and bolted?"

Trace's eyes wanted to bulge again, but somehow, they hooked on the tiny girl dressed in pink. Scruffy hair told Trace Wyatt had probably been the one taking care of her overnight.

Jealousy roared through him. Until his loss, he'd always wanted a family. Wanted the responsibilities and the joys—

As quickly as he thought that, Joshua sprang to his mind. He'd had his chance and failed.

Pushing all that out of his mind, he walked over. "She's cute."

Wyatt said, "Looks like her mom."

"Where is her mom?"

Wyatt blew out his breath. "I don't know. Uganda. United Kingdom. United Arab Emirates. All I got was a heavy *U* sound, as she was shoving the kid into my arms and draping me with diaper bags."

Trace could picture it, and if suddenly becoming guardian for a child hadn't been so serious, he would have had to swallow back a laugh.

"DNA tests have already been arranged. But I have this feeling—a weird sense—that she's mine." Wyatt shoved the little girl into Trace's arms. "Here, hold her. While I get the papers you have to sign."

Having no choice but to take the baby, Trace settled her across his arm, the football hold he'd been taught when Joshua was first born. The baby smiled at him and his heart tumbled.

Good God. She was beautiful. So small and soft.

She gurgled a greeting and he laughed. "Hey, little one."

Wyatt stopped in his trip down the hall and turned to face him again. "Her name is Darcy."

"Darcy." He glanced down at the baby. Yearning wove through him. Memories of being a dad popped into his brain. The joy. The fulfillment. A love that surpassed anything he'd known. "Hey, Darcy."

As he spoke, her scent wafted up to him. The special combination of baby soaps and powders. Joshua had smelled like that. He'd loved his bath. And Trace didn't have to think at all to recall his blue eyes. His round face with chubby cheeks and tiny lips.

This time when his heart tumbled, it was painfully. He'd had a child, had a family, and he'd lost them.

He'd lost them.

Wyatt reappeared, stacks of papers in his hand. "I'll take her."

He glanced at Wyatt. His limbs had frozen. The baby powder scent filled the air now. If he closed his eyes, he could see his apartment with Skylar. Hear Joshua's laugh.

When he didn't move, Wyatt took his baby from his

arms and handed him three packets of papers before he led him and Cade to three big offices at the end of the hall.

"I see why you chose this building, this space," he said, trying to be light and friendly, but the cruel memories of his son, his other life, haunted him.

"Everything's equal," Cade said, picking up the conversation as Wyatt guided them into the office with no desk, three folding chairs and a play yard filled with baby toys that sat beside a swing.

Wyatt slid the little girl into the padded seat of the swing.

Trace saw Joshua in a swing very similar to that one, laughing, as he talked to him while he made dinner and Skylar sat on the sofa reading a magazine. For the first time, the memories made him angry. And not at himself. Not even at Skylar. At the injustice of it.

He blinked away the images, forced himself into the conversations about the formal offers Wyatt had written for two of the companies and forgot about his son, his ex-wife, the life he'd tried to create.

But it lingered, haunted him, every time he looked at Darcy.

A week later, he stood by the wall of windows behind his brand-new desk, working to erase even one of the memories. His view of Manhattan stole his breath. He loved that it appeared as if he could reach out and touch the buildings around him, even though some of them were blocks away. But every time he saw Darcy, he saw Joshua. He remembered Skylar's snippiness, actually heard the discontent in her voice and wondered why the hell he hadn't seen it while it was happening.

"What are you doing?"

Trace spun away from the window to see Wyatt in his doorway. "I was looking at the..." He glanced at his desk. "Forecast for Green Peas and Ham." He sighed. "I still think that's a stupid name for a company."

"Then you should be coherent and vote when we have our meetings. Besides, we're going with the initials GP&H. No one needs to know what it stands for." He plopped on the seat in front of Trace's desk. "And by the way, I didn't buy that you'd been reading the forecast. You were staring out the window."

Trace shook his head, returned to his seat. Hands folded on his desk, he said, "Happy now?"

"No! I like you sharp with eagle eyes that find problems. I don't like this guy who came back from Italy with a broken heart. You said you were the one to end it with Marcia, so why are you moping around like a sad puppy?"

He tossed his glasses to his desk, then ran his hands down his face. "I'm not a sad puppy."

"Oh, please."

Darcy let out a shout and Wyatt sprang from his seat. "Be right back."

Seconds later, he returned with his daughter. Today she wore pajamas the color of a pumpkin. Something Wyatt had found online because he didn't like the clothes her mother had given him for her.

"I thought you hired a nanny."

"I did too. But something about her wasn't quite right." Trace sighed.

"What? You don't like having the baby around?"

Part of him did. Part of him loved watching her, hearing her tiny voice. But every time he saw her, he thought of Marcia, then Joshua, and it was killing him. "She's no trouble... Now."

"Oh, I get it. She's no trouble now, but she will be when we hire employees."

"You know if you pawn her off on an assistant, someone hired to do accounting or write strategic plans, that woman's going to have grounds for a lawsuit."

"What if I ask a guy to watch her?"

Trace frowned. "I don't know."

"See? That's it right there. That's the problem. The old Trace would have known."

"Are you telling me I've gone soft?"

"I'm telling you something's wrong."

While orange-pajamaed Darcy crawled up her dad's chest, Trace tapped a pencil on his desk. His children with Marcia would have had black hair and his blue eyes. "I'm fine."

"You better be. We have a lot on the line here."

Right on cue, thoughts of Joshua drowned out his thoughts of Marcia, of their babies. Reminding him that life wasn't simple. Wasn't something he could conjure because he wanted it.

The next week, he tried to be sharper. He made spreadsheets. He created complicated to-do lists and made lists that reminded him of things. He swore to himself that nothing would get by him. He'd been present and helpful when they hired a receptionist and three assistants to handle the easy prep work. But twice Cade had to snap his fingers in front of Trace's nose when they were having a planning meeting.

Carrying Darcy, who wore blue jeans and a T-shirt that morning, Wyatt said, "Maybe you need to read up on government contracts some more."

"Okay. Yeah. I'll do that." He turned to go out of the room, embarrassed that he was slipping so much, but Darcy caught his eye. She gurgled and laughed.

His heart rolled into a ball, then expanded again.

Wyatt's shrewd eyes narrowed. "You know, if it bugs you or distracts you that Darcy is here, maybe you should work from your penthouse."

His breath stuttered. "I'm not that bad." But every time he looked at Darcy, he saw the potential kids he could have with Marcia, the family. Then he'd think of Joshua and the vision would fade, kicked to the curb by the reminder that he hadn't been a good dad.

"You *are* that bad. It's been weeks since your return from Italy, and you're the saddest person I've ever seen."

Exhausted, about at the end of his rope, he took a seat on the chair in front of Wyatt's desk. He, Cade and Wyatt had never had a secret, and his current feelings suddenly felt like one. Especially since it was clearly affecting his work.

He took a breath. "Okay. I'll come clean. Every time I see Darcy, I think of Marcia."

Wyatt's eyes sharpened. "You see yourself having kids with her?"

"I don't know. Maybe. But it doesn't matter. As soon as I get the warm, fuzzy, oh-my-God-I-want-that feeling, I remember Joshua and the feeling turns to horror."

"Or fear."

Trace frowned. "Whatever."

Wyatt sighed. "Don't you think it's natural that you'd be afraid to start another family?"

Trace shrugged. "Sure. I guess. I don't know."

"Hey. Don't shrug that off! When you had too much time on your hands, you thought about your family. So, to get rid of that, you bought a business thousands of miles away so you could forget again. But you didn't forget. You found a woman, fell in love, and all your old longings came back—and you remembered your son. So, you ran again."

"I'm not running from having another family."

"No. You're running to stop the memories of losing a child." Wyatt glanced down at Darcy. "Honestly, Trace, I can't imagine the pain." He looked up and caught Trace's gaze. "And for you, I'd probably toss in a sense of failure. But twelve years have passed. You're not a kid anymore. And you're back to wanting the dream."

Trace swallowed. "Dreams don't always turn out the way we want."

Wyatt laughed, bouncing Darcy when her lips puckered and she looked like she might cry. "Don't I know it." Wyatt shook his head. "This is life," he said, angling his chin down at his baby. "Surprises. Pains. Wins and losses. You can't run from it. You can't hide. And you sure as hell shouldn't be blaming yourself for something that wasn't your fault."

When Wyatt seemed so sure, Trace groaned. "How do you know it wasn't my fault?"

"Because I know you. You make lists. You go over plans a million times looking for flaws. You do more than your share of the work and then some. Trace, you didn't fail. Something went wrong with the worst possible results. But it wasn't your fault."

Trace said nothing. He felt frozen. Tired. Tired of running.

"Go to Italy. Tell that woman you love her."

Everything Wyatt had said fluttered through him. With his defenses down, new questions filled his brain.

What if he hadn't been at fault? He wasn't so foolish that he didn't realize that some things really were out of a person's control. Even if that person was a nitpicky, detail-oriented brainiac.

Still, he was tired of going over it in his head, looking for a mistake.

Maybe it really was time to let go?

To try again.

With Marcia.

Time to let himself be himself. He would never forget his son, but he couldn't stop living. Or he'd lose Marcia to another man, and unless he got rid of Giordano Vineyards, he'd watch her fall in love, marry and have kids with someone else. While he sat at a desk, buried in work because he was afraid to try.

* * *

Marcia kept herself busy hiring staff. Her dad talked non-stop about what a great guy Trace was, but her mother was wise enough to see Marcia wasn't interested and she constantly changed the subject.

At nights, she'd sit by the pool, missing Trace, going over almost every word they'd said, trying to find a way to bring him back to her, but nothing stuck out. He'd told her about losing his child. He'd given her details about his ex. He could have talked forever about Cade and Wyatt. But he couldn't tell her he loved her.

Except in a note. And then only as a sign-off. A throwaway word.

She supposed she understood. His commitment to his business partners was just that. Business. His sorrow over his son and the loss of his marriage… Those might be the past, but he'd loved the life he'd set up for himself, and she genuinely believed he wanted it back.

In a weird kind of way, she realized he didn't want a future. He wanted his past back.

It was nuts to want something he couldn't have… But maybe that was the point. He didn't want a future filled with twists and turns and surprises. He wanted his past fixed. Or maybe a future he could control.

Once or twice she slept on the chaise by the pool instead of her room, but after two weeks, she'd compartmentalized her feelings for him and worked to be her old self again. When her mother invited her to have lunch with her in the village, she hesitated, but knew it was time to move on.

With everything.

They entered the tavern, their eyes adjusting to the lack of light, and Mama told the hostess there would be just two of them.

When they were seated, Gina raced over with her order pad, a silly smile lighting her face.

"Hello, Gina," her mother said, her normal sweet self.

"Hello, Mrs. Giordano."

"How have you been?"

"I'm great." She held out her hand, showing off an engagement ring. "Look."

Marcia's mother gasped. "That's beautiful! Congratulations!"

Marcia looked at the ring too. Her heart tugged and she thought of Trace, but she shoved those memories out of her head. "It's lovely. Your fiancé has great taste."

"It's not as fancy as the ring you got from that guy… What was his name? Adam? But at least we know my guy will stick around."

Marcia smiled. Funny how the mention of Adam barely registered. He was so far in her past that her heart didn't even tweak. "That's true."

"Rumor has it you ran off Giordano Vineyards' new owner too." She leaned in and added, "There was gossip you were sleeping together, but I stopped it."

Marcia counted to ten. Did this woman never let up?

Her mother pressed her lips together.

"I told people there were plenty of reasons the two of you were living together. That it might not be about sex."

This time Marcia heard the baiting in Gina's voice, so she only smiled.

"Besides, it's not like every man in the world is smitten with you," Gina said on a laugh.

Finally done with this, the gossip, the speculation, the out-and-out stupidity of caring what this woman thought, Marcia shook her head. "You know what, Gina? You need to get out more. If the only thing you can think about is my love life, you have got to be really bored." She smiled thinly. "Go to a museum. Take a ride somewhere out of town. Broaden your horizons."

Gina gave her a puzzled look before she took their

drink orders. When she scampered away, Marcia's mother laughed.

"That was interesting."

Marcia rolled her eyes. "No. It wasn't. I've heard something from her every damned time I've come into this tavern since Adam left me. Today, I just got tired of it and turned it back on her."

Her mother patted her hand. "And you did it so nicely I'm not even sure she knows what hit her." She patted her hand again. "That's the Marcia I love."

"Really?"

"Yes. Now I think what you need to do is go to Manhattan and tell that Trace a few things."

This time Marcia laughed. "I pushed him as hard as I could push when he told me he was leaving. Deep down, Trace is a wonderful guy. He lost a marriage and a child when he was young. He will never get over them."

"But he loved you. I could see it in his eyes."

She shook her head. "Doesn't matter."

She said it simply, easily, but her mother frowned. "Of course it matters. Just like getting the last word with Gina mattered. Marcia, you cannot let everyone walk all over you just because you made one mistake. You need to go to Manhattan."

"And do what?"

"Tell him you're not letting him leave you. Tell him he needs to come back to Italy."

"He can't. He and his partners have new projects now. New businesses they are buying."

A shaft of light from the front door opening skimmed over their table, then retreated as the door closed.

"Plus, I'm not begging a man to stay."

"You wouldn't be begging. You'd be putting your foot down."

Marcia laughed, but stopped suddenly when she saw

Trace out of the corner of her eye. Within seconds he was at her table. The chatty, noisy bar silenced.

"Hey."

She looked up at him. "Hey." He looked great. A little thinner, but his face was different. Not tight. His eyes weren't shrewd or calculating. His face looked—

Relaxed?

"Can I sit?"

Mama quickly shifted to the seat next to hers so Trace could have the chair beside Marcia. "Sure."

"Did you come back for grape harvest?"

His eyes widened. "Oh, my gosh! Is that this week?"

"My dad is thinking Saturday."

"I…" He laughed. "You know what? Yeah. I want to be here for grape harvest."

Marcia worked up a smile. "Great."

"But first, there's something we need to talk about." His eyes shifted to her mother, then back to her.

Mama said, "I think I'll go to the ladies' room," and was gone within seconds.

Marcia noticed the whole bar seemed to be watching them and she groaned internally.

"What is it about the vineyard that concerns you?"

He took a breath. "It isn't the vineyard. It's about me… well, us. I made a big mistake…or maybe not really a mistake. I saw a future for us, and every time I did, I would think of my son and make the assumption that I couldn't have other kids because I'd always think of him when I saw them."

"I believe we talked about something like that the last night we slept together."

"Yeah. But it didn't hit home enough. I knew that every time I'd think about the future, thoughts of Joshua would drown it out. Making me feel I had no options but work.

But it took seeing Darcy—Wyatt's baby daughter—to make me think of Joshua—"

"I'm so sorry."

He sniffed. "Don't be. At first she brought back awful memories. Then she made me want a baby so much I couldn't even be around her. She smelled like him. She even looked a little like him and I just kept longing for another chance."

"She broke you."

"Her and a talk with Wyatt. It was like seeing her every day pushed me past that point of fear that always rose up when I'd think about having another child...with you."

She said nothing. Her heart filled with sadness for him, but she also saw what he was saying.

"Did you ever stop to think that maybe your longing for a child started after you sold your business? That time on your hands didn't have you thinking about your past. It had you thinking about your future..."

"Yes. I figured that out once I got back to Manhattan. In fact, I think that was the thing that was bugging me. The thing that didn't fit. I hadn't thought of my past in a decade. I thought it had popped up because I had too much time on my hands. But what actually happened was time on my hands had me thinking about a future. When I did, the past came back to haunt me. Making me think I couldn't have a future."

"So you're good?"

He smiled. "Very good. Good enough to be able to say that I want to spend the rest of my life with you. To have kids running around all over the vineyard. But most of all, to just watch it all and do it all *with you*." He pulled a jeweler's box from his jacket pocket, lifted the lid and exposed a diamond the likes of which Marcia had never seen before. Her gaze leaped to his.

"Will you marry me?"

Her breath stuttered. Her heart expanded with joy. "Oh, my God."

Silence stretched between them.

The bartender shouted, "Answer already!"

A general rumble of laughter rode through the tavern.

Tears filled her eyes. "It seems everyone is on your side."

His eyes filled with humor. "Oh, I'll bet half of them are hoping you say no. If only for the gossip."

She laughed but said, "That means the other half is hoping I'll say yes."

He took the ring from the box. "If you add me in, that tips the scales."

She held out her hand. "Wouldn't want to ruin your equation."

The ring hovered over her finger. "You need to say the words."

She blinked back tears and said, "Yes. I will marry you."

When he slid the ring on her finger, they both rose and she threw herself into his arms. "I never thought you'd come back."

He rained kisses on her face. "Wyatt's baby wasn't the only thing that made me sad. Every time I saw her, I thought of you…"

She pulled back. "So, you missed me?"

"Every damn second of every damned day."

She laughed through her tears. "I missed you too."

"Let's go home."

From behind her, Mama said, "Leave the Maserati and I'll be fine."

She laughed. Trace laughed. "Should we leave her the car? I have a rental."

"Yes. Let's leave her the car."

Trace tossed his set of keys to her. "No scratches or dings."

Mama caught them. "I'm not promising anything."

They left the bar amid shouts of congratulations, and when they stepped outside, the sunlight burned their eyes.

"This would have been so much more romantic at night… under the moon."

She stood on her tiptoes and kissed him. "I couldn't have waited that long."

He slid his hands around her waist. "I couldn't have either." He paused a beat. Then he looked into her eyes. "I am so sorry I left you."

She grinned. "I'm not. It might have been a few long weeks, but if that's what it took for you to work it all out, then it was worth it."

He kissed her long and deep, happiness singing through his soul. "Oh, it was definitely worth it."

EPILOGUE

THE FOLLOWING SPRING, on White Gates Vineyards, Trace stood at a makeshift altar, waiting for his bride. The place had been spruced up, and Antonio and his sons were making progress toward getting the winemaking up and running again. Deciding to be married on her parents' vineyard had been a way to honor them, and Trace had taken it.

With Wyatt and Cade at his side, he watched the arch decorated with white roses, waiting for Marcia and her dad. Her friend Janine, serving as bridesmaid, appeared first. Smiling, glad to be with Marcia after months of mourning her mom, she looked elegant in her pale blue gown.

Then Marcia and her dad stepped under the arch and his breath stuttered. After her myriad shopping trips when she accompanied him when he was needed in Manhattan, he'd expected her to wear something bold and outrageous. Instead she wore an old-fashioned lace dress and an airy tulle veil that billowed in the breeze.

The ceremony was quick, and his eyes had misted as they said their vows. He would never hurt her. She would never hurt him. Not because they were perfect but because each understood real love. Each knew *trust* was a verb.

They also wanted the same things, came to this relationship as mature adults, ready to face the future together.

They posed for pictures for over an hour, then ate an early dinner under white tents decorated with roses. Wine flowed freely. Everyone danced late into the night. His parents and sisters had become close with Marcia's parents and brothers, and though Trace suspected a little hanky-panky between the Jackson sisters and the Giordano brothers, he said nothing. From here on out, he let nature take its course. He didn't brood. He didn't overplan. He let himself be himself.

When they could finally leave, he carried Marcia to the Maserati. Because the top was down, he dumped her in the passenger's seat without opening the door, and she laughed.

"Is this how I can expect you'll be treating me now that we're married?"

He hopped into the car, caught her hand and kissed it. "Oh, I expect to treat you very well tonight."

Her laughter rang out as they roared down the lane of White Gates and headed for their home.

Their home.

A real home.

A combination of his parents' common sense and the Giordano love of life, it would be a very happy home indeed.

* * * * *

AN OFFICER AND
A FORTUNE

NINA CRESPO

Chapter One

Nicole Fortune strolled through the food section of the outdoor flea market or, as the locals called it, Mariana's Market, located in a rural area just outside the town of Rambling Rose.

The items her fellow shoppers chose from tables shaded by green canopies illuminated who they were as clearly as the sun lit up the Texas morning sky.

Adventure seekers lived for the challenge of trying something new. Easygoing types tended to love all things sweet. But those tiny tells were just the basics.

The young brunette soothing the baby securely tucked in a gray striped wrap while carefully examining the organic peaches—most likely, she was making baby food. The silver-haired older couple smiling at each other as they sampled raspberries handed to them by the vendor—they would probably enjoy them over breakfast along with the eggs they'd purchased. And the redhead wearing blue workout clothes—she had the willpower of a saint to ignore the alluring scents of cinnamon bread and apple pastries flavoring the breeze. Veggies were undoubtedly high on her list.

A couple of yards away, the redhead picked out a head of romaine from one of the stalls. After paying for the lettuce and slipping it into a cloth bag, she went across the graveled aisle and bought cucumbers and a pint of grape tomatoes.

I knew it. As Nicole purchased a loaf of cinnamon bread, a light wind blew her blond hair back over the shoulders of her white fitted tee. She tucked a stray strand behind her ear, unable to hold back a small smile at being right about her prediction.

If someone had asked her about her own story of food, it was a simple one. As the executive chef of Roja, she lived to create dishes with flavors that raised anticipation for the next bite.

Her phone buzzed with an alarm in the side pocket of her black cargo pants. A reminder that as much as she loved her Saturday visits to Mariana's, she had to get back to her restaurant.

Switching her netted market bag filled with lemons to her other hand, she took out her phone and turned off the alarm. She still needed rosemary for the chicken recipe she wanted to test out as a special for the upcoming summer menu. The first day of the warmest season of the year was only seven weeks away, and she was way behind in selecting entrées. Last time she'd visited the marketplace, she'd found a nice selection of herbs midway down the aisle.

"Excuse me." A man walked past her from behind, gravel crunching under his beige Lugz boots.

As she scooted over, his arm bumped Nicole's, raising tingles on hers. The appealing woodsy scent trailing after him woke up her senses like the first whiff of coffee rising in the steam from her favorite mug.

Perfect-fitting jeans encased his long legs. A deep tan pullover shirt stretched along his back. His unhurried pace emanated purpose and confidence as his wide shoulders made room for him in the crowd.

Where had he been hiding? She hadn't seen him around town before. But then again…he looked familiar.

As she walked forward, he veered right to a table with red apples, giving her a partial glimpse of him from a distance. His dark hair cut in a high-and-tight fade emphasized what looked to be an interesting light brown face. His muscular-looking chest and biceps naturally flexed under his shirt with the sleeves pushed up to his forearms.

He moved to the next stall, and Nicole took his spot in front of the apples. His wonderful scent lingered. Disappointment hit as soon as the breeze took it away.

Farther down, he paused at a stall laden with squash. Skipping over the more familiar varieties of long yellow necks and zucchini in front of him, he selected a round green tatume variety.

That was an interesting choice. How was he preparing it—grilled, sautéed, baked? Was he a fellow chef or a foodie?

"Is he single?"

Ashley's and Megan's voices echoed in her thoughts. Had her sisters been there, they would have encouraged her to go after him and find out.

"Hey, Nicole," Louella O'Brien called out to her.

Nicole dragged her attention away from the guy and looked back over her shoulder.

Thin but sturdy-looking in jeans, a green plaid button-down and a red apron, the eightysomething woman with pulled back, dark gray-and-silver hair, waved her over to her stall.

Nicole slipped her phone back into her pocket and walked back to greet Louella.

Lou's Luscious Jams was one of her and her sisters' favorite vendors. "Hi, Lou. How are you?"

"I'm good." Lou smiled and fine lines creased

her tanned face, friendliness reflected in her clear green eyes.

"How's business?"

"Booming." Lou pointed to her half-empty table. "I've only been here a few hours, and this is all I have left. Now that we have a revamped farmers market section, lots of new people are stopping in."

"That's wonderful."

The area with matching canopies lined up on either side of the gravel aisle really did bring more attention to the produce, baked goods and other tempting food items offered by the vendors. It was also close to Mariana's food truck, the central point of the market, placing it directly in the flow of foot traffic. And the changes also showcased the spirit of togetherness bringing the ranchers, farmers and other longtime residents there to sell their goods.

That sense of small-town closeness was one of the things that had prompted Nicole to relocate from Florida to Rambling Rose.

Lou held out an eight-ounce quilt-patterned jar of red jam to Nicole. "I thought you might be interested in having some of your favorite before I sold out. Made it fresh this week."

Roasted strawberry. Nicole's mouth watered as she imagined the jam slathered on warm buttered toast and spooned over vanilla ice cream. "Thank you."

"Need a bag?"

"I've got one." Nicole reached inside her net bag, pulled out a folded cloth tote and put the jar inside it. "I'll take two more if you have them. I had to pry the last jar out of my sisters' hands just to get some."

She'd stored the jam in the back of the pantry, but as usual, her sisters had sniffed it out. But that wasn't surprising. As triplets, they'd never been able to keep anything from each other for very long.

Chuckling, Lou handed her two more. "Here you go. But I suspect your sisters eating the last of this won't be a problem for you anymore. You're living on your own now, aren't you?"

As Nicole paid Lou for the jam, images flickered through her mind. A week ago, Ashley had gotten married to Rodrigo Mendoza. Their ceremony at the Texas Mission—a beautiful, historic adobe structure near town with terra-cotta floors, timber arches and a ceiling inlaid with colorful Mexican tiles—had been lovely and sweet. And the day had become even more romantic when Rodrigo's brother Mark had proposed to Megan. Now that they were engaged, Megan was spending most of her free time with him instead of the suite of rooms she and her sisters had once shared at their family's Fame and Fortune Ranch.

Lou was right. Ashley had her own home now with Rodrigo. Megan spent most of her time with Mark in Austin. She didn't have to worry about having enough jam anymore.

Happiness for her sisters along with a teensy bit of loneliness and envy rose inside Nicole. "Yes, I'm on my own now."

As Lou slipped the money into the pocket of her apron, she gave Nicole an all-knowing look. "Well, you know what they say. Good things come in threes. I'm sure you'll be following in their footsteps soon enough."

Chapter Two

Good things come in threes...

The words echoed in her mind as Nicole accepted a sample jar of a new jam flavor, triple-berry jalapeño, from Lou and walked away from the stall.

Over the past twenty-four years, Nicole, her sisters and their parents had encountered that saying a lot.

And it was true that many of her, Megan's and Ashley's experiences had lined up in threes. From learning to crawl at the same time as babies to triple dating as teens to venturing into the hospitality industry. But as far as her finding Mr. Right, as her sisters had done...well, that would have to come later.

Since she'd moved from being a sous chef at Provisions, the restaurant she and her sisters opened in town last year, and stepped into the position of executive chef at Roja a few months ago, she'd barely had time to keep up with doing her laundry, let alone date. Attracting loyal clientele, building a solid staff and maintaining quality service required her full attention. Along with designing menus that enticed guests at the hotel and the residents of Rambling Rose to visit the restaurant.

The summer menu was high on her to-do list but making it a reality was a challenge. Her creative muse had unexpectedly taken a long vacation and didn't appear to have plans on returning anytime soon. Lately, just thinking about the menu or trying to research new recipes left her feeling overwhelmed instead of motivated.

One of the reasons she'd come to the market was to find inspiration in the outdoor, farm-to-table atmosphere. There was something special about farmers or home-based fruit and vegetable gardeners who had the knowledge and patience to grow food.

She recalled the guy who'd run into her earlier. Seeing him handle the squash had been inspirational, too, in its own unique way. She couldn't stop a smile as the clear image of him came back into her mind. But now wasn't the time to daydream about him. She needed to concentrate on finding the rosemary.

Weaving through the growing crowd, she glanced left and right. Just as she was about to give up her search, she spotted the herbs and a host of leafy green vegetables. Harris Farms…that was the vendor she was looking for.

But the baskets were almost empty.

Picking up the pace, Nicole moved to the side, squeezing between the people strolling down the center aisle and the ones perusing items at the stalls.

Almost there…

A few steps from the table, a dark-haired woman cut in front of Nicole and set down the numerous full bags she'd been carrying at her feet. Leaning over the table, she blocked the rosemary basket as she flagged down the vendor. "Do you have more basil? What's out here is wilted."

"Pardon me." Nicole tried to snag some of the rosemary, but the woman calling out to the vendor wouldn't budge.

Releasing a sigh of frustration, Nicole scooted around her, battling the crowd like a salmon swimming upstream. By the time she made it to the other side of the woman, only one bunch of rosemary tied with a thin red band remained.

As she reached for it, a familiar woodsy cologne and alluring body heat surrounded her like an embrace. Distracted from the basket, she glanced left at the guy standing there. It was *him*.

Stunning coppery eyes met hers, and her thoughts

short-circuited, leaving her mouth momentarily un-
censored. "You are so…" She barely swallowed the
rest of her sentence, preventing it from slipping out.
Gorgeous.

"I'm what?" He picked up the last of the rosemary. The corners of his eyes crinkled slightly as
his mouth quirked up with a quizzical smile.

Nicole pointed to the tied bunch of herbs in his
hand. "You are so lucky. That's the last one."

"It is? I guess I am." The deep tone of his voice
settled inside of Nicole, making her tingle from the
inside out. As he held her gaze, she couldn't bring
herself to look away.

Stop staring! What was wrong with her? She was
acting like he was the first sinfully hot guy she'd
ever laid eyes on.

His gaze moved from her face to her free hand,
still hovering in the air.

She snatched up some parsley.

Okay, it wasn't what she came for, but she'd
looked silly just standing there practically drool-
ing over him. It wasn't like she didn't need it. Parsley was in the lemon rosemary chicken recipe and
a dozen other dishes at Roja. They could always
use more.

The sixtyish brown-skinned man behind the
table, dressed casually and wearing a tan cowboy
hat, came over and smiled broadly at the gorgeous
guy. "Collin, good to see you again."

Collin... Now she remembered. He'd attended an event at the Hotel Fortune a few months ago. She hadn't gotten a chance to meet him, but Grace Williams, the hotel's general manager, had been talking to him at the get-together. After he'd left, she'd overheard Grace mention his name and that he was a friend.

"It's good to see you, too, Mr. Harris." He shook the older man's hand.

Not wanting to seem as if she was eavesdropping on their conversation, Nicole busied herself sorting out dollars for her purchase.

"Thanks again for reminding me about this place yesterday," Collin said. "You saved me a trip to Ellington Field."

"There's no need to make the drive all the way out there," Mr. Harris replied. "You can find most of what you need here."

Ellington Field... That was the joint military reserve base near Houston. Was he stationed there? With his haircut, and the way he carried himself, she could easily imagine him wearing a uniform.

Mr. Harris accepted Collin's money. "How's Sam?"

"He's..."

Collin's pause as he slipped the rosemary into his bag made Nicole glance at him.

"He's doing okay." His smile dimmed, and for a brief moment sadness was in his face.

A sudden wish that it wouldn't be strange for her to lay her hand on Collin's arm in a gesture of comfort hit Nicole square in the chest.

"Be sure to let him know I'm thinking about him." Empathy reflected in Mr. Harris's expression.

"I will." Collin gave a nod and left.

After paying for the parsley, her path continued to mirror Collin's as she made her way through the crowd.

As more people swarmed into the market, a bottleneck landed her at his side.

Her bag with the jars bumped his leg. "Sorry."

"No problem. We seem to keep running into each other." The smile he'd lost at Mr. Harris's stall returned, full force, making her smile back.

"We do." Nicole slipped the strap of the bag over her shoulder. Maybe it was a sign that she should introduce herself? She could mention that she recognized him from the event at the hotel. Or she could ask him what he was making with the items he'd bought.

Spotting an opening in the crowd, they slipped through it at the same time.

As they exited the market and headed to the parking lot, he chuckled. "Looks like the entire population of Rambling Rose just showed up."

"I know, right? So…what's on your menu?"

His brow rose. "My menu?"

From the hint of amusement in his face, her

question had sounded like a really bad pickup line. "What I meant is, what's cooking in your kitchen." That didn't sound any better. The heat of embarrassment crept into her face. "You bought a squash. Or some people call it a tatume. It just depends, really…" And she really needed to stop talking.

"I'm making *calabaza con pollo*." He pronounced the Spanish vowels perfectly. "Have you ever had it?"

If she hadn't had the dish he'd mentioned, or recognized the other name for the squash, the way he'd said it would have made her want to sample the dish right away.

Relief that they were finally speaking the same food language made her smile up at him as they slowed down at the edge of the parking lot. "It's one of the specials at my restaurant."

"Which one?"

"Roja. I'm the executive chef."

"That's in the hotel the Fortunes built, isn't it?"

"Yes." Should she tell him she was a Fortune? But how many times had that revelation caused a friendly conversation to go sideways?

Her brother Callum, a real estate developer and contractor, had invested in revitalizing Rambling Rose almost two years ago. The town had been in decline with a dwindling population and even fewer employment opportunities. She, Ashley and Megan, along with their other four siblings, had joined him in the venture. So far, it had been successful.

Recent retirees from outside the area were moving in. Millennials were returning because of jobs and more social activities. The Gen Z demographic now saw Rambling Rose as a place they wanted to live instead of one they wanted to move away from. The rebuild had also attracted millionaires seeking a quiet refuge, just off the beaten path. Because of the new residents, Rambling Rose was experiencing a housing boom, with subdivisions being built in the area.

Some of the locals appreciated the improvements that included Roja and the Hotel Fortune, while others saw the changes as an intrusion and viewed her and her family as interlopers.

She could never deny who she was. If Collin felt that way about her family, it was best to find out now before she kept talking to him.

Nicole stretched out her hand. "I'm Nicole Fortune, by the way."

"Collin Waldon."

His hand enclosed hers, not too tight but firm, feeding a heady buzz of happiness in not seeing disapproval in his eyes.

A truck and an SUV drove past.

"Careful." He quickly released her hand and took hold of her arm, urging her to move farther away from cars cruising through the parking lot.

She gravitated in his direction, feeling safer just being near him.

He released her but remained close enough for her to map out the soft flecks of gold and amber in his eyes. "So it's your turn to confess."

She'd tell him anything he asked. "About what?"

"What are you making with the parsley and lemons in your bag?"

"I'm testing a recipe I found for lemon rosemary chicken."

"Are you preparing it with fresh pasta?"

"That's the only way to make it." Excitement over the recipe and the intensity in his gaze, as if every word she said mattered to him, fueled a ramble. "But I can't decide which pasta to make. Angel hair, spaghetti, fettuccini or rigatoni. Or maybe a veggie-based pasta for a little more flavor."

"Whichever one you decide on, you'll need this." He took the rosemary from his bag and held it out to her.

Nicole reached for it but caught herself. "I couldn't." She released a quiet laugh and smoothed hair from her forehead. "You need it for something you're making."

"But you need it more. Fresh rosemary is a must for lemon rosemary chicken. Its pungent, lemony undertones accent the dish perfectly. You know I'm right."

From the flavor profile Collin had just described,

he really did understand. As Nicole accepted the bundled herb, her fingers grazed his. Tingles along with a secret wish to see Collin again and make something wonderful and delicious with the rosemary for him to taste, came over her.

"I'm taking it on one condition." She slipped a business card from the back of her phone case and held it out to him. "You have to come to Roja for lunch on Monday and taste it. I'd love to get your opinion."

Collin's expression sobered as he offered up a shadow of a smile. "My schedule is full next week. I can't promise I'll be there."

As Nicole stared up at him, hopefulness remained in not seeing an outright no in his eyes. "Just try."

Chapter Three

Collin scooped up fresh kernels of corn from the glass cutting board on the white marble counter and added them to the cooked, seasoned chicken, calabaza and other diced vegetables gently simmering in the skillet on the stove. He put a lid over it, but the wonderful, savory aroma of the food still escaped, filling the kitchen at his father's house.

"What's cooking in your kitchen..."

From the sincerity in Nicole's face that morning when she'd asked him the question, along with what was on his menu, she hadn't been trying to hit on him with bad pickup lines.

Recalling Nicole's self-conscious blush turning

her cheeks pink pushed a chuckle out of him. Coming from her, the lines had actually sounded cute. With her being a Fortune, he'd been a little surprised she was embarrassed over what she'd said and didn't have a privileged "look at me" attitude. That had made her even more interesting. Along with her being an executive chef.

Her genuine excitement over what she'd planned on making had been as infectious as the happiness in her blue eyes. If she cooked with that level of passion, the dish would be perfect. Her enthusiasm was what had prompted him to give her the rosemary. Okay, and maybe he hadn't missed that she was pretty. Still, being wrapped in her positive, almost addictive energy for those few short minutes had been like a breath of fresh air he hadn't realized he'd needed, until he'd walked away from her.

In the adjoining dining room, the French doors opened and closed, and the memory of Nicole's blue eyes filled with excitement and the generous upward curve of her mouth dissipated in his mind.

The sound of ripping Velcro prompted Collin to see the image of his father, Sam, on the other side of the wall, leaning on the jamb for support as he took off his tennis shoes and traded them for the slippers sitting on the rug in front of the glass doors.

Long seconds ticked by with the cadence of Sam's slightly labored breathing. From the sound of it, his father hadn't just sat on the back porch like he'd said he'd planned to do. He'd walked around the yard as well.

"Dad," he called out. "Do you want to eat lunch in the living room instead of the dining room?"

"No, I don't want to eat in the living room." Weariness tinged his father's borderline snappish response. "The dining room's fine. Just give me a minute to wash my hands."

But if you sit in the recliner, you can prop your feet up... Collin held back from saying it.

During the past few days since he'd been home again, anything he mentioned to his father seemed to cause them to butt heads. That morning, when he'd discovered Sam at his desk in the home office and simply asked why he was awake so early, his father had claimed he was hounding him.

The uneven scuffing sound of Sam's steps and the thump of his cane on the wood floor slowly faded.

Fighting aggravation, Collin took a bowl and plate from an upper cabinet. As a thirty-year-old captain in the army, his training had prepared him to lead, mentor and strategize. But not even a near decade of military experience and discipline had prepared him to handle his father's increasing stubbornness.

Collin set the table then returned to the kitchen and ladled the room-temperature soup he'd also made into the bowl from a pot on the counter.

After spooning some of the *calabaza con pollo* onto the plate for himself, he brought the food to the table along with glasses of water for him and his father. Taking a seat in the chair at the side of the wood oval, he waited.

Sun shining through the French doors created a shadow of a checker-like pattern on one of the slate blue walls.

Out back, beyond the covered, raised wood deck and the lawn, rosebushes near the fence sprouted past their usual manicured shape.

Last weekend, Sam had been trimming the roses when he'd passed out.

Grace's parents, Barbara and Mike, had noticed the gas trimmer idling for an extended period of time and peeked over the side gate between his father's house and theirs. What if they hadn't found him?

Collin mentally pushed aside the ugly possibilities.

The couple he'd known since childhood had contacted him in Grafenwöhr, Germany, where he was stationed, to let him know an ambulance had rushed Sam to the hospital. Two agonizing hours later, Sam's personal physician had called to update him on his father's condition—a bump on the back of the head, a badly bruised knee—and the shocking news Sam had hidden from him for months. His father had terminal lung cancer.

Maybe a year...

That's how much time his dad had left.

Sam's footfalls grew louder from the living room, and a short time later, he walked through the archway.

Remnants of the disbelief he'd felt days ago when he'd first seen the changes that had occurred during the few short months since he'd last visited his father pushed a breath out of Collin now. The changes were even more startling compared to how his dad had looked last spring.

His father's salt-and-pepper hair had turned mostly white. His face that had once been lightly tanned from puttering around in the yard and playing golf on the weekends was pallid. A thirty-minute-a-day routine on the rowing machine in the home office had kept Sam fit since retiring four years ago, but now, the blue slacks and gray shirt he wore were at least a size too big. And the zeal that had once filled his dad's hazel eyes was gone.

As his father went to the chair facing the doors, a fifty-foot hose trailed after him. The nasal cannula secured by loops around his ears was connected to an oxygen concentrator in the living room.

"What kind of soup is this?" The outer metal rim of the medical alert device on his father's wrist gleamed as he leaned heavily on the cane to sit down. "Does it have milk in it? You know I can't have dairy."

Multiple medications had affected his father's digestion. But the soup's texture, mild seasoning and cool temperature wouldn't upset his stomach.

"It's chicken and potato. I pureed it with broth."

His father tasted the soup, then pointed the spoon at Collin's plate. "That's *calabaza con pollo*. Is it your mother's recipe?"

"Close. The seasoning's off. I can't tell what's missing."

His father released a gruff chuckle. "There's no telling what it is. Remember how your mom used to taste something she'd made, decide it needed a little pepping up, then go outside to find herbs in the garden to fix it? A pinch of this or a little bit of that. She just knew."

Collin followed his father's faraway gaze out the French doors.

Daisies, sunflowers, lavender and herbs along with thriving vegetables had once been planted near the back fence, melding seamlessly with the lawn.

For a brief moment an image of his mother, Beth, pinching leaves from a plant with a satisfied smile on her flawless brown face appeared in his mind.

But then the pink, red and white roses refocused in front of him. They were out of place.

After throwing out his mother's things, Sam's second wife, Sharon, had uprooted the garden and planted the rosebushes four years ago, a year after his mother's death. But they didn't belong there any more than Sam had belonged spending last weekend trying to trim them.

Frustration laced with concern drove Collin's attention from the view of the roses.

His gaze collided with his father's.

Sam lowered his eyes and ate his soup.

Collin tucked into his own meal, allowing the flavors of the dish to soothe him. The past was over. Sam had outlived both of his wives. As his father's only child, it was up to him to help his dad sort out his affairs now and after he'd passed away.

Turning the conversation in a different direction, Collin broke the silence. "I saw Wayne Harris at Mariana's Market selling herbs from his farm. He said to tell you hello."

Wayne, an army veteran and retired US marshal, had sometimes played golf with Sam.

"Harris was there, huh?" Sam gave a wheezy laugh. "So he finally drank the Fortunes' Kool-Aid. The last time I spoke to him, he'd been skeptical about the changes being made at Mariana's. But I don't blame him for giving in and joining everyone else."

"Haven't the changes the Fortunes have made so far been good for Rambling Rose?"

"Maybe. But it doesn't matter either way. Like it or not, we're stuck with them. Might as well get used to it."

From what he'd overheard, not everyone shared

his father's "just deal and get over it" attitude. Despite the growth happening in Rambling Rose, there were still a few longtime residents who saw the Fortunes as outsiders and opportunists who'd swept in, taken advantage of the town and created a playground for the rich that suited their own needs for profit.

Collin thought back to that morning at the market. Nicole had looked a little wary before she'd introduced herself. Had she expected some kind of judgment from him over her being a Fortune?

Spoonfuls away from finishing his soup, exhaustion flooded Sam's face.

"Maybe you should lie down in bed for an hour or two."

"I'm not tired." Using the cane, his father pushed up from the chair. "I just want to relax and watch TV, if that's okay with you."

Collin held up his hands in weary surrender. "Fine, whatever you want."

After finishing lunch and cleaning the kitchen, Collin walked into the living room carrying his mug of coffee.

His father slept soundly in his black recliner while a past episode of a series drama played on the flat-screen television against the far wall.

Collin checked the reading on the concentrator sitting on the floor near the tan couch before he crept to the home office.

While his father rested, he could check his emails.

Sitting at the wood desk, he powered up his laptop. In charge of field and training operations for the division, he'd had to hand off a few key tasks before he'd left. For the next twenty-seven days while he was on emergency leave, one of the operations sergeants was keeping him abreast of things.

As Collin pulled up his email, his phone rang on the desk, and he glanced at the screen.

It was the life care manager he'd hired to guide him and Sam.

He answered the call. "Hello, Ruby."

"Hi, Collin. How are you?"

"Fine."

"And Sam?" From her caring tone, she understood the question wasn't a simple one.

"He's having a decent day. We just had lunch. His appetite was fairly good. He's resting now. Switching the times for his medications seems to be cutting down on the nausea."

"Ian mentioned the same."

Ian, a private nursing assistant, came by every other afternoon to check on Sam.

"Speaking of medications," Ruby added, "have you and Sam talked about the new therapy?"

Sam had tested positive for a gene that responded to a drug cocktail that could extend the outcome of his prognosis by months, possibly years.

"Yes." Collin took a breath and released a slow exhale. "He still says no."

"Do you think it would help if I talked to him?"

"No. He said he's made up his mind and he doesn't want to talk about it anymore."

"I see." Empathy hung in Ruby's voice. "With the upcoming move and his health, he's facing a lot at one time. He may have a change of heart once he's settled into his new place. Be patient with him. He still has time to decide."

No. His dad didn't have time. Frustration sank with Collin back in the chair. For his father, time was being measured in weeks and months, not years. He couldn't afford to wait. His dad had won a chance that had the equivalent odds to winning a lottery, but he wouldn't take it.

"I have a bit of good news," Ruby said. "You were interested in seeing more places that your father could move into. I found one I think both of you might like in Houston. It's called the Highlands."

"How does it stack up against the last one we visited in Austin?"

The place he and Sam had gone to that past Friday had seemed to cater to mostly bedridden patients. The grounds and the small private and double rooms were stark and stifling. He'd been against his dad living there, but his father had insisted he wanted to move in as soon as the spot became available in three weeks. At least he'd talked his dad out of giving them the deposit until they'd had a chance to check out some other options.

Ruby continued, "This place is more of a community with a mix of residents, from people who have very minor health issues to those who need full-time care. I'm uploading the brochure to Sam's online profile now, along with a link to their virtual tour. Take the tour and let me know if I should set up a meeting with them."

"Okay, I'll take a look."

"Right now, they have three vacancies. They're all shared cottages with two or three people, but they're still pretty spacious—separate bedrooms and full baths with nice-size sitting areas. Because of your father's health prognosis, he's at the top of the list for one of them. As long as he meets the financial requirements, he can move in. He has until the end of the month to decide and put down a deposit, but sooner is better."

"I'll let you know what my dad says. This sounds like it could be a good place for him."

"I agree. If you have any questions, don't hesitate to call me. Oh, one more thing—I'm also uploading our new family caregiver's guide. It has lots of helpful tips on how to relieve stress. It may feel counterintuitive to focus on your needs right now, but one of the best ways you can be there for Sam is by looking after yourself."

Caregiver's stress. He'd read about it in an article. But he'd handled tours in the Middle East, and he was only home with his father for a few weeks. As difficult as his father was being right now, he could deal with it.

"I appreciate the information," Collin said.

He ended the call with Ruby and went back to reviewing his emails. After sending out the necessary responses, he logged in to his father's online account with the care adviser service, found info for the Highlands and took the 360-degree virtual tour.

Basic modern apartments in a three-story building and cottages on the grounds had ample amenities and a few extra touches. Wider doorways. Hospital-grade electrical outlets for medical equipment. A monitoring system with a keypad in every room. It was a huge upgrade from the institution-like feel of the place in Austin. But it was pricey.

He needed to go through his father's financial records. Between Sam's savings, investments, pension and the proceeds from selling the house, they could probably make it work.

Tomorrow, he'd planned on sorting out the things in the garage. He'd crunch numbers and research Realtors on Monday.

"You have to come to Roja for lunch on Monday and try it out... Just try."

If only he could take Nicole up on her lunch invitation. He would have enjoyed talking to her again. And it would have been interesting to find out what other food topics lit up her face besides rosemary and pasta.

Under different circumstances, he probably would have even asked her out after having lunch at Roja. But with all that he had going on with his dad, connecting with her on a personal level wasn't something he could consider. He had to change his father's mind about moving to Austin, and he didn't know how to make that happen yet. And time wasn't on his side.

Chapter Four

Nicole cleaned a stray drop of tomatillo sauce from a plate of chicken-stuffed avocado. She slid it farther down the long pass-through pickup window that separated the kitchen from the servers' area.

It was one of the daily specials, and a lot of them would be ordered by customers that afternoon. On Mondays, the buses from an antiquing tour on their way back to Austin from a long weekend stay in nearby Round Top stopped for lunch in Rambling Rose. The travelers were free to eat wherever they wanted, but many of them chose to dine at Roja.

Behind her at the center island, a cook took a sheet pan of baked chicken from the top of a double-tiered convection oven while another cook sautéed vegetables at one of the stoves.

A helper in the far corner of the red-tiled space rapidly chopped vegetables at a stainless steel table in the salad and dessert station. In the other corner, the general prep space was empty.

The cook that would have been there getting a jump on dinner preparations had quit that past Saturday.

Nicole slid an order ticket under another grouping of entrées. She'd found out about it shortly after she'd returned from Mariana's Market. It had been a total blindside, and the timing couldn't have been worse. Members of the kitchen staff were already covering the duties of the storeroom supervisor, who was out for a few weeks after major surgery. And the first Fortune's Give Back fund-raising barbecue, an event to raise money for nonprofits and outreach projects in Rambling Rose, was in three weeks.

Until they found another cook, Mariana had agreed to put in more hours to take up the slack.

Mariana, the founder of the eponymous Mariana's Market, who helped out in the kitchen a few days a week, carried two blackened-tilapia entrées from the cooking station.

The middle-aged woman with ruddy cheeks, brown eyes and bleached blond hair was dressed similarly to Nicole in navy Crocs, black cargo pants and a chambray chef's coat and apron tied around her waist. But instead of a wide blue band holding back her hair like Nicole had chosen that day, she wore a black chef's skullcap.

Even though she'd been awake before dawn setting up at the market with the employee who was running her food truck for the day, she exuded energy.

"Do you want me to take over for you?" Mariana set the plates in the window. "You mentioned you wanted to research recipes."

"Thanks, but I can wait until after the rush. But there is something else you can do for me later. Can you check the butter inventory and add what we need to our order? It's uploading to the distributor's site at three."

"Sure."

"Thanks."

As Mariana went back to the cooking station, Nicole garnished the tilapia entrées with sprigs of parsley.

Parsley, rosemary and butter were on a tray in the walk-in refrigerator along with the other items she'd need to make the lemon rosemary chicken. She was still crossing her fingers that Collin would make it.

After leaving him on Saturday, she'd come back to the kitchen with a spark of creativity and found another recipe to test for the summer menu.

The combination of the market and Collin had

done the trick. Or had it just been the inspiring combination of Collin, his beautiful eyes and his understanding of fresh rosemary?

What had he planned to do with it? Collin had picked up the herb for a reason.

"You are so lucky. That's the last one."

"It is? I guess I am."

Remembering the deep tone of his voice and being caught up in his gaze brought a smile to her face and raised goose bumps on her skin now.

She could ask him what his plans had been for the rosemary when he came to lunch…during a very brief conversation with him. She had work to do. Feeding him lunch wasn't a date. She was just thanking him for giving her the last bunch of rosemary, the one he'd been lucky enough to get.

A couple of hours later, the pace of the orders slowed. And hope over Collin showing up for lunch waned. It wasn't like he'd promised to come. Actually, his answer had leaned more toward him not being there.

Truthfully, him not stopping by was a sign that she needed to stay focused and eliminate distractions. She needed to research recipes and clear paperwork from her desk, and not spend the afternoon wondering why Collin didn't show up…or thinking about how hot he was…or how much she really had been looking forward to seeing him again.

Laughter from the staff unhurriedly running

plates and glasses through the dish machine traveled from the other side of the kitchen.

The cooks and the kitchen helper also worked at a pace that was more relaxed than usual for this time of the day.

Lunch service had been a little sluggish. But the tour group hadn't arrived yet. Usually by now, her dining room supervisor, Lesly, had already popped into the kitchen, alerting them to their arrival.

Mariana came out of the small walk-in fridge built into the side wall and joined Nicole at the window. "I checked the butter, and we actually don't need any. I found some stored in the wrong place. While I was looking around, I also checked the inventory for a few more things and made an adjustment to the order."

"Were we running low on something?"

"No. The opposite. We had more on hand than we usually do. This past weekend was slow."

"Today isn't that busy, either. Did you hear anything about the antiquing group? They haven't come in yet."

"Oh." Mariana's brows rose. "Lesly didn't tell you?"

"Tell me what?" The change in Mariana's expression during the silence raised concern. "Oh no—were they in an accident?"

"No, nothing like that. They—"

A brunette server picked up an order at the counter.

Mariana paused until the young woman walked away. "We should probably have this conversation in your office. I'll get Lesly."

A few minutes later, Nicole sat behind the desk in her kitchen corner office. A wide window in front of her, to the left of the door, provided a view of Mariana talking to one of the cooks.

Lesly, with curly dark hair, naturally tanned skin and a light sprinkling of freckles on her cheeks, came into the kitchen and walked inside the office with Mariana. The petite, twentysomething dining room supervisor, neatly dressed in a long-sleeved chambray shirt and dark slacks, appeared troubled.

Mariana shut the door behind them, and the two women sat down in the chairs in front of the desk.

Nicole looked between Mariana and Lesly. "From the looks on your faces, I'm guessing the news you have to tell me isn't good?"

"No, it's not." Lesly's shoulders fell. "The Roadside Diner made a deal with the bus tour company. They're the official dining stop for all the company's tours. It's in the information for the tour along with a discount coupon."

"What?" Nicole sat straighter in the chair. "But Roja is a popular choice with the group, and we already offer them a really good discount. Why choose the diner over us?"

Mariana crossed her arms over her chest. "I'm just as confused as you are. I know one of the tour guides, and she never said a word to me about it."

"From what I understand, they didn't know." Lesly sighed. "I hate to keep heaping on the bad news, but discounts aren't the only thing the diner is handing out." Lesly took a folded blue paper from her pocket. She opened it and handed the paper to Nicole across the desk.

It was a flyer with the Roadside Diner's logo on the top along with a tag line: *Don't have an unFortunate dining experience. Drop on into the Roadside Diner for happy, worry-free dining...*

Below the huge tag line on the top of the page, an illustration showed worried people falling through the air and landing in restaurant booths with huge smiles on their faces.

It might look innocent enough, but anyone living in Rambling Rose would clearly see the connection.

Four months ago, before the hotel had opened, the balcony had collapsed outside of the second-floor area that was used by Roja for parties and catered events. Grace, who'd been a management trainee at the time, had gotten hurt. What happened wasn't something to joke about or use in an advertising campaign.

"This is unbelievable." Nicole handed the flyer to Mariana.

As Mariana stared at the paper, her cheeks grew

cherry red and her lips flattened. "This isn't just unbelievable, it's low and it's libelous. We have to do something about this."

"I agree," Lesly chimed in. "And whatever it is, it needs to be soon or we're going to lose more staff. Jan, one of our best servers, used to work at the diner, and now she's going back because they offered her a raise. And a couple more of the waitstaff are considering jumping ship, too."

Irritation rose in Nicole. "So the diner isn't just trying to steal customers, they're stealing our staff, too?"

Lesly shook her head. "Not everyone is interested in getting a job at the diner. There's also the Hot Spot Bar and Grill near Houston. It was recently reviewed by *Texas Eats Quarterly*, and now it's packed every night. Supposedly, the servers there are making more just in tips Thursday through Sunday than our servers make here all week. Even with the commute, it's tempting to the staff."

"So money is the driving factor?" Mariana said.

"Not just the money, but job security," Lesly replied.

"Job security?" Nicole said. "Why would anyone here be afraid of losing their jobs? Especially since hiring more people is my priority."

"Well…they don't think you'll have a choice in whether or not the staff is let go."

"Why would they think that? I'm in charge of

running Roja. Hiring or letting someone go is up to me."

Lesly shifted in her seat as if it had suddenly become uncomfortable.

Apprehension intertwined with Nicole's frustration. Had the staff lost faith in her ability to run Roja?

Lesly met Nicole's gaze. "They're not questioning whether or not you're in charge. But with the restaurant not being as busy as they imagined it would be, they're worried about the future. They're afraid Roja won't be in business for long."

Chapter Five

Collin left the bank office in downtown Rambling Rose. His sunglasses muted the sunlight, but not his headache or the frustration growing inside him.

Yesterday evening, he'd approached his father, wanting to access his father's checking and savings accounts online to get an idea of his financial situation, but his dad had been evasive, claiming he didn't know the password or the email associated in retrieving it.

Rather than dealing with his father's defensiveness, he'd gone to the bank with the financial power of attorney his father had given him, one of the many legal documents his dad had contacted an attorney to prepare.

But the visit with the customer service rep at the bank had been much longer and more illuminating than anticipated.

Payments over the past year to a high-interest loan company had whittled down his father's savings. But one major transfer to the company a few weeks ago, along with a generous down payment to the care facility in Austin, had almost completely wiped out the account. And the house was no longer paid for. His father had taken out another mortgage last year. He was relying solely on his pension from his years of working as a dental equipment sales rep to take care of himself and pay the bills.

The revelation of his father's financial position pounded into Collin's temples along with one big question. Why hadn't his father come to him for help when he'd started experiencing financial problems?

More questions zipped through Collin's mind as he joined pedestrians on the sidewalk, hurrying or strolling in and out of the older brick and newer glass-front buildings lining the street.

As he stood at the corner, two tour buses nestled in the steady flow of traffic drove past, releasing exhaust fumes and a blast of heat that circled him in the wind.

Collin's headache grew worse. He needed to sit down and think things through before talking to his father. He also needed to eat. The eggs and coffee he'd consumed that morning had worn off more than an hour ago. His gnawing empty stomach was growing just as uncomfortable as his head.

Collin grabbed aspirin and water at the corner pharmacy. Standing in the space between the outer and inner sliding glass doors of the building, he immediately took the pills. While he stood there, he texted Ian letting him know he wouldn't be returning right away. Ian texted back that he could stay for a couple more hours.

Ian was working on his nursing degree. He lived with his sister, her husband and their three kids, and he appreciated having a quiet place to study. And Collin paid him extra for staying with Sam outside of his normal visits.

Sam didn't require 24-7 care. But Collin felt more at ease having someone with him, or at least checking on him regularly, when he wasn't there.

Back outside, as Collin looked up and down the street, he reoriented his mental map of food establishments in Rambling Rose. Back in the day, the Roadside Diner and Mariana's food truck had been the most notable places. Now, there were more options.

The Shoppes at Rambling Rose, the two-story building that had once been the abandoned five-and-dime store, was close. The retail space not only had boutiques but a couple of small café, coffee and bistro-type establishments. Provisions Restaurant was on the next street over. He'd been there once before, and the food was good. But his T-shirt, athletic pants and sneakers might be too casual for the upscale restaurant.

There was also Roja a short drive away.

"I can't decide which pasta to make. Angel hair, spaghetti, fettuccini or rigatoni. Or maybe a veggie-based pasta for a little more flavor..."

As Nicole's voice played through his mind, his stomach growled, and the ache in his temples lessened.

That past Saturday, he'd arrived at Mariana's Market with a lot on his mind about his father. He'd just started to relax when Mr. Harris had asked how his dad was doing, and the tension he'd been fighting had landed right back on him.

But then he'd run into Nicole on the way out, and their simple conversation about food, along with hearing her laughter and seeing her smile had been a huge moment of relief. Something he hadn't realized had helped him back then, until now.

For a brief moment he closed his eyes, imagining himself sitting at a table, talking to Nicole about the pasta choice she'd made and tasting the dish. As he thought about it, more tension fell away. Taking advantage of Nicole's lunch invitation to see her again would be a nice change from the frustration of trying to figure out his father's finances.

A short time later, he parked his gray rental in

front of the light-colored stucco four-story Hotel Fortune.

In the terra-cotta-tiled lobby of the boutique hotel, wrought iron wall hangings and leather chairs reflected luxury and relaxation.

He bypassed the front desk on the left and walked down a short corridor to the entrance of Roja.

A young blonde woman in a chambray shirt and black jeans stood behind a dark-colored restaurant host stand with Roja emblemized on the front in raised red lettering. She greeted him, and after confirming he was on his own for lunch, he followed her into the restaurant.

Natural light from windows along the side wall brightened the cozy, half-empty dining space with cream-colored walls and a wood-beamed ceiling. The unoccupied wood tables with burgundy upholstered chairs were set with silverware rolled in white napkins.

After seating Collin at a four-top next to the window with a view of the pool, she gave him a menu and let him know his server would be there shortly.

He glanced at the menu then laid it on the table next to his keys and phone. The selections were tempting, but he'd shown up for the dish Nicole had talked to him about.

As promised, a brunette server arrived. "Hi, my name is Jan." She flashed a customer-friendly smile.

"Welcome to Roja. What can I bring you to drink today?"

"Water and iced tea, please."

Her gaze dropped to the menu on the table. "Do you need a few minutes to decide on your order?"

Collin's mind went back to what he'd envisioned earlier, sitting at a table talking with Nicole. "I'm ready. I know exactly what I want."

Nicole laid her phone on the desk. She'd just sent Grace a text with the flyer, but she probably wouldn't hear from her for a while. Grace's assistant had said she was in a meeting.

Fighting impatience, Nicole straightened the top of her desk. There had to be some kind of action they could take against what the diner was doing, but what? She'd mentioned what Mariana said about the flyer being libelous in her text. Was legal action an option? She could call her brother Wiley and find out. But as the hotel's attorney, he might have been one of Grace's first calls about the flyer, especially since she and Wiley were dating. It was probably best to hold off on contacting anyone else until she'd spoken with Grace.

Maybe she could hash things out with Ashley and Megan? Honestly, she was surprised they hadn't called her already. They joked about having some sort of triplet telepathy, but if something was wrong with one of them, the others seemed to sense it. At least most of the time it happened that way.

But Ashley and Rodrigo had just left for their extended honeymoon and just arrived in Fiji. After Ashley and Rodrigo left the island, they were mixing business and pleasure, attending a hospitality conference in Vegas.

And Megan had her hands full keeping an eye on Provisions while Ashley was gone. Plus, she was still handling tasks as financial director for both restaurants and commuting to Austin whenever possible to spend time with Mark.

Her sisters were busy with their own lives. And they were in love.

A pang of loneliness, similar to what Nicole had experienced when talking to Lou about her sisters at the market that past weekend hit her now. She swept it away.

If she were to call them now, all she could do was vent about the situation. They couldn't help her. She could handle this on her own, and maybe, she'd fill them in later when she had something more substantial to tell them other than she was frustrated with the competition.

As she sat in the chair, she pushed out a sigh. She wouldn't mind having more of the worries that came with the type of success the Hot Spot Bar and Grill were probably experiencing right now.

Curiosity and the need to live vicariously for

a moment led her hands to the keyboard. A quick search of the internet brought her to the website of the bar and grill. Pictures on the website showed a full establishment of happy people and tempting entrées.

A line from their review by *Texas Eats Quarterly* was front-page news. As it should have been. They'd earned it.

Continuing to fall down the rabbit hole of the internet, she landed on the *Texas Eats Quarterly* website.

The online guide and quarterly magazine directed people to the best restaurants, small and large, across the state. If she was remembering a past conversation with her sisters correctly, getting *Texas Eats Quarterly* to review a restaurant wasn't an easy feat. And of course, no one knew who the reviewers were or their selection criteria for which places to visit.

But at the bottom of the contact page, they did have a restaurant-recommendation suggestion box.

The form didn't ask for the names of the recommender, just the suggested restaurant along with the location.

Nicole filled out the form. She wouldn't be the first chef or owner of a restaurant who'd recommended their own place.

A knock on the doorjamb drew her attention.

Lesly stood in the doorway. "Sorry to bother you,

but there's a Collin Waldon in the dining room. He wants to order something that's not on the menu— lemon rosemary chicken and pasta?" Lesly gave her quizzical look. "He said you'd understand."

He showed up. Barely suppressed excitement waved through Nicole. She hit Send on the website form. "I do. I'll take care of it." Cooking for Collin and talking to him again was exactly what she needed to get her mind off the competition.

In the kitchen, she gathered the ingredients for the dish and got to work. As she prepared the recipe, mindfulness plus a dash of perfectionism blended with her skill. Peacefulness settled inside her as she moved through the tasks.

Cooking had always been her bliss. The only thing that topped it was witnessing the satisfaction of someone enjoying the first bite of something she'd made. Would her meal rate a smile of satisfaction from Collin when he tasted it?

She worked a little faster, eager to find out.

A little over a half hour later, she plated fresh fettuccini and laid one of the sliced chicken breasts on top. After ladling some of the buttery sauce over it, she garnished the dish with an artfully twisted lemon slice and carried it out of the kitchen.

In the dining room, she spotted him at a table near the window.

Grace sat across from him, crisp and professional-looking in a gray pantsuit and blue blouse. As she talked to him, Grace nodded and brushed her brown hair back from her face.

Their expressions were solemn.

Nicole slowed down. Was she intruding on their conversation?

Collin glanced over at Nicole, and his smile drew her closer.

She set the plate in front of him and smiled. "Lemon rosemary chicken, hot from the oven."

"This looks great."

"Thank you. I'm glad you were able to make it."

"My schedule changed." He pointed at the plate. "And how could I not show up for fresh pasta?"

"Well, then…" Grace rose from the chair with a slightly amused smile on her face. "I'll let you two enjoy lunch."

Oh no. How could she have completely ignored Grace? Nicole stalled Grace with a hand on her arm. "Would you like to try it? It's one of the entrées I'm testing for the summer menu. I could use your opinion, too."

"I'll have to take a rain check. The front desk needs me. Oh, and I got your text." She met Nicole's gaze. "Are you free to talk about it later?"

"Absolutely."

"I'll come by your office." Grace turned to Collin. "If you need anything…"

"I know." He nodded once. "Call you."

Grace left, but the seriousness of her conversation with Collin lingered.

He also looked worried and…sad.

Was he okay? Did this have something to do with Sam? Either way, that wasn't her business.

Feeling as if she was hovering around him while he ate, Nicole started backing away, planning to retreat to the kitchen. "Enjoy. I'll come back later so you can tell me what you think."

"Or you could join me." Collin pointed to the chair where Grace had been sitting. "Please? I'd rather not eat alone."

Eagerness leaped up in Nicole, but she hesitated. Hadn't she just given herself a pep talk earlier in the kitchen about not letting herself get distracted by him? And how could she sit down and relax with the flyer and the staff situation going on?

But he looked as if he was having a hard day and could use a lunch date.

Wait, no, not a date—he just needed some company. And as far as the flyer and everything associated with it, she couldn't really do anything about it until after she talked to Grace.

Collin raised his brow a fraction and tipped his head toward the chair.

And she really did want to see his reaction after he took the first bite.

Chapter Six

Nicole sat down, and some of the tension he'd carried since leaving the bank lifted from his shoulders.

"I have to admit, I'm anxious to hear what you think." She rested her hands on the table and interlaced her fingers.

The prim and proper gesture failed to mask the anticipation that practically shimmered around her like an aura. It was in the upward curve of her full light pink lips, the hint of color in her cheeks and the glimmer in her eyes—not blue like the ocean or the sky, but the color of bluish-purple rosemary flowers.

The coincidence made him stare at her longer.

She looked to his plate then back up to his face, cuing him into what he wasn't doing.

He took a bite, and tangy lemon melded perfectly with the rosemary and a hint of garlic in the buttery sauce. "It's good."

"And?" She rolled her hand in a keep-talking gesture.

"And I can definitely see this on a summer menu." He drank some iced tea.

"But there's more. It's written on your face. It's okay. Be honest with me."

Be honest? From the beginning of time, those two simple words had ended marriages, torpedoed friendships and possibly led to a few wars.

Though he was planning to reassure her that the food was better than good, the earnestness in her expression got to him. "Thyme."

"Thyme? Really?" Her expression grew pensive. "It's earthy and a little bit sweet."

"And it's also slightly warm and peppery."

The spark of understanding grew brighter in her eyes, and she nodded slowly. "You are so right. Thyme will add another layer of flavor. That's exactly what's needed to make this dish a bit more interesting. Thanks for the insight."

"You're welcome."

Curiosity about her stirred inside him. Her smile. Her quiet laugh as she tucked a strand of hair behind her ear. The spark in her eyes that grew brighter in an instant. Was it only conversations about food that caused them? What else made her smile?

No, he needed to back up. He'd come to Roja to taste the lemon rosemary chicken and maybe have a side conversation about food. Not to find out more about Nicole.

He cleared the questions about her from his mind. "So what else is on the summer menu?"

"Other than what you're eating? I'm not sure yet." Anxiety tinged her quiet laugh. "What I do know is that it's going to feature a mix of smoked barbecue and light, seasonal entrées."

"A nod to Texas and the summer season. Sounds good. I'm guessing brisket is top on the list?"

"It is, along with smoked chicken and sausage. The challenge is what to serve with them." She held up her hand, holding back a response. "I know. Coleslaw. And trying to change that around here would be as welcome as dropping off a bunch of porcupines at a nudist colony. So I've been told."

He'd actually heard that comparison made quite a few times while growing up in Rambling Rose for things people thought were a terrible idea. He hadn't heard it used in a while.

That realization and the teasing smirk on her lips pulled a chuckle out of him. "True, but on the other hand, sometimes people don't realize what they want until they experience it. Once they get a taste of something that they like, they're on board."

"What would you serve instead of coleslaw?"

He mentally sorted through his catalog of food experiences. "The last time I had brisket, it was served with a melon, cucumber and tomato salad."

"That sounds interesting. Where did you have it?"

Stalling, Collin took a bite of food.

The way he recharged and found peace—he'd only shared that with a few people. Compared to anyone he'd told in the past, she should understand. But would she? He'd thought that before a few times, believing that people wouldn't put him in a box because of his looks or what he did for a living. But instead of basic acceptance, he'd received negative to dumb to straight up ridiculous comments.

"I never would have guessed you had that talent... Seriously? You're joking, right? That's an interesting thing to do..." Which was usually just another way to say they thought it or he was boring. *"You do it alone?"* Or the all-time classic—*"Tell the truth. You just do it to impress women."*

Why people seemed to think he couldn't possibly enjoy his pastime as much as watching his favorite sports team play, swimming in an ocean, skiing fresh powder or putting on the perfect green baffled him. Wading through people's opinions about the topic exhausted him. Which was why he'd quit bringing it up.

But Nicole had asked him for honesty a minute ago, and he'd given it to her. Offering her less than that now felt wrong.

"I prepared it. During a culinary boot camp I attended in New York."

Her brows inched up. "You went to a culinary boot camp?"

"Yes. I like to take cooking vacations."

Almost every year for the past five of them, except during back-to-back deployments, he'd squeezed in a long weekend or taken leave for a week of cooking to unwind and reset.

And here it comes... Which variation of a response that he'd already heard would she give him? Or would she come up with a new one?

"Really?" She leaned toward him. "Tell me everything. I want details. What have you made?" From the smile on her face, it was as if he'd told her he'd hung out with her favorite celebrity.

"Well... I made *tagliolini al limone* on the Amalfi Coast. In the class I was a part of, we also made Sorrento-style gnocchi and stuffed calamari."

In his mind, he traveled back to the excursion he'd taken a couple of years ago. The memory made him smile. "It was a six-day trip with four cooking classes and plenty of time to explore. Where I stayed was in walking distance of Sant'Agata. It's a quiet village in the hills above Sorrento. There was a local spot that had the best coffee and pastries topped with fresh cream. Practically, everything we cooked with or ate at the restaurants in town came from one of the nearby farms. I had some of the best mozzarella I've ever tasted at one of them."

"Cooking with fresh ingredients is amazing." She gave him a wide smile. "And doing it there must have made it even better. From what I've heard, that part of Italy is beautiful."

A recollection of the breathtaking views of lush farms, sandy pebbled beaches and of towns perched on cliffs overlooking the sea swept into his mind.

Nicole seemed to be the type who would dive right into the experience, soaking it in along with the sunshine. For a brief moment, an image flickered in of Nicole doing just that.

What would be more satisfying? The Amalfi Coast or seeing her taking it all in?

A sudden longing to discover that answer, standing by her side, rose up. He tamped it down. This conversation was about food, and his past cooking vacations. Nothing more. And if she did happen to choose to visit the Amalfi Coast, he wouldn't be with her.

"So." She leaned in. "You said cooking classes. Where else have you gone?"

"You honestly want to hear more?"

"Yes. I do. Right now, I'm living vicariously through your experiences. Have pity on me."

A chuckle escaped him. "Right, I'm pretty sure you've had some great experiences yourself working with chefs. Tell me about your latest one?"

"No." Laughing she shook her head. "Where I went to cook in no way compares to your excursion by the sea. Where else have you gone?"

"I'm not giving up the details until you tell me about yours." He took bites of his food and waited.

Her sigh ended on a laugh. "Fine. It was a vegetarian cooking intensive in Denver."

"What did you make?"

"A lot of dishes with vegetables." She held up her hand warning off his response. "I answered your question. Let's get back to your adventures being my mental escape."

A mental escape? How could he say no to that? Especially since that's why he'd showed up to see Nicole. And honestly, he was enjoying reliving the moments he was sharing with her.

Collin laughed. "Okay, let's see…"

Tapas in Madrid. Sea scallop ceviche in Maine. Jerk-rubbed ribs in Texas. After every destination he mentioned, he'd planned to stop talking, but her enthusiasm pulled him back in and took him to the next place he'd been.

Then they moved on to other topics. Favorite restaurants—his was a hole in the wall place in

Miami. She'd never heard of it. Hers was an up-scale restaurant in New York—a place he'd always wanted to try. Most underrated spice, they both agreed—cardamom.

"I've got another one." She pointed at him. "Best impromptu meal you've made in the last six months."

Breaking his "only food topics" conversation rule, he prefaced his answer with a confession. "Before I tell you my answer, you should know that I'm in the army."

"Oh really? Are you stationed at Ellington Field?"

"No. Grafenwöhr, Germany."

"Germany?" Her brow rose in surprise then slowly fell. "Oh, that's a long way from Texas."

"Yes, it is."

Why are you here? That was probably her next question, and he didn't want to get into it. Sure, he could just say that he was visiting his father and leave it at that, but she'd made a point of asking for honesty, and once again, he didn't want to lie to her. This was his fault. He should have kept the conversation strictly on food.

Disappointment wove in with the tension ready to spring up inside of him. Collin drank from his glass, waiting for the dreaded question.

Nicole stared at him with an expectant expression.

"You want the answer to the impromptu meal question?" Baffled that she wasn't going to pry into why he was in Texas, his own question had slipped out.

"Impromptu meal and army as part of the answer? Did you really think I was just going to let that go?"

Relief and surprise pushed a huffed chuckle out of Collin. "No, probably not. The best impromptu meal I've made in the last six months is a chili mac MRE."

Nicole's brow furrowed with a disbelieving frown before shooting back up. "A chili mac MRE? You can't be serious. Oh my gosh, you are."

"One hundred percent. Add in some hot sauce, crush some saltines on top—perfection. Now, it's my turn. Go-to comfort food. Don't overthink it. Tell me exactly what popped into your mind when I asked the question."

"I don't have to overthink it." She offered up a delicate, nonchalant shrug. "Vanilla ice cream topped with roasted strawberry jam. It's a recent thing. Don't judge me."

He held up his hands in mock surrender. "No judgment here."

She laughed. "What about you?"

"Red beans and rice."

Nicole studied him. "So who or what got you so interested in cooking?"

Collin relaxed back in the chair. "My mom—she was a great cook. And she firmly believed I should be able to fend for myself, so she taught me." She'd also taught him how food had the power to teach, to bring people together and shape how people viewed the world. "What about you?"

"I come from a big family, so preparing meals was always a huge production. I loved being a part of it."

Jan swept in and cleared away his plate. "How was everything?"

"Delicious."

"Would you like to see the dessert menu?"

"No, I'm good." Collin took out his wallet. "I'll just take the bill, please."

"It's on the house." Nicole looked to him then the server.

"Okay, then." Jan nodded then smiled politely at Collin. "Thank you for dining with us."

Collin slipped bills from his wallet and handed them to Jan. "Thank you."

"You're welcome." Jan gave him a wide smile and walked away.

Collin looked to Nicole. "And thank you. I really enjoyed lunch."

As Nicole shrugged that same glimmer of happiness he'd spotted at the market was in her eyes. "It was the least I could do for you giving me your rosemary."

The least she could do? She had no idea what she'd actually done for him. He'd walked in feeling like crap, and she'd helped him feel better, getting him to talk about food and places he hadn't thought of in a long time.

As he looked into her eyes, the urge to tell her that almost overwhelmed him.

Collin shook off the feeling and glanced around the dining room. Except for the waitstaff, the restaurant was empty. "I should go."

Nicole followed his gaze. "And I should get back to work."

As they rose from the table, what felt like a fifty pound rucksack of reality and responsibility clawed its way back onto his shoulders.

Nicole looked at Collin, frowning as if she saw the invisible load he was carrying. She lifted her hand as if planning to reach out to him, but lowered it instead. "Bye, Collin."

As her hand fell, something that felt like hope went with it. "Bye."

Collin walked out of the restaurant. After a few short hours of being with Nicole, he was already missing her.

Chapter Seven

After Collin left, Nicole went back to the kitchen. Anticipation and the need to create flowed restlessly through her like a current on an endless loop. She'd spent almost two hours talking to Collin. Nerding out with him about food had been such a release.

But it felt like an uneven exchange. Collin hadn't been smiling when he left. As he walked out of the restaurant, it was as if she could see an invisible weight settling on him and him adjusting the weight on his shoulders to accommodate the load.

Sadness had been in his eyes at Mariana's Market the morning they met. Mr. Harris had mentioned someone called Sam. Did he have anything to do with Collin's unhappiness?

Back at her desk, Nicole used the creative energy to look through a few cookbooks in the low book-shelf behind her desk. She found another recipe that she wanted to play around with and make her own.

Her phone buzzed with a message from Ashley to her and Megan.

Nicole glanced at it. Ashley had sent a photo. From the looks of it, she'd snapped the picture lying in a hammock while taking in the view of the white sandy beach and the clear blue ocean sparkling in the sunlight.

Jealous, Megan messaged back.

Yes, please, Nicole added.

Too bad Ashley couldn't send that view special delivery.

They signed off with "I love you's" to each other.

Nicole hesitated in setting her phone back down.

But she hadn't heard from Grace yet about the flyer.

As she started to send her another text, Grace walked in. "I've got a good twenty minutes before my next meeting. Are you free to talk?"

"Yes." Nicole slid the cookbooks aside.

Grace dropped into a chair in front of the desk. "In case you were ever wondering, technology gremlins actually do exist."

"Uh-oh. What's happened?"

"We had another minor glitch with the reservation system right before we got a wave of check-ins.

But it's handled, and now I'm all yours. How did your lunch with Collin go?"

"*We* weren't having lunch. He was. I asked him to come in and give me an opinion on the entrée."

Just as Nicole was about to explain the how and why of what happened, Grace said, "I'm glad he came in to help. He could use a distraction with all he has going on with his dad."

"Is his father's name Sam?"

"Yes. Did Collin mention him?"

"No. Collin and I were both at Mariana's Market on Saturday. I overheard someone ask him how Sam was doing. Collin said he was fine, but he looked really sad."

"He and his dad are going through a hard situation."

Was that what Collin had been talking to Grace about at the table? They'd both looked so serious. Nicole wanted to dig deeper, but the empathy in Grace's expression morphed to friendly professionalism, a hint that talking about Collin was over.

"So," Grace said. "About the flyer. I checked in about it with Wiley."

Nicole's attention perked up. "And?"

"He'd love to have a long talk with the diner's management. I would, too. But from a legal angle, it's not worth pursuing. Even though we all know the diner is taking a swipe at us, since they're not mentioning the Hotel Fortune or Roja by name, it's not libelous. And then there's the optics. If there was a legal avenue, it could end up being spun around as unfair—the big, bad Fortunes going after the little guy."

"What's unfair is that we're getting used as target practice by the diner."

"I know. But we're taking a milder approach to the problem through Ellie. We conferenced her in on the call."

"What did she say?" As mayor, Ellie had been and still was instrumental in helping those long-time residents who strongly objected to changes in Rambling Rose see reason.

"She totally agrees the diner's ad campaign is underhanded. But as your sister-in-law, if she gets too involved, she could be accused of playing favorites. But she does think she can get one of the town council members to have an informal talk with the diner's management about how trashing their fellow business owners isn't a smart thing to do."

"And if they can't get through to them?"

"We'll still survive. The only reason the balcony incident is coming back to haunt us is because nothing bigger has happened in the town yet. Once that magical moment materializes, people will move on and forget about it."

Nicole sat back in the chair. "I'll be so glad when that happens. And I'll also be glad when I fill the restaurant's vacancies. It will help settle down the staff and hopefully debunk the myth that we're going under. We wouldn't be hiring new people if that were the case."

"Agreed. I already spoke to our human resources manager. She's working on setting up ads about the vacancies on major job sites. And she's taken your advice and reached out to the culinary programs in Austin and Houston. The initial conversations with them have been favorable."

"That's good news. Having knowledgeable interns working in the kitchen on a regular basis will be a big help. And I'm looking forward to mentoring upcoming chefs and helping them hone their practical skills. If more experienced chefs hadn't invested time in me, I wouldn't be here today."

"Same for me. I wouldn't be here without the Hotel Fortune's internship program."

"Or you could have been working somewhere warm and tropical with endless sunny beaches and no computer glitches, staffing shortages, malicious competitors or unfounded rumors about your employer's impending demise."

Grace laughed. "And exactly where would that be? Fairyland? Bottom line, we're going to be okay." She stood. "We just have to keep our energy focused on our own positive promo and the experience we want to create when people come here."

"People don't realize what they want until they

experience it. Once they get a taste of something that they like, they're on board..."

As Collin's comment played through Nicole's mind, possibilities rose up, along with a plan she'd sidelined a few weeks ago.

"Earth to Nicole." Grace waving her hands brought Nicole out of her thoughts. "Where'd you go just now?"

"Sorry, I didn't mean to space out, but what you just said about positive promo and creating experiences made me think of something. I know I said last month that I didn't want to preview Roja's summer menu at the fund-raising barbecue, but I'm changing my mind. It's the kind of positive promo Roja needs right now, and it's a chance to create a buzz about the menu that we can keep capitalizing on until the menu goes live on the first day of summer."

Grace nodded. "I like it. In fact, a couple of free dinners from the summer menu could be prizes in the raffle at the fund-raiser. But are you sure about doing this? The fund-raiser is right around the corner. Will you be ready by then?"

Nicole weighed the pros and cons of pushing ahead with the idea. A chance to have positive news circulating about Roja outweighed everything. After all, she'd invested every part of her life in this restaurant, and she couldn't fail. "I'll have to be."

Chapter Eight

Collin entered the house and shut the door.

Voices from the television echoing from the living room greeted him.

He'd really lost track of time talking to Nicole and didn't get a chance to finish his errands. But he'd had to come straight home. Ian had left to attend class about twenty minutes ago.

He'd mentioned in his text that he'd left Sam dozing in his recliner, but he wasn't there.

"Dad?" Collin went down the hall on the right and peeked into the bathroom on the left. Finding it empty, he checked the guest bedroom where he was sleeping, the office and then his father's room at the end.

The navy comforter on the king-size bed was wrinkled on one side, as if his father had once been sitting there. A hardcover book was on the nightstand with his father's reading glasses and bottles of prescription medication. The second oxygen concentrator sat between the bed and dark blue side chair. In the corner by the dresser were oxygen tanks available as a backup source if the electricity went out.

A quick check in the adjoining bathroom confirmed his father wasn't there, either. Collin tamped down the concern threatening to take hold in his gut.

His father wasn't an invalid or a prisoner in his own home. He could go anywhere he wanted. And he had his medical bracelet. If something went wrong, he could press the button and immediately reach out for help.

Still, Collin's pace was quicker back down the hallway as he walked toward the dining room and kitchen.

Outside, past the French doors, his father walked near the rosebushes in the backyard, watering the roses with a garden hose. A pack with a small portable oxygen concentrator was around his waist.

A strange mix of relief and agitation settled over Collin. Quelling the impulse to open the door and yell at his father for being outside alone, he paced the opposite direction. How he felt now—this was what he'd have to deal with if he moved his father to that place in Austin. Since his father wasn't bed-bound, he'd worry about the staff keeping tabs on his father or if they were needlessly sedating Sam to keep him there.

Collin released a pent-up breath. He had to convince his father that Houston was the best option. Maybe it was selfish of him, but he needed the peace of mind the Highlands would bring if his dad were there.

The money his father had paid to the loan company could have helped cover it. What had his father spent all his money on?

Agitation made him walk back and clutch the door handle, but he resisted the urge to storm outside and confront his father for answers. He didn't need a crystal ball to know how that conversation would turn out. It was better to focus on what he had to get done. And that was convincing his father that he needed the best care possible for whatever length of time he had left, no matter what the cost. And that was at the Highlands.

Collin opened one of the doors. Heat greedily consumed the cooler air and expanded into the dining room. Closing the door behind him, he walked toward his father.

"Dad," he called out. "Can you come inside a minute? There's something important we need to talk about."

His father briefly glanced at him. "In a minute. These roses are dry. They're practically shriveling. There's something wrong with the sprinkler system. I don't think I've seen it come on all week."

As his father shifted more to the right, he wrestled a bit with his balance as his cane sank into the wet ground.

Unable to just stand there and watch him struggle, Collin asked, "Why don't you let me do that?"

To his surprise, Sam handed him the hose. "Make sure you water near the fence behind the bushes, too. That's where they need it the most." He headed to the house.

His father not arguing with him about letting him help was a good sign. Maybe he was in an agreeable mood. If he was, they could get somewhere on the moving issue.

Collin sprayed water on the ground near the fence line. As he sprayed a little more over the top, the sweet floral scent of roses engulfed him. It was too much. He finished up and rolled the hose around the holder at the back of the house.

Inside the house, his father drank a glass of water in the kitchen. "What do you want to talk to me about?"

"I need to show you something on the computer." Collin poured himself a glass of water from the pitcher in the fridge. "We need to use your desktop, if you don't mind."

His father released a weary sigh. "That's fine. I hope this isn't going to take too long. I have episodes of *NCIS* to catch up on."

Minutes later, with his father settled in the desk chair, Collin pulled up the virtual tour of the Highlands. "I know you're interested in moving to that place in Austin, but Ruby called the other day about another possibility. They have a virtual tour. So why not take a look?"

He gave control of the computer mouse to his father.

Just as Collin had hoped, the modern-looking mixed-living community appeared even more impressive on a larger screen. And his father seemed interested, leaning in as he clicked the arrows and controls that gave him a 360-degree view of the grounds and accommodations.

His father ended the tour on an image of an impressive aerial shot of the community.

Sam sat back in the chair. "It looks like a really nice place."

"They have three vacancies. All we have to do is put down a deposit, and you'll be able to move in before the end of the month."

"I see. Well, tell Ruby I appreciate her looking into it, but I've already got a room waiting for me in Austin."

"But you just said the Highlands is a nice place. Wouldn't you rather be there? It has lots of amenities. It's even close to a driving range, and you're more familiar with Houston."

"I'm fine with what I got. It's not like I'll be there for years."

"How long you'll be there doesn't matter. It's about you living in a comfortable place."

Sam scooted the chair away from the desk, forcing Collin to step back as he planted his cane and stood. "I'm comfortable with Austin."

"But I'm not. You don't belong there."

"This isn't about you. It's about me and what I want."

"Is it? Or is it about the money?"

His father gave him a hard stare. "This conversation is over." He walked around the desk, heading for the door.

Collin gripped the back of the chair his father had vacated. Without the truth, this discussion wasn't over. "I went to the bank this morning and took a look at your accounts."

With his back to Collin, his father paused. As he stared at the ground, his shoulders sank. "You shouldn't have done that."

"Dad, it's okay." Collin walked toward him. "I know—"

"No!" His father banged his cane on the ground. "You don't know." Sam almost lost his balance as he turned to face Collin. Anger snapped in his eyes. "You don't know because it's my business, not yours. Who gave you permission to go through my finances?"

"You did. You gave me a power of attorney to handle your affairs."

"Handling my affairs doesn't include you sticking your nose into places you shouldn't."

Frustration poured out of Collin. "Dad, I'm trying to help. I want to help. But all I keep getting from you is pushback. Why?"

"Because I don't want your help."

"You may not want my help, but you need it. And you being stubborn won't change that."

His father opened his mouth to speak but then snapped it shut. As he pressed his lips together in a thin line, his breathing grew heavier and his hand quivered on his cane.

Collin released a harsh exhale. The two of them barking at each other in anger. His father straining himself by getting upset. That's what he'd hoped to avoid during this conversation.

He modulated his voice. "You don't have to go to the Highlands if you don't want to. But you don't have to go to Austin, either. The deposit you gave them—it's not too late to get it back. We can make arrangements for you to stay here with a live-in companion, and Ruby can set up private nursing and doctor visits."

"Enough." Sam threw up his hand, halting the conversation. "I'm done talking about it. You say you want to help me? Then sell this house, pack up my things and move me to my room in Austin." He turned and hobbled toward the door. "And get the damn backyard sprinklers fixed."

The next morning, Collin jogged down the street toward the weak watery light of the sun creeping up on the darkened predawn sky. Hard-earned sweat clung to him under his gray tank and loose running shorts. His steady footfalls echoing in the silence counted down his final ten-minute mile. No music came through the buds in his ears that were synced to his phone tucked into an armband. But his heartbeat drummed in his ears. Energy, strength, power, accomplishment—they clicked together in perfect unity.

As he rounded the corner, his legs burned, reminding him of just how human he was. As much as he might like to keep running, he couldn't. He had to go home and face his father and spin the wheel of Sam's moods. Which one would it land on today? Frustrated? Stubborn? Unreasonable? Dissatisfied? Noncommunicative?

Yesterday, after their argument, his father had stayed in his room the rest of the day, bullheaded enough to starve versus joining Collin at the dinner table.

He'd taken a tray of food to his father. As he'd set it on the bedside table, Sam, sitting in the side chair, had acknowledged him with a peering-over-the-top-of-his-glasses stare and refused to talk to him.

The iciness growing between him and his father wasn't doing either of them any good. It was just heaping on resentment. Something that shouldn't exist between them, especially not now. As much as he hated doing what his father was asking, maybe he should just sell the house, drop him off in Austin with his things and stay out of his business. Well, as much as he could.

With his father's situation, it didn't matter where he moved or if he stayed in the house monitored by private care. He'd still need financial assistance to maintain it. But he wasn't telling his father that. Sam might decide to live under a rock just so he could avoid getting help from him.

Frustration washed over Collin, and his legs felt even heavier. The desire to quit started creeping in.

No. He needed to focus on something to distract himself. Or someone.

He let his mind wander to being with Nicole the day before at Roja. She'd been able to get him out of his head. He couldn't remember the last time someone had been able to take him from pissed off to smiling even laughing in under a couple of hours. How had she done it?

"Tell me everything. I want details..."

That's what she'd said to him. What if he could tell her everything about his father, and what lay ahead in the future? Would talking to her make it easier? Or would she pity him?

No. Her feeling sorry for him would actually make things worse. But that wasn't a problem he would face. Going to Roja for another meal wasn't happening anytime soon, possibly not at all, since he didn't have a reason to drive to that side of town. And even if he did go back to Roja, there was no reason for her to take time out of her busy day to sit down and talk to him again.

Near the final stretch, Collin's smart watch beeped. He was almost at the end. But if he wanted to finish his run in the next four minutes and stay on track with the pace he'd set for himself, he had move it.

Collin picked up speed. As he lengthened his strides, the sky grew brighter and streetlamps lighting his way home flickered off.

People slowly ventured out from brick homes built in the '80s to bring trash bins to the curb or to get into their cars, most likely heading for work.

He blocked it all out, including the discomfort of his heavy legs and feeling as if his heart was suddenly taking up too much room in his chest, and finished strong.

Done with his run, he paced the driveway, sucking in the air his lungs demanded. It was already laden with warmth, an indicator of just how high the temperature would soar in a few hours.

He'd made it. Once again, Nicole had managed to get him out of his head. What would she say if she knew she'd just helped him finish a tough couple of miles?

Seriously? You're losing it. If you told her that, she'd probably walk away and never talk to you again. Stop thinking about her and get to work.

Still, a smile he couldn't stop came over his face.

Inside the house, he showered, skipped a shave and dressed for the day—a T-shirt and a pair of shorts. He wasn't going anywhere. A call with the Realtor that was helping him sell the house and finding a moving company were at the top of the to-do list.

As he scrambled eggs for himself and his father, his phone chimed with a call. He ran through a mental list of who might call him this early. When he looked at the number on the screen, it wasn't any of them, but the number looked familiar.

He answered. "Hello."

"Hi, Collin. It's Nicole Fortune. I hope I didn't wake you up."

Wow. He'd just told himself to stop thinking about her, and now she was calling him. What were the odds of that happening?

The same smile he'd failed to stop in the driveway returned to his face. "Nope. I've been up for a while."

"Up at dawn, guess that's a military thing? What

am I saying? Lots of people wake up early. I'm up right now, too."

A flashback to Nicole at Mariana's Market rambling on about squash came to mind. She'd been nervous then, but she'd just met him. They'd had a long conversation yesterday, and she hadn't been tense around him. What could she be nervous about now?

As Nicole released a quiet laugh, it prompted the remembered image of her smoothing hair from her forehead. "In case you're wondering, I got your number from Grace. I hope you don't mind."

"Not at all." The smile in her voice created a vision of her face, and he smiled even wider as he divided eggs between two plates sitting on the counter with strawberries and grapes and forks already on them.

"Is that a skillet I hear in the background?"

"Yep. I made scrambled eggs."

"Cooked in butter with a little salt and pepper?"

"That's the only way to make them."

Mirroring back what she'd said to him about fresh pasta being the only way to make rosemary chicken gave him what he wanted—she laughed.

Warmth filled his chest, and tingles raised on his skin.

"I guess I should get to the point of why I called."

A reason for the call. He'd forgotten there should be one.

As Collin turned off the stove, Sam's footsteps filtered in from the dining room.

"Hold on a sec," Collin said to Nicole. He put his phone on mute.

A moment later, his father came into the kitchen dressed and ready for the day in his tennis shoes. His sour expression hadn't changed from last night, but based on the bags under his eyes, his father hadn't rested well. Which was unusual. Pain meds usually knocked him out.

He handed his dad a plate of food.

His father took it from him then walked back out of the kitchen.

A moment later the television came on.

Well, that answered his question about the mood of the day. Irritated and stubborn with no end in sight. Collin lowered his head and released a quiet sigh. The frustration he'd lost during his run now waited at the periphery.

Unmuting his phone felt like a lifeline. "Sorry about that. You were saying?"

"I was wondering if you're free for lunch today."

Meeting with the Realtor, hiring a moving company, finding out what was wrong with the sprinklers, he really needed to get on all of that today. But seeing Nicole again…the prospect of that kind of outweighed everything on the list. What about her? Did she just want to see him or was there another reason?

Collin picked up his mug of coffee and leaned back against the counter. "So…are we trying a new recipe?"

"Well, now that you mention it, trying out a new recipe wouldn't be a bad idea. Would you mind?"

Mind? As he released a breath, frustration moved from his periphery into his rearview. "As long as you're having lunch with me, I don't mind at all."

Collin, pretending the work of coffee and leaned
back against the wash of ... ... me with any issues
further ...

"Well, now that you promised it's true, on a few
more you will, it's a bad idea? Would you mind?"

"And A.J. he cussed at you?" Ian angrily moved
Copp, the part, her, into his reserves. "As long as
you're buying breakfast with me, I don't mind at all."

Ian ... the ... ... he said ... ... the ...
the ... ... back out of course ... ... went ...
Past ... ... the before ...

... ... and it ... ... the ... ...
directly ... he ... ...
learn it that much of the game ... ... It's her

Chapter Nine

Walking into Roja later that morning, Collin reflected on how leaving the house had already ac-
complished two things. His day had already taken a
turn for the better, and before he'd walked out of the
house, his father had broken his silence to ask him
where he was going and when he was coming back.

Ian wasn't scheduled to visit his father and he
was also in class, but Ruby had been happy to arrange for a home health aide to stay at the house
for as long as needed. His dad hadn't been thrilled
about that and had insisted he didn't need anyone
there. But with his father's current disposition in
play, Collin didn't trust him not to spend too much

time in the sun messing with the roses, or worse, digging around in the grass trying to fix the sprinkler system.

The same dark-haired hostess from the day before sat Collin at the corner table he'd been at yesterday. She smiled. "I'll let Nicole know you're here."

Like yesterday, the dining room was less than half full. Most likely, the restaurant was busy during the noon rush and at dinner. This was probably just the calm between the storms.

A server left two glasses of water at the table.

Shortly after, Nicole emerged from the archway leading from the back of the house, expertly carrying two plates of food in one hand and four smaller plates stacked in the other.

She set everything on the table. "Lemon rosemary chicken *with* a hint of thyme. I want you to taste it and see if I got it right. And as a thank-you, I'm including chili-dusted shrimp over a corn relish."

Enjoyment in seeing her made his heart kick in an extra beat. Like yesterday, she wore dark-colored Crocs and black pants, but this time her chambray chef's coat had black side panels that dipped into her slim waist. And her hair was tucked under a black chef's hat, bringing all the attention to her face and luminous blue eyes.

Suddenly he was glad that he made a little bit

of an effort and put on a navy button-down shirt with his jeans.

Nicole sat across from him and doled out empty plates. "I hope you don't mind if we share this."

"Not at all." He unrolled his silverware and laid the napkin across his lap.

Nicole did the same.

He took some of the lemon rosemary chicken and put it on his plate while she went for the shrimp. But she paused in taking a bite, waiting for him to taste his first.

The savoriness of the rosemary, lemon and garlic was still present but with a gentle layering of what he knew was also there—thyme. To the untrained palate, the blend of flavors would just make them want more.

"You nailed it."

"Yes." She gave a small fist pump and smiled widely at him. "Thank you."

Too tempting to pass up, he put some shrimp on a second empty plate and squeezed a lime wedge over it. He took a bite of shrimp, and spice, tangy and sweet awakened his taste buds.

He polished off another shrimp. "Are you going to keep me in suspense or tell me why I'm being treated to another great lunch?"

Nicole set down her fork. "Like I mentioned yesterday, I'm testing recipes for Roja's summer menu. But I need to step things up to get it done. I want to introduce some of the entrées at the Give Back barbecue. It's a fund-raiser my family is sponsoring the weekend after next. I was wondering if you'd consider helping me test recipes and develop the menu. Maybe a few hours a day or every other day? I wouldn't be able to pay you much. And for legal reasons, I'd have to bring you on as an intern."

So this wasn't just a friendly lunch, but he probably should have suspected it. "You wouldn't be able to pay me at all. I'm an officer in the army. I can't have a second job. And even if I could, I don't need one."

"Maybe you don't need a job, but what about an outlet? With what's going on, wouldn't doing something you enjoy help?"

With what he had going on? What did she mean by that? Was she referring to his father being ill? He hadn't mentioned that to her…but someone they both knew probably did. So much for confidentiality in friendship. "What did Grace tell you?"

"About?"

"My father."

"She just mentioned that he isn't well. But I kind of already knew that. I heard Mr. Harris ask about him." She offered up a small shrug. "And I saw your face when you answered."

He'd been that transparent? She probably viewed him as a charity case. Disappointment dulled his appetite, and he put down his fork. "So you feel sorry for me."

"Am I sorry your father's sick? Of course I am. Any feeling person would be."

She was right. And he was being extra touchy. That was actually one of the symptoms of caregiver's stress that was in the article he'd read. Maybe the situation with his father was starting to get to him more than he realized.

Collin released a long breath. "My father is more than just sick. He's terminal. I'm here to help him move to…" He couldn't bring himself to say *Austin*. "To a place where he'll receive care for the time he has left."

In a compassionate gesture, Nicole reached toward him and laid her hand on the table. "I can't imagine what you're going through."

"I definitely wouldn't recommend it."

His hand itched with the impulse to take her hand in his and unburden himself of the difficulties he faced with Sam.

Collin drank from his glass as he squared his thoughts away. *You have a lot going on…*

But helping her wasn't totally out of the question. And he could volunteer to do it. In a way, it would be like one of the cooking intensives he'd attended. And he'd never planned a restaurant menu. It would actually be an interesting challenge.

Yeah, right. Who are you kidding? You like her…

As Collin set down his glass, he let reality sit inside of him. Spending time with Nicole and getting to know her was the true bonus. Not that it could go anywhere. It would just be a basic exchange. She would keep him from getting too far into his head over the situation with his dad. He'd help her develop the menu. So there really wasn't a reason for him not to help Nicole. But still…

He set down his glass. "I'm sure you have plenty of qualified applicants to choose from. Why do you need me?"

Nicole slid her hand back. It was a legitimate question that deserved an answer. She toyed with her water glass, debating how to explain.

"We're still in the beginning stages. Roja has only been open officially a few months. I've been busy with service, training the staff…"

And she was hedging around the truth. But how could she explain what she hadn't told anyone, not even Megan and Ashley?

That morning, Megan had called to ask a question about one of Roja's invoices. Megan had also mentioned the diner's smear campaign—she'd heard about it from someone at Provisions—and had asked how she was doing.

Nicole had mentioned the plan of introducing the summer menu at the barbecue but skipped over her lack of inspiration. And how her anxiety over it had awakened her hours before dawn.

Remnants of anxiety stirred in Nicole now. But how could she expect Megan, who worked with numbers and facts, to relate to her lack of creativity? Especially when she wasn't quite sure she understood it herself?

Nicole released a breath and the words that came with it. "I'm creatively blocked. Every time I sit down to work on the summer menu, nothing feels right, and then I just get anxious about it. It's become a vicious cycle. But when I spoke with you at Mariana's about making lemon rosemary chicken, I felt excited about the recipe and the menu. And sitting here yesterday with you, just talking about food, gave me another boost and I came up with the shrimp recipe."

Collin crossed his arms over his chest, and muscles formed under the front of his shirt. "If you're trying to use me as your good-luck charm, it's the wrong approach. It's better if you just accept that you're working hard to get the restaurant off the ground. That takes a lot of energy. It's not surprising that your creative spark isn't there. It's temporary. Like my assistance will be if I agree to help."

He hadn't shut her down completely, so maybe she still had a chance. "I don't see you as a good-luck charm, but I think you'd be a great sounding board to bounce ideas off. And I know your help would be temporary, but it would also be a boost to get me over the finish line and get the menu done in time for the barbecue. That's what I need right now. That and the chance this new menu will give me to shut down the naysayers."

"Naysayers? What are people saying?"

Sharing her problems with a guy she barely knew wasn't something she'd done before. But Collin didn't feel like a stranger. When they talked about food, she didn't feel self-conscious. Or that she was boring him by being such a food nerd. And something told her a collaboration with him was what she needed. So telling him everything was worth the risk.

Nicole took her phone from her side pocket, pulled up the photo of the flyer, then handed him her phone.

As he used his fingers to widen the photo for a closer look at the wording, a "what the hell?" expression came over his face. He released a heavy breath and gave her the phone back. "That's way out of line."

"Unfortunately, it seems to be working…" Needing to confess her concerns to a neutral party, she told him about losing staff, the bus tour business choosing the diner over Roja and the rumbles about the hotel and restaurant being a sinking ship.

And what the tiny voice in her head wouldn't shut up about—one of her greatest fears. "I can't maintain a high standard of quality if my entire staff leaves."

"Your entire staff won't walk out. Deep down

you have to know that. Sure, you'll lose people who are easily stirred up by rumors and assumptions. But those are usually the ones who are just looking for an excuse to leave. The ones who value having a job and don't mind hard work are the ones you want. Rambling Rose is a small town. From my experience, once the next new thing pops up on the radar, they'll move on from Roja to something else."

Feeling lighter already after talking to him about her problem, her exhale fueled a quiet laugh. "The next new thing popping up. That's what Grace said. So what about my proposition? Will you consider being my *unpaid* intern and work with me on the menu?"

"No."

Her heart sank. "Oh."

"At least I won't until we clear something up."

How much more transparent did she need to be? "What?"

"How do you know I can cook?"

That was an easy question. "Instinct. When it comes to food and people, I'm never wrong."

Collin chuckled. "Nope. Not buying it. You wouldn't just snag a random stranger off the street and give them a uniform and a chef's knife because you had a good feeling about them. At least that's how it will go down with your staff if you just drop me in your kitchen."

He had a point. But she had a solution. She stood.

"Then let's eliminate that as a potential problem. Cook for me, right now. Your choice of one of the two dishes on the table."

Collin rose from the chair. A confident smile hitched up his mouth. "Sounds fair. But I don't have to choose. I'm making both."

In her office, she gave him a black cook's skull-cap and an apron. After he put them on, she handed him a chef's knife from one of her own personal sets. It was perfectly balanced and able to create masterpieces in the right hands.

She got him situated in the general prep area, out of the way of her staff. But curious about what was going on, Mariana, the cooks and the kitchen helper kept glancing in his direction as he got to work.

Nicole stood in her office and watched him through the window.

Lesly, one of the many who'd been drawn to what was happening, wandered into the office, most likely on a scouting mission. The staff undoubtedly had questions.

"Is he going to be working with us?" Lesly asked.

"We'll see." Things were definitely looking good so far.

After gathering the ingredients he needed, Collin peeled, chopped, diced. His economical movements showcased his skill…and his flexing biceps.

Not that she was fixated on that. She was observing his cooking technique. And he definitely had it…hands down.

Collin picked up a mango. As he ran his palm over it, Nicole's skin tingled.

When he finished with the mango, he went on to the next steps, folding in ingredients, drizzling juices and pinching in spices.

Sometimes his touch was gentle, barely handling the ingredients. At other times, he was all about control, picking up the pace and slowing down at just the right times. He treated the ingredients lovingly, respectfully and with attention to detail.

To be a fruit or vegetable in his hands… As Nicole thought about how it would feel to be caressed by him, she swallowed against the sudden dryness in her throat.

He slid a lemon rosemary chicken breast from a pan onto a perfect mound of pasta.

As he rested a slice of lemon on top, a sigh slipped from her lips. He was definitely a keeper… as a temporary intern, working at Roja.

Nicole wiped produce fantasies from her mind and walked out to the table where he waited with both of his plated entrées.

Collin handed her a fork.

Would they taste just as wonderful as they looked?

Nicole took a bite of corn relish from under the shrimp, and a mix of sweet flavors filled her mouth.

He'd gone one step further and added bits of mango. She loved mango.

She tasted his version of the rosemary chicken and barely contained a moan of pleasure as the perfect balance of flavors floated over her tongue.

A confident sexy smile that shouldn't have been allowed near a flame for fear of setting something on fire came over Collin's gorgeous face. "So… did I pass?"

Chapter Ten

Nicole unwrapped the fresh flank steak and laid it on a cutting board on the table.

Once it was cooked, she'd combine it with a variety of fresh mushrooms, sliced poblano peppers, warm spices and toppings and serve it in a soft corn tortilla. She could already taste the goodness. It had been Collin's idea to use a mix of mushrooms instead of just one kind.

She glanced over at him working on a recipe for vegetarian patties at the opposite end of the long table. He was dressed in Roja's standard kitchen uniform of a chambray chef's coat and black pants, along with a black chef's skullcap that fit close to his head.

He'd worked well with the staff over the past seven days, sharing advice as well as learning from the other cooks, lending a hand when needed and not just helping her work on recipes. The first time he'd helped out the staff, that moment had bonded him to them for life.

And they seemed to follow his lead when it came to professionalism. The cooks were more focused with their time, and their uniforms at the start of shift were as crisp-looking as Collin's.

The other day, when Megan had popped in for a moment to say hello, she'd also noticed the changes in the staff and had even joked about borrowing him for a few days to get the workers at Provisions in shape.

Nicole smiled to herself. Her answer to that request, joking or not, had been a definite no. Collin hadn't just been good for the staff. He'd brought out the best in her, too.

At times, during a rush, it would feel as if she was operating in a frenzied haze, but he'd walk in at twelve thirty sharp, and like the addition of a much-needed lens, her day would snap back into focus.

"Let's go through it one step at a time..."

That's what he'd always say when they analyzed a recipe, trying to determine what was right or wrong about it.

Collin snagged a skillet from the shelf, started to walk away, then went back for a second one.

He put both on the stove. One was for him and the other was for her.

Anticipation of what was needed—they'd fallen in sync that way the first moment they'd cooked together, but him doubling back because he'd forgotten something, that was the first time he'd ever done that.

In fact, today, Collin seemed slightly off his game...preoccupied. Earlier, he'd even gotten irritated over not finding the cooking oil. After she'd pointed it out to him, he'd seemed even more annoyed at himself for not seeing it.

Collin took the patties he'd shaped to the stove.

Wait...wasn't he supposed to add fresh cilantro to the bean mixture? Was he changing the recipe? Usually he mentioned something like that ahead of time.

On a hunch, Nicole stripped off her disposable gloves, picked up a stem of cilantro and joined him at the stove. "Did you change your mind about adding this to the patties?"

Frowning at the cilantro, Collin shook his head. "No, I didn't change my mind. I forgot. Good catch. Thanks."

While she moved on to cooking the flank steak, he dumped the patties into a clean bowl and chopped cilantro to add to the mixture.

Collin's behavior was more than just a little strange. Had something happened with his father?

He never talked about what was going on. But she'd made it clear from the start that if he had to leave early or not come in to help at all, she completely understood. His dad came first.

They finished prepping the entrées, and like they'd done since starting the testing, they shared what they made with the staff in exchange for them filling out a brief comment form.

Later on, they sat at what had become their table by the window in Roja's dining room. They went over the comments about the entrées from the staff and shared their own impressions about the dishes.

A few customers remained from the lunch crowd on the other side of the space, but they were far enough not to disturb them.

Nicole sorted through the forms. "The consensus on the patties seems to be the same. They were good but they need more salt."

Collin rubbed the back of his neck. "Actually, I think I forgot to add it. I can swing by tomorrow and make them again. That way we'll know the recipe will be good for the tasting with your family."

That coming Sunday at Roja, a few of her family members were participating in a tasting of the completed summer menu to help decide which items she should feature at the barbecue. It was a last-minute thing, and everyone was still sorting out their schedules to see if they could come. Lately, connecting with her family had consisted of brief phone calls and text messages, mainly with Megan and Ashley. It would be nice to catch up with everyone and get their opinions about the menu.

"I can do it. Don't you have something to do tomorrow with your dad?"

"Yes. I have to take him in for a physical. It's one of the requirements for him to move into where he's going." Collin's jawline ticked as he muttered under his breath. "If I had a choice, we wouldn't be doing it."

Nicole stopped making notes on her phone. "I thought getting your father moved out of the house was a top priority."

"It is, but…" As he released a breath, a bleakness she'd never spotted in him reflected in his eyes.

"But what? What's going on?"

"Nothing." Collin shook his head. "Sorry. I didn't mean to bring my problems with me into the kitchen today."

"It's okay. You're human."

"Doesn't matter. It's unprofessional."

Nicole failed to suppress an eye roll. "It does matter that you're human, and emotions are real."

Collin gave her a side-eyed look.

"It might help to talk about it."

A server passed by, and his mouth snapped shut.

Nicole moved her chair closer to him for a little more privacy. "You can tell me as much or as little

as you want. If you don't want opinions on anything, I'll just sit here and listen."

Collin studied her a long moment. He raised and
dropped his hands. "I don't like the place my father is moving into. If he was at the stage where he
spent all day in bed, maybe I could see it, but even
then, I wouldn't be okay with him moving there. It
looks like a place where people go to…"

Die. The word landed in Nicole's thoughts, a
single drop all on its own without a frame of ref-
erence to group it in. Sure, she'd lost people in her
life, but she couldn't imagine losing one of her parents. Of course it had to happen. But someday far
in the future, not now.

Nicole quelled the instinct to rest her hand on his
arm. She'd said she'd allow him to talk. He wouldn't
appreciate her using the moment to coddle him.
"Is there someplace else that he could go that you
do like?"

"Definitely. It's in Houston. But he's refusing to
go there. Hold on a minute, I'll show you." Collin
picked up his phone from the table and tapped the
screen. He scooted over, and as he pulled up the
site, his knee rested lightly against hers.

Hints of something clean-smelling and wonderful wafted from him. He'd only been in the kitchen
a few hours. His clothes hadn't absorbed a half day's
worth of food odors.

Hers had. The bacon she'd cooked that morning. The onions she'd chopped and the flank steak tacos she'd just made. The combination might have worked well for food but wasn't a great smell for people. In a self-conscious gesture, she leaned slightly away from him, but he leaned closer to show her his phone.

As Nicole breathed more of him in, she couldn't stop her gaze from wandering to the top buttons of his chef's jacket that were unfastened. He wore a snug black T-shirt underneath his jacket today. She'd been treated to the full appealing view when he'd walked down the outer aisle of the kitchen to the staff locker room, carrying his chef's jacket on a hanger.

Most of the women waitstaff paused to stare at him when he walked in each afternoon. She really couldn't fault them for doing it. Sometimes, she did, too. But she couldn't let herself dwell on how good he looked. She'd learned that the first day they'd started working together. When her mind had wandered that direction, she'd kept dropping things.

"This is the Highlands in Houston," Collin said, flipping through a series of pictures showing manicured outdoor areas and modern, state-of-the-art apartments and accommodations. It was easy to understand why the people in the photos were smiling and why Collin would want his dad there.

"That does look like a really nice place. Is there a reason why he doesn't want to be there?"

"Money." Collin paused. "My father's finances are in bad shape. I don't understand how he lost all his money, and he doesn't want to discuss it, and that's fine. I don't care. I'll pay for him to go to Houston. At some point, I'm probably going to have to help pay for him to be at the place in Austin. I just don't want him to end up in a place where he doesn't belong." He swiped the site closed on his phone and dropped it on the table. "Sometimes, I wonder if he's actually trying to spite me by going there."

"Or he might feel that's where he deserves to go." Nicole searched for the words to explain. "Place yourself in his shoes. He has to accept your financial help. If he's anything like my parents, that may feel wrong to him. Especially if he's holding on to the belief that parents should take care of their children. He might also feel ashamed about it."

"So you think he's not punishing me, he's punishing himself. That makes sense." Collin gave a nod. "But if that's true, he'll never admit it."

Nicole wrestled again with what to say. In her family, they all had their stubborn moments, times where they wouldn't budge because of their opinions. How had they gotten through it?

The answer formed in her mind. "Your father doesn't have to admit it. But you have to leave room for that understanding."

"So I should just let him have his way and not do anything about it?"

"That's not what I'm saying." Nicole laid her hand on his forearm and solid strength met her palm.

Collin had the physical ability to fix what was broken. As an officer, he had the authority to give orders, but he couldn't fix the situation with his dad or order his father to change his mind. And that's what she'd guess was irritating him the most.

"What I'm saying is, all that frustration you're feeling, right now—channel it into what you can do. Keep talking to him. Don't give up on him."

"That's a big ask."

"But I know you can do it."

"You do? How?"

As he looked deeply into her eyes, Nicole's heart thumped an extra beat. "Because you haven't given me a reason to believe you can't."

Did she really believe in him? Collin searched Nicole's face, looking for hints of pity or that she was just telling him that in an attempt to make him feel better.

But as his gaze roamed over her face, all he saw was truth. It was in the slight raise of her brow and the light in her eyes. It was in the curve of her cheeks, and the hint of a reassuring smile lifting up the corners of her mouth.

The realization that she meant it along with her hand resting on his arm, and how close they were to each other hit him at once. Just hearing her voice, let alone being near her, knocked his frustration from high to basement level. And amped up what he'd been fighting since they'd started working together. His attraction to her.

So far he'd managed it by keeping his head in the game and minimizing contact, but this was the first time she'd really touched him. All he wanted to do was lay his hand on hers and feel more of her warmth seeping into him.

"Excuse me." Mariana stood beside the table.

Nicole took her hand away and he leaned further back in the chair.

"I'm sorry to bother you guys," Mariana said. "But I just sent the kitchen helper home. He wasn't feeling well. Now we're behind on dinner prep. I have an appointment, but I could try and cancel it."

"No." Nicole stood. "You've been here all day. You should go. I'll handle it. What's left on the prep list?"

"I just put the prime rib in the oven. And one of the cooks has started on the baked potatoes. A couple of the side dishes aren't done. And we ran out of *calabaza con pollo* at lunch. It's one of tonight's specials."

Collin stood, buttoning his jacket. "I can handle the *calabaza con pollo*."

Nicole looked his direction. "But don't you have to leave?"

He'd planned on going by the hardware store to pick up paint, but that could wait. He couldn't leave Nicole in a jam. "I've got time and can knock out the vegetable patties recipe while I'm at it."

In the kitchen, they went their separate ways and Collin got to work on both dishes. Instead of making the *calabaza con pollo* in a skillet, he had to start baking the chicken in the oven and cook the vegetable mixture in a stockpot on the stove. He'd combine everything in the pan just before the chicken was done.

He followed Roja's recipe for the vegetables, but just like when he'd made it a little over a week ago, something was off. More salt or pepper? Garlic, maybe? What was missing?

Nicole walked to the nearby rack with all of the dry goods for that day's meal prep. "Where's the cumin?"

As soon as she said it, the flavor profile for the spice popped into his mind. Curiosity and inspiration came with it as he picked up the container. "I've got it." He'd been using it for the vegetable patties.

"Can I use it?"

"Sure."

Nicole walked over to him. Puzzled, she stared up at him when he didn't hand it over. "Is something wrong?"

"No, just the opposite. Hold on a minute." He

took the cumin to the stockpot on the stove and stirred some into the bubbling mixture.

Nicole joined him. "I don't remember cumin being in the *calabaza con pollo* recipe."

"It should be." He snagged two plastic spoons from a box on the counter. Confident in his decision, he spooned some out and held it near her lips. "Taste it."

As she blew over the hot food on the spoon, the cooling air from her mouth blew over his fingers.

Leaning in, she carefully consumed the bite. Nicole released a low sound of approval and his own mouth watered, imagining what she tasted in the cumin. She smiled up at him. "You were right."

He knew he was. The spice was warm, earthy, spicy and a bit peppery in a way that brought excitement. Just like her.

A small drop of the tomato-based liquid sat on the corner of her mouth. Before Collin could stop himself, his hand was there, and the pad of his thumb was swiping across her bottom lip to wipe it away.

Her mouth parted slightly. Surprise, wonder and something that made his gut tighten with oncoming need was in her eyes.

A pot banging to the floor made them both jump.

And brought Collin back to reality. "So, I think I'm done." He held out the cumin.

Nicole took the container and almost dropped it. "Thanks." She hurried away.

Collin forced a long exhale. Willing his heart to stop thundering in his chest. Touching her like that. What had he been thinking?

The answer bubbled up along with the vegetables simmering in the pot. He knew full well what had been in the back of his mind. He'd wanted to kiss her.

Chapter Eleven

Nicole sat on the blue couch in the living room in her suite at the Fame and Fortune Ranch, ready to enjoy her late night dinner. A grilled cheddar cheese and triple berry jalapeño jam sandwich and a glass of chardonnay.

It wasn't the most exciting way to spend a Friday night. But after a busy week at the restaurant and finalizing the menu for that Sunday's menu tasting with her family, lounging around the house in her favorite purple-and-gray sweatpants and a tank top was excitement enough.

As she crossed her legs under her and settled back into the sumptuous cushions, her mouth watered. She hadn't eaten a meal all day—only small bites and tastes of entrées and side dishes, making sure they were up to par for service. When she got home, she could have gone full-blown chef on a three-course meal, but at almost eleven at night, that was way too complicated.

Nicole took a bite and the sharpness of the cheese blending with sweet spiciness prompted a moan of contentment. This was exactly what she'd wanted. But it was weird not to have made it with her sisters.

In the past, she, Ashley and Megan had usually tag teamed their cooking efforts in the ranch's large kitchen. Ashley had always handled prep, Nicole cooked and Megan took care of what she did best—filling their wineglasses. Once the meal was done, they'd always gone to their spot—the huge couch in the living room adjoining the kitchen—and chatted about anything and everything as they ate.

A pang of loneliness hit as Nicole took another bite of sandwich. It was still good but suddenly not as satisfying. She picked up her glass of wine from the side table and took a long sip, temporarily numbing the feeling of missing them so much.

As if on cue, her phone buzzed on the wood coffee table in front of her. Megan's face and number flashed on the screen.

Nicole answered. "Hey."

"Hi." The sound of rapid strokes on a computer keyboard filtered in on Megan's end.

"Are you still at work?"

"I'm at Mark's, but I'm weeding through last month's budget reports."

The budget. Ugh. Roja's didn't look that great. But it wasn't bad enough for Megan to call her this late. "I'm surprised Mark hasn't dragged you away." Nicole took a bite of her sandwich.

"He says I have until midnight. If I'm not done by then, he's coming to get me. Oh, before I forget. We can make it to the menu tasting Sunday night."

"Good. That makes six."

"Who else is coming?"

Nicole filled her in. Their brother Steven and his wife, Ellie, and their other brother Dillon and his fiancée, Hailey, had already confirmed they would be there. Callum and Becky couldn't make it.

"I wish Callum and Becky could be there," Megan said. "And Ashley and Rodrigo."

"I do, too." Giving into hunger, Nicole nibbled on her sandwich.

"What are you eating? Hold on. It's Ashley. She's trying to FaceTime me. You want in?"

"Of course I do."

"Okay. Hang up."

The call ended, and less than a minute later, a group call rang in. Nicole answered and two smiling faces identical to her own appeared on screen. "Hi."

"Hi… Hey," her sisters replied in unison.

"Look at you, little Miss Beach Bandit. Don't

you look cute," Megan said, referring to Ashley who had a light, glowing tan, and wore a cute woven hat and what looked to be a lime-green bikini top. It was daylight where she was.

"Thanks. And it's Mrs. Beach Bandit." Ashley beamed a smile as she wiggled the fingers on her left hand, showing off her wedding ring.

"Where's Mr. Beach Bandit?" Megan said.

"Checking on a snorkeling tour we want to take. It's the perfect day for it. Check out this view." Ashley flipped the camera around, showing them a stunning beach.

"It's so beautiful," Nicole said. "Are you completely bummed about leaving Fiji this weekend for the conference in Vegas?"

"It'll definitely be a change in scenery." Ashley grinned. "But a few visits to the casino could make up for it."

As Megan joined Nicole in coveting Ashley's beach view and upcoming trip to Nevada, Nicole took more bites from her sandwich.

"What are you eating?" Megan asked. "You never told me."

"Eating? I'm not eating anything," Ashley replied.

"No, not you. Nicole."

Two pairs of eyes peered at Nicole as she swallowed. "A grilled cheese and triple berry jalapeño jam sandwich."

"Lou's got a new jam flavor?" Megan asked. "How come you didn't tell?"

"Or share it with us," Ashley piped in. "Or were you holding out because Megan ate all of the roasted strawberry the last time you bought some?"

"You're blaming me?" Megan's mouth dropped open with a shocked look. "I wasn't the one eating it straight out of the jar."

"Well…" Ashley smiled with a sheepish look. "Now that you mention it, that was me. But I had legit reasons. I was a stressed bride-to-be."

"Seriously?" Nicole and Megan groaned at the same time then all three of them laughed.

"Don't worry." Nicole put the saucer with the rest of her sandwich on the side table. "I'll pick up jam for all of us. I still have jars of roasted strawberry for each of you. I keep forgetting to bring Megan's with me to Roja."

"Well, considering who's in the kitchen, I'm not surprised that you're distracted," Megan said.

Nicole took in her knowing look and paused in sipping wine. "Wait. You don't mean Collin."

"Who's Collin?" Ashley said. "I leave for a few weeks and I miss everything."

The memory of Collin feeding her a bite of the vegetables from the steaming pot came into her mind. As she remembered what happened next, it was as if she could feel his thumb caressing her mouth. She pulled her lower lip through her teeth.

Nothing had happened. He'd just saved her from running around with food on her face. That's it.

Nicole mentally shook off the memory and the feelings that came with it. "You're not missing anything. Collin is a friend. He's helping me out in the kitchen. He's just a friend."

Ashley snorted a laugh. "You just said friend twice. Maybe you should say it one more time. You might be able convince yourself that it's true, but I'm not buying it."

"Neither am I," Megan chimed in. "And honestly, why aren't you interested in him? He's cute and you're both single."

"Hello," Ashley added.

"It's a little more complicated than that."

Her sisters waited for Nicole to say more. Usually she talked to them about guys without hesitation, but a protectiveness she'd never felt before came over her as she thought of Collin. He probably wouldn't appreciate her sharing about his dad being terminally ill.

She chose her words carefully. "Collin is in the army. He's stationed in Germany. His dad isn't well, and he's here to take care of him, but he's leaving in a few weeks."

"Sorry to hear that about his dad." Ashley's expression grew empathetic. "It says a lot about Collin that he came home to take care of him. But even in the midst of everything, he's making time to help you out at Roja. He sounds like a really good guy."

"He is." Nicole sipped her wine. She'd never met a guy like Collin. He was honest, dependable, confident but not arrogant. Guys with egos completely turned her off. And his sense of humor, subtle but not too over the top. She liked that as well. And when he did laugh it was...

"Nicole, are you still there?" Ashley called out. "Her screen looks frozen. Did we lose her?"

"I'm still here." Nicole set down her glass.

"So." Megan smiled knowingly. "I'm guessing from that dreamy look we just saw on your face you were thinking about Collin. You know, Ashley's right. In the midst of everything, he's finding time to help you. I don't think he'd do that unless he was interested in you, maybe you should..." She glanced right, away from the screen and did a double take. Her gaze stayed there as she smiled. "Umm... Hate to cut things short. But Mark needs me to help him...handle something. Talk to you later. Bye."

Megan dropped from the call.

Ashley snickered. "I bet he needs her to handle something."

Nicole laughed with her. "The way she and Mark have been cuddled up at his place lately, you'd think they were on their honeymoon."

"I know, right?" Ashley's expression sobered to

a soft smile. "She did have a good point about Collin. I think he is helping you out because he likes you, and probably not just in a friendship sort of way. And you feel the same about him, too. A good guy who can put a dreamy look on your face just thinking about him doesn't come along every day."

Nicole sighed as she sank back on the couch. "But he's only in town for a few more weeks, and I really need to stay focused on Roja right now. You know what it takes to open a restaurant."

"I do know what it takes, and I'll be the first to admit that I'm telling you this from a newlywed I'm-so-totally-in-love place, but you can't put the rest of your life on hold while you run Roja."

Nicole almost let the problems she faced with Roja slip out. Ashley would listen, but she might start worrying about her, too, and that wasn't the way it should be. Ashley was on her honeymoon and Rodrigo deserved to have one hundred percent of her attention.

She conjured up a small smile. "Putting all of my time into Roja won't be forever. Just until things are a little more settled."

"But Collin is there now." Ashley stared directly into Nicole's eyes from the screen. "If you two like each other, spending the next few weeks together could be a really good thing. Don't rule it out. Beyond that, who knows what could happen? Planes don't just fly from Germany, they actually fly there, too. It could end up not being a short-term thing. But you won't know unless you test the waters and find out."

"I'll think about it."

They chatted a couple minutes more and ended the call with virtual air kisses.

Nicole cleaned up her dishes in the kitchen then came back to her suite.

As she lay in bed, what Ashley and Megan had said about Collin, played in her mind. She did like Collin a lot and they got along well. And the other day in the kitchen, she'd thought she'd spotted a glimpse of something in his eyes that had reflected how she'd felt, a longing to get closer and move out of the friend zone. But what if that hadn't been what he was thinking? What if she was wrong?

Chapter Twelve

Nicole added two more sets of silverware and art-fully folded burgundy napkins to the round white linen-covered table.

The head count had gone up. Originally, only Steven and Ellie, Dillon and Hailey, and Megan and Mark had been coming to the Sunday night menu tasting. But then Callum had called a little while ago to let her know that he and his wife, Becky, would be able to come. As the parents of two-year-old twin daughters, they were consider-ing the dinner a date night.

The table separated by a partition from the rest of the dining room did have a romantic feel with low lighting, a floral centerpiece and votives floating in glass on the table, and a wide window view.

A few people sat outside at the bar near the pool enjoying drinks and the clear starry night.

Jay Cross, the twentysomething hospitality intern at the hotel, set up water and wineglasses at the additional place settings.

He'd helped in housekeeping earlier that day and had changed into the semiformal catering uniform for the restaurant. With his clean-shaven, lightly tanned face and neatly clipped hair, he complemented the uniform aesthetic of a white button-down and blue-and-black striped tie, with black pants and a crisp chambray apron.

"Is there anything else you'd like me to set up?" Jay asked politely.

"No." Nicole smiled. "Thanks for doing such a nice job. The table looks wonderful."

"You're welcome." He looked less uneasy than usual. Hopefully, he'd remember to keep smiling and look her family in the eye while he served them. Being that he was Lou's grandson, and she was so outgoing, it was surprising he was that quiet.

In the kitchen, after checking in with the cooks on the night shift handling dinner service for the restaurant, she went to Collin at the corner station.

Like her, he was wearing the usual kitchen uniform and twinning it with matching black chef's hats.

He scanned the list lying on the table with the

food items they were preparing. "I adjusted every-thing for two more people. We're good to go."

"Perfect."

This was the first time she'd seen him since he'd confessed his problems with his father...and he'd fed her in the kitchen. The texts they'd sent each other during the days he wasn't at Roja had only been about tiny changes in recipes or shifts in the menu. And Collin had mentioned having to run out several times for more tape and boxes as they packed for his father's move.

Collin must have accepted that his dad wasn't going to go to Houston. And forgotten what hap-pened when he'd been preparing the *calabaza con pollo*. He was a little more serious than usual, but he'd been on top of things as they'd prepped for the meal earlier that evening.

Jay walked into the kitchen, gave them a thumbs-up and walked back out to the dining room.

Collin huffed a chuckle. "I guess that's his way of telling us your family is here. I just don't get that guy sometimes."

"Jay is just quiet. And yes, he does act a little strange sometimes, but he's perfect for tonight. He memorized everything I told him about the menu so he can explain the entrées to my family."

"Speaking of family, go out there and say hello. Spend some time with them." Collin tilted his head toward the dining room. "I can handle kicking things off back here."

Excitement and nerves bubbled inside her. She'd cooked for her family before, but this time felt different. She was serving them her first summer specials menu as an executive chef in charge of a restaurant, all on her own.

"Okay. When I come back, Jay can take out the salads."

"Once he does, I'll start firing up the chicken for the lemon rosemary entrée." Collin winked at her. "We got this."

We. Her heart fluttered. They really did make a good team.

In the restaurant, sounds of her family's laughter reached her before she got to them.

Just past the partition, the four couples stood near the table, absorbed in multiple conversations as they enjoyed the drinks Jay had brought them from the bar.

Her dark-haired, blue-eyed brother Steven stood the tallest at over six feet. Since they'd moved to Texas, jeans and cowboy boots had become his standard. As the oldest of her siblings, in his early thirties, he exuded confidence. His tall, willowy wife, Ellie Fortune Hernandez, the mayor of Rambling Rose, stood beside him. As she smoothed her dark hair from her cheek, quiet self-assurance shone in her naturally tanned face.

Callum, also dark haired and just as lean and tall as Steven, kept an arm loosely wrapped around the waist of his wife, Becky. The dark-haired nurse's upbeat attitude reflected in her smile.

Blond-haired Dillon, the most laid-back of everyone in the group, held hands with his fiancée, Hailey Miller. Like Ellie and Becky, the slim petite blonde had worn a casual dress but had worn cowboy boots instead of heels.

Megan and her dark-haired fiancé, Mark, co-owner of the Mendoza winery in Austin and a marketing expert, stood close to each other as they chatted with the group. They'd consciously, or maybe unconsciously, done the couple thing with their clothing, wearing black shirts and dark jeans.

Megan laughed at something that was said. Mark's brown-eyed gaze remained on her face as he smiled, seemingly oblivious to the conversation, totally mesmerized by her.

Nicole paused, taking in the sight of the people she loved.

Becky was the first to spot Nicole. "There she is." Smiling, she slipped away from Callum to embrace her. "Thanks for the invite. Everything looks so beautiful."

Nicole returned her tight squeeze. "I'm glad you two were able to make it." She continued to make the rounds, hugging and trading kisses on the cheek.

Steven pointed at the table. "There's only eight chairs. Aren't you joining us?"

"Not for dinner. Maybe afterward. Collin and I are cooking for you tonight."

At the mention of Collin's name, Megan grinned at Nicole, and mischief was in her eyes. Undoubtedly, she was remembering their Friday night chat with Ashley about him being just a friend.

Nicole shot her look she hoped translated into Megan not teasing her about it in front of everyone.

Message received, Megan remained quiet as she sat down at the table.

"We're tasting food for a new menu, right?" Becky said.

"Yes," Nicole replied. "We have two salads and seven entrées for you to sample that are going to be summer menu specials. You're also helping me choose what to showcase at the fund-raising barbecue. So I hope you came hungry."

"I'm starved." Callum patted his flat stomach. "Let's eat."

As everyone else headed to their seats, Steven spoke directly to Nicole. "Collin—why is that name familiar? Have I met him?"

"Maybe. He was at the business mixer earlier this year. He and Grace are friends."

A pondering expression came over his face. "Come to think of it, Wiley may have mentioned him. But why is he cooking here tonight? Isn't he in the military?"

"Yes. But he's home on leave for the next few weeks. I needed an assist, and he's helping me."

Before Steven could launch into twenty questions, she nudged him toward his seat. "Go sit next to Ellie and let me go do my job."

As Nicole walked across the kitchen, Jay passed her going the opposite direction, shouldering an oval serving tray with sample plates of melon, cucumber and tomato salad and a tropical kale salad.

After washing her hands, she joined Collin and fell easily into the rhythm of preparing and plating the food.

"Knife…"

"Firing the flank steak now…"

"Hot behind…"

At that cue from Collin, her mind was anywhere but on the steak dish in front of her. *Don't look down. Don't look down.* But she couldn't help but glance over her shoulder as he walked by with a hot pan.

Collin really did have a hot behind.

The flush that reddened her cheeks had nothing to do with the heat radiating from the cooktop. So he wouldn't see, she kept her head down and finished plating the steak tacos.

As the last plates went out, Nicole looked at Collin. Grinning, they exchanged a high five. "We did it!"

For a moment they clasped hands, and the heat of his palm seeped into hers as they looked into each other's eyes. Their connection, that thing that had allowed them to work and create together in the kitchen, held all the words they didn't need to speak.

They let go.

As they cleaned up the area together, Nicole glanced over at him, and he smiled at her. She smiled back, but a pang of sadness hit her. The menu was done. After tonight, he wouldn't be there with her in the kitchen. He'd come in maybe one day before the fund-raising barbecue that coming Saturday, but that was it. And then in a couple of weeks, he'd fly back to Germany.

Nicole shook off the feeling of loss. Of course, they'd connect before he left. Lunch or even dinner at Roja. Or maybe at her place. Would he accept if she invited him over?

Jay came to the table. "No one was interested in dessert. They want to know when the two of you are coming out there."

Nicole stacked dirty pans. "Tell them we're almost done."

Jay nodded and left to deliver the message.

Collin wrapped and labeled pans to be put into the walk-in. "Go ahead. I can finish cleaning up."

She shook her head. "They asked for the two of us. We're going out there together."

When they stepped into the dining room, her

family clapped, and Collin surprised her by giving in to the playful demand that the two of them take a bow.

Two extra chairs were pulled up to the table, and they sat down.

While Jay discreetly cleared dishes, conversation turned to the food from the tasting—what they'd liked and the five items they'd enjoyed the most that they thought should be featured at the barbecue.

Dillon inquired about Collin's cooking background, and Collin shared his experiences.

Happiness and a bit of pride blossomed in Nicole as she took in their impressed expressions and asked for his recommendation on the best food vacations to explore.

After Ellie and Becky both took a minute to check in with their babysitters, the joys of parenting came up. Ellie and Steven would be facing potty training down the road with their one-year-old son, George. Becky and Callum gave them tips and warned about the terrible twos stage they now faced with their twin daughters, Luna and Sasha.

Dillon and Hailey, and Megan and Mark were teasingly warned about what to expect as parents once they started a family.

The engaged couples took it in stride. Dillon and Hailey nudged shoulders and exchanged smiles. Megan and Mark stared at each other with love in their eyes as they shared a brief peck on the lips.

The topic switched to future construction and community projects the family had in mind for Rambling Rose.

Steven, sitting between Nicole and Ellie, stretched his arm out on the back of Ellie's chair. "One of the things we're interested in doing, Collin, is better supporting the military members and their families that are part of our community and in the surrounding area. We've been kicking around offering a weekend with discounts and specials. Maybe even connecting it to an event similar to the barbecue but honoring the military. And offering special opportunities for the spouses as well. What do you think?"

"Those are great ideas," Collin said. "Like everyone else, military members, especially ones with kids, are budget conscious, so discounts and specials are definitely appealing. You mentioned doing it for a weekend. A town near one of the installations where I was stationed offered a standing five percent discount to residents in the military in addition to having special weekends. A standing discount might be something you want to consider."

"That's not a bad idea." Callum slowly nodded. "The military members are supported and so are the businesses. Anything else come to mind?"

Collin sat back in the chair. "You mentioned targeting military spouses. That's always good, but keep in mind, military spouses include women *and* men. Sometimes the guys are forgotten when it comes to special offerings. And something else you may want to do is target military couples. A weekend package including a stay at the hotel and meals is something that would appeal to anyone married or dating. And give them a chance to get away. That can be critical for a couple who've been separated for a while."

"We've added some new couples' massages to the menu at Paz," Hailey piped in. She was the assistant manager at the spa. "And we're also looking into offering services for guys that are popular at barber spas."

"Ooh, pampering for a date weekend," Becky interjected. "And maybe add in his-and-hers sample gift bags."

"That's a great idea," Hailey replied.

Callum chuckled as he stroked Becky's shoulder. "You mentioned date night earlier. And now date weekend. I'm sensing a theme coming from you."

She laughed. "Maybe a little. It's great to do things with the kids, but being together like this is nice, too."

"I agree," Ellie added.

More ideas for the military and other topics were tossed around the table, and Collin joined in.

Jay caught her eye, and Nicole nodded at him, letting him know he could leave.

Steven leaned over and whispered to Nicole, "Make sure you invite Collin to the next date night.

It sounds like we're going to have a few more in the future."

Wait, did Steven think…? Nicole cupped her hand near Steven's ear and whispered, "He and I are just friends. We're not dating."

Steven whispered back, "That's too bad. I like him."

The conversation around the table slowed to a trickle.

Ellie tried to stifle a yawn, but it started a chain reaction with Becky, then Callum and finally Steven joining in.

"Sorry." Ellie gave a slightly sheepish smile. "These days I turn into a pumpkin by ten at night."

"I know the feeling," Becky said. "Having kids does that to you." She looked to Callum. "And we need to get back so our babysitter can go home."

Everyone stood.

After hugs and kisses on the cheek were exchanged, Becky thanked Nicole and Collin again for a delicious meal. "I'm looking forward to seeing both of you at the next date night," she said.

"I am, too," Megan added. "We'll have even more fun with you and Collin there."

Nicole's head swiveled to Megan. *We're not dating!*

Megan smiled, clearly satisfied with herself for stirring up trouble supporting Becky's suggestion. She returned Nicole's death stare with a slight eye roll.

Fearing Collin might be uncomfortable with the

expectation of being her date at the next family get-together, Nicole almost announced their status out loud.

But as Collin shook hands with Mark, he smiled, seemingly taking the comments in stride.

Nicole shook off her concerns as they followed the four couples past the partition.

The dining room was empty. The customers and staff had left.

Nicole and Collin paused as the others went ahead to the exit.

"See you guys at the barbecue," Steven said to the group as he and Ellie led the way, strolling hand in hand to the exit. "And make sure you bring your dancing shoes. We're line dancing to a live band."

Megan shot her a pitying look as everyone else shared his enthusiasm about the band. She knew exactly how Nicole felt about it.

Dancing. *Ugh.* Nicole mentally shook her head. She'd avoid doing that at all cost.

Collin quirked a brow at her. "Your brother said get ready for dancing, not torture."

Nicole released a quiet laugh. "It is torture. And extremely dangerous if you're dancing with me."

He huffed a chuckle. "You can't be that bad at it. You're joking, right?"

Chapter Thirteen

Collin walked with Nicole to the table to clear the remaining glasses. She hadn't responded to his question about dancing. She actually couldn't? Or was it something she just believed?

The way she worked seamlessly with him in the kitchen required a level of coordination. "You can't be that bad of a dancer."

"I am." Nicole winced as she released a breathy laugh. "The last time I was at a club, a very long time ago, the two guys brave enough to risk dancing with me nicknamed me the Impaler because I stabbed their feet with my stiletto heels so many times."

A laugh shot out of him, and she gave him a glum look.

From what he saw in her eyes, she was really bothered by what happened. She was such a perfectionist, and always hard on herself. She was probably so caught up in doing it right, she'd forgotten to just have fun. "I'm sure it was them, not you. Dancing is all about who's leading." He took his phone from his pocket. "Come on, I'll show you."

"Here? Now?"

"Yes."

Laughing self-consciously, she waved him off. "No…just no."

Collin pulled up the music service app on his phone, chose a random free country music playlist and tapped Play. As he set his phone on the table, she turned to scurry away.

He caught her by the wrist. "We're doing this."

"No," she pleaded as he tugged her toward him. "Don't do this to me. Don't do this to yourself."

"You can't hurt me if we're dancing side by side with space between us. But you can hurt yourself trying to dance in a pair of Crocs. Kick them off."

Collin held her hand as she did what he asked. In her sock feet, he led her to an open space near the table. Dancing wasn't something he'd had time to do in the past few months. Getting back into the flow of it would be good. "You can do almost any line dance to country music. So should we do a recent one like the wobble, go old-school with the cupid shuffle or traditional with the cowboy cha-cha or the tush push? Which one do you want to try first?"

"I don't know." Nicole shrugged with a bewildered look. "The cowboy cha-cha, I guess."

"I haven't done that one in a long time, but I think I remember how to do it." Collin found a song on the playlist with the right tempo. "We'll go slow. Dancing is like a recipe with ingredients. Put them together in the right way, and you end up with something good."

"Or a complete disaster."

Ignoring her comment, he demonstrated. "The first few steps are rock forward, cha cha cha. Rock back, cha cha cha."

Nicole stared at her feet and his as she moved stiffly through the rocking step and kind of marched in place on the cha cha cha.

"See? Not bad. You just need to put a little more rocking motion into your rock step and loosen up on the cha cha cha part. Let's do it again."

They went through the step a few more times until she got it right.

"Good," he said. "Now let's add in some turns." He demonstrated again. "Rock back, cha cha cha. Half turn and rock back, cha cha cha."

"Are you serious? I can't do that."

"You can. You just have to keep practicing."

"Hold on." Nicole stopped dancing. She took off

her chef's hat and freed the elastic from her pony-tail. As she shook out her hair and smoothed it back with one hand, she flung the elastic and the hat onto a chair. Put together, the innocent gestures, ending with her opening the side buttons on her jacket, had a sexy quality that riveted his attention.

The unconscious reveal of her dark shirt under-neath clinging to her full breasts and dipping into her waist ticked up his heart rate.

Next she dropped the jacket into the chair. "Okay. Now I'm ready."

He wasn't. All he could think about was fitting his hands into the curves of her waist and bringing her close. But they weren't slow dancing.

The track on his phone ended and moved to the next, and it was a bit too fast.

Collin went to his phone. *Get it together, Waldon. It's just a dance.*

Focusing on the playlist, he found another song with the right tempo. "Okay. Let's try it again."

"Oh my gosh," she laughed. "I think I got it."

He turned and looked at her.

Nicole executed the rock step and cha-chas with an easy sway in her hips. She made the half turn and with her back toward him she did it again. Her butt rocking side to side made his mouth dry out.

She looked over her shoulder at him. With her hair tousled around her face and the smile curving on her lips, she was nothing but pure temptation.

"I don't think I'm doing it right. Do I turn then cha cha cha or do I rock step? Come show me."

Oh, she was definitely doing it right, and this dance lesson needed to end.

But while his mind worked through a ten-second delay in making that decision, his legs had minds of their own.

Dancing side by side, he became distracted by how she came alive with a glow in her eyes and cheeks and her hair swirling around her as she turned.

On the next sequence, Collin spun toward her instead of away. They faced each other.

She was confused. And he was confused by his lack of willpower to leave.

Trying to right their steps at the same time, they jumbled them.

"Whoops. Wrong way again." Nicole faltered as she turned, stepping on his boot.

He caught her by the waist, and she latched onto his arms. "Shoot. I did it again. See? If I'd been wearing heels, you would have been in pain right now."

"That mistake was on me." And he was making another one by not letting her go.

He hadn't allowed himself to think about how much he'd wanted to kiss her in the kitchen that day he'd stayed later to help out. Or how the scent of something that reminded him of wildflowers emanated from her hair. How one innocent touch from her ignited sparks under his skin that could easily turn into fire if he allowed his mind to wander into the dangerous territory of imagining himself kissing or holding her. Like he was now.

She'd been right. Dancing with her was dangerous.

Unable to stop himself, he leaned in.

Nicole stared up at him and laid her hands to his chest, not to push away but to balance herself as she lifted slightly to her toes. The warmth from her mouth bathing his lips made it impossible for him not to pull her in and close the distance.

A low groan came from inside his chest as she released a soft sigh and parted her lips, welcoming him in. The taste of her was decadent and sweet. Something he could easily come to crave.

Collin broke from the kiss and closed his eyes for moment, blocking out the desire in her eyes and her pouty, just-kissed lips. "We can't do this." He took his hands from her waist.

Nicole's remained in the air near his arms.

The ringtone for his phone, loud and jarring, interrupted the music.

It was the one he'd programmed for Ian. He wouldn't be calling him unless something was wrong.

Collin moved the side chair in his father's room closer to the bed and sat down.

As his dad adjusted his position on the wedge pillow propping up his torso, he winced and closed his eyes. Ten minutes had passed since he'd taken some heavy-duty pain meds, but from his father's drawn face, they hadn't kicked in yet.

Ian had called him that night because his father was in extreme discomfort and couldn't find the higher-dosage pain meds he rarely took. He usually claimed they made him too groggy. His father really was in pain if he asked for them.

Chronic and worsening back pain was one of the symptoms his father would struggle with more and more in the coming months. But he'd also found Sam looking through boxes in the garage early that morning. Was overexerting himself the cause, or was this part of the prognosis?

Collin rested his elbows on his thighs and looked to his booted feet. He'd refilled the prescription for his father before he'd gone to Roja late that afternoon. The bottle had been stored in a locker with his stuff in the staff locker room.

He'd left Roja as soon as he'd gotten the call. He should have come home right after cooking for the tasting. Socializing with the Fortunes and dancing with Nicole never should have happened.

His father looked him up and down. "Are you going back to the restaurant?"

"No. I'm home now."

"Won't the Fortunes be upset? You just started working for them and you're leaving early."

"I'm not an employee. I'm just giving Nicole a hand." Technically he was an intern, but there wasn't any point in making that distinction. He was done assisting Nicole.

"So they aren't paying you for your work?"

"No. I can't have a second job. And I don't need one. I'm good financially. I've made smart investments, just like Mom taught me, and my career is solid. I'm on track to make my next promotion."

His father gave a weak smile. "Good. You listened to her. Your mother was really smart when it came to handling money. The people she kept books for around here still miss her."

Beth had been an accountant. The day she'd died, she'd been driving back from a meeting with a rancher who was one of her clients, in the middle of a severe rainstorm. A tire blew and she'd lost control of the car.

Between her life insurance policy and the money she'd saved for them over the years, his dad should have been more than good financially. But now the money was gone. Did Sharon have anything to do with it? Would his father ever tell him how he'd ended up almost broke?

"So you'll be Major Waldon soon?" His father sighed deeply, and tension relaxed in his face as he closed his eyes. "That's wonderful. Your mom would be so proud of you."

As his dad drifted off to sleep, the grief that would always remain with Collin over his mother's loss swelled with a single solid heartbeat.

Collin crept out of his father's room and went to the spare bedroom where he was staying.

He tapped the light switch, and a ceiling lamp illuminated the teal comforter and blue-and-white throw pillows covering the king-size bed. The light wood bedroom furnishings made the room seem unusually bright.

When he came out the bathroom from taking a shower, wearing a towel around his waist, he spotted a text bubble on his phone sitting on the dresser. The message from Nicole had been sent just a few minutes ago.

Is your dad okay?

Collin replied, Yes. He's good now.

I'm so glad.

Text bubbles indicating she was typing floated, disappeared and floated again on the screen.

Was she writing something about their kiss?

We can't do this... That's what he'd said before

Ian's call, and she'd started to reply. What had she planned to tell him?

I think you're right.

I don't agree.

I didn't mean for this to happen, either. It was a mistake.

Her message finally popped up.

If I can help, let me know.

A mix of relief and disappointment that she hadn't brought up the kiss settled with his exhale.

Collin typed his reply. Thank you.

He put on a pair of sweatpants and got into bed. As he propped an arm behind his head, he used the remote to flip through channels on the flat-screen television across from him on the wall. Instead of the images on the screen, what happened with Nicole a few short hours ago played in his thoughts.

Up until tonight, he'd kept his attraction to Nicole under control. He'd just never let his mind go there. But tonight he'd been riding high on the success of the tasting. Impressing her family had been important to Nicole, and they'd done it.

Part of the reason he'd sat down with them was to gauge their reaction and see if her family put pressure on Nicole to excel as a chef. But after seeing them together, it was clear Nicole put that pressure on herself.

She may have worn the title of executive chef, but she didn't fully trust herself. And that lack of self-confidence was what caused her to freeze up when it came to creating the summer menu…and line dancing. Like with the menu, he'd just wanted to give her a boost of confidence, but now he'd opened up something he couldn't ignore or continue with her.

He not only needed to look after his father, he was returning to Germany soon. All he could offer her was a few nights together. She deserved more than that, but he just couldn't give it to her.

Sure, at some point, in the next few months, he would make it back to see his dad, but he had no idea when that would happen or how long he would be able to stay. And her being a part of his life in the midst of what was happening with this father, knowing that it was just a matter of time before Sam passed away—that was a hard situation. And not the best circumstances in which to start a relationship.

He was also career military. Today he was stationed in Germany, but in the future, possibly sooner than later, he would receive orders for his next assignment. He could still be overseas or if he was stateside, he could be at an installation that wasn't close by.

Nicole had a restaurant to run. Her family lived in Rambling Rose. She wouldn't want to give that up to be a part of his unpredictable life…would she?

For a moment, he allowed himself to consider what her being a part of his life would mean. Phone calls and video chats with text messages in between. Matching up their calendars to figure out when they could see each other again.

The distance unconsciously growing wider between them as they missed celebrating holidays, birthdays and other special occasions together. Or her simply growing tired of not being able to share everyday moments with him and date nights and other gatherings with her family.

He'd tried casual long-distance relationships in the past, and they'd only lasted a few months. He'd also witnessed his colleagues trying to make the situation work, and more often than not, those relationships ended because of loneliness and broken promises.

The reality of the situation—more cons than pros when it came to him and Nicole—dropped inside of him and he let it settle in.

They were headed in different directions. It just didn't make sense for them to get involved.

Chapter Fourteen

Nicole parked her sporty red two-door next to the curb in front of Sam's modest, light brick home. At nine in the morning, the middle-class neighborhood was peaceful. Collin had given her the address before he'd started helping out at Roja when she'd needed to send him an official letter offering him the intern position.

The driveway in front of the house was empty. Maybe Collin's gray two-door was in the garage.

Before she got out, she picked up the rolls of packing tape sitting next to her chef's jacket and then grabbed one of the two extra-large rolls of Bubble Wrap from the back seat. The packing supplies had just been sitting in a closet at her place. She'd decided to drop them off before going to Roja.

During her last few moves, Bubble Wrap and tape were the two things she'd run out of just before she'd gotten ready to pack the final boxes. And of course, it always happened after midnight. If she could prevent Collin from dealing with the same fate, why shouldn't she? After all, they were friends. Who'd kissed. No big deal, right?

A huff blew past her lips. *Who are you kidding?* And honestly, Collin would probably see right through her excuse for stopping by to see him.

They hadn't spoken to or seen each other in the past two days since making dinner for her family. But the memory of dancing with him, and their kiss, remained stuck in her mind and was as hard to ignore as a wooden spoon beating against the back of a metal pot. How could she forget what it felt like to lean into his strength as he brought her close? To feel his hands tighten possessively on her waist. Or the way he'd skillfully explored her mouth.

As the memory replayed, warmth rose on her skin, making her light blue T-shirt and black chef's pants feel as warm as two layers of winter clothes.

Since he'd had to leave after it happened, she'd envisioned them talking about it that week, facing a small awkward silence before they chuckled and blamed it on adrenaline after a successful night of impressing her family. And her excitement over getting the steps to the cowboy cha-cha half right without maiming him.

But then he'd sent her a text. A spot had opened up sooner than anticipated for his father, and Sam was moving to Austin the day before the barbecue. Because of that, and meetings with his real estate agent, he might be late to the barbecue or he might not make it at all.

We can't do this...

That's what he'd said about the kiss. And as much as a part of her wanted to dispute that, she understood why it was a bad idea to explore where that kiss might take them. But she didn't want to share that with him in a text message or a phone call. Or try talking about it the day of the barbecue. Or worse, not talking about it at all.

After working together so easily and sharing creative synergy, it didn't feel right ending their working relationship, or possibly ruining the memory of it, over a kiss that shouldn't have happened... despite how wonderful that moment had been.

She shut the door and walked up the paved path leading to the small porch.

As she stood in front of the hunter green door, the muffled noises of what sounded like a television reached her.

She rang the doorbell.

A few moments later, a thin, pale older man with white hair wearing a nasal cannula opened the door.

His slightly watery-looking hazel eyes landed on the Bubble Wrap. "Why did he tell you to bring that? We need boxes, not Bubble Wrap."

Nicole wasn't sure what to say. "Are you talking about Collin?"

"Who else would I be talking about? Come in and stop air-conditioning the neighborhood." Leaning on a cane, he moved aside to let her in and shut the door behind her. "Mind the hose."

Her gaze followed the long hose that led from him to a machine in the living room near the tan couch. "Mr. Waldon…"

"You can call me Sam." As he walked left toward the living room, he leaned slightly forward, planting the bottom of the cane on the floor as if impatient with the slowness of his gait. It was easy to envision him as a man who'd once walked at a faster pace and with a purpose. Like Collin did.

She followed, making sure to avoid the hose trailing behind him.

As they passed closed packing boxes against the wall, she left the Bubble Wrap and tape on top of them. "Sam, my name is Nicole. I work with Collin at the restaurant. I was hoping to talk to him. Is he around?"

Sam's breathing had grown a little heavier during the walk to the recliner. He sat down. "Nope. He's out, but he should be back soon. Are you in a hurry?"

"No, not really."

His phone rang. He fished it out of the front pocket of his gray shirt and answered it. "Hello." Sam's expression grew exasperated. "No, I haven't been exerting myself. I'm sitting in the living room exactly where you left me. Oh?" His brow knitted together with concern, and she saw traces of Collin in his face. Collin did the same thing with his brow when he was mulling over a problem. "I'll be fine until you get back. Nicole is here. Yes, the one from the job where they don't pay you. Sure." Sam held the phone out to her. "It's Collin. He wants to talk to you."

She accepted the phone from Sam. "Hello?"

"Hey, Nicole." On Collin's end of the line, the sounds of moving cars growing louder then fading as if passing by filtered in. "I didn't know you were coming to the house. Did I miss a message?"

"No. You didn't."

Sam turned the volume down on the television, clearly listening in on the conversation.

She continued, "I found some extra moving supplies at home. I thought you could use them. And I was hoping we could talk."

"Sure. It'll be a few minutes before I get home, though. I have to change a flat. Can you wait there with my dad or do you have to get to Roja?"

"I have some time. I don't need to be at Roja until eleven thirty."

"Okay. No need to hand the phone back to my dad. He knows about the tire. See you when I get there."

"Bye."

Collin hung up.

She gave the phone back to Sam.

He pushed up from the chair. "Do you like roses?"

"Yes."

"Come on, then. You can help me with them and tell me what my son did to screw up."

"Screw up? He didn't."

Sam snorted a laugh and a cough. "I was married to Collin's mother for over twenty-five years. Whenever she said, 'Can we talk?' it meant I'd messed up big-time. I just need to grab my portable concentrator. Can you check and see if my gardening tools are on the back deck near the door? If not, we'll have to grab them from the garage."

Tools meant work, and hadn't Collin just been questioning his father about not overexerting himself? "Maybe we should wait for Collin."

"Looking after the roses will help pass the time until he gets here." Sam smiled.

"I don't think you're supposed to work in the yard."

"We won't be working in the yard. Just taking care of the rosebushes. We'll be fine." He winked and patted her arm. "Besides, a pretty woman like you deserves flowers."

* * *

Sam opened the French doors and walked across the deck, headed for the roses. A mini oxygen concentrator was strapped to his waist, and he carried pruning shears in his gloved hands.

Nicole followed him carrying a blue mason jar. "I still don't think this is a good idea."

"Help me or watch me."

Helping wasn't the option she wanted to take, but she couldn't just watch him work outside. At least she'd managed to talk him out of raking and weeding. Five minutes and then they were going back inside.

They reached the bushes, and a contented, loving expression crossed his face as he examined the blooms.

Compassion lessened her concern. Tending to the roses clearly made him happy. How could she not let him enjoy the moment considering he might not have many of them left? She'd give him ten, maybe fifteen minutes, tops, before she suggested they sit on the porch. At least he could see them from there.

Sam clipped a pink rose stem from the bush. "So, how did my son end up working with you?"

Nicole held out the blue mason jar, and he dropped the stem inside it. "We had a conversation about cooking. I was impressed by his background, so I asked if he'd help me with some recipe testing and menu planning."

And then Collin had insisted on cooking for her before giving his answer. Did he realize he had a stubborn streak just like his father did?

Sam shifted farther down and clipped more roses. "Did he tell you how he got interested in cooking?"

"He did. Collin said his mom wanted to make sure he could fend for himself."

"Yes, that's right. She used to say that if she could teach him how to make a salad, prepare a sandwich and boil an egg, he'd never starve."

"My mom was the same way. She wanted us to be able to take care of ourselves and each other."

"How many brothers and sisters do you have?"

"Seven."

He chuckled. "With that many kids, I can see why she'd want all of you to be self-sufficient. For Collin, cooking gave him independence, too, but his mother also taught him that it was a way to reach people. Everybody eats. Friends and the power of food. That wasn't an easy lesson. I wonder if he still remembers what happened." As he put the white roses he'd clipped into the jar, his expression grew nostalgic and a bit sad.

Sensing there was more to tell, Nicole stayed quiet as he moved down and inspected the red roses, deciding which ones to snip from a grouping of flowers.

"I was on the road one weekend when I got a call

from Beth. Collin had been in a fight with someone, and he wouldn't tell her who it was. She finally got the truth from little Gracie next door. A new kid from their second-grade class had started making fun of Collin and calling him names because of the color of his skin. He'd also gotten other kids involved."

"A child was bullying him like that? That's terrible. Did you talk to the child's parents?"

"We would have, but we'd already met them, and knew they were a big part of the problem. Ignorance breeds ignorance." Sam released a derisive snort. "Beth came up with another idea. With the teacher's permission, and the help of other parents with children in the class, they baked cupcakes for the kids—all different types from flavors to the frosting. During snack time, she and the parents used the cupcakes as a way to open up a conversation about race and why bullying was wrong."

"Did the kid that had bullied Collin understand?"

"I don't know that he did. But he lost the support of the other children. And with the help of the teacher, and the other children's parents reinforcing the message with their kids, he lost his power. At the end of the school year, he and his parents moved away."

Sam wiped sweat from his brow, raising concern in Nicole. She fanned her face and feigned discomfort from the heat. "Can we take a break and sit in the shade?"

"Sure. There's some lemonade in the fridge. We can have some and cool off." He followed her to the raised deck and sat down on one of the padded green outdoor chairs.

In the kitchen, she put water in the mason jar with the roses and left it on the counter. As she poured lemonade—a glass for her with ice, a smaller one for Sam with no ice, as he'd requested—she imagined a seven-year-old Collin facing the situation his father described. She'd never gone through anything like that. And like Sam had mentioned, she'd also had siblings to lean on.

Nicole took the drinks outside, handed Sam his and sat in the chair next to him.

For a long moment, they sipped lemonade in companionable silence.

As Sam absently skimmed his fingers over his leg, she spotted a thin line of blood on the back of his wrist.

"You're hurt." Nicole set her glass in the cup holder in the arm of the chair and sprang up. "Why didn't you tell me?" She grasped his hand.

"Oh, that's nothing but a scratch from handling the roses." He tried to tug his hand away.

"It's still bleeding."

"It's the damn blood thinners they make me take."

"Where's your first aid kit?"

"Pick a room. They're everywhere."

"Can you be a little more specific?"

As she gave him a hard stare, he relented. "In the kitchen, first bottom cabinet on the right."

Nicole located the large first aid kit and sorted through the color-coded packs that covered conditions from airway to burns to bleeding to hydration. Locating the alcohol swabs and adhesive bandages, she took out what she needed, washed her hands and went back to the porch.

Sam held up his wrist for her to see. "It's almost stopped bleeding. Told you it wasn't a big deal."

"Good. Now let's get it cleaned and covered." She pulled the chair she'd been sitting in closer to him, ripped open the swabs and gently cleaned the cut.

"You do that well."

"I work with knives. I've gotten lots of practice taking care of cuts, mine and other people's." She put on a bandage that completely covered the thin wound. "You're all set."

"Thank you." He gently laid his hand over hers. "Sometimes, I think Collin forgets that just like in the second grade, he doesn't have to handle difficult problems or situations on his own. That he has friends, and he needs to reach out to them." Sam looked into Nicole's eyes. "I need someone like you to remind him of that when I'm gone."

As she thought of Sam not being there for Collin,

soft sad emotions formed in her chest. Of course, she'd be a friend to Collin, but Sam wasn't gone yet. There was still more he could do for his son. Like not move to Austin. Maybe it wasn't her place to share what she knew, but if there was a chance it could make a difference for Sam and Collin, she'd face the risk of one of them or both being upset with her.

She held Sam's hand in both of hers. "Of course, I'll remind him. But you could show him yourself now by moving to Houston instead of Austin."

Sam made a face. "He told you about all that. He shouldn't have."

"Collin wants the best for you—a place where you can be around friends while he's away from you. Where he doesn't have to worry about you."

Sam shook his head. "If he's worried, he won't have to be for long."

"Is that how you felt when he was facing that bully in the second grade? Did you and your wife just let Collin suffer through it because he wouldn't be in that class for long? No. You did what you could to make it better for him. Why not let Collin do that for you? Why not do that for him?"

"Dad? Nicole?" Collin's voice came from the house.

Just as she stood to greet him, he rushed out the French doors. "Who's hurt?" His gaze landed on Sam's wrist. "What happened?"

Nicole laid a hand on Collin's. "He's fine. Your father got scratched by a rose thorn, that's all."

Collin's gaze landed on his father. "Was staying away from the roses and not exerting yourself too much to ask?"

Sam glared. "You didn't ask me. You *told* me. I'm not a child. And what happened had nothing to do with exertion. I'm fine."

Nicole gave Collin's arm a light squeeze, gaining his attention. "Really. It's just a scratch. It's okay."

He looked back at Nicole. "Okay? No, it's not okay. But hey, thanks for doing such a good job of looking after him." Collin stomped back inside.

Startled more than stung by the remark, Nicole stared after him. He was always so even-tempered and patient. What had gotten into him?

Sam released a wheezy sigh. "I'm sorry. I shouldn't have dragged you out here with me. None of this is about fault, though. He worries too much."

"He worries because he loves you." Giving in to impulse, she leaned down and hugged him. "Please, think about what I said."

"I will. Because you asked me." He hugged her back. "See you next time."

Would there be a next time? A quick hit of sorrow stole her voice. Time. After meeting Sam, she'd never take that four-letter word for granted again. And no matter what happened between her and Collin, she would visit him.

Pulling herself together, she returned his smile as she moved away. "I have to get going. Thanks for the roses."

Sam beamed. "You're welcome."

Nicole walked through the French doors Collin had left open.

In the kitchen, Collin glanced over at her as he repacked the first aid kit. "I'm sorry for what I said. I know it's not your fault that he was outside." He stuffed the final item inside the container and shut it. "He does what he wants when he wants. I'm just glad you were here to look after him. Thank you."

"I enjoyed his company."

Collin chuckled wryly. "He does have his moments. So what did you want to talk to me about?"

Actually, she didn't need to talk to him anymore. She'd already gotten her answers. The kiss was insignificant, under the circumstances. They both knew where it couldn't lead. He had more important things to worry about.

"I just wanted to make sure you knew that I'm not expecting you to show up at the barbecue. You have a lot going on." She forced a smile. "And I better leave or I'll be late." She walked around him to get the roses.

As she reached for the mason jar, Collin caught her by the hand.

"You came all the way out here just to tell me that?" As he turned and leaned back on the counter, he gently tugged her in front of him. "Or did you want to talk about the kiss?"

Facing him again and feeling his body heat radiating over her skin momentarily made her mind go blank. She dropped her gaze to his chest and the smudge on his beige T-shirt. "I...no. You said it shouldn't have happened. I agree. What more is there to talk about?"

"A lot. Starting with how much we both enjoyed it." As he cupped her cheek, intensity filled his gaze. "I can't stop thinking about it." The huskiness in his low tone seeped into her. "Can you? Be honest with me."

Hearing his request, the same one she'd given him that first day he'd come to Roja, stilled the lie she'd almost told him. She held his arms and felt his muscles grow taut under her fingertips. "No. I can't."

Collin leaned in, and she met him for a kiss.

Want, heat, the promise of passion—it was there in the slow sweeps and glides of the deepening kiss that awakened desire. It grew into a slow-rising flame curling inside her.

The need she tasted in that kiss was what she'd hoped to find by coming there that morning. She had to know if Collin had felt it, too. And it was selfish of her to want that validation.

Sweetness turned to sadness as she broke from his lips. "What you said was true." She laid her hands on his chest, hating that she had to hold back. "We can't do this, and we just confirmed it."

"We did?"

"Yes, because kissing each other would lead to more, and there are so many reasons why that's a bad idea for us. You have things to work out with your dad. I need to stay focused on Roja."

Collin's chest fell with a long exhale as his thumb stroked her cheek. He dropped his hand from her face.

She took a step back. "Thanks for helping me with the menu. I wouldn't be ready for Saturday without you."

"You're welcome. I'm glad I was able to help." His eyes seemingly held the same wistful sadness that made her words almost stick in her throat.

"But I mean it about not expecting you to be there on Saturday. It's important that you look after your dad." Nicole reached to pick up the flowers.

He caught her hand. "I'll still be at the barbecue."

"You don't have to. Really, the staff and I can handle it."

"I know you can." Collin gave her hand a squeeze. "But we need to take care of one more thing."

Chapter Fifteen

A loud banging noise woke Collin from sleep. Years of instinct and situational awareness kicked in, and he quickly oriented himself. Throwing back the covers, he ran down the hall toward his father's room.

Another crash sounded, and he rushed even faster to get there.

A rim of light peeked from around the closed door that he flung open.

Startled, his father, dressed in his blue striped pajamas, raised his cane as if planning to whack him with it.

Seeing Collin in the doorway, he wheezed out a

breath of relief and a cough as his shoulders sagged. "You scared the hell out of me. Why are you busting down the door?"

"What are you doing up? I heard a crash. I thought you'd fallen or that we had an intruder in the house." He followed his father's gaze to the photos scattered on the floor and to the album at his father's feet. "What were you doing?"

"I finally remembered where this photo album was. It was so far back on the shelf, we missed it when we were packing. I was trying to get it down." His father leaned over, holding his cane with one hand and trying to snag the album with the other.

"I've got it." Collin picked up the album and handed it to his father.

Sam cradled it to his chest and sat on the side of the bed. He sighed. "I've made a mess of it. I hope I can figure out where all these pictures went."

As Collin gathered the photos from the floor, he noticed that they were pictures of his father and mother with people he didn't recognize. Based on the age of his parents and the clothing they and other people had on, he'd guess they were taken in the '80s.

So his father hadn't thrown away everything that reminded him of Collin's mother, Beth.

He handed the photos to his father and got the ones that had scattered under the side chair. Another had made it all the way under the bed. "I'll help you put the album back together, but can we tackle it in the morning? It's late."

"I guess so." His father looked through the pictures he'd just given him.

Collin got on his knees near his father and stretched his arm under the bed, but he couldn't snag the photo. "Can you hand me your cane? This one's too far under here for me to reach." Still looking under the bed, he held up his hand for the cane, but Sam didn't hand it to him or respond.

Collin rose.

His father held the album on his lap and was staring misty eyed at a photo.

"Dad, you okay?"

As Sam stroked his finger over the photo, his chest deflated with a long breath. "I'd forgotten how beautiful your mom was, especially on our wedding day."

Collin glanced at the photo. It was one he'd seen before. It was of his mother, slim and elegant-looking in a white lace and satin dress with flowers on one side of her hair, carrying a bouquet of white, purple and pink flowers. Her eyes sparkled, and she smiled as if someone had made her laugh.

He sat next to his father on the bed. "She was."

"That day was the happiest of my life. I was a lucky man. To this day, I still can't believe she chose me."

Collin knew the story well. At twenty-six and

a college dropout, his dad had drifted from job to job. He'd just become a dental supplies and equipment representative and was about to give up the new gig when he'd walked into the Atlanta dental practice where his mother had been the bookkeeper for her uncle. She'd been a senior in college at the time finishing her degree in accounting.

According to his father, he'd invented reasons to stop by the dental practice in hopes of seeing Beth, who he'd fallen in love with at first sight. His father's persistence eventually paid off, and she finally gave him a chance. But her parents hadn't approved. They'd wanted their only child to marry someone who'd matched their stature in the community.

They'd refused to come to the small ceremony held at one of Beth's friends' home. And they'd never really accepted Sam.

His father sorted through the photos in his hands, putting the ones from the wedding together. Sam paused on one of a pouting dark-haired girl, about five years old, wearing a frilly dress. He chuckled. "This one caused so much trouble. What was her name? Annabelle, or was it Ariel? She got upset over who knows what and stomped on all the flowers, including your mom's wedding bouquet, right before the ceremony."

"What? Seriously?" Collin angled toward him. He'd never heard this story before.

"Yep. Your mom's friend, the one who held the ceremony at her house, ran to her next-door neighbor's. They had white, pink and red roses in their yard. She snipped a few and with what was left of the original flowers she remade your mother's bouquet. And your mom actually liked it better than the first one." He coughed a laugh. "I just saw a picture of it in here someplace." He pulled out a photo and handed it to Collin.

The picture showed his parents taking their vows. His mom was holding a different bouquet in this photo, one with white, pink and red roses.

"The roses in the backyard..." Collin looked to his father as he pieced it together in his mind. "Are they connected to this photo?"

His father nodded and took the photo back. "Sharon realized how much I regretted digging up your mother's garden. So she planted them as a way to commemorate your mom."

"*You* dug up Mom's garden? Sharon told me she did it."

"She what?" Sam looked stunned. "I didn't tell her to do that. I just assumed you knew I did it. But that sounds exactly like something Sharon would do. Generous and caring to a fault...but also reckless."

Reckless? Collin went with his gut. "Did Sharon have anything to do with your financial trouble?"

Sam stared straight ahead. His breathing filled

the long silence as his lips remained tightly closed. They trembled a little. He nodded his head. "When we got married, I didn't know she'd had a past problem with gambling. She'd kept it under control for years, but then she took a trip to visit her niece in California. On the way back, her plane was rerouted through Nevada because of a storm. She lied about her flights being canceled. She was gambling at a casino. From there it progressed to underground poker games. She'd taken out multiple high-interest loans to cover her tracks, but they also ended up feeding her addiction."

Collin ran his hands over his head, trying to make sense of it all. "Why didn't you tell me?"

"It was illegal. Bad people were involved. I couldn't risk hurting your career."

"And after she died?"

Sam wheezed a long breath. "I know you hated Sharon. I wasn't going to ask you to help pay for what she'd done."

Collin mulled over the misunderstandings between them. With him living overseas and going through multiple deployments, he and his dad hadn't really gotten a chance to talk. And he hadn't gotten to know much about Sharon.

"I didn't hate her. Did I believe Sharon was the right choice for you? No. I felt you were rushing into things when you married her."

His dad looked down at the photos. "Maybe I

was." He blinked as if holding back tears. "But that's not an excuse for my mistakes. I should have paid more attention and stopped her."

His father blamed himself for what Sharon did? Nicole had mentioned his father might feel ashamed over what had happened with the money. From his experience, blame and shame showed up together.

Collin laid a hand on his father's shoulder. "You helped Sharon the best you could. She was your wife, and I know you cared about her. But punishing yourself over what happened won't solve or change anything. And I don't think that's what Sharon would have wanted you to do."

His father stared at the packed boxes in the corner. "A parent is supposed to leave their child some kind of legacy. I'm leaving you nothing. I don't deserve to live in a comfortable place. I failed you. And I'm leaving you all alone."

As Collin wrapped an arm around his dad's fragile shoulders, a lump formed in his throat. "I'm your legacy. You being proud of me is all that matters to me. It's all I need."

His father looked at him with tears streaming down his cheeks. "I'm very proud of you. You're the best of me and Beth. You're the one thing in this world that I know I did right."

Chapter Sixteen

Nicole walked out the side door near the back of Roja's dining room that opened into the pool area. Warm sun and a hint of breeze created the perfect spring morning with a promise of an even better afternoon.

Mother Nature had given her blessing of good weather for the Give Back barbecue kicking off in a little over two hours.

The blue covering on the pool rippled as she walked past the tables shaded by blue and beige umbrellas that had replaced the lounge chairs—backup seating just in case they needed it.

Up ahead, the large, empty grassy space had

been transformed. In the middle, round tables and chairs were arranged under a large white tent positioned in front of a stage. Food tents were positioned on either side: the smoked barbecue buffet on the right and the new summer menu preview buffet on the left.

Beverage stations, yard games and face painting for the kids, as well as a dessert station that would serve ice cream, cookies and Popsicles, were also spaced out in the area.

Under the barbecue tent, Mariana checked the propane tank on the large grill, preparing to cook hamburgers and hot dogs. Then she went to the smoker. As she opened it to rearrange sausages and chicken on the grate, smoke curled up in the air.

As Nicole walked toward the grass, Mariana gave a smile and a brief wave. Smoked barbecue was an art, and Mariana was an artist in that department. She'd mostly taken over the task of slow cooking the brisket since midnight in the kitchen's electric smoker, and despite them having had a late night, she'd gotten up early to get a jump on grilling the rest of the meat.

Nicole walked under the summer menu tent, mentally mapping out what would go where on the buffet tables arranged in a U around the perimeter. They'd settled on three items to feature: rosemary chicken, seasoned flank steak tacos and cold mango shrimp skewers served over corn relish with a spicy puree, and a few of the sides her family had liked the most the night of the tasting.

Excitement and anxiety swirled the coffee and bagel she'd forced herself to eat earlier. Everything was in place and ready to go.

"Testing…one-two, testing."

The deep, resonant voice of the person talking in the mic came through the speaker system.

Nicole looked to the stage and did a double take. Jay the hospitality trainee was at the mic. He'd apparently fixed the problem they were having with the sound setup for the live band.

Wow. He had a really nice voice. Why didn't he speak that clearly in general?

As her gaze landed on the dance floor directly in front of the stage, Collin's voice drifted in.

"But we need to take care of one more thing…"

Dance together. That's what Collin had said they'd needed to do that day she'd stopped by his house and they'd shared a second unforgettable kiss. And since then she'd been watching line dancing videos and practicing in her living room.

One of the instructional dance videos had featured partners doing the cowboy cha-cha not in a line dance but together. And she'd dreamed about dancing that way with Collin.

But that was just a dream. If she could just get through one dance without tripping over him or her own feet, she'd count it as a win. Honestly, she was just looking forward to seeing him. And the two of them celebrating the success of the summer menu.

When she and Collin started working together, she'd envisioned both of them working in the kitchen today, one last time, guiding the cooks through the recipes the two of them had perfected.

Nicole headed back toward the pool.

Grace walked out the side door. Dressed in a gray pantsuit and flats, she was pulling double duty, managing hotel issues and being Wiley's date for the barbecue.

Today was close to a Fortune family reunion. Aside from Wiley and everyone who'd made it to the tasting last weekend, their sister Stephanie and her husband, Acton Donovan, were coming along with their cousin Brady and his fiancée, cousin Adam and his wife, and cousin Kane and his fiancée. It would be so great to see all of them and catch up.

Ashley had texted her earlier that morning. She and Rodrigo were enjoying their last weekend in Vegas, but they were also kind of sad about missing the chance to see everyone.

"How are we looking out here?" Grace said.

"Everything looks good. And it sounds like the sound system issue they were having earlier on stage is fixed."

"Oh, good. That's one of the things I came out here to check on."

Grace peered at an umbrella rocking above a table by the pool. "I better get someone on that. And have them check the other ones, too. The last thing we need is an umbrella flying away or knocking someone out." As Grace turned her focus back to the pool, she took a two-way radio from her pocket and radioed the groundskeepers.

Nicole went through the side door.

In the back of the dining room, Lesly briefed waitstaff and runners who would be working the barbecue. There were a few unfamiliar faces. They'd borrowed staff from Provisions to help out. To free up Lesly and Mariana for the fund-raiser, they'd also moved senior staff members into their positions in the kitchen and dining room.

As soon as Nicole entered the kitchen, she was swept up in the orderly chaos of handling the restaurant plus monitoring the preparation of the food for the fund-raiser.

Ten minutes before go-time, the buffets were ready as guests started to arrive at the venue.

Nicole took a minute to say a brief hello to her family. They'd claimed seats at their reserved tables a half hour ago and were mingling with the special guests, the heads of the nonprofits and projects that would benefit from the fund-raiser.

Unfortunately, there had been an accident on the interstate, and Megan and Mark were stuck in traffic.

A couple of reporters and their camera operators, as well as news photographers, circulated the area as well, interviewing guests, recording footage and taking pictures.

Callum and Steven, standing near the stage, had both gone full Texan for the occasion with cowboy boots, jeans, Western shirts and Stetsons. Wiley was with them, and the three were deep in conversation. Before the buffets opened, Callum and Steven would kick off the event by welcoming the attendees and sharing what the fund-raiser was about—the Fortune family's commitment to giving back to the community now and in the future.

Mariana closed the lid on a chafing dish. "I hope your brothers know the meaning of a brief welcome. There's nothing worse than dried-out barbecue and wilted coleslaw."

"I think they'll stick to the plan."

Nicole glanced at the smoked barbecue buffet. She'd included the classic side dishes: coleslaw, baked beans and corn bread. But she'd also added the melon, cucumber and tomato salad for a refreshing change. It was also on the other buffet.

Nicole's gaze strayed to the other tent. The cooks were making the hot food for the summer special buffet in small batches to keep up the quality. The cold food was also being put out the same way. She should probably check and make sure they hadn't put out too much of everything to start, just in case things on stage did get a little long-winded.

Mariana nudged her. "They need you." She pointed to Steven, Callum and Wiley.

Wiley motioned for Nicole to join them.

When she reached her brothers, Callum wrapped an arm around her shoulders and leaned in, and Steven and Wiley did, too, forming a huddle as he spoke to her over the low music playing from a nearby speaker.

"The reporters want to interview us about the fund-raiser, and a couple of them want to know more about Roja's summer menu. Wiley thinks we should do one interview all together right after the welcome. Are you up for that?"

"Sure," Nicole said. "As long as the interview isn't too long. I really need to keep an eye on the food."

"It'll be brief," Wiley said. "Just you, me, Steven, Callum and of course Ellie. We're staying on message. Rambling Rose is our home, and this fund-raiser is about us supporting our community. As far as Roja, anything about the restaurant and the new menu is fair game, but we're not addressing the flyer the diner distributed or the balcony incident."

"Got it. Where are we doing the interview?" Nicole said.

"By the summer menu food tent," Wiley replied.

"That works for me. I'd planned to be there when the buffet opened."

"All right, sounds like we're set." Wiley gave a nod. "I'll let the reporters know the plan."

Nicole spotted Becky and Stephanie holding down the fort at the family tables while the rest of the family continued to mingle. She made a pit stop.

"Hey, I've got to do an interview. Do any of you have any gloss or lipstick?"

"I do." Stephanie flipped her red hair over her shoulder, dug through her purse and handed her some lip gloss.

"Thanks. Where are the twins?" Nicole asked.

"They're at the face-painting tent with Dillon and Hailey." Becky smiled. "It's good practice for the future. Here." She handed Nicole a tissue. "You're a little shiny."

Nicole blotted her face. Luckily her hair was tucked under her chef's hat. On the fly, how she looked now was the best she could do. "Any word from Megan and Mark?"

"Nothing's changed." Stephanie put the lip gloss Nicole handed her back in her bag. "They're still stuck in traffic."

Hopefully they'd make it before things started.

Nicole headed to the summer menu tent and snagged Jay, who was helping monitoring the buffet. "I have to do an interview, but I'll be nearby.

When I give you the signal, can you and the runners uncover the food on the buffet?"

Jay nodded. "Of course."

Some of the press started gathering next to the tent as the MC for the event, a dark-haired man who was also a popular regional news anchor, took the stage.

He encouraged everyone to find their seats. After welcoming everyone, he launched into an introduction highlighting the new businesses, renovations and other developments the Fortunes had been a part of in Rambling Rose.

Long minutes later, he welcomed Steven and Callum to the stage. They explained the purpose of the fund-raiser and how the proceeds from the cost of admission, as well as the raffle tickets sold during the event, would be distributed to nonprofits and other projects serving the community.

They turned the stage back over to the MC, who spoke about the raffle items—goods and services in Rambling Rose—that were up for grabs.

While he continued to talk and entertain the crowd, Nicole joined Steven, Ellie, Callum and Wiley to meet with the press.

She took in a deep breath and quietly let it out. Since moving to Rambling Rose, she'd done her share of interviews, but no matter how many she'd done, a seed of apprehension over saying the wrong thing or being interrogated on a hot topic was always there.

"Tell us how the plans for this fund-raiser came about," one reporter said.

Callum fielded the question. "The Fortune family considers Rambling Rose home, and we're committed to this community. The nonprofits and projects this barbecue supports provide important services, and we want to make sure they have the funds to do it. That's why we're matching every dollar raised at today's event."

"Your family has met some resistance about some of your building projects, especially where we are today at Hotel Fortune. Do you think that's changing?" another reporter asked.

Ellie handled the question. "Yes. There were some challenges in the past, but the Fortunes, the town council and the residents of Rambling Rose are working together to make sure we address everyone's needs and concerns as we rebuild our town."

"And with Roja..." The mention of her restaurant focused Nicole's full attention on the reporter. "What would you tell the people who are still hesitant to dine there because of the balcony collapse?"

Wiley laid a hand on her arm, stopping Nicole from answering the question.

He responded instead. "The balcony collapse was an unfortunate accident. Safety is our number one priority. The only occurrence our guests will find at Roja is a top-rate dining experience."

Attention shifted to the new summer menu and Nicole breathed easier, happy to answer questions about the entrées and the theme. She borrowed Collin's words from that day she'd asked him to assist her in developing the menu. "It's a nod to Texas and the summer season."

As her brothers and Ellie answered more questions, Nicole's attention wandered to the stage.

"All right, everyone," the MC said. "We've waited long enough for this feast. Our special guests will lead the way."

Nicole looked to Jay and gave him a nod as the guests rose from their seats.

He and a couple of the other staff opened the chafers and uncovered the food.

After a few questions about upcoming Fortune Brothers Construction projects, the interview ended.

Wiley murmured, "Good job, everyone."

A reporter nabbed a blond-haired man leaving the buffet with a plate of food. "What do you think about Roja's summer menu selections that Chef Fortune is introducing?"

"I think it's fantastic. Especially the shrimp." To emphasize the point, he dunked one in the container of mango puree on his plate and ate it.

"How is it?" the reporter asked.

The man stopped chewing. He gagged as his eyes bulged. He gasped. "Hot...hot." He dropped his plate and ran off.

Callum and Wiley went after him.

"What's happening? Is he choking?" The reporter rushed to follow them.

Alarm rose in Nicole. He'd said the shrimp was hot, but they were on ice.

"What did he eat?" someone asked.

Good question. On a hunch, Nicole snagged a cup of the puree from a startled woman's plate. She dipped the tip of her finger into it and tasted it. As soon as the sauce hit her tongue, pinpricks of fire spread into her mouth.

Ultra-hot peppers!

Up ahead, Wiley handed the now red-faced and sweating blond man a bottle of water.

"No!" Nicole shouted. "It will only make it worse."

As she rushed toward Wiley and the man to stop him from taking a drink from the bottle, a scream erupted in the tent.

"Oh my god! Something's moving in the corn relish!"

Chapter Seventeen

Nicole dropped down into her desk chair, feeling like she'd been slapped, rolled through a pasta machine, then boiled to oblivion.

Outside her office, the subdued mood of the employees as they tidied the kitchen reflected that of the rest of the hotel's staff still cleaning up the aftermath of the barbecue.

Roja was closing for the rest of weekend. No one could work after what had happened. She had to tell the staff and address their concerns. But first, she needed a minute.

As she closed her eyes, the cascade of bad to worse that had occurred in the past two hours played through her mind.

She didn't make it to the poor guy who'd eaten the mango shrimp in time to stop him from drinking water. He'd ended up hyperventilating and rolling on the ground in agony. Others who'd left the food tent before him, as well as a few people who'd gone through the buffet in Mariana's tent, had met a similar pepper fate after eating the melon, cucumber and tomato salad.

Tiny bugs crawling in the corn relish had actually fallen low on the scale of events.

Thankfully Becky and other medical first responders had gone into action. Becky had advised that they call the paramedics for two of the attendees who'd had the worst reactions. As a precaution, she'd also instructed others to go to the hospital as well. She and Callum had followed the ambulances.

Steven, Wiley and Ellie were handling damage control with the press, trying to stop the massive flow of misinformation that had spread faster than the people scrambling to leave the fund-raiser.

"The food was poisoned..."

That was the main rumor going around. No, it hadn't been poison. The truth was more insidious and appalling. Sabotage.

Nicole's tongue still burned in that tiny spot. She'd tasted an ultra-hot pepper before, and whatever had been in the mango puree had packed a lot of heat.

But who would do something like that? It was too incredible to believe.

Maybe it was a good thing Collin hadn't shown up. All the hard work he'd put in to help Roja, to help her, had ended in total failure.

The quiet rustle of clothing made her open her eyes.

She met Collin's gaze as he stood in the doorway. The way he was dressed reminded her of the first time she'd spotted him at Mariana's. Was he really walking into her office or had she conjured him up because she wanted him there so badly?

"Nicole…"

Hearing him say her name shot her up from the chair.

He caught her in his arms, and she sank against him, burrowing her face into his shoulder. "Oh, Collin…"

The despair she'd held back for the past couple of hours, trying to keep it together and remain professional in front of everyone, swelled from her chest into her throat. It stole her voice, consumed her breaths.

"I've got you." He tightened his embrace and kissed her temple.

Nicole sank into his solid strength even more. "So you heard what happened?"

"Yes. I stopped for gas on the way here and heard people talking about it. I got here as soon as

I could." He held her tighter. "I think I scared your sister Megan. I saw her when I walked into the lobby and thought she was you. She filled me in."

Megan and Mark had arrived and walked right into the middle of the disaster. But like the rest of their family, they'd jumped in to help.

Collin leaned away and cupped her cheek. "I'm so sorry I wasn't here. I should have been here for you."

"You couldn't be here. You had to move your father and take care of the house, and—"

He kissed her firmly on the mouth, absorbing her words, taking away some of the misery.

She wanted to live in that kiss. To disappear with him to a place where the worst day of her life wasn't still unfolding.

Collin eased away and laid his forehead to hers. "I called and you didn't answer. I was afraid something had happened to you."

"I'm sorry. Everything was in chaos."

"Answering your phone wasn't a priority. I know you needed to make sure everyone was okay and then work on figuring out what happened."

Nicole met his steady gaze. He really did understand. She still wondered how he had managed to get there in such a short period of time. "I'm so glad you're here."

He stroked her cheek. "Tell me what you need."

"Help me figure out how this happened."

"You know I will."

A knock on the doorjamb drew both their attentions to Wiley and Grace standing at the door.

Wiley stared at them a moment with questions in his eyes.

"Is this a good time for us to give you an update on some things?" Grace asked.

"Yes, come in." Nicole moved out of Collin's embrace.

He released her but remained close.

"Hey, Collin." Grace gave him a subdued smile that he returned as she walked in first.

"Hi, Grace." Collin acknowledged Nicole's brother. "Wiley."

"Collin."

The two men shook hands.

"I heard you were back in town," Wiley said. "I wish we were meeting under better circumstances."

"So do I," Collin replied.

Greetings over, Grace and Wiley sat in the chairs in front of the desk. They were firmly in hotel manager and attorney mode.

Collin turned to leave, but Nicole laid her hand on his arm. "I'd like you to stay." She looked to Wiley and Grace. "Collin needs to know everything. He's going to help us figure out what happened."

"I don't have a problem with it." Wiley looked to

Collin, Nicole and Grace. "But remember, most of what we're going to talk about in here stays here."

They all nodded in agreement.

Declining the offer of a chair, Collin leaned a shoulder against the wall and crossed his arms.

"I have good news," Wiley said. "Becky and Callum followed the ambulances to the hospital, and they were able to give us an update. Everyone who was transported or went to the hospital on their own like she advised is fine. One gentleman was treated for an allergic reaction. Everyone received something for digestive discomfort, but no one will be kept overnight."

Relief whooshed out of Nicole. "I'm glad they're all okay."

"Yes," Wiley said. "We were lucky."

"I know." A fleeting thought went through Nicole's mind of just how bad things could have turned out, especially for the gentleman who suffered an allergic reaction. "Did the person who spiked the food with pepper even realize how dangerous this could have been? Did they think it was a joke?"

"Good questions." Determination was in Wiley's eyes. "And we're going to get those answers, but first, we have to establish that this *was* a pepper contamination and not something else."

"The symptoms of the people who went to the hospital," Grace interjected. "Isn't that proof enough?"

Wiley shook his head. "Right now, it only supports a theory. I've sent the food samples Nicole and Mariana collected to a lab in Austin for analysis. The results will tell us just what types of contaminants were in the food. We need to know just how high the SHU rating is on the pepper that was put into the food, as well as the origin of the bugs."

Revulsion turned in Nicole's stomach. She'd almost forgotten about the bugs in the corn relish.

Collin released an audible breath. "Based on the symptoms I've heard described, the Scoville heat unit of the pepper put into the food is high on the chart. That's definitely not the type of seasoning Roja would ever serve."

"Exactly." Wiley nodded. "And that will work in favor of our claim that someone brought it in and spiked the food."

"Our claim?" Grace's expression grew concerned. "Do you see lawsuits in our future?"

"Sadly, yes. And an investigation. Ellie's already heard from members of the town council about wanting the police involved."

"The police?" Internal alarms had Nicole sitting up straighter in her seat. "Is that necessary?"

"We need all the help we can get in finding the person who did this. Otherwise, if we can't prove sabotage, there's only one other explanation people will latch on to."

Collin filled in the blank. "Negligence."

Nicole breathed against the weight of disbelief in her chest. "And that would be my fault. It is my fault. I should have been paying more attention to what was happening in the kitchen."

"No." Collin shook his head. "We don't know that it happened in the kitchen."

"He's right," Grace added. "It could have happened during the event, and that's a security issue. That's on me."

"Stop." Wiley raised a hand, halting the conversation. "No one, especially the two of you, is taking blame for anything. And as legal counsel for this hotel and Roja, I strongly advise you not to say that to anyone. Understood?" His expression softened with a bit of empathy as he looked to both of them, especially Grace. "Look, I get it. You're viewing this as something that happened on your watch, and you think you're responsible. But you're not to blame. You two didn't contaminate the food."

"We need to find whoever did this." Anger sparked in Collin's eyes. "They have to be held accountable."

He spoke for all of them, especially Nicole. But she knew getting to that point was going to be a long haul. "One of the things we'll need to prepare for right away is a restaurant inspection," she said.

"Under the circumstances, they could show up as early as today or tomorrow."

Grace and Wiley exchanged a look.

Wiley nodded, and Grace spoke up. "As it turns out, the woman who first spotted the bugs in the corn relish is the sister of a county food safety inspector. Other complaints have already been lodged with the health department. The contaminated food and people needing medical attention were enough for them to issue an emergency order."

Nicole's heart sank as Grace's gaze met hers. "They called a half hour ago. Someone is on their way with the paperwork. I'm sorry, Nicole. They're shutting Roja down."

In the dining room of Roja, Collin sat at a table behind the ones where restaurant staff gathered, listening to Nicole.

I should have been here…

The thought kept pinging back and forth in his mind. He could have come back to Rambling Rose last night after dropping off his father instead of spending the night. The meeting with the Realtor that morning could have been handled over the phone.

Frustration turned in his gut, but pride and concern made him look to Nicole.

On the outside, she was calm, but when he'd looked into her eyes after the meeting with Wiley and Grace, he could see that her composure was holding on by a thin thread.

She was keeping it together for her staff, trying to set an example.

They were all somber and clearly shaken up. Some looked as if they'd been crying.

Nicole took a deep breath and met their gazes. "I know you want to get home, so I won't keep you much longer, but I just wanted to share a few things with you before you left. First, thank you for all you did to help during a really tough moment. You looked after our guests, and you looked after each other. I'm proud of you for doing that. I'm relieved to tell you that everyone who went to the hospital was released. They're fine."

A collective exhale of relief was followed by multiple questions all at once. "Was the food poisoned?" "Did they get sick because of the bugs?" "How did it happen?"

"Listen to me, please." She spoke over the hubbub. "Food poisoning wasn't the reason people had to go to the hospital..."

Nicole's answer reflected what Wiley had told her before she'd walked into the dining room a minute ago. He'd cautioned her not to share too many specifics and to choose her words carefully.

"Do we have any idea who might have done it?" someone asked.

A red-haired cook fired back. "Why is everyone

looking at us? We're not the only people who handled the food. And we weren't the ones monitoring the buffet."

"That's enough." Nicole held up her hands, halting the speculations. "Blame won't get us anywhere. Facts will. We're having samples of the food analyzed, and we're going to examine every step from preparation to when the food reached the buffet for answers. We'll be talking to each of you so you can help us fill in the gaps."

"Are we working tomorrow?" a cook asked.

"No, but I'm asking everyone assigned to work on Monday to come in, plus anyone else who's free, for a cleaning day." Silence lingered a beat before Nicole continued. "As expected in a situation like this, the health department has closed Roja for the next two weeks. Once we pass our inspection, which we will, Roja can reopen. During the time that we're closed, everyone will be paid."

Nicole expertly fielded more questions, but fatigue started to shadow her face.

Just as he debated whether or not to step in, she ended the meeting. "Monday. Seven a.m. sharp. I'll see you then."

As everyone began to disperse, Collin hung back. He returned greetings from the staff as they left, but he kept an eye on Nicole.

Lesly and Mariana were the last to leave, sharing tight hugs with Nicole before they left.

When Nicole faced him, the recollection of what happened with Megan in the lobby swept in. They looked exactly alike.

He'd grasped Megan by the shoulders and almost hugged her before he'd realized she wasn't Nicole.

Luckily, Megan's fiancé, Mark, had heard him say Nicole's name before he'd grabbed her. From the look in Mark's eyes, he'd understood how helpless he'd felt in those long minutes driving to the hotel, not knowing if Nicole was safe.

Collin embraced Nicole. She wrapped her arms around his waist. Now that he had her in his arms, he didn't want to let her out of his sight. But he was there to support her in any way she needed, not invade her space. "You ready to go home?"

"No." She laid her cheek to his chest.

"Nicole, I know you're anxious to start mapping things out, but you're exhausted. We can tackle it in the morning."

"I know, I'm not worried about that." She laid her forehead against him, and her deep sigh warmed his chest. "My family…they're all at the Fame and Fortune Ranch right now, and I don't want to be there. I know that sounds terrible, because they're all on my side. They want to support me, but I just…" Her voice broke down to a whisper. "I just can't."

But someone needed to be there when the exhaustion fully kicked in and the barrier she'd built to hold back her emotions finally fell. He wasn't leaving her alone.

Collin leaned back to look at her. "You don't have to go there. You're coming home with me."

Chapter Eighteen

Nicole walked into the house with Collin. It took a few seconds for her to reconcile why the sunlit living room was devoid of furniture and packed boxes.

Sam had been moved to his new home. A place that Collin hated.

She looked to Collin as he shut the front door, carrying Megan's overnight bag. When she'd told her sister that she wasn't going home with her and Mark, but that she was going to Collin's, Megan hadn't argued. She'd just retrieved her own bag from Mark's car, told Nicole she'd loved her and given her a tight hug.

As she stared at the empty room, a sudden wave

of emotion hit, and Nicole blinked back tears. What she was doing was selfish. She had a family that loved her, but she was avoiding them because she was all up in her feelings about what had happened at the barbecue. While Collin had no choice in his father not being there.

Maybe she should leave and let him adjust to his father's big move. But she didn't have her car. She'd have to call Megan. She wouldn't inconvenience Collin more than she already had by asking him to drive her to the ranch.

Collin set the bag by the door and stood beside her. "It's a big difference, not having furniture in here."

"It is." Nicole hugged herself as she nodded. "Did you sell everything or donate it?"

"We donated the couch. His television and the recliner fit well in his… I'm not sure what they call it. It's not a living room, more like a small alcove. But I doubt he'll spend a lot of time there. He and his roommate really hit it off."

"Oh? I thought he was moving into a private room. What happened?"

"He does have a private room. It's kind of a suite, actually." A dawning of realization came over his face, followed by a smile. "I was going to tell you this afternoon. Sam's not in Austin. He changed his mind. He's at the Highlands."

"What? He's in Houston?" Thrilled to hear good

news, she wholly embraced it with a smile. "When did this happen?"

"Early Thursday. Once he agreed, everything just fell into place and it happened."

Smiling, she clasped her hand over her heart as happiness lightened some of the heaviness. "Thank you. I needed good news."

"It is good. Dad and I talked before he moved. We're in a good place."

"I'm really happy for the two of you."

Collin pulled her into a loose embrace. "And I'm happy that you're here."

"Really?" She rested her palms on his chest. "Because I wondered if I was getting in your way. Your dad just left. Me being here doesn't even give you time to adjust."

"You're not in the way. I'm here for you. You can stay with me for as long as you need."

His declaration was like a soothing balm, but a strange mix of gratefulness and fatigue tightened her throat. "I can?"

"Absolutely, as long as you don't mind that the house is nearly empty. But there is a bed, and the dining room table. I haven't packed up the kitchen yet, so there are plates. And there are towels and sheets, too."

"I don't mind at all."

"Good." He mocked a contemplative expression.

"But I do have to ask one very important question. How are your room-painting skills?"

"My room-painting skills? Well, I'm handy with a roller and a paintbrush. And I'm pretty darn good at matching colors using a color wheel."

"Oh really? Then I have to ask. Will you be my intern? Now, I can't really pay you. Just a few good meals, some coffee…"

Hearing him repeat a variation of what she'd asked him a few weeks ago made her laugh. "Well, you should probably audition me first. My two-year-old nieces could have better painting skills than I do."

"Yeah, that's true. As a precaution, I should probably check you out. But that can wait until morning." He dropped a kiss on her mouth. "Right now, you're going to get comfortable, turn off your phone and relax. While you do that, I'll go to the mini-mart and grab some wine for tonight and some eggs so I can make you breakfast in the morning. Do you need me to pick up anything while I'm out?"

A complete do-over of her day to erase what happened at the barbecue. But that was impossible.

Collin tipped up her chin with his finger. "Do you want to come with me."

"No, I just want to get out of these clothes and take a shower."

"Will you be okay?"

Wanting to erase the concern in his eyes, she

forced herself to conjure up a smile. "Yes, once I get comfortable, I'll feel a whole lot better."

"You do that. Make yourself at home. First bedroom on the left." Collin gave her a lingering kiss. "I'll be back in a minute."

He left and she stood in the entryway. A weird type of exhaustion, a mix of too much coming at her at once, too little sleep and near crushing disappointment, landed on her. But she wasn't ready to give in to it yet. She needed a distance from it.

What Collin was doing for her right now, letting her pretend that everything was normal for a few hours. It was exactly what she wanted. She hadn't been able to define it, standing in the dining room of Roja after the meeting with her staff, but he'd just known.

She'd thought their connection had just existed at the restaurant, but it extended beyond that. She couldn't imagine being with anyone at that moment but him. It felt good…right and more normal than anything she could have imagined, all the way down to him bringing home mini-mart wine.

In the picture-perfect guest room with light wood furnishings, Nicole unzipped the green paisley bag sitting on the turquoise comforter.

Whoever had decorated it had bought every piece shown in the advertisement they'd come across, all the way down to the lamps and bookends, and dropped it into the space.

The only personal touches were the lingering scent of Collin's cologne, his clothes, which she could see through the cracked open door of the closet, and her sister's overnight bag.

She definitely needed a shower.

She sorted through Megan's things packed in the bag. Jeans and T-shirts. A cute red sundress and heels, a satin and lace teddy—yeah, she'd skip wearing that. Collin probably wouldn't mind loaning her a shirt to sleep in.

Suddenly eager for a shower, she took off her uniform, not bothering to search the multiple pockets to remove her pen or thermometer. After she rolled it up, she set the bundled uniform next to the bag.

In the adjoining white-and-gray-tiled bathroom, she slipped out of her pink bra and panties, turned on the glass-encased corner shower and, as soon as the temperature was good, stepped in.

The scent of Collin's body wash, something that reminded her of spice and evergreen, wafted around her as she showered.

While rinsing off under the wide showerhead, she closed her eyes and lifted her face toward the spray. A tiny stream of warm water entered her mouth, drifting over the tiny numb spot on her tongue. Numbness turned into a faint sting that spread like wildfire as memories from that afternoon rolled in.

If only...

If only she hadn't been in the interview, she might have noticed something, tasted something, felt something that would have staved off the disaster. She might even have caught the person in the act.

If only she'd done a better job, she wouldn't have failed her staff, or the people who'd trusted her to feed them, or her family, who now had to deal with her falling short.

Emotion struck hard, and she exhaled on a sob of despair. The sound was amplified by the glass shower doors.

Collin must have heard it, because he walked into the bathroom, concern filling his face.

As she waved him off, she closed her eyes and turned away, fighting tears and choking back sobs that made her shake. When he'd brought her to his home, he hadn't signed up for handling emotional outbursts.

Clearly he was undaunted. He stepped into the shower, and his strong arms embraced her from behind as he fit her back against his T-shirt and jeans. "Let it out," he whispered in her ear. "It's okay. I've got you."

Sadness, fatigue and frustration rolled up into one found its way out of her. It echoed off the tiles.

Flowed down with the tears from her eyes and merged with the water streaming down the drain.

She started shivering harder under the spray that had gone cold.

Collin turned off the water and let her go long enough to grab a thick blue towel hanging on the rack. He wrapped it around her. Fighting past the feeling of being drugged and detached from her body, she secured it over her breasts.

He turned her toward the door, and she walked out and curled up on her side under the comforter, feeling too heavy to move.

A short time later, Collin came to the side of the bed dressed in a dry T-shirt and sweatpants. He reached down and smoothed hair from her cheek. "What can I get you?"

She grasped his hand. "Nothing. Just come hold me. Please?"

He nodded and crawled under the comforter. She turned toward him, and he held her close. As she cuddled against his chest, her breathing naturally synced with the rise and fall of his, and she closed her eyes.

Nicole awakened in Collin's arms. Sometime during her nap, she'd turned and was spooned back against him. The semidamp towel had twisted around her like a vise.

She wiggled around, trying to dislodge the bulk

of the terry cloth stuck under her. As she pushed her hips back, Collin released a quick breath that blew over her nape. Goose bumps and tingles of awareness rose on her skin.

As she wrestled with the towel and turned, he loosened his hold.

Facing him as they lay on their sides with only inches separating them, she saw the desire that was simmering inside her burning strongly in his gaze.

Collin stroked his fingers over the curve of her cheek. "I know what you're thinking. But are you sure that's what you really want?"

Escaping with Collin and finding normal for a few hours—that's what she'd said she wanted. And right then, letting the desire they had for each other take hold felt more than just normal.

Nicole reached out and laid her hand on the middle of his chest. His heart beat hard against her palm. "Yes. I am. And I know there's an end date and it's soon. But I have enough 'if onlys' in my life right now. And I don't want to add us to that horrible list when I know being with you isn't just what I want…it's right."

Collin curved his hand to Nicole's hip and rolled her to her back. As he stared down at her his grip slightly tightened, and the internal debate reflecting in his eyes went away. "It feels right to me, too."

As he leaned in, she slid her hand up and curved it to his nape. He kissed her, and his slow, thorough exploration of the curves and hollows of her mouth ignited a need inside her that one kiss wouldn't satisfy.

She tugged at the hem of his shirt, and he sat up. The reveal of his abs and chest as he pulled it over his head made her mouth water. Nicole untucked the towel and pulled it apart. His gaze sweeping over her was like an invisible caress. Her breasts grew heavy. Her belly quivered as her breathing shallowed. An ache grew between her thighs.

Collin kissed her eyelids, swollen from her tears, and swept his lips down her cheek. His gentle, slow caresses and the heat of his mouth as he made his way down her body teased, soothed and worshipped. She was lost in pure want, mesmerized by the feel of her palms gliding over his heated skin, caught up in a sensual exploration of each other where they learned what brought each other pleasure.

Soon it became too much for both of them.

He stripped off his sweatpants, and after sheathing his erection, he fit himself between her thighs. Collin glided into her. She stroked her hands down his broad back and felt his muscles flexing and rippling underneath her fingertips. They moved as one, lost in a heady desire that shifted into pure bliss as she arched up underneath him, reaching her climax at the moment he found release.

Chapter Nineteen

Nicole separated the pink, green and yellow index cards and stacked them separately on the dining room table.

Wiley had sent her a text earlier that morning. The police investigators were going to start interviewing the staff tomorrow during the Monday cleaning shift at the restaurant. He'd mentioned they'd want her take on what happened, and she needed to work out her theory beforehand.

Collin walked from the kitchen carrying two mugs of coffee. He set hers on the table next to her, then dropped down in the chair beside her, holding his mug.

T-shirt, sweatpants, coffee and him. It was the perfect Sunday recipe for relaxation. But she couldn't. Not until she figured out what might have happened at the barbecue.

As she wrote Storage, Prep/Hold, Transport, Hold, Buffet under each other on the lined side of the cards with a blue pen, he stroked her back. The soothing gesture calmed her anxiety and awakened the temptation to crawl right back into bed with him.

Escape didn't begin to describe what they'd shared. Just like when they were cooking together, Collin had been able to anticipate what she'd wanted. And afterward, he'd held her in his arms and told her how good it had felt to be with her.

His remembered words moved over her, heating up her skin, like his kisses and caresses the night before and in the wee hours of that morning.

Nicole closed her eyes, seeing it in her mind. But she couldn't think about that now. She needed to figure out what happened at the barbecue.

She glanced over at Collin and pointed at the titles of the dishes she'd written on the blank side of the card earlier. "Pink represents the mango shrimp. Green is the melon, cucumber and tomato salad, and yellow is for the corn relish. These are the food items I know were contaminated. Like Wiley said, the lab results will tell us more."

"Where do you want to start?"

"With the corn relish." Shuddering, she shook off the remembered image of the corn relish teeming with fruit flies. "I say no to contamination during the storage and the prep phases. We all would have noticed them because they would have been flying all over the place. And corn wouldn't be the first place we'd find them."

Collin sipped coffee. "That's true."

As they discussed phases, she put a checkmark next to the ones where someone could have most likely contaminated the food. They did the same with the mango shrimp and the melon, cucumber and tomato salad. Both had been contaminated with the spicy pepper.

Collin peered at the cards. "Since you or the cooks are usually doing quality control checks and tasting the food during and after prep, it's unlikely someone did it in the kitchen. Someone would have picked up on it."

Nicole ran the scenario of who and when through her mind. "That leaves the waitstaff and runners overseeing the buffets. They would have had the most contact while stocking and monitoring the food."

"That's something you'll want to share with the investigators along with who else spent a lot of time under the tents. They may want to talk to them first about what they saw."

But that would include Mariana and Lesly. And

Lou's grandson Jay. She knew none of them was involved. "I can't wrap my mind around any of Roja's or Provisions' staff doing something like this. They just wouldn't."

"But someone did. I know it's hard to accept that it could be one of them, but you have to open yourself up to the possibility. One of them could be holding a grudge against you or your family because they think you have too much money or influence in Rambling Rose. Or they're upset at you as their boss because you reprimanded them over something they did or didn't do."

"Someone wanting to get back at me or my family. That sounds so…harsh."

"So you're telling me there's never been anyone who's held resentment toward you or your family?"

"Yes, of course. My dad was successful in the video game industry, and sometimes that attracted people who thought being our friend would gain them access to something they wanted. But no one's ever…" The face of the woman who'd caused problems for her entire family came to mind.

He put his mug on the table. "You've thought of something. What is it?"

"Charlotte Robinson—she was a relative. Sort of. She was married to Gerald Robinson, who turned out to be the long-lost Jerome Fortune." She shook her head. "It's a long, convoluted story, but they split up after a long marriage, and, well, she terrorized a lot of Fortunes."

"Oh?" Collin leaned in.

"But she can't be involved in this. She's in a psychiatric hospital."

But the possibility of someone coming after her family was becoming more of a reality lately. Incidents from the past year rose in her thoughts.

"But you're right." She closed her eyes for a moment, but that didn't block out the truth. "The balcony collapse was most likely caused by sabotage, and we keep having issues with our reservation programs."

Grimness shadowed his face. "So what happened with the barbecue is just part of a series of incidents against the hotel and the Fortunes."

"And without any suspects, it *could* be anyone, and I have to accept that. And balance that with the possibility that what happened at the barbecue could still just be someone who thought it would be hilarious to see people eat food spiced with a hot pepper. Videos pop up on the internet all the time of things happening to unsuspecting people. It's all about the likes, not the consequences. Whoever it is, we have to find them."

"And that's why you have to let the investigation run its course." With one hand, he slowly massaged her nape and then between her shoulders, kneading away the tension. "You, me, everyone close to

Roja has to be looked at so there's transparency. And trust."

"But what if we don't find out who did this? How will I or anyone else ever feel safe or comfortable at Roja again?"

As her anxiety rose and knots started to retighten in her neck and shoulders, Collin's magic touch found them. "You'll put cameras and safeguards in place. You'll get input from experts. You'll figure out a way. I know you will."

He stopped massaging, and she groaned at him in disappointment. "That felt so nice."

"Glad you liked it." He leaned over and kissed her. "I promise to give you a full-body massage from head to toe…after we paint the dining room." He punctuated his plan with kisses. "And the living room…and the kitchen."

"So I get a full-body massage every time we finish a room?"

As he kissed her again, Collin's chuckle rumbled against her lips. "Not quite the plan I had in mind, but I should have phrased it better."

"No. I actually like the way you phrased it."

"I bet you did." He stood, tugged her to her feet and into his arms. One long, wonderful kiss later, flavored with coffee and growing passion, he released her with a groan. "Let's get started before you completely distract me."

A short time later, Nicole helped him lay down a

drop cloth and apply painter's tape along the trim, baseboards, windows and door frames. With each task, the pressure she'd felt that morning about Roja lessened.

Her thoughts shifted to the text messages she'd traded with her sisters and brothers that morning. They'd wanted to know if she was okay. If she was going back to the Fame and Fortune Ranch. Not yet.

In the morning, on her way to Roja for cleanup day, she was stopping by her place to pack a few things. She was taking Collin up on his offer to stay with him for as long as needed. Admittedly, now that they'd grown closer, spending as much time as she could with him during his final week in town fueled most of that decision. But as much as she loved her family, at times like this, outside of Megan and Ashley, her other siblings and cousins could be a little too protective. And she understood. They wanted to shield her from getting hurt and to fix what was wrong.

Collin wanted to protect her, too, but he did it by keeping her away from the land mines in her thoughts. Once again, he was the lens that helped her to see things more clearly. And that's what she needed the most right now. Especially if she was going to get through tomorrow and the start of the investigation.

Chapter Twenty

In the back of Roja's empty dining room, Nicole shook hands with the dark-haired police investigator wearing a blue suit and tie.

"Ms. Fortune, I'm Detective Vale. I'm helping out with the preliminary interviews today. Please have a seat." The thirtysomething investigator with a slightly crooked nose flashed an easy smile, but gravity lurked in his gaze. She got the sense that he missed nothing and assessed everything.

Feeling a tad slouchy in an old pair of faded green chef's pants, she tugged down the long sleeves of her bleach-stained fitted yellow T-shirt as she sat down at the four-top table with him.

The smell of commercial cleaning products lingered in her nose. She probably reeked of oven, stainless steel and floor cleaner. She and the staff had been at it for three hours already, scouring every piece of equipment, surface and corner in the kitchen and storage areas.

He opened a small notebook and as he clicked his pen, he glanced at her. "With your family's tech background, writing things down must seem pretty old-school to you?"

"Not at all."

Answer the questions truthfully and succinctly. That's what Wiley, Callum and Steven had told her earlier that morning in their separate phone calls. And just as Collin had mentioned, Wiley had reminded her that everyone, including her, was under suspicion for contaminating the food.

Vale continued the interview. "Right now, we're just trying to get everyone's account of what happened the day of the barbecue. Tell me what you remember?"

"Where would you like for me to start?"

"When you first arrived here at Roja that morning."

She'd anticipated the investigators asking her this question. But knowing this still didn't relieve the feeling of dread that tightened like a rubber band around her chest as she gave her account of events.

As she also shared her theory about the most

likely time the contamination would have happened, her own internal questions ping-ponged in her mind about what she'd missed and how she could have prevented it.

"So," he said, "you mentioned that while you and your family were being interviewed, you signaled to one of the runners to start preparing the buffet for people to come through. Who was that?"

"Jay Cross."

"That name keeps popping up." He looked through his notes. "Someone mentioned that he'd worked some sort of special event involving this new summer menu."

"Yes, but it wasn't a special event per se, just a tasting with some of my family to get their opinions on the selections for the menu."

"Why him?"

"He's a hospitality intern. He has a really good memory. I needed someone who could remember the details about the dishes so he could explain them as they were served."

Vale's brows shot up. "Details as in what's in each dish?"

"Uh…yes, exactly."

"Okay…" As he jotted down notes, Nicole tried to read between the lines of what he wasn't saying, but she didn't like where he was going. How did Jay understanding the recipes make him a suspect?

Vale kept writing notes. "One more thing, Ms.

Fortune, and then I think we're done. Collin Waldon, he's the intern that helped cook for the recipe testing and so forth, is that right?"

"Yes. He did."

Vale lifted his head and looked her directly in the eyes. "And the two of you are in a relationship, right? So is it just a casual hookup, or are you two in it for the long haul?"

Relationship. The way Vale framed the word with Collin being an intern and possibly just a hookup made it sound wrong. And why did Vale need to know?

"You, me, everyone close to Roja has to be looked at..."

"Succinctly and truthfully..."

Collin's remembered words reasoned with her while Wiley's cautioned her.

Nicole met Vale's gaze. "Yes. Collin and I are seeing each other. He's done volunteering at Roja. And as far as the future, we haven't decided that yet."

"Got it. From what I understand, he's only in town for a short time. Do you happen to know when he's leaving?"

"Next Monday."

Vale's brow rose a tad. "I see."

Minutes later, she left Vale and went back to the kitchen.

As she attacked the wall in the prep area with a scrub brush, a text buzzed in from Collin.

How did it go?

As she took off her gloves to text him back, the look on Vale's face when he'd said, "I see" played through her mind.

The detective thought that she and Collin were in a just-sex relationship.

She started typing in the conversation she'd had with Vale about them, framed with rolling eyes emojis. But that was silly.

Nicole erased what she'd started to text Collin and typed in a new message.

It went okay. Lots to process. Tell you the details later.

Collin texted back.

Can't wait to hear them. And to see you.

Happiness warmed inside of her. What the detective thought about her and Collin didn't matter. And it didn't have anything to do with the investigation. She and Collin just hadn't defined this new level in their relationship.

Reasonable as it sounded to her, as Nicole stuck

her phone back in her pocket and returned to scrubbing the wall, one lingering questioned remained.

She and Collin hadn't put any labels on what they had...but should they?

Collin passed the paint roller over the wall in the living room in a V pattern.

Nicole was supposed to be helping him, but she stood in one place moving the long-handled roller over one section of the wall.

She'd come home from cleaning day at Roja clearly preoccupied. When he'd asked her how things had gone with the investigators, she'd mentioned they seemed to be taking a hard look at Jay Cross.

Jay was the last person he'd pick. Sure, Jay was strange, but he didn't see him as a saboteur.

In the silence, his mind went to a call he'd received from his father earlier that day. His roommate, Roy, had a birthday that Thursday. Sam had wanted to throw a small afternoon party for his new friend. Nothing fancy he'd said, just lasagna. Collin had told his father he'd help.

His father was happy and thriving in Houston, and he had Nicole to thank for it. His dad had made that confession during their drive to the Highlands. He'd refused to go into details. Sam had just said that Nicole had helped him see things differently. She'd changed his mind.

Collin glanced over at her. And last night, being with her had changed him.

When he'd brought her to the house, he hadn't planned on the two of them sleeping together. She'd been tightly wound after the barbecue incident, and he'd understood what she was going through. The need to stay strong even when a part of her felt powerless. To put managing the crisis over dealing with the anger, the sadness, the disappointment and self-recrimination. He'd been there, and known she'd need a soft place to fall. That's all he'd planned to be.

But then he'd held her in his arms in the shower and as they lay in bed afterward. She'd mentioned not wanting to add what they had to a horrible list of "if onlys" in her life. And he couldn't deny not wanting that regret, either. Now, he just wished that he hadn't tried to keep her at a distance. And that they'd had more time together…and that he could continue to be there for her in the weeks ahead as things unfolded about what happened at the barbecue and the fate of Roja.

As Collin looked at her, a strange ache of protectiveness, longing and frustration, all rolled together with emotions he couldn't define, swelled in his chest. He breathed them away.

Dwelling on what he couldn't change wouldn't help Nicole. He needed to focus on making every day they had left together count. And support her in any way he could in dealing with what happened at Roja.

He'd planned on asking if she wanted to visit his father and lend a hand with the party. It could be a good distraction for her as she waited on the lab results and news from the investigation.

She ran the roller through the paint tray but didn't move far from the place where she'd just been.

He set his roller down and went over to her. Wrapping his arms around her from behind, he placed his hands over hers.

She glanced back at him over her shoulder and smiled. "What are you doing?"

"You looked lonely over here."

"I'm doing that bad of a job, huh?"

"I didn't say that." And honestly, it was kind of nice to just hold her.

There were a lot of things he wished they could do, places he wished they could explore before he left.

As he guided her hands in painting the wall, the evening sun shining through the window warmed his face. "Let's go for a walk."

Moments later, they strolled the neighborhood, his fingers interlaced with hers.

The streets were quiet with only the occasional car driving past.

Her expression grew pensive. "Did you like growing up here?"

"Rambling Rose or this neighborhood?"

"Is there a difference?"

"I think so."

Actually, it was a big one. The town was a place to go. The neighborhood was a place to be. But Nicole lived in a suite on a ranch. Maybe she didn't understand.

He nudged her. "Something's on your mind. What is it?"

She offered up a half shrug. "A conversation I had with your dad. He mentioned something that happened to you when you were seven. That someone had bullied you."

"He mentioned that, huh?" His mind traveled back all those years. It had been a hard moment for him. One of many experiences that had taught him about life. And how he'd have to find his way through it.

Collin wrapped an arm around her waist. "At times, outside this neighborhood felt like a different place, but living here…" He pointed around him. "I felt accepted. It used to be a lot smaller. Everyone knew each other, and they looked out for each other. If someone knew you were sick, they made you chicken soup. If they had something extra, they shared it with you. A lot of families with kids also lived here. We rode our bikes, played ball, hung out." He pointed to a corner oak. "I had my first kiss right there."

"Was it Grace?"

"No. Her name was Penny Ortiz. I was thirteen and she was fourteen."

"Ooh. An older woman. How long did it last?"

A chuckle shot out of him. "About as long as that kiss. She broke up with me on Pie Share Day."

"Pie Share Day?" She frowned up at him as if he'd just spoken a foreign language.

"It was one of the town fund-raisers. A couple of days before Thanksgiving, people would bring a pie they'd baked to the local elementary school. The pies were given a number. Corresponding numbers were put in a box, and for ten dollars, people got to draw a number and they got that pie."

"That's so sweet."

Her smile prompted him to say more. He told her about apple picking at a local home orchard. Hayrides and bonfires. Pageants and parades. Things he hadn't thought or talked about in a long time.

An almost wistful expression came over her face. "When did it all go away?"

Collin mulled over the question. "Little by little, businesses in Rambling Rose closed. People had to drive to the next town for jobs or to buy the things they needed. I think people just kept driving."

They reached the house as the sun started to lower below the horizon, weaving oranges and reds in the darkening sky.

As he started to walk up the pathway, she stopped

and held on to his hand. "Will you miss Rambling Rose?"

His answer to the question should have been immediate and simple. He'd moved away from Rambling Rose close to a decade ago. The past three and a half weeks had been the longest he'd spent there since then. While he'd been away, other than his father, he hadn't thought much about the town, the neighborhood or the home he'd grown up in… until now.

He stroked her cheek, committing to memory its gentle curve and silky smoothness. But he knew full well it wouldn't sustain in the months to come when he'd wake up in the middle of the night, wishing he could hold, kiss and caress her.

The strange ache he'd felt earlier at the house attached itself to his heartbeats. He still couldn't define all of the emotions trapped inside of it, but, somehow, it was able to provide him a clear answer to her question. Surprise and a sense of loss struck deep. He would miss Rambling Rose because of her. Every time he thought of it, she would be a large part of his memories.

Collin leaned in and kissed her. "I will now."

Chapter Twenty-One

Nicole smoothed the skirt of her casual peach dress, slipped off her wedge-heel sandals and settled back into the passenger's seat in Collin's rental car.

Collin looked over at her from the driver's seat. Sunglasses hid his eyes, but his smile clearly conveyed his mood. "Ready?"

"Yes."

"Let's go." He pulled out of the driveway, and minutes later, they were on the interstate.

Miles later, a stretch of construction made the road uneven, and the car shook.

Nicole glanced to the two coolers in the back seat. A veggie and a beef lasagna, a packaged Caesar salad kit, and a small decorated cake were inside them. She and Collin were headed to the Highlands to see Sam and set up Roy's party.

"Everything good back there?" Collin changed lanes as cars slowed to a crawl.

"I think so. Nothing's tipped over."

"I hope this bottleneck lets up." He tapped the map on the car's built-in GPS. "Once we're past this, it doesn't look like we're dealing with construction all the way there."

"If we're running too late, we'll have to call Sam so he won't worry. He sounded so excited about the party when you talked to him last night."

"He is." Collin chuckled. "I'm glad Dad's adjusting well. He's settling in, making friends. The move's been good for him."

Since his dad had moved to Houston, Sam called Collin every day, sometimes twice. They were getting along so well. Right after the calls, Collin was usually quiet, and she hadn't been able to read him. It was good to hear him say he was happy for Sam. She'd wondered how Collin was adjusting to his father being in the Highlands…and him having to leave. He was flying back to Germany that Monday.

A thin layer of sadness covered her heart. The first of many over the next five days, she was sure. She was the one who had to adjust. After their walk the other day, Collin had said he'd miss Rambling

Rose, but he hadn't said he wanted to come back and visit the town…or her.

But a look had passed through his eyes, as if he'd had some kind of realization before he'd kissed her. A seed of hope started to sprout, but Nicole squashed it.

She was letting Detective Vale's questions and assumptions about her and Collin get to her again.

Imagining she saw something in Collin's eyes was just setting herself up for hurt feelings. When she and Collin had agreed to take their relationship to the next level, they'd both understood it was for the short term. But short term didn't make what they shared a meaningless hookup like Vale seemed to imply. They cared about each other, right? Was that what she saw in Collin's eyes, that he cared about her?

She could ask him.

No, she couldn't. With her going through a rough time with Roja, asking him how he felt about her would come off as a sympathy move or worse a way to trap him into telling her he cared. Collin wouldn't lie to her, but he was the type of guy who wouldn't want to hurt her feelings. It wouldn't be fair to put him on the spot like that, especially since he was so happy about finally being in a good place with his father.

They got through traffic and later arrived at the Highlands just outside Houston.

As they drove into the gated community, Nicole was drawn to the unfolding expanse of grass and brick cottages sitting back from the road. Residents walked or drove in golf carts on wide sidewalks. The landscape conveyed a sense of welcome.

Collin pointed to the tall building up ahead. "That's the main building I showed you on the website."

She remembered the photos he'd shown her. There were apartments, common spaces, a dining room, a specialized care section and the main offices.

He turned left, and a few yards up, he pulled into the driveway of a cottage on the right.

They unpacked the rolling coolers. She walked ahead of Collin, pulling one of them down the paved path toward the front door.

Before they reached it, Collin's father opened the door.

Pleasant surprise made Nicole pause and smile.

Sam looked genuinely happy, and there was a twinkle in his eyes. He smiled and opened his arms. "There she is."

She reached the landing and gave him a tight hug. "You look wonderful."

"Not as good as you." He tugged her inside the foyer. "Come in."

"Wow," Collin teased. "Am I still invited to this party?"

"Did you bring food?" Sam mocked a serious look.

"I've got the lasagna you wanted, right here."

"Well, since you brought me food *and* Nicole, I'll let you in."

Collin chuckled as he followed them inside. "Just remember, you can keep the food, but she's leaving with me."

"Oh, we'll see about that…" Sam squeezed her hand.

Watching Collin and his dad wrap an arm around each other in a hug made her heart swell.

Collin took over the cooler she'd rolled in and nudged her toward Sam, who still held her hand. "Go on. He wants to give you the grand tour."

Sam guided her past the blue couch that was part of a living room with simple wood furnishings and a television on a wood cabinet on a far wall.

A short hall to the right took her to his part of the cottage. It consisted of a bedroom with a sliding door separating it from a small seating area. There was also a bathroom and a corner laundry space.

Sam explained his roommate, Roy, had the same setup on the other side of the living room.

The setup reminded her of the suite of rooms she shared—well, used to share—with Megan and Ashley. She understood the appeal of sharing a home while having separate areas as retreats.

When they returned to the living room, Collin

spoke with a shorter, older man with white hair, a horseshoe-shaped mustache and round glasses.

Collin paused to introduce her. "Nicole, this is Roy."

"Hi, Roy. Happy birthday."

Roy offered up a shy smile as he dipped his head and shook her hand. "Thank you. And thank you for making me dinner."

"You're so welcome."

While she and Collin heated the medium-size lasagnas in the oven, Sam and Roy set the table then went to the living room.

The doorbell rang, and a couple who appeared to be at least in their seventies entered and joined Sam and Roy in the living room. Mary and Jack, she was told, lived down the street. They brought folding chairs and the after-dinner entertainment—Scrabble. Apparently they played board games regularly with Roy, and since Sam had moved in, he'd started joining them.

After the food heated, dinner was served, and Nicole and Collin took the folding chairs, her thigh pressed to his as they squeezed in at the small table.

Mary, an energetic woman with a cute white-haired bob, looked to Nicole and Collin. "You two are just like how Jack and I used to be, putting together dinner parties for our friends. Everyone came to our house, didn't they, Jack?" She nudged her thin, bald husband, who nodded.

Jack hadn't said much beyond hello since he'd arrived. It was hard to imagine him once being the life of the party.

"How did you two meet?" Nicole asked.

"Oh, boy," Roy muttered, looking down at his plate of salad and lasagna.

"You said it," Sam, sitting next to him, mumbled back.

The reason for their quiet comments quickly emerged as Mary launched into the story of her and Jack's lives, from the moment they'd met working on a cruise ship and thrown caution to the wind by marrying each other two weeks later to the places they'd traveled as a couple to finding themselves settled in Texas when Jack took a job on an oil rig.

Mary managed to talk and eat, finishing her square of lasagna at the same time as everyone else.

"It sounds like you've had a wonderful adventure together." Nicole stacked her plate on Collin's empty one on the table to save room.

"We did, and we still are. When we got married, we promised each other we wouldn't waste time and that we'd have adventures. People think time is about minutes or years passing by. No." She shook her head. "Time is measured by what you do and what you don't do with the people you care about. And after fifty-two years, we have no regrets, right, Jack?"

She nudged him, and Jack turned to look at her. He nodded.

As they held each other's gazes, you could see the love in their eyes.

As Jack turned his attention to his iced tea, Mary eyed Nicole and Collin. "How long have you two been together?"

Applying Wiley's rule of being truthful and succinct during an interrogation, Nicole answered, "Not long."

Mary pointed her finger between Nicole and Collin. "I can see it. You two are just like me and Jack. And you're a chef. You know what they say. The way to a man's heart is through his stomach."

"You're behind the times," Roy scoffed. "They don't say that anymore. Nowadays, they quote that singer. Something about if you like her, then put a ring on it. Oh, what's her name? I can't remember."

"Beyoncé," Mary and Sam chimed in at the same time.

Jack muttered, "I still say with lasagna like this, he'd be a fool not to stick around."

"My son's no fool." Sam turned to stare at Collin. "He knows how lucky he is."

Mary, Sam and Roy segued into a debate over the lyrics to the song.

Nicole, torn between laughter and feeling a bit self-conscious over their blatant matchmaking, especially coming from Sam, hazarded a look at Collin.

Amusement was in his eyes as he glanced toward Sam and his friends. As his attention shifted to her face, his laughter faded, but not his smile.

Collin took her hand and as he intertwined their fingers, she let herself imagine the type of whirlwind romance that Mary had described with Jack all those years ago. A great adventure…instead of a relationship with an end date.

A vision slowly rose in her mind of her and Collin taking cooking vacations, discovering new restaurants and out of the way places that would become their new favorites. Of them cooking and enjoying a meal together after a long day. Of watching him teach all that he'd learned from his mom about food to his own children someday…their children.

He'd be so patient with them, encouraging them to taste and try new things in the kitchen and in life. He'd make them laugh with his father's same teasing sense of humor, and he'd be the type of dad who'd make eating vegetables fun.

As she let the memory form in her mind, she saw herself smiling and laughing with him, loving every moment…loving him.

The images faded, but the intense connection, the comfort and unwavering trust, and the happiness from the vision remained.

But was it real or was she just caught up in Jack and Mary's description of their life together?

As Nicole met Collin's gaze uncertainty warred

with exhilaration, a bit of fear and a vulnerability she'd never experienced before in her life.

A small tremble momentarily vibrated through her.

As if he'd felt it, Collin briefly gave her a quizzical look. He smiled and as he squeezed her hand, his warmth seeped into her, stirring up the unexpected feelings inside of her even more.

Still in awe of it all, and trying to sort it out in her head and heart, Nicole conjured up a smile and squeezed back. She turned her attention back to the conversation, but the question in her head was louder than anything that was being said.

Was she in love with Collin?

Chapter Twenty-Two

Late in the evening, returning from Houston, Collin pulled into the driveway of Sam's house.

He turned off the engine, and Nicole woke up from dozing in the passenger seat.

At the start of the drive, she'd been so quiet, he'd started to wonder if something was wrong, but she'd just been tired.

She stifled a yawn. "Sorry, I didn't mean to knock out like that."

"After the spanking you and my father received playing Scrabble against Mary and Jack, I'm not surprised that you did."

Nicole laughed. "That wasn't a spanking. It was a total beatdown."

"Wasn't *beatdown* one of the words they played?"

"Yes. Along with *twerk*, *bizjets*, *kex* and *zorilla*— an African polecat. I'll never forget that word. And Jack, I still can't believe it."

The mild-mannered man had transformed during the game, exchanging whoops, high fives and fist bumps with his wife.

Nicole unfastened her seat belt and started slipping on her shoes and gathering her things.

Collin unfastened his own belt. For him, the part he wouldn't forget was Nicole. Her laugh had been so carefree. Especially when she'd been joking with his father about how badly they were losing.

And the way she'd taken the Beyoncé song comment in stride along with all the others about them as a couple. It made him wonder if she saw them lasting after he returned to Germany...

The other day, when she'd asked him if he'd miss Rambling Rose, he'd said yes, but he hadn't admitted that she was what he'd actually miss. It had felt too risky to say it. They'd only known each other a few short weeks, but it was true.

She was staying with him tonight. Maybe they could talk about their relationship. If she was interested in exploring more with him, they could talk about what that looked like.

Her phone rang in her bag at her feet. Nicole dug it out and checked the screen. "It's Wiley." She answered. "Hey. Sure, I can talk. Go ahead."

Collin started to get out of the car to give her some privacy, but she grabbed hold of his arm.

"Oh?" She looked at him as she spoke into the phone. "What did the results indicate?"

He sat back, knowing they were discussing the lab tests on the food from the barbecue.

Her grasp tightened on his arm. Depending on the results, the news could either help or hurt Roja…as well as Nicole.

A troubled look came over her face.

So much for their relationship talk. Tonight wasn't the right time for it. Setting aside disappointment, Collin laid his hand over hers. She'd been so happy a minute ago, and once again, the barbecue had stolen her happiness. Whoever had peppered the food needed to experience their own special level of hell for putting her through this.

Nicole said goodbye and hung up. "The food taken off the summer menu buffet and the melon, cucumber and tomato salad from the smoked barbecue buffet tested positive for concentrations of capsaicinoids for two varieties of pepper—the 7 Pod Douglah and the Carolina Reaper."

The first one he wasn't familiar with but the second… "The Carolina Reaper is considered to be one of, if not, *the* hottest pepper in the world. It packs a punch two hundred times hotter than the average jalapeño pepper. Do they know what form it was in?"

"They found traces of powder for both. All the culprit did was sprinkle it in."

Anger fueled his next breath. Whoever had sabotaged the food hadn't just wanted to disrupt the barbecue. They'd wanted to cause pain. And he wanted to know who that was…but he probably wouldn't get to unless the coward was unearthed from the hole he or she was hiding in before Collin left in five days.

Keeping his frustration in check, he turned to face Nicole. "This is good news. Your inventory records will back up that you've never ordered or used anything close to those two ingredients. It proves that it was brought in by someone."

"That's what Wiley said. And since they only found it in samples of food that were from the buffet table, it narrows down when it happened. During the barbecue and not in the kitchen." She paused. "Wiley shared the results with the health department. They moved the inspection up. It's the day after tomorrow. Aside from inspecting the kitchen, they want to know about the safeguards I'm putting in place to track who's handling the food."

A flash of uncertainty came into her face, and he squeezed her hand. "You've already written your action plan. We can go over it again to be sure, but you're ready."

"I know." She released a breath. "But that still doesn't change the fact that unless we find whoever did this, they could still be working at Roja, waiting to hatch their next plan."

"And that's why more cameras have been installed in the kitchen and around the hotel. They're not only in place to keep watch, but as a deterrent. And honestly, I doubt whoever did this will risk taking another chance. Don't let them scare you."

"You're right." Determination came back into Nicole's eyes. "I won't let them win. I can't."

Nicole walked through the dining room of Roja. No rattling of dishes, the clinking of glasses or the low hum of voices. Just the rustle of her uniform and the thump of her Crocs on the carpet filled the cavernous silence. It felt strange to be there without the hum of activity filling the place.

The restaurant inspector was supposed to show up sometime between eight in the morning and noon. She'd use the time to take inventory and get her food order ready. Once she got the green light from the inspector, she'd hit Send.

Nicole went to her office, put her bag down on the desk and sat behind it.

The stillness in the kitchen mirrored the dining room.

Months ago, before Roja officially opened for business, she used to sit there and visualize the success of the restaurant. What she'd experienced over the past few weeks was nothing she could have ever imagined. The diner's shady advertising, the barbecue…and she certainly hadn't seen Collin coming into her life.

Tonight and Sunday…that's all the time they had left together. Understandably, he was spending Saturday with Sam. It was hard to imagine that she wouldn't see him next week or the week after or anytime soon. Waking up together. Sharing meals. Helping him paint and fix up the house. Going for walks around the neighborhood. Ordinary things that she didn't want to stop doing with Collin. Because she'd fallen for him. She knew that now, especially after yesterday.

She'd been stressed over the inspection, going over the notes and diagrams for the action plan over and over again.

Collin hadn't complained once or told her she was being obsessive. He also hadn't given her empty reassurances. Instead he'd urged her to reach out to other people she trusted for their insight into her plan.

She'd ended up having a Zoom call with Adam, who helped run Provisions, then Megan, as well as Mariana and Lesly. They'd all given her valuable insight as well as reassurances about what she'd mapped out for Roja.

By the end of the day, she'd felt more confident.

And then he'd fed her one of the most delicious homemade lasagnas she'd ever tasted. And for dessert, he'd surprised her with vanilla ice cream topped with Lou's roasted strawberry jam. While she'd been in meetings, he'd tracked down Lou and gone to pick up a jar.

The memory of sitting at the dinner table with her eyes closed, struggling not to peek, and feeling the coldness of the spoon near her lips prompting her to let him feed her the ice cream made her smile now.

Falling for Collin wasn't just about all of the things he'd done for her. It was about him caring enough to do them. And her wanting to be there for him in return.

Her phone buzzed, and she fished it out of her purse. It was a group text from her family sending encouragement her way for the inspection. Nicole sent back her thanks.

Love you...

Text bubbles with only those two words popped up more than once. As she smiled, tears pricked in her eyes. She loved them all so much. Once she passed the inspection, they could celebrate. Maybe an impromptu date night at Roja before Collin left? Ashley and Rodrigo were coming back today. They could join them. It would be fun to be there as a couple with the rest of her family.

As plans started forming in her mind, footsteps echoed from the kitchen.

Grace walked in, looked at her behind the desk and smiled. "You have no idea how good it is to see you there."

Nicole exchanged a brief hug with her and sat down again. "I've missed you, too."

Grace sat in a chair in front of the desk. "You look rested. I'm glad you didn't let what happen totally stress you out."

"I can thank Collin for that."

"He's a good guy. I'm glad he was there for you. And that you were there for him. When is he leaving, by the way?"

"On Monday."

"That soon?" Grace gave her an empathetic smile. "I guess that answers the question I was going to ask."

"What?"

"When do you want to reopen Roja for business? Should we shoot for Wednesday, maybe?"

"That works."

On Monday, she probably would be emotional after Collin left. Tuesday, she and the staff would be buried in food preparation for the next day's service. Wednesday, she'd be focused on the reopening, and the rest of the week, she'd hopefully remain too preoccupied to dwell on how much she missed him.

More footsteps echoed in the kitchen. A moment later, a tall, thin, neat-looking auburn-haired man in a gray shirt, tie and slacks came to the doorway. He carried a clipboard and a small bag in his hands.

He gave a nod and a quick smile. "Chef Fortune?"

Nicole rose from the chair. It was time for the inspection.

Nearly three hours later, she dropped the inspection results form on her desk. They'd passed! Roja could reopen its doors to the public.

A seal on the pot-sink faucet and a light in the storeroom that had literally flickered out while they were standing there were the only two issues the inspector had noted.

Nicole dropped into her chair and sighed in relief. He'd be back next week to see if the safeguards she'd mentioned were working.

She texted the good news to her family and Grace. And then sent one to Lesly and Mariana. They'd agreed to reach out to the staff about their work schedules starting on Tuesday.

And now Collin. He'd told her to let him know what happened.

She called him, but he didn't answer. Collin had mentioned mowing the lawn and trimming the rosebushes. Maybe he didn't have his phone nearby. The line switched to voice mail, and just as she went to leave a message, he called.

Smiling, she answered. "What are my chances

of enticing you into coming over here for an early lunch?"

"Nicole." Collin paused. His voice sounded strange. "It's my dad…"

Chapter Twenty-Three

Nicole picked up the empty tray from the table.

Was there enough food out? Should she make more coffee?

Was Collin okay?

The last question had run through her mind so many times over the past five days since Sam had died from heart failure. And she wasn't sure of the answer. Stoic, neutral and unreadable had been the extent of his emotions, and today he'd grown even more distant since the funeral that morning.

Tray in hand, she peeked into the adjoining living room.

The polished wood floors gleamed under the folding chairs that were positioned near the recently painted walls. Only a few of the fifteen or so remaining people who'd come to pay their respects sat down. Some were people Sam had worked with at the dental company. Some were fellow golfers he'd played with on weekends before he'd gotten sick. Others were people he'd lost touch with over the years. And then there were his new friends.

Mary, Jack and Roy had come to the funeral and stopped by the house. Sam had touched them during their short time together, and it was clear to see they felt his loss.

Her eyes lit on Collin as he stood speaking with Mr. Harris, the vendor from Mariana's Market. In his charcoal suit, gray shirt and black tie, Collin looked even taller, leaner.

As Collin shook Mr. Harris's hand, she saw gratitude flicker on his face.

Grace came up next to Nicole, stealing her attention. Grace and Wiley had been at the funeral along with Grace's parents, Sam's neighbors. They'd left earlier, but Grace had stayed to assist with the repast she'd helped Nicole organize with chairs from the hotel and food catered by Roja.

Megan and Mark and Ashley and Rodrigo had also attended the funeral. But having just met Collin, and not knowing Sam, they hadn't wanted to intrude on the private gathering of Sam's friends and colleagues paying their personal respects to Collin.

Grace pointed to the tray Nicole held. "Do you want me to take it?"

"That's okay. I'm heading to the kitchen to make more coffee." Nicole lingered.

Grace slipped the tray from her grasp. "Go check on him. I'll make the coffee."

"I don't know what to do for him. He's so closed off. I don't think he's even cried."

Nicole's worries about Collin slipped out on a whisper and landed on a hitched breath partially stolen by grief. Sadness swelled inside her, making the knee-length black dress she wore feel overly tight and warm.

Grace gave her a subdued, understanding smile. "Just be there for him."

"Okay." Composing herself with a cleansing breath, Nicole walked to Collin. On the way, she stopped at the beverage table set up along the side-wall for a small bottled water.

As she walked up, a blond, linebacker-size man who looked to be in his thirties said goodbye to Collin.

"Thank you for all you did for my father, Ian."

"No thanks needed. He was a good man." Ian shook Collin's hand and acknowledged her with a polite smile before he left the house.

Collin glanced over at her. She offered him the water, and he took it. "Thank you."

"Can I bring you anything else? Some food, maybe? You haven't eaten."

"No. I'm fine." He gave her a tight-lipped smile.

That's what he kept telling her. But he wasn't. His walled-off emotions were apparent in the stiffness of his shoulders, the tight angles of his jawline and the flatness in his eyes.

Soon, everyone trickled out the door.

Grace was the last one to go, giving Collin a tight hug. "Don't forget. We're all here for you."

"I know. Thanks." He nodded, swallowing hard.

Helplessness rose in Nicole as she watched him walk away.

Grace clasped Nicole's hand and gave it a squeeze. "Don't give up on him. When he's ready to reach out, he will."

As Nicole tidied up the dining room and kitchen, Collin folded the chairs. Then he took off his jacket, laid it on the table, then walked out the French doors.

She finished up and joined him where he stood staring at the roses.

Was he remembering how much his father loved to tend to them or the connection to his mom and Sharon that he'd told her about during one of their evening walks?

They'd talked about a lot of things. He knew he could talk to her now, didn't he?

She touched his arm, and it hardened like steel

under her palm. "Collin, it's okay not to be fine. I only knew Sam for a short time, and I'm not."

He bowed his head and shut his eyes. "I'm sorry you're not fine."

She tugged at his arm, turning him away from the flowers, and stood in front of him. "This isn't about me. This is about you. I can see you're hurting. You can't just keep it inside. Talk to me. I'll listen."

Collin's jaw angled even more as emotional pain intensified in his eyes.

She threw her arms around him, and as he hugged her back, his heart beat hard against her cheek. He wasn't saying anything, but he wasn't pushing her away, either. It was a start.

Nicole opened her eyes, startled awake in the darkness by the coolness of the sheets instead of Collin's furnace-like warmth. She sat up, turned on the bedside lamp and checked the time on her phone laying on the nightstand. It was a little after two in the morning. Where was he?

Listening for him in the house, she encountered silence. Should she lay there and wait for him or should she get up and see where he was?

She got out of bed, tugging down the hem of her loose gray tank over the waist of her comfy pink shorts as she walked out of the room.

The light was on at the bedroom at the end of the hall.

She'd at least check on Collin and remind him that she was there to listen or just sit with him, if that's what he wanted.

She paused at the entrance to what had been Sam's room.

Collin, dressed only in a pair of sweats, sat against the wall with his knees drawn up, arms resting on his legs, staring at a photo in his hand.

"Hey." She walked slowly into the room. Did he need space or should she go to him?

He stared at her blankly for a moment before his gaze focused on her. "Hey, it's late. What are you doing up?"

"I woke up and you weren't in bed. I came to check on you."

Nicole sat down close beside him, her shoulder pressing to his. She glanced at the picture in his hands.

It was a photo of his father, who looked to be in his thirties, sitting on a couch, cradling a baby wrapped in a blue blanket in his arms. A pretty brown-skinned woman sat beside him. Both of them stared at the baby with soft smiles on their faces, clearly mesmerized.

Nicole pointed at the photo. "Is that you with your parents?"

Collin nodded. "Before my dad moved to the

Highlands, a crashing sound woke me up in the middle of the night. For a second, I thought someone had broken into the house or that he was hurt. I found him in here standing in front of the closet. When we'd packed up his things, a photo album was missed on the top shelf. Instead of waiting until morning when I could help him get it, he'd used his cane to pull it down. There were photos all over the floor. I thought I got them all, but I guess I missed this one."

Wanting to handle getting the album himself, that definitely sounded like Sam. But Nicole held back the comment and just listened.

"A lot of them were wedding photos. The roses out back, I always thought his second wife, Sharon, had just planted them for no reason. But she'd done it for my dad as a reminder of my mom. The same type of roses had been in her wedding bouquet."

Nicole swallowed against tightness in her throat and willed herself not to cry. Collin didn't need her getting emotional. He needed her to sit in this moment with him and just be there as he told her about Sam and his mom.

She slid her hand around his arm, and his bare bicep flexed under her fingertips as she laid her head on his shoulder. "Really? That's so sweet. How did they meet?"

Collin told her how his parents had met and how

his dad had fallen head over heels for his mom, Beth, and pursued her.

He also shared a few of his own memories about his parents. How whenever Sam wasn't on the road, traveling for his job, he'd brought Beth a cup of her favorite tea in the mornings so she could enjoy it in bed before she got up. And how Beth used to always curl up in his father's chair during Sam's nightly calls when he was away. How his parents had always been a beacon for him in the crowd during ball games and ceremonies. And how proud they'd been when he'd graduated from Officer Candidate School and received his commission.

Collin stared at the photo in his hand. "Earlier when I couldn't sleep, I came in here. I don't know what made me look in the closet, but I did, and this was there turned over, flat against the wall, stuck in the molding. Like it was waiting for me. But it was just a coincidence." But a hint of hopefulness, as if he wanted to believe in happenstance, was in his tone.

She lifted her head from his shoulder, and as she looked at his face, for a brief moment, she glimpsed the young boy of the past—loved by his parents and loving them back. In the man of today, she saw the shadow of grief in his eyes.

She gently traced his brow with her fingertips. "Sometimes coincidence is a compass. It shows you the way to something you need."

"Do you really believe that?"

"I do."

In the midst of his emotional pain, he'd needed to be reminded of his parents' love, and the picture had been there for him. But he wasn't ready to hear about his grief or his emotions.

She went a different direction. "That day in Mariana's Market, I'd needed inspiration and I bumped into you."

"So coincidence brought us together?"

As she stared into his eyes, she felt like his parents looked in the picture. Mesmerized by him. Awareness spread over her as the heat of his arm seeped through her shirt and into her breast. Desire uncoiled inside of her, and she couldn't stop her gaze from dropping to his mouth a short distance from hers.

Nicole's breathing shallowed. "Possibly."

He leaned in, closing the distance between their lips to a fraction of an inch. "I'm glad it did."

Collin kissed Nicole and the brief kiss he'd planned expanded into longer ones more urgent than the last.

He set the picture beside him and curved his hand to her cheek, fully capturing her mouth.

Her moan hummed into him as she glided her palm up his chest, igniting a fire inside of him, melting some of the coldness that had burrowed into him the moment he'd heard his father had died. He needed more of her warmth. He needed her.

Collin broke away from the kiss and stood.

Nicole's gaze held his as he helped her to her feet and swept her up in his arms.

As he carried her down the hall, her soft kisses to his jawline and the side of his neck almost weakened his legs.

In the bedroom, as they undressed, the unveiling of her lush breasts as she lifted off her top, and her shorts sliding down the flair of her hips revealing her sex, made his mouth water.

She was so beautiful.

Nicole wrapping her arms around him, rising on her toes and clasping his nape to bring his lips to hers snapped him out of his trance. He crushed his mouth to hers, palmed her hips and melded her softness against him.

Laying her on the bed, need fueled kisses that traveled from her mouth to the peaks of her breasts, down her belly and lower still. She was sweetness, desire and heat. And he couldn't get enough of her.

Long moments later, sheathed in protection, he glided into her sex.

Nicole laid a hand to his cheek, the glow of passion on her face and soft emotions in her eyes. "Oh, Collin," she whispered, "I don't want this to end."

Was she referring to that moment or the days they had left together?

His own emotions, and all he felt for her, welled inside him. He couldn't put it into words. But he could show her.

As they moved as one, he made a conscious effort to slow down, to hold her gaze, to extend the moment of making love to her for as long as he could.

Until her climax overtook her, and pleasure and release along with an intensity he'd never experienced before ruled him, and made his heart beat even faster as realization hit him squarely in the chest.

His heart belonged to Nicole.

At dawn, Collin jogged down the street. He'd left Nicole sleeping in bed, needing to get out of the house.

Even though he knew his father was gone, a part of him still waited to hear his footsteps in the house. In his mind, he could still see him outside fussing over the roses. He longed to battle with his dad's stubbornness...just a few more times.

When he'd moved his father into the Highlands, not looking too far ahead and keeping things in perspective had been his strategy for dealing with the future. He'd looked forward to a few more phone calls with his dad. To celebrating a holiday or two— Thanksgiving and Christmas with his father and his new friends. And to bringing Nicole along with him and seeing her and his dad laughing together while losing at Scrabble one more time.

Fresh grief hit Collin like a sharp blazing hot knife cutting into his chest. He sucked in an extra breath and momentarily lost a step.

Regaining his pace, he tried to clear his mind, but the picture he'd found of him and his parents in Sam's room flashed into his thoughts.

Nicole had said finding the photo was a compass, leading him to something he needed. But right then, it felt more like a reminder of all he'd lost.

Heaviness dropped down on Collin, slowing him to a full stop.

He'd thought he'd been ready to accept losing his dad, but he'd been wrong. Just like he'd been wrong about his plan to talk to Nicole about dating each other long-distance. And from what he'd witnessed in her eyes as they'd made love earlier that morning, she would have said yes.

A week ago, before Sam died, that answer would have made him happy and optimistic about the future. But he didn't feel that way now. It wasn't that he didn't care deeply about her. Actually, he loved her.

But not even love could erase the fact that so many things could go wrong that had nothing to do with being apart from each other. Nicole could simply be taken from him in the same way he'd lost his mom and dad…in an instant.

He'd faced other losses in his life, but losing the people closest to him brought a different type of pain. And the possibility of one day losing Nicole without warning was more than he could bear.

Chapter Twenty-Four

As Nicole pulled up to Collin's house, a truck from the Hotel Fortune pulled out of the driveway.

She hadn't expected them to come by for the chairs until later that day. Had they woken up Collin?

Early that morning, after taking a shower after his run, he'd crawled back into bed with her. She'd left him sleeping while she'd gone to Roja to check in with Mariana and Lesly and make sure the food prep safeguards were in place.

On the way home, she'd picked up eggs, bacon, cinnamon bread and orange juice from the mini-mart.

A late breakfast wouldn't take away the grief of losing Sam, but maybe preparing it together would lessen it. And allow them to talk and be honest with each other. After what they'd shared last night, and with only a few short days before Collin left Rambling Rose for good, she couldn't hold back how she felt for him anymore. What she felt for him went beyond a few weeks together. And she believed it was strong enough to expand past Rambling Rose and the ocean that would separate them.

Since she'd awakened that morning, what Mary had said at Roy's birthday party kept echoing in her mind.

"Time is measured by what you do and what you don't do with the people you care about..."

It was clear to her now. She and Collin shouldn't waste the time they had.

Nicole got out of the car and grabbed the large canvas tote that held all she'd bought, along with her purse, from the back seat.

As she walked into the house, the smell of fresh paint greeted her.

Collin looked up from where he had obviously touched up the wall. But the jeans, pullover gray shirt and boots he wore were his nice clothes, not the paint-stained shirt and jeans he'd worn previously while doing work around the house.

Sadness shadowed his smile as she walked over to him. In time the sorrow would fade. The house was on its way to a new beginning. And they were, too.

"Good morning." She paused to give him a kiss

on the way to the kitchen. He tasted like coffee. "I've got bacon, eggs, cinnamon bread and juice. I thought we could make breakfast."

As she went to walk away, he took her hand. "We really need to talk."

"I know we d—" The words halted when she saw Collin's packed bags in the hallway.

The day after Sam had passed away, she'd mentioned to him about staying at her place until he left. That way, he could take the bed and the dining set to Goodwill in the next town over now. Was that what was happening? Was that what he wanted to talk about?

She met Collin's gaze and found her answer. Disappointment sank deep in her stomach. "You're leaving?"

Collin slipped the canvas bag from her loosening grasp, set it on the floor and took her hand. "I'm staying in billeting on the military installation until I fly out. The Realtor is going to take care of clearing the house. Dad's gone. Most of his affairs are in order, and what's not, I can take care of when I get back to Germany. Right now, I need to get back to my normal life, my responsibilities. And you do, too. You have Roja to take care of. Our lives are moving in two different directions."

Nicole looked into his eyes, searching for doubt, for answers about what had changed since last night, but his guards were up, veiling his emotions. "Collin. Why don't we sit down and talk about this?"

"Talking about this won't change the outcome." He paused, visibly swallowing as if it took effort. "Ending it now is the best thing for both of us."

As she looked into his eyes, she saw the belief in his decision, and her inability to change his mind. She couldn't make him see things differently.

Nicole suppressed the urge to scream, to shout at him. She also wouldn't beg. She'd give him what he wanted. For things to end between them.

Rising on her toes, she pressed her mouth to his, lingering for a moment. The spark of love and desire that rose naturally inside her added a bittersweetness that drove her away.

Unable to look at him and willing herself not to cry, Nicole picked up her bag and walked out. She loved him, and she knew he loved her, too, but she had to get out of his way. She had to let Collin go.

Collin slowed down and eased his foot on the brake.

Down to one lane, bumper-to-bumper traffic moved at a crawl through the part of the road under construction.

He tapped the screen synced to the car's GPS system, and a map of the interstate illuminated. Red flags indicated construction for the next ten miles. Great.

It was an even longer bottleneck than when he and Nicole were driving to Houston for Roy's birthday party.

As he adjusted his sunglasses, his gaze strayed to the passenger seat. Instead of seeing his small duffel bag, in his mind he saw Nicole on that day. She'd been so happy, and she'd looked so pretty in that dress. Had he told her that?

All the things he had said to Nicole that morning seeped into his mind.

"Ending it now is the best thing for both of us."

And it was.

Collin's phone rang through the car's speaker system. He clicked a button on the steering wheel and answered.

"Hello, Collin. It's Ruby. How are you?" As always, concern and compassion flowed easily in her tone.

It resonated with the dull heaviness in his chest. "I'm okay."

"I'm so sorry I couldn't make it to the funeral. I had a personal emergency. You have my deepest condolences for your loss. I know you'll miss him."

Collin cleared his throat, thick with emotions he struggled to define. "Thank you. And no apology needed for not being there. I hope everything worked out."

"Yes, thankfully it did. I just wanted to let you know that I was thinking of you. And if you still need my help as you start to settle his medical bills and insurance, please feel free to call me."

Collin let the car roll forward, shortening the gap between him and the car in front of him. "I will. Thank you. Take care."

"Wait…before you hang up. I think there's something you should know. Sam didn't want to mention it to you, but under the circumstances…"

He pressed down on the brake. What had his father kept from him? "Go on."

"Your father had agreed to take the drug cocktail. He was supposed to start the week after he died."

His dad had been so adamant about not doing it. "Do you know what changed his mind?"

"I believe I do. He'd mentioned that you'd met someone, and he was looking forward to the two of you joining him for the winter holidays." Ruby chuckled softly. "He'd also said that by then he'd hoped you'd wake up and propose. That maybe he'd make it all the way to your wedding day."

Collin blinked, clearing his eyes that had suddenly gone blurry behind his sunglasses. "He said that?"

"Yes. I just thought you'd want to know how happy he was that you were happy."

He thanked her, and they said their goodbyes.

Ruby's words came with him as he continued to move through traffic.

He imagined the day his father had longed for and what Sam's smile might have looked like. Collin saw himself standing with Nicole on their wedding day, awed by her, devoted to her, all in on the commitment of living the rest of their lives together.

The emotions Collin hadn't allowed himself to define a minute ago surfaced full force inside him and became a one-two gut punch that made him suck in a breath.

Fear. He loved Nicole, but he was scared that maybe she didn't love him as much. He was afraid of not being there when she needed him and failing her. That what he had to offer her wasn't enough.

Collin tightened and loosened his hold on the steering wheel as he acknowledged what else was there. Profound loss. Not just because of losing his father, but over losing Nicole. The very thing he'd thought he could avoid by leaving her.

Chapter Twenty-Five

Her phone buzzing on the coffee table awakened Nicole on the couch. She blinked her gritty eyes that were swollen from too many tears and not enough sleep.

The light from the screen illuminated the darkness. The microphone on the doorbell camera that synced to her phone echoed and amplified whispers.

"I know it's in here someplace. Where's yours?"

"I left it at home. Use the key code."

"I would if you'd give me some light. I can't see."

Recognizing Megan's and Ashley's voices, Nicole pulled herself up from the couch. By the time she left her suite and padded down the main hallway to the foyer, they'd gotten the front door open.

Standing outside, just beyond the threshold, she met matching blue gazes.

In the next instant they rushed in on their high heels, bringing filled plastic grocery bags, rolling suitcases and compassion through the door with them.

As they enveloped her in a tight three-way hug, she connected the dots of how they'd come to arrive there.

After leaving Collin that morning, she'd gone to Roja, hoping to lose herself in the kitchen. Within the first thirty minutes, she'd snapped at her staff, burned a pan of gravy, nicked herself chopping carrots and spilled a bag of dried beans in the storeroom.

Red beans and rice. Collin's comfort food. That's what she'd been thinking about when she'd dropped the container. Grace had come to the kitchen to talk to her about something. She'd taken one look at Nicole and ushered her out of the kitchen and to her office in the hotel.

Nicole had told Grace the basics—she and Collin had broken up. As soon as Nicole had said it, she'd realized being around hot surfaces, knives and heavy objects was the last place she needed to be. She'd come home.

By the time she'd gotten there, Wiley had called then sent a text when she hadn't answered. Before long, more calls and texts started coming in from her other family members. She'd assured them in a group text that she was okay. She just needed time alone.

Megan and Ashley were the only ones who hadn't responded. She'd known then that they were heading to see her.

A long moment later, an unexpected sensation made Nicole ease back a little. "Something cold is on my butt."

Ashley slipped out of the embrace first, holding up a plastic grocery bag. "Ice cream. I came prepared."

"I did, too," Megan added. "I brought wine."

Nicole looked into her sisters' faces, and the compassion in their eyes threatened to unleash fresh tears. She hadn't known she'd needed her sisters so badly until that moment.

Megan and Ashley wheeled their bags to their old rooms in their suite.

Nicole went back to the couch.

The familiar sounds of them moving around their suites soothed her.

"I'm on my own now..."

That's what she'd mentioned to Lou all those weeks ago. And that's truly how she'd felt. Not just with Megan and Ashley moving out but also with Roja. And then she'd met Collin and her world had changed.

Nicole closed her eyes and a vision of Collin that day in the market appeared, crystal clear.

If she'd known that heartache was ahead of her that day, would she have walked away from him?

A cool hand smoothing over Nicole's warm cheek alerted her to the tears that had leaked past her closed eyelids.

"Oh, sweetie." Megan dried her tears. She set the full wineglass she carried on the coffee table and hugged Nicole. "It'll be okay."

Ashley, now comfy like Megan in shorts and a loose tee, came in with a bowl of ice cream topped generously with Lou's jam.

The ice cream and the wine were both for Nicole.

Nicole chose the ice cream. She'd already had a bowl that day, but more couldn't hurt. She could always have wine later.

Megan's phone chimed on the side table. She picked it up. After reading the text, she wrapped an arm around Nicole and gave her a squeeze. "That's from Stephanie. She said she loves you and she'll call you tomorrow."

"Tell her thanks and send her a kiss back."

Megan set down the phone, and she and Ashley crowded closer to Nicole, leaning against her like bookends, holding and supporting her.

Ashley rocked against her. "Tell us what happened."

Nicole let the whole story pour out of her. She finished and her heart ached.

Megan hugged her a little tighter. "Collin's grieving his dad. Maybe he'll come around once he's had some time."

"Time?" Ashley scoffed. "Think of how stubborn Mark and Rodrigo can be. Sometimes guys need a nudge in the right direction. Nicole, you should just tell him how you feel."

"And what if he still says no? What if I misjudged him and he doesn't feel the same?" Both prospects added to the lump in Nicole's throat. She set her melting bowl of ice cream and jam on the coffee table. "We said our goodbyes. And now it's time for me to move on."

Chapter Twenty-Six

The chic ranch and Texas-cool atmosphere of Roja Restaurant is part of what makes it a diamond in the rough. Their menu delivers on its promise. Every offering will lure you back for more. I'll definitely be back for the calabaza con pollo...

Nicole sat back in her desk chair. Shock and disbelief made her mouth drop open as she read the glowing review.

Filling out the restaurant suggestion box on the *Texas Eats Quarterly* website weeks ago had been long forgotten, but there it was. One of their reviewers had come to Roja before the fund-raiser buffet disaster and loved the restaurant.

Mariana and Lesly beamed wide smiles on the other side of the desk, too happy and excited to sit down.

"Is it okay if I print this and post copies for the staff to read?" Lesly said. She'd been the one to deliver the news after finding out about it from a friend and hunting down a tweet with a link.

"Absolutely."

"We need to send copies to the Roadside Diner. Better yet, we should hand out flyers in front of their building that say, 'Fall into this spectacular review and suck it, Roadside Diner.'"

If only...

Nicole sent the link to Grace. "We're not going to waste energy on the diner. A good review like this one beats a smear campaign, hands down."

Lesly and Mariana hurried out of the office to share the good news.

At her desk Nicole read the full review again. They'd come to dinner the day Collin had made the *calabaza con pollo*...and added cumin. Remembering that day in the kitchen and the way he'd looked at her with desire in his eyes and touched her, made her chest ache with her pulsed heartbeats. She swept the image of Collin from her mind and got up from her desk. Roja had a review to continue to live up to. She didn't have time to slack off.

In the kitchen, she seamlessly joined her cooks, taking up her position at the pass-through window.

The usual lunch rush didn't happen, but with the hotel being fully booked, business was fairly steady.

Lesly came to the window on the service side. "One of our guests has a complaint. They said something isn't right."

Dread rose in Nicole. *Oh no.* She grabbed a plastic tasting spoon from a nearby container. "Which entrée is it?" A protocol list from the safeguards she'd created lined up in her mind.

"No, it's not the food." Lesly frowned. "I'm not sure what it is, but they'll only talk to you."

"Which table is it?"

Lesly gave her the number.

"Tell them I'll be right there." So much for ending her day on the high of the *Texas Eats* review. But complaints were just as much a part of running a restaurant as good reviews, she reminded herself.

Pasting a customer-friendly smile on her face, Nicole entered the dining room and went to the table. No one was there.

Her gaze was drawn to the next table over by the window. It was where she and Collin used to sit.

A bouquet of red, white and pink roses along with tiny purple flowers, tied with a pink ribbon, lay in the middle of the table. They looked so much like Sam's roses. Curiosity pulled her closer. She recognized the tiny green fronds with purple flowers. It was rosemary.

"If you're wondering whose they are, I'll tell you. They're for you."

Hearing Collin's voice behind her made her heart pick up its beat. Why was he there? Hadn't they already said their goodbyes? Was this second time some kind of official end to them? Sadness and frustration settled in her chest.

Mary had said time consisted of the things you did and didn't do. There was one more line that should be added to that advice. It also consisted of what you did and didn't say.

She needed closure. And being honest with him would give her that.

Nicole spun around, bolstering her courage and ignoring how impossibly wonderful he looked in a blue pullover, jeans and beige Lugz boots. Like that day he'd first bumped into her at Mariana's Market, she couldn't help but stare at him.

But frustration over their breakup kicked in, and she advanced on him. "Before you say whatever it is that brought you here, I have something to tell you. I don't agree that ending things was best for both of us. It was just better for you. We're good together, and I love you. And think you feel the same, but you're just too afraid or blind or stubborn to see it."

Collin's patient expression increased the frustration that tightened her chest. "Are you finished?"

"No. Sam was wrong about you. You don't know—"

Collin cupped Nicole's face and touched his lips

to hers. Each slow drift of his mouth against hers and the even slower glide of his tongue as he explored her mouth stole every last one of her words.

He broke from the kiss and looked into her eyes. "Dad wasn't wrong. I do know without a doubt that you are and will always be the best thing that ever happened to me."

"Then why did you push me away?"

"I was scared of losing you."

"Lose me?" She laid her palms to his chest. "Why would you think that would ever happen? I love you."

"I know." He closed his eyes a moment. "But I've already lost the two closest people in my life. It hurt too much to think I could lose you the same way, in an instant. But not having you in my life at all hurts more. I want a chance to build moments with you. A life with you."

Happiness welled up, and tears pricked in her eyes. "I want that, too. I know we have a lot to work out with me running Roja and you being in the army, but I know we can figure out how to make a long-distance relationship work."

"No." He shook his head. "I can't do a long-distance relationship."

Nicole blinked up at him. His kiss must have gone straight to her head. She was confused. "Then how can we be together?"

Collin took a knee. He held up a ring with a

marquis-cut diamond that sparkled in a beam of sunlight coming through the window.

"I love you." He didn't have to say it. All he felt for her was written on his face and shone in his eyes. "Nicole Fortune, will you marry me?"

"Oh…" Happiness momentarily lodged her quick intake of breath.

"The answer isn't 'oh,'" Megan called out to her. "It's yes."

Nicole glanced up from Collin, surprise made her laugh in seeing Megan and Mark and the rest of the date night bunch there: Steven and Ellie, Callum and Becky, Dillon and Hailey. Plus Wiley and Grace and Ashley and Rodrigo.

Customers in the restaurant, along with her staff, looked on.

Ashley motioned for Nicole to get back to Collin patiently waiting for an answer to the most important question of their lives.

Smiling through tears, she held out her left hand to him. "Yes."

As Collin slipped on the ring, cheer and applause erupted along with the popping of corks on champagne.

Collin rose to his feet and Nicole met him halfway for a kiss. Without a doubt in the world. She was his and he was hers. Forever.

Chapter Twenty-Seven

Seven days later...

"Ladies and gentlemen," the DJ said. "Let's welcome the newlyweds to the dance floor."

Applause and cheers erupted from the guests sitting at the round white linen-covered tables in Roja's second floor at the Hotel Fortune.

Happiness radiated through Nicole as she took hold of Collin's hand and stepped into his arms for their first slow dance as husband and wife.

Two hours after their wedding ceremony, held by the pool, it still felt like a wonderful dream to her.

Images flashed through Nicole's mind from that

morning of being with her sisters, Ashley, Megan and Stephanie, in an upstairs suite. In between laughter, happy tears and champagne, they'd swept her hair into an updo, put on her makeup and helped her get dressed.

Just like the first time she'd tried on the close-fitting lace-over-satin strapless dress with the slightly flared hem at the bridal shop in Houston, she'd fought back tears over how perfect the dress was for her. With the chapel-length train trailing behind her as she'd walked down the aisle and the magnificent bouquet of Sam's roses mixed with rosemary flowers in her hands, she'd felt like a princess.

And Collin, her gorgeous prince times twelve, had been waiting for her, standing under an arch of white flowers, along with the minister.

When her father had walked her down the aisle created between the chairs occupied by her family and their friends who could make it to the ceremony on short notice, she was so anxious to get to him. But as she'd gotten closer to Collin, her steps had almost faltered. She hadn't been fully prepared for the up-close view of him in his dress uniform. The light blue trousers with a gold side stripe and dark blue waist-length jacket with gold shoulder knots over a snowy white shirt and black bow tie emphasized his height, trim waist and broad shoulders.

The certainty in his eyes as they recited their

vows fully echoed how she felt. They were in this together.

"I Won't Let Go" by Rascal Flatts crescendoed from the speakers. They could have chosen a song with more overt lyrics about love, but the lyrics to this one had spoken to them so clearly.

You think you're lost... But you're not lost on your own... I will stand by you... I will help you through...

They'd found each other, supported each other and loved each other through some of the hardest moments in their lives, and they hadn't let go. And they wouldn't, even when miles separated them in the future.

His extended leave was coming to an end, and he was flying out in three days, but in two months, she was going to Germany to spend time with him. And she'd get a chance to meet and talk with other military spouses. Making Roja one of the best restaurants in Texas was still on her to-do list, and Collin was proud of her ambition. But being there for him as he served his country, that was important to her, too.

For now, she'd continue to travel from Texas to Germany to see him. And he'd come back at least once in the next few months on leave. He would receive new orders before the end of next year. She'd join him, making their home there.

Collin dropped soft kisses near her shoulder

along the sensitive curve of her neck then whispered in her ear, "What do you think the odds are for us not being noticed if we sneak out after this song?"

Smiling, Nicole wound her arms around him and pressed closer to whisper back in his ear. "Well… since it is *our* wedding reception, I don't think the odds are exactly in our favor. Especially since we still need to cut the cake, you haven't taken off my garter and I haven't tossed my bouquet."

He leaned away from her neck and groaned. "Who agreed to us doing all that?"

She laughed. "I think we did."

Collin smiled down at her. "Are you happy, Mrs. Waldon?"

Nicole looked around the room at all of her family and their friends. She paused at the table where Roy, Mary and Jack sat with Wiley, Grace and Grace's parents. Mary was chatting away as usual and nudging Jack. Three lit candles flickered in the center of the table. One for Sam, one for Beth and one for Sharon.

Collin had mentioned how concerned Sam had been about him being alone. Not only did Collin have her and her family now, but when Sam had made friends at the Highlands, he'd brought Roy, Mary and Jack into Collin's life, and they'd already made it known to Collin that they were his family, too.

The people who mattered most to them were there in that room.

She looked up at Collin. "I'm very happy."

He gave her a lingering kiss. "That's all that matters."

A couple of hours later, in their suite at Hotel Fortune, the hours of waiting to be together were finally over.

Urgency rose with every piece of clothing that was stripped away. As they lay in the king-size bed, Collin trailed kisses down her throat. The heat of his mouth bathed the peaks of her breasts. His slow, torturous caresses up her thighs made her bow up from the mattress, pleading and chanting his name when he finally reached where she ached for him the most.

By the time he glided into her, she was more than ready for him, quickly falling into an orgasm that consumed her in pleasure.

Afterward, she lay with her head on his shoulder, legs intertwined with his as he held her close. She cataloged the moment in her mind, a moment that she would latch on to in the weeks to come when she missed him the most.

Collin rested his large hand on her hip, and she fit herself against him. He tipped up her chin. "What are you thinking about?"

As she looked into his eyes, a future that made

her heart swell with happiness played in her mind. A future of them being together. Of the places they'd call home. Of the children they'd bring into the world.

She couldn't explain it all to him, but it was easy to define. Nicole cupped his cheek. "I was thinking about how much I love you."

Collin smiled as he leaned in to kiss her. "I love you, too."

* * * * *

MILLS & BOON

Coming next month

THE PRINCESS AND THE REBEL BILLIONAIRE
Sophie Pembroke

Isabella had to admit to herself that she was just postponing the inevitable. She had the whole rest of the week here in this glorious villa, beside this beautiful lake, with Matteo. Not making the most of it would be a terrible waste.

Throwing open the doors to the shared balcony that joined their bedrooms, Isabella let the morning air rush in, and felt her own breath rush out.

Once again, Matteo was already sitting at the table on the balcony. There were shadows under his eyes that suggested his sleep might have been as disturbed as her own. But he looked up as she appeared, and a slow smile spread across his face at the sight of her, making him look instantly younger. More free.

Was he remembering that moment last night, too? The one when he'd been close enough for her to kiss, if she'd moved her head just ever-so-slightly? Was he thinking about the suggestion he'd made to her?

The smirk on his face suggested he probably was.

"Good morning," he said, his voice low and warm. "Sleep well?"

She took her seat. "Like a baby." It wasn't a lie. Babies were notoriously bad sleepers, weren't they?

"Me too." The smirk hadn't gone anywhere. "So, how are we going to spend our second day in secluded paradise? Chess? Poker?"

He was teasing her now, but she didn't rise to it. Instead, she looked out over the lake, the balcony suddenly claustrophobic, despite all the fresh air. This villa was huge, and she knew that if she asked for space Matteo would give it to her. He wasn't the kind of man to press where he wasn't wanted, she could tell that already from the way he'd backed off last night after the merest suggestion of more.

The problem was, she wasn't at all sure she wanted him to keep backing off. But she wasn't certain enough to let him in, either.

She wanted him; she wasn't lying to herself about that anymore. But it was so against The Rules. And beyond anything she'd let herself want for so long—ever since Nate. The desire she felt for Matteo…it was overwhelming, and terrifying.

And it felt amazing, all the same.

She stared out over the water and the mountains in the distance. The June air was warm and welcoming, but the breeze from the water kept things fresh in the shady trees that surrounded the villa.

She didn't want to be trapped inside today—otherwise, this villa was no better than the palace in Augusta that she'd escaped from.

Maybe she wasn't ready to take the risk of letting Matteo in quite yet. But perhaps she could take the tiny risk of letting herself out. Just a little bit.

One small first step towards where she was almost ready to admit she really wanted to go.

To bed, with Matteo.

Isabella placed her empty coffee cup down on her saucer. "I'm going for a walk, down by the lake," she said, before she could change her mind. That would give her time and space to keep figuring out what she wanted from this week. Time away from the allure of Matteo's smile, or those green eyes that pulled her in whenever she caught them.

Matteo grinned. "Great! I'll come with you."

Continue reading
THE PRINCESS AND THE REBEL BILLIONAIRE
Sophie Pembroke

Available next month
www.millsandboon.co.uk

COMING SOON!

We really hope you enjoyed reading this book.
If you're looking for more romance, be sure to
head to the shops when new books are
available on

Thursday 27th
May

To see which titles are coming soon, please visit

millsandboon.co.uk/nextmonth

LET'S TALK
Romance

For exclusive extracts, competitions
and special offers, find us online:

 facebook.com/millsandboon

@MillsandBoon

@MillsandBoonUK

Get in touch on 01413 063232

For all the latest titles coming soon, visit
millsandboon.co.uk/nextmonth

MILLS & BOON

THE HEART OF ROMANCE

A ROMANCE FOR EVERY READER

MODERN

Prepare to be swept off your feet by sophisticated, sexy and seductive heroes, in some of the world's most glamourous and romantic locations, where power and passion collide.

HISTORICAL

Escape with historical heroes from time gone by. Whether your passion is for wicked Regency Rakes, muscled Vikings or rugged Highlanders, awaken the romance of the past.

MEDICAL

Set your pulse racing with dedicated, delectable doctors in the high-pressure world of medicine, where emotions run high and passion, comfort and love are the best medicine.

True Love

Celebrate true love with tender stories of heartfelt romance, from the rush of falling in love to the joy a new baby can bring, and a focus on the emotional heart of a relationship.

Desire

Indulge in secrets and scandal, intense drama and plenty of sizzling hot action with powerful and passionate heroes who have it all: wealth, status, good looks…everything but the right woman.

HEROES

Experience all the excitement of a gripping thriller, with an intense romance at its heart. Resourceful, true-to-life women and strong, fearless men face danger and desire - a killer combination!

To see which titles are coming soon, please visit

millsandboon.co.uk/nextmonth

JOIN US ON SOCIAL MEDIA!

Stay up to date with our latest releases, author
news and gossip, special offers and discounts, and
all the behind-the-scenes action
from Mills & Boon...

 millsandboon

 millsandboonuk

millsandboon

It might just be true love...

GET YOUR ROMANCE FIX!

MILLS & BOON
— *blog* —

Get the latest romance news, exclusive author
interviews, story extracts and much more!

MILLS & BOON

HISTORICAL

Awaken the romance of the past

Escape with historical heroes from time gone by. Whether your passion is for wicked Regency Rakes, muscled Viking warriors or rugged Highlanders, indulge your fantasies and awaken the romance of the past.

MILLS & BOON

HEROES

At Your Service

Experience all the excitement of a gripping thriller, with an intense romance at its heart. Resourceful, true-to-life women and strong, fearless men face danger and desire - a killer combination!